ZEBRA BOOKS
KENSINGTON PUBLISHING CORP.

ZEBRA BOOKS

are published by

Kensington Publishing Corp.
475 Park Avenue South
New York, NY 10016



First Printing: February, 1993

Printed in the United States of America

# EVENING RENDEZVOUS

Evon had retraced Dominique's steps that afternoon, finding footprints along the outer edges of the beach. After careful examination he found the path where she and the dog had entered the woods. Fearfully he had followed their trail to the deserted cottage. Suddenly, Dominique burst through the cottage and into his arms. His relief gave way to anger and his dark-brooding eyes raked over her body.

He kept his tone harsh as he demanded, "Come. The night air grows cool."

Who did he think he was that he could order her around? Dominique ignored him and stomped back inside the hut.

"Dominique!" he roared. Evon was right behind her. He reached out and jerked her around to face him. "What do you think you're doing?" he asked angrily.

"You are no longer my guardian. I do not have to do as you say," she hissed, her breath ragged.

His eyes were black and dazzling with fury. He stood there, tall and angry.

The dog whined and tried to step between them, but there was no room and he backed up and circled around them.

The silence became unbearable. Evon had a fiery, angry look that was familiar to Dominique. She inhaled and tossed her head. "I will leave when I'm good and ready and not before," she said insolently.

Evon remained silent. He reached out and lifted her in his arms. She gasped and glared at him. "You are right *chérie,*" Evon said. "I am no longer your guardian. I am your husband," he whispered and instead of leaving the hut, he carried her toward the pallet, his eyes never leaving hers . . .

## CAPTURE THE GLOW OF ZEBRA'S *HEARTFIRES!*

CAPTIVE TO HIS KISS (3788, $4.25/$5.50)
by Paige Brantley
Madeleine de Moncelet was determined to avoid an arranged marriage to the Duke of Burgundy. But the tall, stern-looking knight sent to guard her chamber door may thwart her escape plan!

CHEROKEE BRIDE (3761, $4.25/$5.50)
by Patricia Werner
Kit Newcomb found politics to be a dead bore, until she met the proud Indian delegate Red Hawk. Only a lifetime of loving could soothe her desperate desire!

MOONLIGHT REBEL (3707, $4.25/$5.50)
by Marie Ferrarella
Krystyna fled her native Poland only to live in the midst of a revolution in Virginia. Her host may be a spy, but when she looked into his blue eyes she wanted to share her most intimate treasures with him!

PASSION'S CHASE (3862, $4.25/$5.50)
by Ann Lynn
Rose would never heed her Aunt Stephanie's warning about the unscrupulous Mr. Trent Jordan. She knew what she wanted – a long, lingering kiss bound to arouse the passion of a bold and ardent lover!

RENEGADE'S ANGEL (3760, $4.25/$5.50)
by Phoebe Fitzjames
Jenny Templeton had sworn to bring Ace Denton to justice for her father's death, but she hadn't reckoned on the tempting heat of the outlaw's lean, hard frame or her surrendering wantonly to his fiery loving!

TEMPTATION'S FIRE (3786, $4.25/$5.50)
by Millie Criswell
Margaret Parker saw herself as a twenty-six year old spinster. There wasn't much chance for romance in her sleepy town. Nothing could prepare her for the jolt of desire she felt when the new marshal swept her onto the dance floor!

*Available wherever paperbacks are sold, or order direct from the Publisher. Send cover price plus 50¢ per copy for mailing and handling to Zebra Books, Dept. 4079, 475 Park Avenue South, New York, N.Y. 10016. Residents of New York and Tennessee must include sales tax. DO NOT SEND CASH. For a free Zebra/ Pinnacle catalog please write to the above address.*

# One

*New Orleans, Louisiana 1857*

"Christ!" Evon Forest exploded, pulling back hard on the reins of the white gelding he rode. His handsome face darkened as a great ebony stallion plunged from the dense forest of twisted oaks.

"What the hell?" he asked. Great gusts of howling wind tore at his clothes, and hurled his words back at him.

Angry ink-black clouds roiled as streaks of lightning flashed across the turbulent sky to light up the blue-gray afternoon and Evon glimpsed a small figure leaning low over the broad back of the stallion.

Suddenly alerted to their presence, instinct caused the huge stallion to quickly veer to one side. At the same instant Evon skillfully maneuvered his own mount as far off the path as the trees would allow. This action prevented the stallion from trampling them, but his muscular hindquarter grazed Evon's leg. Ignoring the pain, he fought for control as the gelding reared back on his hind legs.

Once more, lightning lit up the black and blue sky, and Evon glanced up as the small dark form was hurled over the stallion's thick neck. The colossal animal came to an abrupt halt beside the still figure as a loud clap of thunder followed.

Marengo, frightened by the collision as well as the noise, reared once more, and the boy and stallion were momentarily forgotten as Evon again brought the white gelding under control.

An angry sigh escaped Evon's lips as he dismounted and moved toward the unconscious boy. "Of all the damn fool . . ." he muttered angrily, but his words trailed away as the stallion arched his wide neck and reared high into the air where he pawed viciously at the blowing wind before dropping back onto the mist-shrouded ground.

Evon slowed his movements and began speaking in soothing, gentle tones to the great black beast.

The stallion's eyes never strayed from his young master, but even so, Evon knew the horse was aware of his presence. He was also aware that the storm was intensifying to hurricane proportions. He inched his way forward until he was near enough to reach out and touch the trembling giant. Evon exhaled, just realizing he'd been holding his breath. When the stallion showed no animosity toward him, he knelt on one knee while he ran his long tapered fingers over the figure on the ground in an attempt to determine the extent of the injuries.

After he had inspected the boy's arms and legs for possible fractures, Evon was about to check the boy's ribs when suddenly his hands were thrust aside as the black horse dipped his head toward the boy.

One thick brow elevated slightly as Evon watched the stallion as he trailed his velvety lips over the pale visage of his master. When the boy did not respond, the stallion clamped his large teeth into the bill of his master's floppy cap, and unceremoniously pulled it from the boy's head.

Evon's dark eyes widened as silver strands of thick hair spilled upon the dew-drenched earth.

He inhaled sharply, and stared as though mesmerized at the silver halo surrounding the exquisite features of the beautiful girl.

Evon whistled softly. Then he whispered aloud, "So, big boy, he is not your master, but your mistress!"

Lightning rent the horizon and explosive thunder signaled that the storm was upon them, and Evon realized he would have to move her out of the weather. But they were miles from the Chandler Plantation, Belle Terre—where he'd been headed—and he knew the long jolting ride could be dangerous if the girl had suffered a concussion.

Then, as the heavens opened wide and large drops of moisture splashed against his face, he remembered passing a deserted cabin less than a mile back. He decided to take her there. They would at least find shelter out of the weather.

Also, he thought, at the cabin he could better determine the extent of her injuries, and they could wait until the storm abated. Having made his decision, Evon gently lifted the girl as the black stallion tossed his head and nickered. He whistled softly, and the stallion followed him as he walked the short distance to where Marengo stood cropping at the wet grass beneath a giant oak.

He mounted Marengo and then he shifted his burden gently against his chest. Lightning lit up the black sky giving him a brief glimpse of dark sooty lashes resting against creamy cheeks. "Who are you, my beauty?" he muttered. Why would a young woman risk her life, and that of a fine horse, to travel at breakneck speed through the thick growth of the bayou, he wondered as he guided his horse back the way he'd come. Despite the chill of the air, her body felt warm against him and he was gripped by a strong urge to protect her. Quick on the heels of that sensation came a tightening in his loins as her full rounded breasts pressed against his chest. He'd been too long without a woman to share his bed, and his response was a logical one, he reasoned silently. The padding of the stallion's shod hooves on the sodden earth claimed his attention, and he glanced over his shoulder to see the big black following at a respectable distance. "I admire your loyalty, big fellow," Evon mumbled. He returned his gaze to the unconscious young woman in his arms, and whispered, "But your mistress doesn't deserve such a fine animal. She's careless and selfish to a fault." He reached out his hand to smooth the silver blond wisps away from her face.

Less than a half hour later, they reached the vacant cabin. Inside, Evon gently laid the girl on the moss-filled mattress and eased her head to a more comfortable position. Her lips parted and a soft moan escaped. He gazed at her delicate oval-shaped face and full, sensuous mouth. His dark brooding eyes moved over her body, taking note of the boy's cambric shirt and breeches she wore. The tight clothing accentuated her fine hips and shapely thighs. The fall had torn the top buttons from her worn shirt and firm uptilted breasts were visible. He swallowed tightly and looked away from that tempting view to examine the lump on her brow. There was an ugly bruise surrounding it, but it did not mar her exquisite beauty. Her features were finely shaped, fragile, and he had an overwhelming urge to taste her full lips. Instead, he reached out and smoothed a damp strand of silver hair back from her face. "Aah *chérie,*" he whispered. "Please wake up. I don't know who you are or what to do for you." Leaving her side, he walked to the window and stared out into the dark, stormy afternoon, thinking about his appointment with the lawyer at Belle Terre the following afternoon. He'd been anxious to view the new property he'd recently purchased; however, he was skeptical of the obligation he'd reluctantly accepted upon the death of Emmett Chandler: the guardianship of the Chandler children—Nicki and

Beau. After seeing to the welfare of Chandler's sons, there was still the distasteful duty of finding a wife. A wife! His father's ultimatum still infuriated him; his father had added a codicil to his will that he must wed before his thirtieth birthday or his father would give Forest Manor to Wye. A wife was the last thing he wanted.

The family plantation meant everything to Evon—it was his life! Wye had no head for business. Wye hated the country life, preferring instead the excitement to be found in the city.

Another moan escaped the girl's lips, interrupting his train of thought. Evon found an oil lamp, lit it, and held it near her face so as to get a better look at the beauty before him. He gazed at her perfect features, then set the lamp back on the crude wooden table beside the chipped glass bowl. He left the cabin to search for a well, and a few minutes later returned with a bucket of water. He found several more oil lamps, and after he lit them, the small cottage was aglow with the soft light. Evon walked back into the room and sat on the edge of the bed, and gently lifted her light frame to a sitting position and placed a cup to her dry lips. "Drink *chérie,* you will feel better," he coaxed softly. The girl coughed, but did not open her eyes as the cool liquid slid down her throat. Easing her back, he dipped his handkerchief in a bowl of water he'd placed on the bedside table and wiped her face.

Her wet clothing had to be removed or she would take a chill, he decided. Evon returned to the main room and found a quilt inside an old chest. Gently, he undressed her and covered her to the chin. A flush of unbidden desire warmed him and he felt guilty. The poor girl was unconscious and he was having trouble controlling his lust, but, sweet Jesus! she was so beautiful! And how was he to know she wore no undergarments? Her body was perfection—fine hips, shapely legs, and softly rounded breasts. "Christ!" he hissed between his teeth and strode from the room. He would simply put such thoughts from his mind. The fire he'd built before tending to the horses warmed the room and he removed his wet shirt and hung it on the mantel to dry next to the girl's much smaller garments. He sat before the fire, enjoying the warmth and listening to the raging storm beating against the cabin. It was as if he and the lovely girl were in a world all their own. "Who are you, *ma petite?* And what were you trying to do out there?" he whispered. At the speed that big black stallion was traveling she was lucky to be alive . . . they were both lucky. Several times in the next few hours, he looked in on her but she was still in a deep sleep. When the rain slackened he rubbed the horses down with an old burlap sack he'd found in a corner of the lean-to. With that job finished, he threw another log on the fire and sat down to wait. His thoughts drifted to the Chandler children. What was he to do with two active boys? The time grew nearer to the meeting with Nicki and Beauregard Chandler. He thought of how Emmett Chandler had asked—no, had begged—him to stand guardian if anything should ever happen to him. Evon had reluctantly agreed, thinking he would never be called upon to honor this agreement.

Emmett Chandler had been a quiet man—surely his sons would take after him? They would have to be fed and clothed; that he could handle with ease, but what of their schooling? He would hire a tutor—but if they were unmanageable, he would pack them off to the academy outside of New Orleans, or perhaps send them to a school in Paris. He heard the girl cry out and he was on his feet and in her room in a matter of seconds.

"Papa!" she cried, her voice pitiful in its pain.

He knelt beside her and stroked her cheek gently.

"Ssh *chérie*. You are all right."

"Beau," she whispered then.

"You are safe, *chérie,*" Evon comforted in a soothing tone. She seemed to settle and turned to nuzzle against his hand. She was so vulnerable his protective instincts were aroused once again. Curiously, he wondered who Beau was? Was he her lover? An unfamiliar twinge of envy pricked him as he wondered what kind of man she belonged to.

He stared at her intently and as if he had willed it, her silken black lashes lifted.

Huge green eyes stared up at him. Dominique Chandler was confused as she whispered, "Who are you, M'sieur?"

Her head ached from the vibration of her own words. Dominique tried to sit up, but knifelike pains shot through her temple, and she gasped at the severity of it. Evon eased her aching head down onto the hard ticked pillow. She stared into his face but his features were blurred. "M'sieur! I cannot see!" she cried. Fear, stark and vivid, clutched at her insides. "What has happened! Where am I?"

Evon saw the panic in her gaze. He gently stroked her cheek, concern furrowing his brow. "There, *ma petite,* you were thrown—" he began, but when he heard her utter a distressing noise, he grabbed for the chipped bowl. He held her tenderly as she emptied the contents of her stomach, and when she finished he wiped her flushed cheeks.

Even as groggy as she felt, she was mortified. She did not even know this man, and she'd just disgraced herself. No one had witnessed such an unpleasantry but her mammy. "M'sieur, please—" she asked. Dominique was miserable, but she needed her questions answered.

"Ssh my dear, you have suffered a concussion. Perhaps you should rest now," Evon urged. He continued to apply the soothing cloth to her face and when he heard her even breathing, he knew she slept. He rose from her side and returned to the kitchen.

He had retrieved the cheese and bread from the pouch he'd brought with him. He put some aside for the girl when she awoke. The rain had stopped, but they would stay overnight in the cabin. Evon knew it would not be a good idea to try to move her too soon. She had suffered a severe blow to her head, and her blurred vision combined with the loss of her last meal convinced him that his first suspicion of a concussion was accurate.

*"Mon Dieu!"* Dominique wailed. "M'sieur!"

At the alarm in her voice, Evon hastened quickly to her side. "Are you in pain, *chérie?*" he asked, concern in his voice at the strange expression on her face.

"How dare you! How dare you undress me, M'sieur!" Dominique had thought her shame complete when she'd suffered the embarrassment of losing her stomach, but to wake up completely unclothed in a strange room, with a strange man—well, who did he think he was to take advantage of an unconscious, unchaperoned woman? "You'd better have a damn good reason for doing what you have done, M'sieur," Dominique demanded. Her fingers went to her temple as she felt an excruciating pain, brought on by her upset.

"Can you see me, *chérie?*" he asked, ignoring her outburst.

"Of course I can see you!" she answered irritably.

"Good. Do you always speak like a dockside whore?" he asked, a smile tugging at the corner of his mouth.

"A dockside—!" she gasped at his outrageous question. She stared at his arrogant, but handsome face. Ebony eyes stared back at her, and she was mesmerized by the intent of his gaze. His hair was as black as a raven's wing, and his aquiline nose told her of his aristocratic breeding. But his mouth, what was it about his mouth that fascinated her so? She felt drawn to those sensuous and perfectly shaped lips. *Mon Dieu!* What was she thinking? This beast of a man had undressed her, viewed her nakedness, and she had been helpless to stop him.

*"Ma petite,* your wet clothes demanded immediate attention. I could not allow you to suffer a lung disease that could prove fatal. Of course I could have left you and your stallion to take your chances in the storm . . ." Evon allowed his words to drift away as he waited for their meaning to take effect. The girl was spoiled and ungrateful. She was a typical New Orleans snob. A Creole prima donna. But why the boy's attire, and where the hell had she learned to use such language?

"You expect me to thank you for stripping me of my garments, I suppose?" Dominique choked, her cheeks flushed several shades of red.

"I expect nothing, *chérie,* except that you have a care from now on. You nearly killed us both riding at breakneck speed, not to mention the horses. What possessed you to do such a foolish thing?" he asked sharply.

How dare he reprimand her as though she were a witless child? She knew what she had done. She realized the danger she had brought to herself and Saladin. But she'd been upset to the point of hysteria, and she had left the house in such a state that she had not even bothered to saddle Saladin. Oh Papa, she thought, with fresh anguish. Dominique closed her eyes tight, refusing to cry in front of this man. She'd suffered enough embarrassment for one day. Men were not to be trusted, she thought, as she remembered the stipulation of her father's will. He had appointed a guardian for her and Beau! A person who would tell them what they could and could not do. A man to bully them and spy on them every waking hour of the day and night. And this man was no different; she would not tell him who she was or where she lived.

Saladin was near. She knew he would not leave her, and when her head stopped aching, she and Saladin would leave this place. She would never see this man again.

"Your lips are sealed, *chérie?* You are not going to tell me who you are?" Evon prodded. His dark eyes were intent on the beautiful creature before him.

"Do not call me *chérie,* M'sieur. I am nothing to you, and I certainly am not your love!" she spat the words at him, but she refused to look into those jet-black eyes. Eyes that could confuse, and maybe even make her say things she did not want to reveal. This handsome stranger affected her in a way she had never before experienced. He made her feel tingly and warm. Warm? Yes, he made her feel warm and protected. Her father had not cared about her. He had not cared for Beau. After her mother's death, he had blamed his son for his beloved Celeste's death. And Dominique? Why had he ignored her? She was a girl, and girls were mindless creatures to serve a man's baser needs. The thinking was a typical Creole thought. But she reasoned, when she escaped this man she would never see him again. "My name is Dominique. But M'sieur, that is all you need to know."

"Dominique. A lovely name for one so beautiful, *chérie,*" he complimented as he smiled at her stubbornness.

"I said—"

"But *chérie* is an endearment used by all Creole men, and after what we have been through together—well, *chérie,* you have become very dear to me," Evon said knowing his words held a double meaning. Evon was not a vindictive person, but the young woman had acted foolishly; endangering both their lives as well as valuable horseflesh. And instead of apologizing for her actions, she had assaulted him with her salty tongue. So, he thought, he had given the little minx what she deserved.

"*Non,* M'sieur! Do not say such things. A gentleman would not take advantage of an unconscious and defenseless woman!" she exclaimed. But as his smoke-black gaze caught hers, Dominique started at the smoldering flames she saw there. She could not breathe, and as his compelling desire captured and held her, she could not look away.

His eyes blazed red coals as they searched her emerald orbs with an intense look of pleasure and pain. He sat on the edge of the bed, and suddenly her rock-hardened nipples were crushed against his firm muscled chest. Dark eyes moved over her perfect oval-shaped face to stop at her parted red lips. At her sudden intake of air, his demanding lips claimed her mouth with a hard, seeking hunger.

Evon stripped the sheet to her waist. Her soft ivory mounds lay against his bare chest, and he felt the warmth penetrate his skin. Evon lifted his head, "I am no gentleman, *cherie*, remember my warning," Evon parried. He released her and rose and walked from the room.

At his words, her eyes widened, her lips still parted, but no sound escaped. Her body felt aflame all the way to the apex between her slender thighs. Dominique struggled to gain control of her traitorous emotions. Anger seeped in to replace the turbulent desire the arrogant man had forced upon her. But his deliberate insinuation brought distorted visions of Saladin nipping and kicking, and after the foreplay at last mating with one of her father's prized mares. She wondered what manner of man this was, that he would take such advantage? Her sea-green eyes narrowed; he would pay for his misdeed when she told her father! But, remembering, she realized her father could protect her no more. He had taken his own life. A lone tear escaped to slide unnoticed down her flushed cheek. Her father had had no time for her or Beau, but this incident would never have taken place had her father still been alive. Dominique tried to sit up, but the movement brought on an excruciating pain to her temple, her vision blurred and she gasped as she eased her aching head back onto the moss-filled mattress. How was she to escape this place or this man if she could not even lift herself from the bed? The pain began to subside and as her lids grew heavy she welcomed the veil of darkness that claimed her troubled thoughts.

Evon stood staring out the rain-soaked pane. What manner of man was he? Dominique was right. A gentleman would not have taken advantage of her situation. She had raised his ire, and he had snapped his anger for his loss of control at her. She had been thoughtless to urge the big black to his full speed in dangerous terrain, and on a gray afternoon filled with mist making the ground unsafe even in sunshine hours. But he, too, had been thoughtless in his actions. Dominique did not deserve to have his attentions forced upon her.

Evon walked back into the room where Dominique lay. Her sooty lashes lay against her cheek, her rounded breasts rose and fell in an even rhythm, and he knew she slept.

"Papa! Ooh please no, no. Papa, don't leave—"

Her cries left Evon shaken, and something tugged at his insides. Quickly, he moved to sit beside her and enfolded her in a gentle embrace. Evon whispered endearments into her tiny shell-shaped ear as he smoothed her tangled silver-blond locks away from her face. "There, there *ma petite.* It is all right. You are not alone. There *chérie,* I will take care of you," he crooned. What was he saying? He did not have the time to take care of this girl. He must leave tomorrow. There were important matters awaiting his attention at Belle Terre; another commitment—two in fact. Yet he did not release her and with his arms still around Dominique, Evon lay down on the firm mattress to hold her against him until the early morning.

As dawn approached, Dominique awakened to find herself not only lying beside the stranger in bed, but wrapped snugly in his firm embrace.

*"Mon Dieu,"* she whispered. If she were to escape this man, she must do so while he still slept. Dominique eased from his arms, and his even breathing brought a sigh of relief from her soft lips. She found her clothes resting over the back of a chair in the kitchen area and quickly dressed. She searched the room for her boots, but when she couldn't find them, she hurried out the door, closing it quietly. She found Saladin in the lean-to with the white gelding. Her silent command brought the ebony stallion to his knees, and in one agile movement Dominique was on his back. They left the cabin behind in a swirl of predawn mist.

# Two

Evon was awakened by Marengo's cry of protest, and the sound of hoofbeats pounding on the wet earth outside brought him to his feet. When he threw the wooden door back, the horse and rider were well on their way back the way they had come.

He felt a strong urge to go after her, but then reminded himself wryly that he didn't need trouble of that sort; he had enough problems already. He turned back inside and began to ready himself for the last of his journey to Belle Terre.

Evon eased back on the reins bringing the white gelding to a halt. The stirrups bore his weight as he drew himself up and out of the saddle to gaze at his newly acquired property. The fields lay barren but soon he would see them tilled and planted in sugarcane. He eased back onto the saddle as he drew his watch from his pocket. Both hands on the face were straight up and he had an hour before his appointment with the lawyer. He had covered quite a bit of ground in the hour since arriving on Belle Terre property, but Evon wanted to freshen up before his meeting with the attorney and Chandler's sons. He reined Marengo in a full circle in the direction of the plantation house when he caught sight of a rider and horse coming toward him. Evon would have recognized that red stallion anywhere, and when the rider brought his stallion to a halt several yards from where Evon sat atop Marengo, Evon's eyes narrowed and he yelled, "Harcourt! Where the hell did you come from?"

"You, M'sieur, are trespassing!" Harcourt bellowed.

Trespassing? What the hell was he talking about? "Look you bastard—" Evon began.

*"Non,* M'sieur! Be warned," Jules interrupted and his nostrils flared as he seethed with hatred, "you got away with murdering my brother, but this is my land!"

"Now wait just a goddamn—" Evon hissed between clinched teeth, but his words ended abruptly as Harcourt spun the stallion around, digging his spurs viciously into his horse's sides as Evon stared after Jules. "His land? What the hell is he talking about?" Evon muttered under his breath as he, too, brought his own horse into motion.

It had been a year since Evon had shot and killed Jules Harcourt's brother, Reynard, in a duel. Reynard was several years younger than Jules and through the years Jules had gotten Reynard out of one scrape after another until the night Evon had sat in on a poker game with Reynard. When Evon had caught him cheating, Reynard had called him out. Evon had shot Reynard through the heart. When Jules was notified, he had sworn to avenge his brother's death. During the past year there had been several attempts made on Evon's life. Evon suspected Harcourt of being behind the attempts. But he had not been able to prove it. "One day you will have to face me yourself, Jules, and when the time comes I will be ready for you," Evon prophesied aloud.

"Daughter! What the hell are you saying, Hamlin?" Evon Forest exploded. He rose to his feet abruptly, slamming his hands on the flat surface of the oaken desk.

"I beg your pardon, M'sieur?" the attorney, Neville Hamlin, asked uncertainly as he stared up into the angry eyes of the large figure looming over him.

"The girl, Hamlin! Where did the girl come from? Chandler asked me to accept guardianship of his two sons. He made no mention of a third child." Evon could not believe his ears. He had been reluctant to accept full responsibility of raising someone else's children in the first place. And the age difference of ten years between the two could pose still another problem. At Chandler's insistence, he'd agreed thinking Emmett Chandler was a relatively young man in good health who had sold him his plantation at a very reasonable sum. The house needed remodeling and the fields stood vacant, but the soil was excellent and would grow thousands of acres of prime sugarcane. But a daughter!

"But M'sieur Forest, Emmett Chandler did not have two sons, nor is there a third child," the attorney explained patiently. However, as Evon's expression darkened, Hamlin's bony fingers shook as they curled tightly around the sheath of papers he held and he quickly continued, "As I said, M'sieur Chandler has two children, young M'sieur Beauregard and Mademoiselle Dominique."

"Two children . . . Beau and Nicki . . . Beauregard and Dominique! Dominique? Of all the underhanded, contemptuous—he tricked me! Chandler tricked me, and damned if I didn't make it easy for him. I do not need the burden of raising a half-grown girl," Evon stated, shaking his ebony head. "Christ! What have I gotten myself into?" Evon was bewildered at his situation. He had given his word and he would not go back on his word, but a girl . . .

The tall, slim girl stood unnoticed at the entrance to her father's study. Her mammy and little brother stood beside her. As she listened to the deep baritone voice of her new guardian, her heartbeat quickened and her mouth went dry. Dominique Chandler had not wanted to be present when the attorney read her father's will, and she definitely did not want to meet her new guardian, but the attorney had insisted. And there was her young brother's feelings to consider. Beau had been anxious to meet the man who would take him fishing and horseback riding. Do all the things their father had never had time to do. Dominique could never say no to Beau, but she feared their new guardian would break her brother's heart. She believed the man was an unscrupulous rogue who had cheated her father out of their home. The man had paid half of what Belle Terre was worth. She realized her father had mortgaged the property to the hilt, but after paying back what her father had borrowed from Jules Harcourt, there was still a sizable amount Evon Forest would deposit in an account for her and Beau.

But as she got over the initial shock that the stranger she'd met in the bayou was indeed her legal guardian, his words filtered through to her, their meaning becoming clear and they both humiliated and infuriated her.

How dare he! her mind screamed. She refused to listen to another word. With lightning speed, she crossed the room and slapped his smooth-shaven cheek. "You bastard!" she hissed. A shocked silence filled the room following her actions and Evon stared at her. His cheek had begun to sting when she raised her hand to strike him again. He grabbed her wrist in a painful grip while smoldering black eyes clashed with flashing green eyes. Evon inhaled deeply as he stared at the beauty he'd held so tenderly the night before. His anger was suddenly tempered with amusement when he realized he'd never been slapped before.

"How dare you come into my father's house and slander him this way? You have no right!" she whispered staring into those now familiar ebony eyes, while she struggled to control the tears threatening to erupt and spill forth. But Dominique would not allow him the satisfaction of seeing how he had hurt her. He had called her a burden and her pride was raw and throbbing. He was arrogant and hateful to treat her as a charity case. Dominique Chandler would never be a burden to anyone and he would regret his rash words.

As quickly as he'd seized her arm, Evon released her. His anger dissipated as he gazed into her emerald eyes that were as changeable as her moods. But her words were condemning and it irked him that she treated him as the villain here. "I have every right, mademoiselle. I am the new master of this house. And as your legal guardian—"

*Non!* His words stabbed at her heart, not this stranger, not the man who had held her tenderly through the stormy night. His warm, protective embrace had eased her heartache, and her fears. But the stranger was in fact Evon Forest; the man her father had appointed as their guardian. *"Non!"* she gasped. "I will not stay even one night under the same roof with you, you—"

"Aah *chérie,* but you will. As your legal protector, I am not only the master of this entire estate, but master of your brother, and master of you," Evon retaliated with a cynical smile on his handsome countenance.

"We shall see, M'sieur!" Dominique threatened angrily.

"You are being childish. If I do not receive your full cooperation I shall send you away to school. Far away. Do you understand fully what that implies?" Evon asked, realizing his words were rash, but she was pushing him beyond his limits.

"School! M'sieur, how young do you think I am? I have been tutored in all things possible, and I am too old to be sent away to school!" Dominique taunted indignantly.

"I can do anything I want as your guardian, Dominique," he said with a thread of steel in his voice. His dark eyes pierced her with his mounting anger. "If you are too old for school, then I will find you a husband." He didn't know why he'd said that, but, damn, the girl could raise his ire. His dark brooding eyes moved over her wholesome beauty as he appraised her with more than a mild interest. Without doubt he knew Dominique was more woman than child. Her attitude was childish, but she had the ripe body of a woman. Suddenly he felt an all too familiar tightening deep within his loins. What the hell was he thinking? He quickly turned his back to her, and pushed his hands into his pockets. How the hell was he to be Dominique's guardian? A guardian was to be trusted with his charge—Dominique Chandler would tempt any man's passion. His instincts warned him to stay away from this silver-haired minx. She was a distraction he could not afford. Turning to face her once more, he began, "I realize neither of you are responsible for this ridiculous situation, but we're stuck with each other, and . . ." His words trailed away as he saw Dominique's angry expression. Her eyes were pools of emerald fire matching the outdated sea foam velvet gown she wore. "Now what have I said to offend you?" he exploded. He would not weigh his every word while in her presence.

Dominique could not believe her ears! The repulsive man considered her and Beau a ridiculous situation. They were to be an imposition? And, how had he phrased it? He thought himself stuck with them? What nerve! "Why you pompous ass! you are not stuck with either Beau or me. We shall move out of *your* house, immediately, M'sieur!" Dominique raged. Once more, she felt moisture gathering behind her eyelids, and before her tears could bring her further embarrassment and give Evon Forest another reason to mock her, she whirled and fled the room.

Dominique rushed toward the staircase, but as the toe of her worn, satin slipper touched the first step, a fist of steel clamped around her wrist, and she was jerked around and pulled up tight against Evon's rock-hard chest, knocking the wind from her lungs. She drew air back into her lungs as she gasped, "How dare you touch—" she began, but her words died away as her eyes locked with his, giving her heart a perilous start. After a moment, Evon released her, and she would have fallen had her hand not caught on the banister.

Evon's heart thudded noisily in his chest, "Damn!" he swore. She made him lose his temper as no one else ever had. He couldn't become involved with this half woman, half—no, he would no longer think of her as a child. He would have to alter his plans. Originally, he had thought to send Chandler's boys to Locust Grove Academy, but upon learning that Dominique was the other half of the Chandler boys, that was out of the question. He could still carry out half of his plan, but the other half . . .

"Dominique—" he began, but the innocent passion he saw in her green eyes took his breath away. He tried once more, "Dominique—" he whispered hoarsely. Evon always kept a tight rein on his emotions, but he felt his reserve slipping. Was she a witch? Had she cast a spell over him? When he'd first gone after Dominique, his intentions had been honorable, but when he pulled her close, her soft curves had molded into the contour of his chest as though they were made to fit together like the pieces of a puzzle. He'd wanted to taste the sweetness of her, he'd wanted—Christ! What had he wanted? Evon knew he'd have to keep a tight grip on his emotions or Emmett Chandler's choice of him as an honorable guardian would have been made in vain.

Dominique had paled visibly at the impact of his embrace. For the short while Evon had held her in his arms, she had felt protected, she had felt a sense of security. When she'd stared into his dark-passion-filled eyes, she had wondered what it would be like to feel his lips on hers. Her face flushed with humiliation and anger at her traitorous thoughts. Evon Forest did not want to be bothered with her or her younger brother, and she did not like him. He was an unscrupulous man who had taken advantage of her father. In a defensive gesture, she folded her arms across her chest and affirmed, "I'd like to go to my room." She did not wait for his permission, but turned and ran up the stairs.

Evon turned and strode back into the study, closing the door behind him. "Shall we continue?" he asked the lawyer.

"Of course, M'sieur. There are papers for you to sign, and the estate will be yours. Everything, that is, except for a broken-down riverboat that M'sieur Chandler left to his daughter. And the mortgage—do you plan to take care of—"

"*Oui,* I will take care of the note myself," Evon interrupted as he walked to the heavily draped window to stare out at the overgrown scrubs. "What I want to know is what Jules Harcourt was doing on my property?" Evon turned toward the attorney, awaiting his answer.

The attorney's brow rose slightly as he said, "M'sieur Harcourt holds the lien against Belle Terre."

"Harcourt? How the hell did Chandler become involved with a lowlife such as Jules Harcourt?"

"M'sieur Harcourt owns the estate that adjoins Belle Terre, and after M'sieur Chandler suffered severe losses, M'sieur Harcourt was kind enough to save Belle Terre; but then M'sieur Chandler had invested in a fraudulent shipping business and—"

"Chandler told me about the shipping business, but he didn't tell me who was behind the swindle. But I bet I can guess," Evon said, jamming his fists into his pockets. When at last the lawyer left, Evon, feeling a need to put some distance between him and his new ward, also left the plantation for New Orleans.

"I'll get even with that bastard, Evon Forest, if it's the last thing I do!" Dominique hissed, as she angrily kicked a piece of overturned furniture that lay among the rubble cluttering the cabin of the *City of New Orleans*.

"*Non petite!* You must not speak with such a whorish tongue. What would your mama say if she were alive?" the attractive mulatto scolded. Her soft-soled slippers made no sound as she walked into the room. "I thought when we left Florrie behind at Belle Terre, you'd leave that sort of talk there, too," Hetty said tersely, shaking her dark curly head. Her large almond-shaped eyes glittered as she glared at Dominique, but they grew wider as she accused, "Or did you sneak off to Annie's while I was at the market shopping this morning?"

"Hetty, please. Not now!" Dominique said irritably. She clenched her straight white teeth. But when she saw the hurt look on her mammy's features, her anger quickly dissolved and she explained patiently, "Hetty, I've been cursing since Mama died, and I'll probably curse until the day I die. And *non,* I haven't been to Annie's since before Papa's death. Please let's not fight, not now," she begged. Dominique put her fingertips against her throbbing temples as her eyes filled with tears of exhaustion.

Hetty saw Dominique's lovely face crumple and put her arms around the girl. What had she been thinking? Why, Dominique was like her own daughter. At the early age of fourteen, Hetty had lost her own child within minutes after giving birth, and the only thing that had saved her sanity was the birth of Dominique. Hetty had been called on to be her wet nurse and had cared for her ever since. *"Ma petite,* I did not mean to upset you, but I worry that you will be recognized even in your disguise. Your reputation would be in shreds," Hetty chided gently.

Dominique understood that Hetty was only looking out for her own good, but her disguise concealed her identity. And the large floppy hats she and Beau wore hid her brother's telltale red hair. She had explained these things to Hetty many times. But the tall mulatto feared they would be discovered, and once again Dominique assured her mammy, *"Mon Dieu,* Hetty, Beau and I have been to Annie's hundreds of times. Our disguise is a good one."

But Hetty was not appeased. "It would take but one gentleman to know that you are Dominique

Chandler, and your future would be destroyed."

"My mother visited Annie on a regular basis, and you accompanied her," Dominique pointed out stubbornly.

"But *chérie,* that was a long time ago. Things were not as they are today. People accepted your mother's friendship with the madam because they knew your mother supplied Annie with her potions, and I went along to help your mother. Now I make the potions and deliver them to the madam, but no one cares where I go, *chérie.* For I am a *femme de couleur;* a woman of color does not have a reputation to uphold."

Dominique knew that what Hetty said was true, but she hated being shackled in a woman's body. She hated being a prisoner of a society so strict it dictated where she should go, how she should act, what she should say, and who she should marry while men were free to do as they pleased. The more mistresses a man kept, the more virile and masculine he was thought to be, and each time he maimed or killed a man on the dueling field, he was not considered a murderer; *non,* he was excused for defending his *honor!* But no matter how furious it made her, she was a woman, and the only way she could escape her role in life, if only for a few hours, was to wear her disguise—the old worn out cambric shirt and breeches that had been the castoffs of the overseer's young son at Belle Terre. But she realized guiltily, Hetty was not responsible for her predicament, only guilty of voicing her concern, and Dominique apologized,

"I did not mean to hurt you, Hetty. I am just upset at the way things are. I hate being a woman."

"I know, *ma petite,* but you are a lady of society and if you expect to make a good match with a fine gentleman, you must not take the chance of going to Annie's where you might be recognized," Hetty warned once more.

A sign escaped her lips. Dominique knew she could not make promises to Hetty she could not keep. When it came to the brothel, her mammy was relentless and Dominique bit back the retort that had been on the tip of her tongue.

The independent streak in Dominique worried Hetty. Hetty wished she would meet a man who would make her forget such foolish thoughts, a man like Evon Forest. Her full lips curved upward, but she sobered quickly as she stared at Dominique and asked, "Why do you blame Evon Forest for this latest escapade of yours? That handsome man did not force you into this abominable situation. *Non petite,* this was your own idea to move to this old riverboat. And Missy, let me tell you, this is your wildest idea yet! No lady of quality would do such a scandalous thing! You have a willful nature, but M'sieur Forest appears to have a stubborn streak of his own," Hetty snorted, hands on her hips. "I sure wouldn't want to be you when M'sieur Forest returns and discovers you and Beau gone."

"You just don't understand. Evon Forest is a roguish bas—" she began, but at the frown on Hetty's visage, she said instead, "You are wrong in this, Hetty, you will see."

The mulatto woman shook her head at Dominique's prediction, and at the determination on her lovely features.

While Dominique was still an infant, Hetty knew she would one day become a beautiful woman. And at seventeen, she was a vision of perfection. Dominique was no longer a girl, and yet not quite a woman. Hetty knew Dominique possessed a contrary nature. When Evon Forest came for her, and Hetty knew he would, he would find Dominique to be a handful. She chuckled to herself. Yes, she thought, Evon Forest was definitely a man who could take charge of the young miss. Again she smiled, the days ahead would not always be sunshine and happiness, but they sure would be interesting!

"What are you smiling about?" Dominique asked, frowning as she bunched her skirts and tucked them into her waistband in an unladylike fashion. She didn't wait for Hetty to answer, but said instead, "When Evon Forest returns to Belle Terre and finds we've vacated his premises, he'll be anything but mad. Mark my words, Hetty, that bully will be glad to be free of us and his obligation as our guardian. Especially since ours was such a distasteful arrangement! Ooh, I hope I never lay eyes on that man again!" Dominique said heatedly.

For all her bravado, Dominique felt a moment of panic as she wondered how they would survive. How could she support Beau, Hetty, and herself? They wouldn't need much, but even the bare necessities cost money . . . and what of Beau's future? He would need an education. Dominique slowly looked around the dusty cabin. Leaving Hetty to her cleaning, she wandered out onto the gangway and into the grand salon.

The tables were turned every way on the expensive, but soiled, Belgium carpet covering the width and length of the room. She inspected the gambling tables more closely, and recognized that the felt tops were not torn and they were in relatively good shape. The germ of an idea began to take shape in her fertile mind. This old riverboat was once a place of business—a floating palace. Maybe it could be again? Umm, she mused, why not? A gambling casino brought in a great deal of money. And it would be the answer to her dilemma. After all, she thought, this was her riverboat—the only thing she owned. And she could do as she damn well pleased! Just let Evon Forest try to stop her. She'd make his life so miserable, he'd wash his hands of her.

One lone tear of relief slid down Dominique's flushed cheek as she hugged herself. She swiped at the tear with the back of her hand. Her spirits soared at the challenging adventure ahead and her lips tilted upward. She realized though that Hetty would never approve of her operating a gambling establishment. Twirling, she contemplated how a new coat of paint and a good cleaning would certainly do a lot for the old tub. Perhaps if she promised Hetty she wouldn't actually run the casino herself, the older woman wouldn't take to her bed. After all she and Beau did need an income. What if she hired a gentleman to run the casino? She would be the proprietress. Surely Hetty couldn't object to that, could she? The more Dominique thought of the advantages to owning her own business, the more appealing her idea became. Dominique took the stairway to the floor above, and stepped out onto the weather-battered boards. She strolled around the deck fixing, in her mind, this and that which needed repair. It became clear to her it would take more than a bucket of paint and elbow grease to make the old side-wheeler operable. She would need money. But then, she reasoned to herself, there was her share of the inheritance—Damn! She suddenly remembered her father had left Evon Forest in control of her funds. Maybe she could borrow the money and use the riverboat as collateral?

Excited at the possibilities she'd arrived at, Dominique made her way back inside. Her excitement was short-lived as she walked into the room Hetty had been cleaning. Black dust flew into her face, blinding her as her eyes filled with grit. Dominique sputtered and wiped her eyes with the back of her sleeve. She opened one watery eye and she saw Hetty making vigorous sweeping motions with her makeshift broom. "Hetty!" Dominique choked, but the slim woman ignored her protests.

She used the hem of her dress to wipe the dirt from her teary eyes, and smiled. With a few hours of daylight left, Dominique reached for a broom and began to sweep the cluttered debris into a neat pile. She had another idea but knew she would have to wait until Hetty was asleep before making the short trip to Basin Street. If Hetty became suspicious, she would tie her to her bed if need be. This time it was Dominique who chuckled out loud, but Hetty was humming a song and didn't hear her.

# Three

"Touch me, Camille, make me hard, make me crazy with wanting you," Evon whispered as he lay beside Camille on the soft feather bed. Camille was beautiful with thick chestnut hair and eyes the color of fool's gold. She was sought after by every gentleman who made Annie's his regular sporting house. And Evon was no different. Camille's sensuous mouth and experienced fingers worked their magic to excite the coldest of men, and Evon wanted Camille to help him erase the silver-maned hellion from his mind. With a giddy sense of pleasure Camille ran her hand tantalizingly down Evon's lithe frame, and her long tapered fingers encircled his swollen shaft. Camille was eager to please. She'd worked for Annie for eight years, and at twenty-six, men no longer brought her the satisfaction she once felt. But Evon Forest was different. He knew how to make a woman feel whole, he could arouse the coldest fish on Basin Street if he'd a mind to. And Camille looked forward to their time together. Evon's experienced hands equaled her own, and Camille gasped at his ministrations. She was fire and passion. But when her lips caressingly inched down the smooth, hard plane of his belly to the thick mass of dark hair, Evon went still. Camille paused. Evon raised his head and shrugged his shoulders as he whispered apologetically, "I'm sorry." This had never happened to Evon before. Evon sat up and swung his muscular legs to the floor. He reached for his trousers on the back of the satin chair beside the bed.

"She must be very beautiful," Camille said in a low, silvery voice.

"What the hell do you mean by that?" Evon asked, but at Camille's knowing look, Evon dressed quickly and strode to the door. Turning his head he said, "Camille, I—" Evon paused, then he called over his shoulder, "Later."

As Evon closed the door softly, Camille smiled sadly as she said aloud, "Somehow I don't think so."

He paused for a moment outside Camille's room and irritably brushed his fingers through his hair. After he'd discovered that Dominique was in fact Nicki Chandler, he had left Belle Terre to drown his frustration in drink at Annie's. When that hadn't helped, he'd made his way up the stairs in search of Camille, thinking she would squelch the burning flame Dominique had ignited in his loins. But he had been mistaken.

Exhaling, Evon walked down the hall to Annie's outlandishly decorated suite of rooms.

Inside, Evon accepted the glass of bourbon Annie offered him. He sat and crossed one booted foot over the other on the red and white Persian rug. Evon and Annie talked into the night, and as the bourbon loosened his tongue he confided in her that his father would disinherit him if he did not marry within the next five months, for then his father would turn everything over to his brother who was not interested in any aspect of plantation life. But he did not mention his present predicament with Dominique Chandler.

Evon's eyelids grew heavy and Annie patted his shoulder as she offered him one of the two vacant rooms across the hall. Annie reserved these rooms for her regular customers who had had too much to drink.

"Nicki, slow down! I can't walk as fast as you," Beau complained.

"Shush, Beau! Someone will hear you. We must hurry if we're to return to the riverboat before dawn. There'll be the dickens to pay if Hetty wakes up and finds we're gone," she said impatiently as she pulled her younger brother along behind her. Dominique hadn't wanted to bring Beau, but she couldn't chance him waking up and finding her gone for he would then wake Hetty. She had wanted to make the trek to Annie's immediately after Hetty had fallen asleep, but after cleaning three cabins she was worn out. As soon as her head touched the musty-smelling pillow, she had drifted into a deep, dreamless sleep. Hours later, when she awoke, she dressed quickly in the stillness of the moonlit cabin. Her disguise consisted of old breeches, a worn cambric shirt, and a floppy hat. Beau's outfit was similar.

They had made it to the brothel without incident and hurried up the flight of stairs. Halfway down the long corridor Dominique stopped abruptly. The hallway was dimly lit and Beau let out a howl as he stubbed his toe on the heel of his sister's hard-soled shoe. Dominique spun around and clamped a cupped hand over his opened mouth, but his squeal of pain had penetrated the silence in the long corridor, and Dominique held her breath as she waited to see if they had disturbed any of Annie's customers. One of the doors opened silently, and a disheveled Annie stood there squinting at the two familiar bedouins, and recognition softened the hardness around her light blue eyes. Without a word, she grabbed the shirtsleeves of both Dominique and Beau, and unceremoniously pulled them inside her elaborate living quarters. She peered up and down the hall before stepping back inside and quietly closed the door. "What in tarnation are you two doing lurking outside my door at this ungodly hour?" the madam asked sternly. There was a hint of irritation in her tone, but the twinkle in her eyes said she was pleased to see them.

"Does Hetty know you're here? No need to answer that. Of course she doesn't, which is why you snuck up here in the middle of the night." She didn't care why they had come, only that they had. Annie reached out and enfolded both of them in her chubby arms, hugging them against her ample breasts until Beau squirmed in protest.

Stepping back, Dominique smiled at the outrageous costume on her friend whom she loved as she loved Hetty. Annie wore a nightdress of scarlet, trimmed in ostrich feathers, and her nightcap, sitting askew on her orange-colored hair, was a deep purple. Her round face was smudged with the remains of makeup, but the love shining from her blue eyes brought tears to Dominique's eyes and she stepped back into the warm circle of Annie's fleshy arms. With her head resting against Annie's shoulder, she said, "Annie, I need to talk to you. But we have to get back before Hetty wakes or she'll send the sheriff after us."

Annie patted Dominique's shoulder gently, and said, "Don't you worry. I'll wake up Lonzo when the time comes and he'll take you back to Belle Terre before the sun comes up."

"We're no longer staying at Belle Terre," Dominique whispered.

"What are you saying, *petite?* Where are you staying?" Annie questioned.

"Belle Terre no longer belongs to us," Dominique explained as she closed her eyes to the pain that threatened to overwhelm her.

"I heard about your papa. I am sorry."

"Thank you, Annie," Dominique said. She blinked rapidly to erase the tears that welled up behind her eyelids, and continued quickly, "I have moved our belongings to Papa's riverboat. It was the only property not included in the sale of Belle Terre," she finished, stepping away from Annie's protective embrace while Beau quickly followed suit.

"Your papa sold the plantation?" she exclaimed, *"Mon Dieu!* But you cannot stay on that broken-down scow down at the wharf. It is not safe there. *Ma petite,* I wish you and Beau could stay here, but . . ." Annie knew it had been ridiculous to make such a statement, but her heart went out to these two children of her beloved friend, Celeste.

"We'll be all right, Annie. But Papa did a terrible thing. He appointed the new owner of Belle Terre to act as guardian over Beau and me," Dominique exclaimed, feeling her anger rise again at the mention of it.

*"Non,* how can this be, *chérie?* I knew things were turning from bad to worse at Belle Terre, but I did not know they were so terrible. Aah, come, *mes petits.* Lonzo will make you a cup of hot cocoa." The old madam ushered them to the blue velvet camel-backed sofa.

"I don't want cocoa, Annie, I'm sleepy," Beau said petulantly, his gray-blue eyes drooping with exhaustion as he yawned.

"Poor *petit,"* Annie chuckled sympathetically. "Dominique, take him into my bedroom and tuck him in while I summon Lonzo. The nosy old thing will want to hear what you have to say." Annie chuckled as she left to wake up her negro coachman who had, over the last thirty years, doubled as her all-around handyman, manager, and, though she refused to admit it, her friend. At sixty-six, the dark-skinned man was still slim and claimed to have the strength of any two men of twenty. Perhaps he exaggerated a bit, but Annie had to admit he was as strong as he'd been thirty years ago when she'd first hired him to keep her establishment free of unruly men who had had too much to drink or who thought they could treat her girls disrespectfully.

Ten minutes later, Annie returned, "Lonzo will be here as soon as he gets dressed," she said as she closed the door. Annie walked to the sofa and sat next to Dominique. "Now what's this about a guardian? Who is this new owner?" she asked, her voice etched with concern. Dominique was unhappy and Annie could not stand to see her this way.

"His name is Evon Forest, a miserable excuse of a man."

"Evon Forest! Are you sure that is his name, *petite?*" Annie asked drawing her brows together in a frown.

Dominique did not notice the surprise on Annie's face as she spat, "*Oui,* Papa met him about six months ago, a man who took advantage of him during his financial difficulties. He talked Papa into selling Belle Terre to him for practically nothing. The small profit after the sale was to go to Beau and me, but that weasel has control of it. It makes me furious, Annie! The funds are ours, mine and Beau's, but that rakehell will steal our money the same way he has stolen our home." Her emerald eyes filled with tears of anger.

"There, *ma chérie.* Sometimes crying helps to relieve the heartache," Annie soothed. Her own sky-blue eyes filled as Dominique sobbed out all the pain and despair of the last week.

Her tears at last stopped, and Dominique felt somewhat better. Annie was a great comfort even if she had no ready solution for their problems. And even her anger at her father had dissipated a bit. But she still resented her father's unreasonable decision in making a man like Evon Forest their guardian. "Thank you for listening, Annie, but I'd better get Beau back to the riverboat. Maybe we can come back later this afternoon."

*"Non, non petite.* Allow the young one to sleep. Lonzo will be here soon, and there is still time to discuss why you have come. There will be no problem with Hetty. After we've had our little talk, Lonzo will drive you and Beau back," Annie insisted. She knew Dominique would not have come at this hour if it were not important. If Dominique and Beau needed her, she would do all she could to help them.

Dominique knew they should be getting back to the wharf, but after making the trip through the dark streets with Beau in tow, she really wanted to stay a while longer so that she could talk with both Annie and Lonzo. She could not carry out her outlandish scheme without their help, and even if it meant bringing Hetty's wrath down around her head, she would stay and explain her plight to her friends.

An hour later, Lonzo dropped them at the end of the wharf. Dominique's lovely face was flushed with excitement as she and Beau quickly made their way back up the wooden gangplank. The sagging side-wheeler groaned beneath their feet as they made their way across the deck and down the stairs. Waves lapped at the sides of the boat, gently rocking it back and forth in the still humid air. They made their way along the hallway to their sleeping cabins.

The riverboat had been magnificent at one time, and now Dominique knew with Annie's help, it would once more rival the finest riverboats on the Mississippi.

Streaks of light filtered through the leaded glass of the porthole in her bedroom and Dominique removed her garments, and donned a cotton nightdress. She lay upon the damp outer cover of her sagging mattress and closed her eyes, but she was too filled with her newfound plans to sleep. Her thoughts returned to the conversation she'd had with Annie after Lonzo joined them.

She smiled as she remembered the look of disbelief on Annie's pudgy face when she explained that she wanted Annie to help her find a man to manage her new casino. And then there was Lonzo's reluctance to hire the men needed to repair and remodel the riverboat into a floating gambling palace. Annie had said no. Lonzo had said no. Together they had lectured her on her station in life, telling her ladies did not do such things, but when Dominique accused them both of sounding like Hetty, Annie had sniffed indignantly and crossed her arms over her bosom agreeing to at least listen to her plans. But when she'd finished, Annie was still not convinced as she argued, "But *petite,* I think you should go into a more respectable business like a millinery shop or—"

"I could never support three prople on what I would earn as a seamstress. And you know I can't sew a straight seam," she said firmly.

"Hetty would help you," Annie reasoned.

"Hetty has enough to do what with making and selling her potions. And I need her to help with Beau. Besides, if I didn't make it as a seamstress I'd be knocking on your door asking you for a job," Dominique teased.

But Annie took her seriously and did not think her words humorous. *"Ma petite!* I did not want to corrupt you with my way of life. Celeste would hate me were she alive to hear you talk this way," the madam said sadly.

*"Non,* Annie, my mother could never hate you. Besides you have done nothing wrong. You have given Beau and me comfort when we needed it, and you have listened to our problems when we brought them to you."

At last Annie had sighed and said, "You win, *petite.* I don't have much money, but I will help you get started."

Her soft palm raised to cover her rosebud mouth and smother a yawn as her lids flickered and then rested against her smooth apricot skin. Smiling, Dominique closed her eyes as sleep claimed her, and she dreamed wonderful dreams of a rich and rewarding future for herself and Beau.

* * *

"Oh . . ." Evon moaned as he sat up in bed and leaned forward to rest his throbbing head in his open palm. He heard someone yelping, and pushing himself off the bed he walked to the door and yanked it open, "Who the hell is making all this racket out here?" he bellowed, but closed his eyes as a piercing knifelike pain stabbed at his temple. He opened one eye to peer out into the hall, but there was no one there and he closed the door and fell back on the bed, grumbling as he went back to sleep.

Later, he was again awakened to a door banging and whispered voices as they moved off down the hall. Once more he jerked open his door to see what looked like one tall and one short street urchin hurrying around the corner of the hall. "What the hell kind of place is Annie running here?" Evon muttered as he banged his own door shut and lay back down. Sleep evaded him, and his thoughts returned to the previous day when he'd discovered his lovely creature from the bayou had been none other than one of his new charges. Dominique Chandler had turned out to be Emmett Chandler's daughter. Evon had not understood Chandler fully when he'd appointed him guardian of his two children: seventeen-year-old Nicki, and seven-year-old Beau. Evon had assumed both children were boys. He had not known that Nicki was Chandler's nickname for his daughter Dominique! A beautiful young woman, that he, Evon, was supposed to protect and oversee. Hell, he thought, how was he going to protect Dominique against himself? Chandler had thought Evon an honorable man. What the hell, he wondered for the tenth time, could the man have been thinking? He had eyes didn't he? He must have known that his daughter was ravishingly beautiful! She could tempt a saint. Why would he entrust his only daughter with him? His reputation was well-known; he was a hot-blooded man with a hot-blooded appetite for beautiful women. All of New Orleans knew Evon Forest. The eldest son of one of the wealthiest men in Louisiana. Indeed, there were many fathers who would have offered Evon a fat dowry to wed their daughters, but they were also aware of Evon's love of the single life, and none wanted their daughters sullied. Emmett Chandler had not heeded this warning, but had instead thrown his daughter to the lion, so to speak. Exhausted, Evon fell back asleep.

Late the following morning, a rumpled and disgruntled Evon left Annie's for Belle Terre. He arrived at the plantation before noon. He'd entered the foyer, and his booted soles clicked against the black and white marble floor and bounced against the wall, echoing his entry.

Looking around he made a mental note to replace the furniture that had been sold along with numerous other expensive pieces in the house. Chandler should have explained the entire situation to him. He would have listened to Chandler's problems, he thought for the hundredth time since hearing of the man's suicide.

With hindsight Evon believed that he would have helped him out of the disastrous situation. He would have loaned him enough money to get him over his phony shipping investment that Evon suspected Harcourt had instigated. Chandler had invested heavily in the shipping business thinking to recoup his losses from the tragic fire that had destroyed his blooded plantation walkers. The mares had been bred to Chandler's prized stallion, Saladin. The colossal black stallion was sought after by every plantation owner in Louisiana and all the surrounding states. The gentlemen plantation owners rode their fields from sunup to sundown, and insisted their ride be one of pleasure. The walker was a must for the southern plantation owner. And Emmett Chandler had owned the finest animal in the South.

When Chandler had approached Evon with his proposition, he had not told him who was behind the shipping investment, only that he was on the brink of bankruptcy and wanted to give Evon first choice of purchasing his estate. The meager amount Chandler was asking for Belle Terre was one Evon could not afford to turn down, and he and Chandler had had an agreement written up the following day. At the lawyer's office, Chandler had approached the subject of his children's welfare. The man practically begged Evon to be their guardian if anything should happen to him. Evon had reluctantly agreed, knowing Chandler was still a young man at forty-two. But he hadn't foreseen the man's inner turmoil, his disgrace at losing everything he'd worked the last twenty years to build. And now, a month later, Chandler was dead, and Evon was responsible for the welfare of his son and his beautiful and sensuous daughter.

The study door was open and Evon walked in and looked around the spacious room. Chandler's leather-bound books lined two walls and his hunting rifle hung over the massive stone fireplace. The fourth wall was lined with six windows that reached from the ceiling to the floor, allowing light to fill the room and brighten the dark browns in the Belgium carpet. The jade-green drapes matched the overstuffed chair, and sofa. Turning, Evon left the study and headed for the stairs, thinking to find Dominique. Yesterday, she had escaped to her room, and shortly after he'd left for New Orleans. But the time had come for him to have a talk with her if either expected to survive this impossible situation.

The door was open to Dominique's suite and Evon looked in. The drawers were ajar, and the armoire doors stood open revealing their contents had been removed. He was left in no doubt that the occupant had departed with bag and baggage for parts unknown.

"Blossom! Where the hell are you?" Evon bellowed at the top of his lungs. He strode through the quiet halls and down the stairs as he continued to yell, "Florrie, Jigger, you'd better show yourself or I'll beat you within an inch of your lives!" His threat was just that, a threat, and no more, for Evon Forest had never laid a hand on any of the slaves at his own plantation, and no one at Belle Terre needed to fear his wrath. But he was the new master here, and no one knew anything about him or what he was capable of doing.

He stormed out the back entrance and down the steps, walking briskly along the enclosed walkway between the big house and the separate washrooms and kitchens. "God damnit, Blossom, where are you hiding?"

"Blossom's here, Massa Forest! Here ah is," Blossom called in a trembling voice, and Evon pushed back the curtained area where she stood with her elbows encased in flour as she kneaded a huge mound of dough.

"Where is Mistress Dominique and Master Beauregard?" he asked, scowling fiercely.

"Naw leans, Naw leans! They's packed up and moved to the wharf," she cried as her eyes rolled back in her head, and the whites were all that Evon saw.

"Wharf? You mean they moved to one of the boats docked there?"

"Yas suh."

"But that's impossible!"

"Nos suh, they's done moved to Massa Chandler's riverboat, and missy say she ain't neva comin' back heres long as yous' here."

"Is that right?"

"Yas suh, missy says—"

"Never mind what missy says, Blossom. We'll just see about that."

"What's yous goin' do wit her? Yous goin' hurt missy?" The terror in the black woman's eyes made Evon realize he'd scared the wits out of the poor woman.

*"Non,* I'm not going to hurt her, but she is coming back to Belle Terre if I have to carry her back. And she'll stay here if I have to lock her in her room."

"Uh umm, po' missy. Po' po' missy," Blossom whispered as tears slid from her coffee-colored cheeks.

His anger mounted, and the woman's tears made him even more angry as he realized he was giving her the wrong impression of himself. But he would have to deal with that later. Evon was determined to reach New Orleans by nightfall.

# Four

At the wharf, Evon dismounted and looped one leather strap around the hitching post, and strode purposefully up the gangplank of the sagging riverboat.

His night-black eyes glittered as he glanced around the deck. Everywhere he looked there was neglect, from the rotted boards on the deck to the cracked and peeling paint. And portions of the top railing were missing. "This old reprobate isn't a fit place for man or beast," he muttered. Evon shook his head. The little vixen had better think again if she thinks I'd allow her to stay in this rubble. His thoughts were interrupted as he paused to test his footing. Then he glanced once more around the vacant deck before making his way to the stairwell and the cabins below.

"Eek! Beau! Get this wretched frog out of my scrub water!" Dominique exclaimed, gritting her teeth in agitation. This was the final straw! Early that morning she and Hetty had begun cleaning their sleeping quarters. They had had to chase Beau out of one cabin or the other. If Beau's frog Napolean wasn't hopping in and out of each neat pile of dirt ready to be picked up, Beau was careening around their skirts pretending he was fighting off an imaginary pirate he had insisted had invaded their vessel.

Both in turn had chased her brother up on deck, but minutes later he was back underfoot. But this was too much, Dominique thought. Poor Hetty had stooped to scoop a pile of dirt from the floor when Napolean had leaped on her shoulder. And when their startled mammy had turned to see what was on her shoulder, she had stared into the bulging eyes of Napolean. Hetty had shrieked at the sight and nearly swooned. Afterwhich Dominique had insisted her brother take his giant frog to his cabin while they tackled the kitchen area. Beau had at first balked at his sister's suggestion, but when Hetty raised her broom high above his head, Beau tucked Napolean into his trouser pocket and scampered out of the room.

Both were tired and out of sorts, and Dominique realized neither she nor Hetty had the patience to deal with the antics of her seven-year-old brother.

Her head jerked up. "It's Lafitte! Man the guns, men! We'll fight to the end!" Beau yelled. Dominique heard his footsteps as he neared the kitchen.

Her patience was sorely tried, and Dominique stepped out into the hallway, "That is enough, young man!" she said, "I think the time has come for you and I to have an understanding, young ma . . ." Dominique huffed, but her words trailed away as Beau skidded to a halt before her, and they both stared into Evon's dark eyes. She gasped and felt impaled by the unyielding gaze he bestowed upon her.

*"Non chérie,* it is you and I who must come to an understanding," he said. His voice, though quiet, had an ominous quality.

His face was black with rage. Dominique was hypnotized by his piercing glare. And when one tapered brow rose slightly she thought how handsome he looked standing before her looking like the pirate Jean Lafitte whom Beau had described. Evon's black trousers hugged his muscular thighs and his white shirt was opened to the waist, displaying a broad chest and spilling forth a mass of dark curls. But it was his mouth that intrigued her. His bottom lip appeared slightly fuller than the top, and although they were parted in agitation, she shivered as she remembered how they had sensuously claimed hers.

"Who gave you permission to leave Belle Terre, madam?"

"Who gave—" Dominique began, when suddenly the meaning of his words penetrated her glazed rumination, and the impact of their meaning made her tremble with rage as she hissed vehemently, "I do not need your permission to do as I please, M'sieur."

"Aah *chérie,* that is where you are wrong. Have you so quickly forgotten that I am your legal guardian? And as my ward you will obey me or suffer the consequence," Evon goaded, his tone ruthless as he cursed himself for allowing a girl to goad him into making threats he would not carry out.

"I have not forgotten how my father, under duress, made such a poor choice when he named a blackguard like you to see to his beloved children's welfare," she blazed haughtily. Dominique was determined that this man should know and understand that he did not own her or Beau. How had she, only moments before, thought him handsome? Evon Forest was a dominating ogre. A tyrant who thought his guardianship gave him the right to make unnecessary demands. He had taken liberties with her that overreached the moral boundary. Why, she thought, the man actually believed he could maul her and do whatever he wanted with her. Well! Evon Forest had another thought coming if he thought she would do his bidding! "I refuse to return to Belle Terre," she reflected adamantly, but her courage faltered as his gaze raked over her body with unabashed interest.

What the hell did she expect of him? Did she think he would allow her and the boy to live on a dilapidated riverboat? A riverboat docked at the wharf with undesirables lurking behind every shadow and doorway?

The gleam in her emerald eyes matched the determination in her voice. But Evon refused to be swayed by Dominique's willful ways. If he allowed her to have her own way the girl would end up in a disastrous situation. She could not fend for herself and the boy in such an unsavory atmosphere. Evon had made his decision as he said, "I must insist that you come back to the safety and normality of the plantation. I will not abide you and the boy living here on this broken-down pile of trash. Nor, *ma petite,* will I stand by and watch you make yourself the subject and delight of every ruffian on the riverfront."

"You will not abide! You will not stand by—M'sieur, I did not ask you to be my protector, nor do I need you to protect me," she yelled into his face, then turned away as she crossed her arms beneath her bosom in protest.

"And *chérie,*" he began as he turned her back to face him, "neither did I ask to be your protector, but I am bound by duty to your father and I do not take such an obligation lightly." Her eyes were large and liquid as Evon gazed upon the velvety lashes damp with tears that Dominique fought hard to suppress. He almost smiled at the beautiful nose wrinkled in anger, but instead he steeled himself as he reached out to encircle her tiny waist as he abruptly tossed her over his shoulder. "Hetty," Evon bellowed as he turned around.

Hetty had been putting the finishing touches on her room when she'd heard Beau yelling something about a pirate and she'd gone to investigate. But by the time she had stuck her head out the cabin door, she saw the new master striding purposefully toward Dominique's cabin. She had quickly stepped back inside, and returned to her task until she'd heard Evon call her name, and she hurried to the door. *"Oui,* M'sieur Forest?" she called.

"Pack your belongings, along with your mistress's and the young master's. Hire a cab and charge the fare to me. Have the driver take you and Beau out to Belle Terre," he called over his shoulder, not breaking his stride as he issued instructions.

"Of course, M'sieur Forest," Hetty reciprocated.

"Hetty, is Nicki going to be all right?" Beau asked.

"Do not worry Beau. Nicki will not be hurt by this man. My guess is M'sieur Forest would like to do many things to your sister, but hurting Dominique is not one of them," Hetty said as she put an arm around his thin shoulders, and hugged a wide-eyed Beau to her.

"Do you think M'sieur Forest hates Nicki, Hetty?" he asked somewhat breathlessly. There was concern in his voice, but his mammy's reassuring words had taken away his fear. Beau had never seen his sister treated in such a manner, and he wondered if Nicki had been right that his papa had been mistaken when he'd made Evon Forest their new father.

*"Non, ma petite.* M'sieur Forest does not hate Dominique, nor does Dominique hate M'sieur Forest, but it will take time to turn their feelings around," Hetty prophesied. She watched the pair disappear up the stairs and her full lips curved upward.

After Evon grasped her around the waist and jerked her off her feet, Dominique had landed with a jolt on Evon's hard-muscled shoulder, and the breath was knocked from her. She inhaled deeply and sputtered indignantly, "Put me down."

When Evon ignored her she became furious,

curling her fingers into her palms, and struck his back repeatedly as she demanded in a shrill voice, "I said put me down, you bast—" but her words were halted as she felt the mortifying sting of Evon's hand on her backside. Her eyes smarted, but she refused to utter a sound.

"You have called me a bastard for the last time, *chérie*. The next time you insult my ancestry I will hike up your skirts and you will feel the flat of my hand on your bare bottom," Evon threatened. He left little doubt in Dominique's mind that he would do as he said.

By the time they reached the gangplank Dominique was fuming, and Evon did not slow his pace as he strode purposefully down the wooden walkway. The impact of each jarring step made it difficult to breathe, and as his grip around her waist purposely loosened she was forced to clutch his waist.

When Evon reached the street where Marengo stood, he undid the reins with one hand. He then clasped Dominique around the waist and lifted her effortlessly, but none too gently onto the saddle, and swung up behind her.

He had made a fool of her. Dominique sat ramrod straight and held herself stiffly away from him while he adjusted his seat. Evon drew her back against him as he nudged Marengo into a walk. Dominique trembled with anger as they rode through the crowded street. She wished Evon would fall from the horse's back and break his thick skull. But she clamped her teeth tightly together until they were through the throng of people. Then as they reached the edge of the city, Dominique jerked from his arms. Evon grabbed her shoulder, and when she felt his fingers dig into her soft flesh, she said in a nasty tone, "Take your filthy hands off of me!" She twisted around and her nose was almost touching his chin as her tone hardened. "Your touch makes my flesh crawl." Evon was silent as she glared at him. When he didn't look away, she quickly gave him her back. Suddenly she was spun around, and his mouth bore down on her parted lips. His tongue darted between her teeth while his hand cupped one firm breast. His touch scorched her skin. The man had the power to make her burn with passion, even when she tried to tell herself she despised him. Warning spasms of alarm erupted within her. Damn him! He could turn her emotions upside down with one blazing kiss. She pushed against his chest with all her might. Evon quickly released her as a half smile crossed his face. Dominique sputtered, but words escaped her. She quickly faced forward as her cheeks flushed a deep crimson at her appalling reaction. How could she respond as she had when she hated this man so? Evon drew her gently back against his well-muscled chest, and Dominique did not attempt to pull away. But she refused to acknowledge the effect his closeness had had on her as she unconsciously strained against his iron-clad grip.

Why had he come after her? He should have left the minx on that damn riverboat. He was wasting precious time when instead he should be finding someone to dangle beneath his father's long interfering nose. He'd left D'Arcy at Forest Manor. And, he thought, if his father's condition worsened no one knew where he was. Wye might, at this very moment, be trying to reach him at Belle Terre, and here he was out chasing this she-cat.

Evon loved his father and didn't want to upset him further, but he hated having his father dictate his future. The days were slipping by and he was in a quandary; he had to find a wife, and soon. There were several women who would readily accept his proposal, but would he find a woman to agree to his preposterous proposal? She would have to agree to marry him and feign a nonexistent pregnancy. Then after his father's death she must agree to give him his freedom. His inheritance depended on his finding the right lady. Should he tell her the truth? No, he thought, then she would have the upper hand. Of course she would be compensated for her trouble, and while the lady occupied his home he would be generous to a fault. In the end he would bestow on her a sizable settlement for any inconvenience he may have caused. The lady would have to be very talented to fool his father. Evon believed that most women were excellent actresses when it came to getting what they wanted. After all his mother had wanted it all; money and social standing she received from his father, and sexual satisfaction she received from his uncle. And his thoughts drifted to his present mistress, the lovely Yvette. What would Yvette's reaction be to such a preposterous arrangement? He smiled. Yvette could act out the plot. Hadn't she in the past put on more than one play for him? The stage was her bedroom and she needed no script. Evon frowned. Yvette hated children. He recalled one evening when he'd escorted Yvette to a ball in New Orleans. A young child had reached out and touched the beautiful satin gown she wore. Yvette had screeched obscenities at the frightened child as she viciously slapped at his hand. Evon had felt sorry for the boy and had given him a coin. Yvette had laughed at him for being so softhearted. She said he was a dirty street urchin and she wouldn't stand for him to touch her lovely gown with his nasty little hands. Evon had been shocked at her honesty. But then he wouldn't be asking Yvette to have his child, he would make sure as he had in the past that that didn't happen. He chuckled softly. Yvette might hate children, but Yvette loved money. Suddenly Dominique stretched against him bringing Evon back to the present. He smiled. He would talk to Yvette soon, and thinking his problem solved, his mood lightened and he rested his chin on top of Dominique's rose-scented hair.

His arms involuntarily tightened around her, and he wondered what he was to do. If she were not so headstrong he could ask her to act as mistress of Belle Terre—that is until he wed. He would bring it up tomorrow, after all what could it hurt? If she would be willing to compromise—sweet Jesus, he had to do something, he couldn't have her running away every time his back was turned.

Dominique sighed as she snuggled against Evon's warmth. She was exhausted. She had at first resisted the temptation to relax in the arms of a man she could not abide. But when her black-tipped lids grew heavy she was too tired to ward off the threatening darkness. She even felt relief as she slumped against him in a deep, but restless sleep.

Her body was soft against his chest and his arms felt good around her, and once more Evon rested his chin on the top of her head. The silkiness of her silver-blond locks against his stubbled cheek brought a longing that started deep within his loins. Evon could not control the urge to touch his lips to her temple. But when she moaned softly, he quickly brought his emotions under control and nudged Marengo into a faster pace. He had to get the vixen to Belle Terre, and soon. She had a way of taking control of his senses. In the future he would have to exert a firm hold on his emotions when he was near her. He ground his heels in the gelding's side sending him into a gallop. If they were alone much longer he feared he would be tempted to take her here in the bayou, with or without her permission.

Marengo walked slowly up the crushed-seashell drive of Belle Terre. Giant oaks lined each side of the drive, and their leaves rustled softly as they swayed gently in the evening breeze. Directly ahead stood the beautiful mansion seeming to Evon to welcome them home. He gazed up at the unusual design of the exterior of the house featuring a semicircular wing and twenty-two immense columns. From a distance Belle Terre gave the impression of ultimate splendor and luxury. But up close the appearance was one of neglect. Several shutters hung loose, and some were missing. Everywhere he looked he saw signs of omission. The exterior would have to be scraped and painted. Evon had had blueprints drawn up, and the reconstruction was to begin the following week. He had purchased fifteen of the finest blooded mares in the state. They were stabled at Forest Manor awaiting the completion of the stables at Belle Terre. Also at Forest Manor, and handpicked by Evon, were slaves trained in various degrees of carpentry, bricklaying, plastering, and other trades. Under the supervision of his brother Wyatt they would leave Forest Manor as soon as they received word that Evon had completed the legalities, and they could proceed to Belle Terre. Evon was anxious to get started. There were several changes he would make at Belle Terre. His major project would be to install two water cisterns in the attic to be used for such an innovative feature as indoor plumbing. He would personally oversee the building of a gas plant where he intended to produce acetylene gas from calcium carbide for the new light fixtures to be installed all over.

Evon was sorry D'Arcy couldn't be with him on this new adventure, but until Evon could replace him, his father would need D'Arcy to oversee Forest Manor. Evon missed his friend. He had purchased D'Arcy Badru in New Orleans ten years ago. The black man had been badly beaten. Evon was sickened by such treatment. He and his father owned more than six hundred slaves, but none had felt the sting of a whip nor was a man ever separated from his family. Taking a man away from his family would break a man's spirit. Evon's father believed that slaves were human and should be so treated. And his beliefs had been instilled in Wyatt and Evon.

The same day Evon purchased D'Arcy, he took him home to Forest Manor where he immediately sent for a doctor to tend the black man's wounds. After which, D'Arcy was nursed back to health. D'Arcy saw Evon when he came to the cabin in the slave quarters to check on his progress. D'Arcy had believed Evon's only interest in him was to protect his investment. But after D'Arcy was able to be up and around, he realized his new master had not just saved his life but was a fair man, working and sweating in the fields beside everyone else. D'Arcy became indebted to his new master. When the overseer at Forest Manor was injured and had to relinquish his position, Evon had offered D'Arcy the job which included a deed to a parcel of land with a three-room cottage situated on the edge of the property. D'Arcy immediately refused Evon's generous offer. He was a man of color, and it was unlawful for a slave to own property. When he said as much to Evon, Evon produced a document that made D'Arcy a freed man of color. Evon said it was D'Arcy's choice. D'Arcy was welcome to stay, but he was also free to leave. D'Arcy chose to remain at Forest Manor.

Jigger was locking the front door when he heard

the muffled sound of hooves on the driveway. When he recognized his new master, he hurried down the steps. Evon stepped down with Dominique in his arms, and the majordomo's eyes widened. But Evon motioned for him to remain silent, and the tall thin man nodded his head up and down and grinned purposefully, showing off the gold tooth he was so proud of, knowing it sparkled in the light of the full moon. Jigger took Marengo's reins and led him toward the stable while Evon made his way up the steps and through the opened doorway. He strode effortlessly up the curving staircase. The soft glow of a lamp beckoned him to the end of the long hall where he paused and glanced inside. The ballerina design on the wallpaper and the soft yellow counterpane adorning a four poster bed left no doubt in his mind that the room had been especially decorated for the exquisite beauty still asleep in his arms. Evon entered the room and walked to the edge of the bed. He gently lay Dominique down upon the coverlet. When he reached for the multicolored crocheted shawl to cover her, Dominique's eyes flew open and she whispered, "How did I get here?"

Evon paused as his eyes took in her disheveled appearance. Her hair was mussed and sleep glazed her eyes, yet she was lovelier than ever. He cleared his throat, and quickly picked up the shawl. "You rode with me atop Marengo," he explained huskily.

A swath of wavy hair fell casually across his forehead. His stance emphasized the force of his thighs and the sleekness of his hips, and Dominique thought, Damn the man for being so handsome.

She shook her head. And as the cobwebs cleared she raised one dark eyebrow and looked slowly around the familiar surroundings. Suddenly she remembered, and she hissed, "You abducted me! You had no right to bring me back to Belle Terre, M'sieur. You cannot force me to stay under the same roof with you. And I do not—"

"Now hold on a damn minute. You and Beau cannot stay on that run-down riverboat. It's unsafe. I will not allow—"

His words sparked her anger. "You won't allow—you cannot make me live here with you. Or were you planning to keep me here against my will? Am I to be a prisoner in your house?" Dominique asked contemptuously. Her flashing emerald eyes blazed as they met and held Evon's own fiery glare. She refused to look away.

Evon was the first to drop his eyes as he unfolded the shawl and lay it across Dominique's legs. When he attempted to tuck the soft wrap around her tiny waist, Dominique yanked the cover back, bounding to the opposite side of the bed where she stepped to the floor before Evon could move. She quickly ran toward the open doorway, but Evon reached the door first and stepped in front of her, his large frame blocking her escape. "Were you going somewhere?" he asked.

"I'm hungry. I—I was going down to the kitchen to see if Blossom will make me something to eat," she quipped. Then she asked bitingly,

"Or, did you plan to lock me in my room? Perhaps you thought to starve me into submission?" she baited him.

"You try my patience, *chérie*. That was not my intention, but since you were the one to suggest it—the idea is an appealing one," Evon threatened as his lips curved upward in a cynical smile.

The look Evon gave her was intimidating, and Dominique realized she had pushed him too far. But he was an irritating man with irritating ways, and he had riled her beyond words. Her courage returned and she snapped daringly, "Do not push me too far, M'sieur."

His eyes darkened dangerously as he grabbed her shoulders, bringing her up hard against him as he looked her over seductively. He would have ground his mouth on hers, but the fear he saw in her eyes stopped him. He quickly released her as he turned and strode out into the hallway slamming and locking the door behind him. He paused outside the door, and when he would have relented, Dominique began pounding on the door as she hurled expletives at him. He pocketed the key and jammed his hands into his pockets. The vixen deserved to be taught a lesson. He was, after all, her guardian. Dominique continued her tirade from behind the closed door.

Dominique stared at the locked door. Her fists throbbed and her words had fallen on deaf ears. She heard Evon's disappearing footsteps, and stepped back from the door. The oaf had actually locked her in her room! Fuming, she rubbed her sore fists. Well, she thought, she was not a child, and she would show him that she would not be treated as such. It was time M'sieur learned a lesson. No man ordered Dominique Chandler around and got away with it. She turned the lamp down low and walked through the French doors and out onto the balcony.

# Five

Evon had been unable to sleep, and several hours later he had made his way back up the stairs. Pausing outside Dominique's room, he inserted the large skeleton key into the lock. He chuckled to himself as he envisioned the irate girl on the other side of the walnut door.

He pushed the door wide, and his dark eyes twinkled with mischief as he scanned the room. Dominique had turned the wick down low, but the full moon allowed him to see clearly. His laughter died as he realized the room was empty. But he noticed both doors leading onto the veranda stood open, and he smiled as he crossed the room to walk out onto the expansive gallery. He quickly scanned the structure, but he didn't see Dominique. Then he saw the large oak branch near the wooden railing, and instinctively he stiffened. A lethal calm washed over him as he turned and made his way back the way he'd come. She'd made a fool of him. He quickened his pace and descended the stairs two at a time. Once outside, he made his way to the stables, never breaking his stride until he came to an abrupt halt at the stall where he had had Jigger put Saladin. The stall stood empty. He quickly saddled Marengo. "You shall regret this trickery, mademoiselle. Why do you prefer that filthy riverboat to Belle Terre and me?" he muttered, but he already knew the answer. It wasn't Belle Terre she was running away from, but him. He gave Marengo a sharp nudge. The gelding started, unused to the sharp heel of his master's boot in his side. The gelding dug his hooves into the soft earth and raced out of the stable, and Evon expertly guided the horse in the direction of New Orleans.

Dominique rode Saladin directly into the stable behind Annie's brothel where she and Beau dismounted and quickly made their way to the stairway.

Several minutes later the disheveled pair stood before Annie. Dominique breathlessly related the incident to her.

Annie stared at Dominique's flushed face. "What are you saying, *petite?* Who locked you in your room?" Annie asked, and there was disbelief in the tone of her voice.

"M'sieur Forest!" Beau volunteered somberly.

"Hush Beau. Let your sister tell me what happened," Annie reprimanded as she raised a hand, but her eyes never left Dominique's face.

"Evon Forest, Annie," Dominique related angrily.

"But you must be mistaken. Evon would never . . ."

"Evon? You never said you knew him!" she accused.

"I'm sorry, *petite,* but I've known Evon Forest a long time and he is . . ." she began, but at the condemning look on Dominique's face her words trailed away. Annie did not tell Dominique that she was having difficulty believing that they were referring to the same man. Nor did Annie tell Dominique that her instincts told her that Evon Forest wasn't a man who took advantage of beautiful young women. And certainly not one as lovely as Dominique.

Over the years Annie had become an expert in judging a man's character. A man could not hide an unsavory or evil disposition from Annie. She could look in a man's eyes and know immediately whether he was good or bad. In thirty years her instincts had never failed her. She knew without a doubt that Evon Forest was a gentleman in the true sense. But Annie didn't say any of these things to Dominique. She realized that Dominique's opinion of Evon was at the moment in total contrast to hers. And Annie was determined to find out why.

"No doubt, M'sieur Forest is one of your best customers . . ." Dominique began, but she quickly apologized. "I'm sorry Annie." Her hateful words were directed at Evon. She hadn't meant to slander Annie.

*"Non, petite.* You have said nothing to be sorry for."

*"Oui,* I have. I may dislike Evon," she hissed, her bitterness spilling over into her voice, "but I'd never purposely say anything to hurt you, Annie." Dominique said it gently and sincerely.

Annie waved away her apology, and asked, "Tell me exactly what happened between you and Evon, *petite."*

"I refused to stay at Belle Terre as long as M'sieur Forest was there. But after we moved to the riverboat, M'sieur Forest came and ordered me to return to Belle Terre. I refused, and he—he abducted me."

"Oh come now, *petite.* Evon would never—"

"But he did, Annie," Beau broke in, then added excitedly, "Then M'sieur threw Nicki over his shoulder. He put her on his horse and he sat behind her and they rode away."

A mental picture of Evon toting Dominique over his shoulder like a sack of flour made Annie chuckle as she said, "I bet that was a sight to see."

"Annie!" Dominique exclaimed.

Annie saw the hurt look in Dominique's eyes and she sobered quickly and apologized, "I'm sorry." Then she spoke with as reasonable a voice as she could manage, "Then what did he do?"

"Wasn't that enough?" Dominique exclaimed.

"Well—I suppose, but I'd like to know why on

earth would Evon lock a lovely young woman like you in your room? What happened after you left the city?" Annie asked gently.

"I, well, we argued—he kissed me, and . . ." Dominique whispered, but was unable to continue.

"Aah. That is more like the Evon I know. Go on *petite,* then what did he do?" Annie asked excitedly, yet not really sure she wanted to hear Dominique's answer.

"We argued. And then I—I guess I fell asleep. After we arrived at Belle Terre, and after he carried me to my room, I woke up. We—we argued again. Then when I tried to go to the kitchen to fix myself something to eat, he, he locked me in my room," she explained in a bewildered voice.

Dominique's tale had aroused Annie's womanly instinct, and she asked angrily, "Where in tarnation was that mammy while all this was taking place?" Annie liked Evon, but Dominique was like her own granddaughter.

"M'sieur had made Hetty pack our belongings and told her to hire a carriage and return with Beau to Belle Terre. Then after he'd locked me in my room I heard their carriage pull up in front. I waited until I was sure he wasn't coming back. Then I climbed down the oak branch, and went to Beau's room. Beau said Hetty was already in her room, and I was afraid if I tried to wake her, M'sieur Forest would hear me. So I scribbled a note to Hetty explaining what happened and slid it under her door. I told her I would send for her,"

Dominique explained.

"But *petite,* you can not send for Hetty. She is now Evon's property," Annie explained sadly. Hetty could be a real pain in the backside, but Annie knew that Dominique and Beau loved her and Hetty returned their love tenfold.

*"Non* Annie! That isn't so. Hetty is our mammy. She belongs to me and Beau," Dominique said firmly.

"I'm sorry, but when your father sold Belle Terre to Evon, Hetty became Evon's property along with everything else on the plantation," Annie said sadly.

"But Annie, that man practically stole our home from Papa and—"

"I'm sorry, *petite.* I wish it weren't so," Annie said as she spread her hands before her.

"Nicki? Is Annie saying that we'll never see Hetty ever again?" Beau asked in a choked voice. His eyes were bright with unshed tears.

Dominique's heart ached at the bewildered look on Beau's face, and she, too, wondered what would happen if they didn't go back. But she was not going to give in to that man. And she said with an assurance she did not feel as she put her arms around her little brother, "Of course we'll see Hetty. Don't worry, Beau. Before you know it Hetty will be back with us, and grumbling about our moldy, smelly old riverboat. Trust me, Beau, everything will turn out fine."

"I don't know, Nicki. Maybe we should go back to our home, our real home. Hetty will be so glad to see us. I know she's worried. Maybe our new papa will be glad we came home, and he won't punish you for running away again," he said hopefully. But the crease forming between his sister's brow said she thought differently, and the small boy dropped his head on his chest.

"Beau, that man is not and never will be our papa. And don't let him fool you. He pretends to take his responsibility seriously, but he'd agreed to Papa's terms thinking to rid himself of us by dumping us at the academy, and getting his hands on Belle Terre, but Papa had the last laugh when he allowed M'sieur Forest to think I was his son instead of his daughter," Dominique explained heatedly as her eyes smarted with angry tears. But the bewildered expression on her brother's face made her realize that Beau was too young to understand what she was trying to tell him. But she knew the kind of person Evon Forest was, he was a thief and a rake who had stolen their home and would take advantage of her. And, she thought, he was probably, at this very moment, finding a way to steal their inheritance. But she knew she couldn't say these things to Beau, so instead she hugged him to her as she whispered encouragingly, "But you're not to worry, Beau. Our guardian likes you. It is me he disapproves of."

Annie watched Dominique as she comforted her brother, and she felt her eyes grow hot. She blinked rapidly. And she said gruffly, "Now *chérie,* don't say such things. I'm sure this is all a big misunderstanding. Perhaps if we all sat down and discussed this situation in a civil manner, well, we might be able to work things out. Come to terms, so to speak." Annie knew she was rambling, and when Dominique opened her mouth to protest, Annie held up her hand, and quickly added, "Beau is in the middle of this, and the little tyke can't understand what's happening."

Annie's comment struck at the heart of Dominique's sibling instinct. Dominique blanched. But then her eyes darkened and grew hard. The look on her young friend's lovely features told Annie that Dominique thought as little of her advice as she had her brother's. Annie stared at Dominique and frowned. The dark circles beneath her eyes also told Annie that Dominique had suffered deeply. Dominique had lost her father, her beloved home. Then her father had appointed a total stranger to act as guardian to her and Beau. Although Annie was well acquainted with Evon, and knew him to be an honorable man capable of taking care of them, she knew Dominique did not.

Annie's thoughts moved to Evon, and unable to stop she chuckled at the thought of the young and fiery miss being thrown over Evon's shoulder. But at the puzzled expression on Dominique and Beau's faces, she quickly sobered and apologized, "I'm sorry, *mes petites.*"

Beau yawned and turned to his sister and said sadly, "I'm sleepy and I miss Hetty."

Annie's heart went out to the young boy and she quickly sized up the situation as she turned to

Dominique and said, "I'm sure that by now Evon is aware of your absence. And since the riverboat is the first place he'll look, you can't go back there. So it looks as though you two will have to stay here until Evon has had a chance to cool off." Annie's eyes urged Dominique to agree. The wise madam knew that Evon would never suspect that they were at the brothel.

"Thank you, Annie," Dominique said. She had no place to go except back to Belle Terre or the riverboat, and she knew Annie was right.

"Where will we sleep?" Beau asked excitedly. The thought of tagging along after Lonzo lifted his spirits, and the seven-year-old was wide awake.

Annie smiled as she put her arms around Beau's shoulders, "Come. You can stay in one of the vacant rooms across the hall," she said, opening the door and ushering them out into the hall.

Dominique chewed on her lower lip as she followed behind Annie and Beau. There was no one in the city she could go to. She trusted Annie. She didn't want Evon to find them. And she knew he would come, if only to save face. She knew she was doing the right thing. Beau loved Annie and he idolized Lonzo. He would be happy here until she could think of what to do.

They made their way across the wide hallway. Annie opened the door. "I usually keep this room for our regular customers when they've over—indulged. I let them sleep off the ill effects," she commented. "Of course there have been times when—um, what I mean is—oh my. What I'm trying to say is, the room will be yours as long as you need it," she finished awkwardly.

"You don't owe us an explanation, Annie. I know that this establishment is more than just your home. I know it's also your place of business, and I promise you, Annie, Beau and I will not cause you any problems."

"How long can we stay with Annie?" Beau asked.

Dominique intercepted his question as she said, "Perhaps a few days. But just you remember young man that the parlor and the rest of the rooms are off limits. And no one must know we're here so you'll have to continue to wear your disguise," Dominique cautioned.

"I'll wear my hat, and I promise I won't get in any trouble," Beau swore eagerly, but he quickly crossed his fingers behind his back just in case he was unable to keep his promise as visions of him and Napolean exploring Annie's cellar and discovering hidden treasure flashed through his mind.

"Just remember what I've said, young man. We don't want to be an imposition," she repeated.

*"Chérie,* you and Beau could never be an imposition. Not to old Annie, and Lonzo will be tickled pink when he hears the good news," Annie insisted archly hugging them both to her before she ushered them into the vacant room.

Dominique thought she saw tears in Annie's eyes, but the madam stepped back and turned quickly to Beau, and Dominique couldn't be sure.

Annie said, "Beau, why don't you run on down to Lonzo's quarters and tell the old reprobate that you and your sister will be staying for a while. And tell him Annie said to fix us all a bite to eat. All this talk has given me an appetite," she declared, rubbing her rotund midsection.

"Sure, Annie. I'll be back in a little while, Nicki," Beau threw over his shoulder, sleep forgotten as he dashed out the door to see his old friend.

As Dominique started toward the center of the room she glimpsed two nude paintings hanging on the wall. She gasped softly, and her step faltered as she stared at the naked men and women who had been painted in various sexual positions that left nothing to the imagination.

Annie looked from Dominique to the paintings hanging side by side on the wall. "Don't fret, honey. I'll have Lonzo remove the pictures," Annie soothed. But as she walked to the first picture nearest her, she reached up and lifted it from the nail Lonzo had hammered into the wall many years ago.

Dominique smiled at her thoughtfulness, and glanced around the room. The walls were papered in a soft gold-leaf design, but the iron-framed bed and windows were decorated in red velvet. After she'd removed the obscene paintings, Annie stood both paintings on the floor, facing the wall as she chuckled, "We wouldn't want the *petit* to see more than he should."

Dominique coughed, but she too smiled at

Annie's remark. She knew Annie's was a sporting house, and she had a good idea of what went on behind the closed doors, but she had never actually seen Annie's customers involved in the artful act of lovemaking.

Annie had always been discreet where Dominique and Beau were concerned. Always insisting that they use the back entrance, and Dominique appreciated her friend's thoughtfulness. There had only been one incident when she and Beau had rounded a corner startling a gentleman who had had his hand spread across one of Annie's girls' derriere. Luckily the girl had seen her and Beau, and had quickly removed the gentleman's hand as she ushered the man into the nearest room. "Thank you, Annie. I'm sure if Beau had seen those paintings he would have had a million questions that I would have found difficult to answer," Dominique said lightly.

Later that evening, after a light meal of venison sandwiches and pecan pie, Annie and Lonzo had excused themselves to ready the brothel for the evening patrons. Dominique smiled as Annie explained away Beau's inquisitive questions about the brothel. Dominique's smile broadened when Lonzo lifted his brow as Annie explained to Beau that the brothel was a place where gentlemen came and relaxed after putting in a hard day's work.

Dominique closed the door softly and glanced over at Beau sitting cross-legged on the floor talking to his bullfrog. The trying events of the day finally caught up with her and she yawned. The wide double bed looked inviting, and she lay down on top of the bright red coverlet. She had not intended to fall asleep, only to rest her eyes while Beau entertained himself with Napolean, but she couldn't keep her eyes open and she quickly drifted into a dream-filled sleep.

Evon had been in a fit of temper when he'd left Belle Terre, and he'd ridden straight to the riverboat. His anger increased after he'd discovered that Dominique was not on board the riverboat. He had no idea where she had gone. He was hot, thirsty, and definitely out of sorts as he stomped off the boat. He felt the need of a stiff drink, and headed for Annie's establishment. Inside, he went directly to the bar where he ordered himself a shot of bourbon.

"What happened, Camille? You and the Stud of New Orleans have an argument?" Sophie asked in a slow Texas drawl as she watched Evon walk to the bar.

"No. But I'll bet you a night's wages there's a beautiful lady out there who has wheedled her way into M'sieur Virility's heart," Camille prophesied sadly.

"The way he walked past you without so much as a howdy-do makes me think you might be right. He didn't even see you. Do you think she strapped an imaginary blinder on him? I wonder if she padlocked his britches as well," Sophie mused as two gentlemen walked in the door, but neither noticed as the two men walked up to Annie and pointed toward them. Annie cleared her throat bringing the women back to the present. As they turned away from Evon, both were reluctant to end their ruminations, but they smiled brightly as they hurried over to the two men.

Evon hadn't come to the brothel seeking pleasure. He'd come to drown his anger at the bar. He'd ordered three glasses of bourbon, and while he'd quickly downed two, the third remained on the bar, untouched. The drinks had soothed his anger, but the liquor couldn't erase eyes, the color of emeralds, from his mind.

Evon shoved the glass away from him with such force it skidded across the bar top to the edge where it tottered, fell, and shattered on the floor below. He reached into his pocket and withdrew several bills and threw them down on the bar. Suddenly Evon felt tired and he glanced around the room searching for Annie, but when he found her she was busy entertaining one of her more prominent customers. He didn't think it was necessary to disturb her and he made his way to the stairway and the room above that Annie had let him use the night before.

A mist swirled around Dominique as she sat beside the riverbank. The inviting water made her want to dangle her feet, and she removed her shoes and stockings and slipped her feet into the clear green water. She leaned back on her elbows on the moss-cushioned ground, closing her eyes, and let her head fall back against her shoulders while she tilted her face up toward the warm rays of afternoon sun. Then suddenly she found herself in the arms of a man. She smiled as the masculine scent of sandalwood and tobacco drifted into her nostrils. She did not want to open her eyes and end the dream. Her flesh prickled at his touch, and her pulse skittered alarmingly as a delightful shiver of desire ran through her.

The dream had become so real she could feel and smell his warm bourbon-scented breath caress her temple. She moaned softly and turned in his arms. His kiss took possession of her very being. She quivered at the strength in his muscular arms, and she tilted her head and felt the tantalizing pressure of his lips. Wantonly she returned his kiss with reckless abandon, pressing her firm breasts against his bare heated chest. She had no self-control as his kiss sent a delicious shudder of heat through her body.

"Aah *chérie,*" he whispered. His voice was low and husky as he caressed her body next to him.

That voice! Frightened, she realized this was not a dream, but a flesh and blood man. Her eyes flew open. "Evon Forest!" she exclaimed. Dominique pulled away, out of Evon's embrace, but he drew her back and held her tight against him as he kissed her. Her throat was raw with unuttered shouts and protests. His kiss sent a delicious shudder of heat through her body, and the small voice of reason was drowned in a passionate arousal.

A small fist banged against the door, and she realized someone was calling her name. Beau! She pulled away with a dazed expression on her visage as in the glow of moonlight she stared incredulously at the dark eyes gazing passionately up at her. She could not believe she had let this odious man paw her. Whatever had she been thinking?

"I'm coming, Beau. Just—just a minute," she stammered as she sat up on the rumpled mattress.

Whatever would she say to her young brother? How could she explain the fact that there was a man in their bed, their guardian at that! Besides, she thought dazedly, she did not know herself why Evon was in her bed.

She jumped out of bed and ran to the door, wrenching it open. Beau stood sheepishly in front of her with Napolean hanging half out of his shirt pocket. "I'm sorry I had to wake you, Nicki, but the door was locked and the hall is kinda dark, and Napolean was scared out here with no one but me to protect him."

Her fingers curled around his shirt collar as Dominique pulled Beau inside. "Why did you leave without waking me? Where have you been, Beau?" she asked shakily.

Evon had sat up in the bed as Dominique padded across the worn carpet in her bare feet. Aah *chérie!* Evon thought as he stared at the back of Dominique's head. Her unbound silver locks fell below her waist to brush against her well-rounded buttocks. He had been accurate back at the cabin when he made the correct assumption that Dominique was definitely all woman. Her honeyed lips tasted like the finest imported champagne, and her firm, full breasts fitted into his hand like it had been designed for his palm alone. His eyes moved to the small boy whose eyes were cast down.

"Whoa! Don't be so hard on him. Come here, Beau." Evon interrupted Dominique's barrage of questions feeling sorry for the boy. Then he asked gently, "What's that hanging out of your shirt pocket?"

Beau looked up and saw his new guardian sitting up on the bed. When Evon called for him to come to him, Beau started to walk around Dominique, but stopped, and his big blue eyes stared up in question.

She needed time to get her emotions under control, and after seeing that Beau was all right, Dominque had acquiesced. "Go on Beau."

What kind of woman was she to allow a strange man to come to her room, get into her bed, and paw her like he had? she asked herself. What kind of person did Evon Forest think she was? What would she say to him? *Mon Dieu.* She looked to where Evon stood talking to Beau in low tones. He draped an arm around her brother's shoulder, then led him to the faded and worn, but clean red velvet sofa pushed against the wall that faced Basin Street. *Mon Dieu,* at least he had put his pants back on. He was bare-chested and her green eyes moved up to his handsome features, and then moved sensuously back to his chest and his tanned skin. Stop it! She admonished herself. She hated him. Didn't she? Of course she did. Besides, what was he doing in the room Annie had given to her and Beau? He had come into her room without her knowledge, and taken advantage of the fact that she had been sleeping.

"How dare you come into my room!" she seethed as she shot him a fiery look of pure hatred.

Evon jerked his head up. "Your room? Since when is this your room? It was not yours last night. I slept here. With, I might add, Annie's permission. In fact several men frequent it on occasion. Aah *chérie*—so, you're upset because I am the man using this room tonight. That's it isn't it? You were expecting someone else?" he asked heatedly. He noticed a gleam of moisture on her sooty lashes, and he felt a twinge of guilt, but he ignored it. If the tart thought she was going to put on an act of purity for his sake, she could forget it. She was in Annie's brothel, using one of Annie's rooms. What was he supposed to think? The lady had missed her calling. She should have been an actress. Her excuse that she had dozed off, and her brother had left the room without her knowledge didn't fool him. His guess was that she had intentionally sent the youngster from the room and had fallen asleep while waiting for a customer to arrive. He had to admit her story sounded convincing. And he would have believed her if she'd been anywhere but in a brothel.

Earlier, Evon had made his way from the bar up the stairs and entered the darkened room. He had had but a few hour's sleep the night before, and, he thought, he wouldn't get much sleep tonight thanks to the disappearance of his ward. Angrily he had shed his clothes, thrown them on the chair, and stretched out on the cool sheet. The last thing he had expected was to find a female asleep beside him. His surprise was complete when a moonbeam caught on her silvery hair, and he recognized his ward, Dominique. He'd wanted sorely to shake her awake. Why had he hesitated? His brows drew together in consternation. He remembered the kick in his stomach when he'd thought Dominique was one of Annie's girls. He hadn't seen her at the brothel before, but then, he usually asked for Camille, and—oh hell, what had it mattered? He had kept a tight rein on his emotions while all along she'd—but she was there, beautiful, tempting, and he had been gripped by desire. His loins had tightened. Even now he saw himself leaning over her. He could feel the fullness of her lips on his—startled, he straightened. What was he doing? She was his ward. He had nearly forgotten his responsibility to her.

Dominique stared at him and saw the play of emotions on his face. What was he thinking? Had her eager response shocked him? How dare he! He had taken advantage of her. Of course he hadn't been the first man who tried to take advantage of her. She'd been kissed before. But the slobbering lips and groping hands of John, the son of her father's friend, had not ignited flames of passion or sent gusts of desire racing through her as Evon's had. Where John's touch had been rough, awkward, Evon's touch was delicate, yet demanding, sending her spinning in a sensual dream. Although Evon was the one who had drunk the liquor, Dominique was the one drunk on the taste of him—the faint scent of his tobacco and the musky male scent that was essentially Evon. Feeling the way she felt, Dominique could not think of one plausible reason for being in that room alone. What could she say? M'sieur Forest, I do not frequent all the brothels, only one, the most popular sporting house in the city of New Orleans. Would he believe the truth if she told him that Annie had been her mother's best friend. That he had found her hiding from him? That she hadn't wanted him to take her back to Belle Terre? She knew he would never believe her for he had drawn his own conclusion, and nothing she could say would convince him of her innocence. She had seen the passion fade to be replaced by a look of disgust, and she cringed beneath his steely glare and knew he was silently condemning her. Then Dominique lifted her chin a notch. Let him think her the most wicked of Annie's lot. She didn't care. She refused to acknowledge the pain his unspoken accusation brought her. But she would not defend her actions to this pompous ass. How could he caress her the way he had, then think the worst of her? Tears smarted behind her eyelids, and she refused to let him see how much he had hurt her as she spun around and ran from the room.

His ward had lied to him, and, he thought, slamming his fist into his open palm, she was damn good at it. Why hadn't he stopped her? Made her tell him the truth? Evon paced the floor finally admitting to himself that he had on more than one occasion enjoyed the delights of the girls working the brothels, so how could he condemn her? Then suddenly he felt sickened. Was it because this particular girl was his ward? His responsibility? Well damn his commitment to Emmett Chandler, and damn his honor! If Dominique didn't care, why should he? He wanted her, and he was damn sure going to have her!

# Six

"Are you *sure* you don't hate Nicki?" Beau asked. He had remained silent while Evon and Dominique had exchanged hostilities, and when Dominique hurried from the room, he had remained with Evon. Beau's blue eyes widened as his scowling guardian stopped pacing and stared directly at him.

Evon hadn't realized the boy was still in the room. He quickly recovered as he said, "Hate your sister? Of course not. Whatever gave you that idea?"

"You act like you don't like her, and she told Annie you hated her."

"Well, she's wrong. I made a commitment to your father to watch after the two of you. It's just that your sister is making my job a little—difficult," Evon explained more gently.

"Nicki doesn't want to stay at Belle Terre. Not if you stay there, too. She said you're a thief. That you enjoy controlling other people's lives," the boy explained. Then he asked innocently, "Did you steal Belle Terre from Papa?"

"Steal? Who the hell put that idea in your head? Never mind. I can guess," Evon barked as his anger mounted.

"Dominique says—"

"Your sister has a way of turning things around to suit herself, Beau," Evon interrupted. His tone held a steel edge and he realized he was frightening the boy. Then more gently he explained, "I did not steal anything from your father and I certainly did not steal your home from you," Evon smiled down at Beau. It was not right that he vent his anger on the innocent youth standing before him.

"Good, because if you had I couldn't like you," Beau said grinning up at Evon.

"Why thank you, Beau. I've grown rather fond of you, too," Evon smiled warmly.

"You have? Then we can be friends. We can go fishing and riding. I have my own pony at Belle Terre, and I ride real good. Would you take me riding tomorrow?" he asked anxiously.

"Whoa, hold on a minute," Evon laughed. He put his arm around the boy's shouldes and ushered Beau over to the bed while Evon explained patiently, "You and I will do all those things, but not tomorrow. I have business to take care of here in the city." And, he thought, your sister and I have some unfinished business to discuss.

"Please don't make Nicki cry anymore. She doesn't cry much, but she sure bellows when you make her mad. Besides, I can't be your friend if you and Nicki aren't friends," Beau said worriedly as he quirked one thin eyebrow up at Evon. He waited patiently for Evon to assure him he would not upset his sister. Beau liked his new guardian, but he loved Dominique and his loyalty was with his sister.

"Don't worry, Beau. Everything is going to work out, you'll see," Evon promised. He smiled, amused that a seven-year-old boy could make a man over six feet tall feel so small. Evon sighed. He knew it would be hard to keep his promise after discovering Dominique's secret, but the boy wasn't aware of his sister's dark side, and Evon was determined to spare Beau that heartache. He knew he would have to watch what he said in the boy's presence.

After Dominique had left them in the room at Annie's, Evon had searched Annie's establishment, but Dominique was nowhere to be found.

A few hours later, dismounting from Marengo, Evon lifted Beau to the ground, and together they walked up the gangplank and onto the riverboat. On board the riverboat, Evon with Beau in hand walked toward Dominique's cabin. Perhaps she had come back to the riverboat, Evon thought, and as he neared her cabin Evon heard her utter a familiar expletive, and knew she had returned. Evon quickly turned to Beau and suggested, "Hey big guy, how about you and Napolean going up to the pilot's house. Maybe keep an eye out for Lafitte and his crew. I have to talk with your sister, and when I've finished, I'll come to the pilot's house and we'll both watch for Lafitte. If you promise to stay in the pilot's house and wait for me, I'll explain a few of the duties of the riverboat pilots, like how they navigate their riverboats, how they read river signs, and things the pilot must learn to ensure a safe journey for his passengers and cargo." Evon purposefully bribed the boy. He wanted a private moment with Dominique. Then when the boy's eyes lit up at his promise, Evon felt a twinge of guilt. But what he had to say to Dominique was not meant for the ears of a seven-year-old.

Beau bobbed his head excitedly up and down as he reached into his pocket to retrieve Napolean. "We'll wait for you in the pilot's house, M'sieur," he called over his shoulder. In his eagerness to get to the pilot's house, Beau did not notice Evon's dark expression.

After she'd left Evon in her room at Annie's, Dominique felt the need to be alone, and she had left the brothel to walk the short distance to the riverboat. She'd strolled lamely along the walkway visualizing the expression on Evon's face. Had it been pain or simply surprise? But then it was acceptable for a man to be in a brothel. Hadn't he admitted that he himself had many times occupied that same room? Well, she thought, at least after what happened tonight she wouldn't have to worry that he'd insist she return to Belle Terre. He thought her a whore and although he might frequent Annie's himself, he wouldn't want one of Annie's girls living in his house. At least now she would be free to carry out her original plan to renovate the riverboat. She realized Evon would no longer care what she did after discovering her in a whorehouse. Nothing she could say would change this newly formed opinion of her. Dominique lifted her chin. She could now forget Evon Forest. She had more important things to think about. The most important was who she should ask for a loan to refurbish the riverboat. She didn't really know anyone except—Jules Harcourt! Jules had been her father's friend and neighbor. He had offered his help when her father needed him. Perhaps he would help her. If she could offer him more than interest on his money perhaps he would not turn her down. She needed the money, and she could pay him back in installments like her father had. And, if she offered him a percentage of the gambling proceeds—she would talk with Jules tomorrow. Maybe by tomorrow afternoon she would have the funds and Lonzo could hire workmen to begin the renovation. She sighed. She knew she should be excited, but she wasn't.

She decided to go to her cabin and pen a note to Hetty. When she'd finished Hetty's missive, Dominique rose to go back up on deck. She turned but Evon's frame blocked the doorway. His muscular shoulder was pressed against the door-jamb, while his dark eyes appeared glazed with that same strange look she'd seen after he'd held her in his arms at Annie's. He'd kissed her with a passion so deep she believed for a moment he'd felt the same delicious stirring she'd experienced; a stirring of something wonderful, something almost sacred. But she had quickly discovered that the look in his eyes was nothing more than lust. He had come to the brothel to slake that lust on a whore—he'd thought her a whore.

What was he doing here? And why was he looking at her that way? She watched him warily. Then suddenly sheer black fright swept through her as she wondered if he had sought her out to have his way with her. Suddenly she knew why he was here, and she knew she must escape, but how? Then she chastised herself. After all, he had not said why he was here on the riverboat. And, she realized, he hadn't made any attempt to attack her—but those eyes—why was he looking at her that way? Sudden panic welled up inside her, and she made a feeble attempt to run between Evon and the narrow space of the doorjamb. But his arm snaked out and brought her curvacious figure up hard against his taller, more masculine frame. Her breath caught in the slender column of her throat, and she paled as he held her spellbound with his ebony eyes.

"Where were you running to this time? Back to the whorehouse?" Evon whispered as his lips curved maliciously. He saw Dominique cringe at his choice of words. "At least you're not a crib whore," he stated cruelly, then questioned, "Why are you always running away from me? Isn't my money as good as the next? Why do you fight me?" he ground out between clenched teeth. Then suddenly his voice softened, and he whispered gently, "aah *chérie,* you are a Venus among women. You do not have to sell yourself." Evon's hands moved down over her rounded buttocks. He kneaded her soft flesh as he molded her against his hard, swollen shaft. Evon frowned at her sharp intake of air, thinking she found him distasteful. Irritably, he dipped his head, but when he tasted her delicious sweetness, his kiss gentled.

Evon raised his head to stare into her sea-green eyes. He wanted Dominique. He felt as though his insides were on fire. She had set his loins ablaze with a hunger he'd never before known. "Aah *chérie,* love me for a little while, and I'll pleasure you like no man before me. I will pay whatever you ask," he whispered, letting out a long audible sigh. He was unable to squelch the twinge of regret he felt as he placed his large palm on one firm, full breast.

What was he saying? He would pay whatever she asked? Love him? She would give him something, but it sure as hell wouldn't have anything to do with love!

Dominique pushed against Evon's chest with all her might, but she couldn't budge him. Then quickly and swiftly she brought her knee up between his legs. She heard his sharp intake of air as he quickly released her.

A million lights exploded before Evon's eyes as excruciating pain engulfed him. He let go of Dominique to grasp his groin as he fought to contain the contents of his stomach. His belly continued to roil and his eyes blurred as he asked tightly, "What the hell did you do that for? I said I'd pay didn't I? Or am I that damn offensive to you?" Evon straighted slowly as the pain subsided.

She could not escape. Her ploy had not worked. "I hate you! I never want to see you again. Now get off my riverboat!" Dominique hissed venomously.

Her green eyes were bright with unshed tears as she pointed her index finger past Evon, in the direction of the hall leading to the upper deck, and the gangplank that would take him off the riverboat, and she thought, out of her life forever.

"What the hell makes you think you're too good to service me? I'm willing to pay—"

"Get out! I am not a prostitute nor am I a dog in heat, and you will not treat me like one! Get out!" she shouted as she pushed him with all her might.

Her tirade so surprised him that Evon allowed himself to be pushed backward out of the doorway, staring at her as she spun around and slammed the door in his face. Dominique sobbed as the door banged closed, and she turned and fell with her back against the closed doorway. Tears washed down her flushed cheeks. He had offered to pay for her services. How dare that arrogant bastard offer her money! She suddenly sobered. What had she expected after Evon found her on a bed inside a brothel? But, she thought, he hadn't given her a chance to explain, but had, in his own mind, found her guilty. Then suddenly Dominique spun back around, opening the door with such force it fanned silver wisps of her hair around her face. Evon was leaning with his elbow against the doorjamb. He gazed at her with something akin to respect. "Evon, M'sieur Forest—I—I apologize for my behavior. There is something—you seem to have the wrong imp—"

"Ssh *chérie,*" Evon whispered as he reached out and enfolded Dominique in his arms. "I will pay double, no *chérie,* I will pay ten times your price."

"What?" Dominique shrieked. She pushed against his chest and, raising her hand palm up, slapped him in the face.

Furious, Evon grabbed her wrist. He swept her, weightless, into his arms. Turning, he kicked the door closed, and in two strides he was beside the bed where he dropped her unceremoniously, landing on top of her. His mouth covered hers hungrily. Her heart took a perilous leap. Evon raised his mouth from hers, he gazed into her eyes. His kiss had sent the pit of her stomach into a swirl. She didn't protest when his hands sought the buttons of her gown. Seeming of their own volition, her arms snaked up around his neck and her lips parted and his lips recaptured hers. His kiss was surprisingly gentle. His tongue explored the recesses of her mouth while his hands moved magically over her smooth breasts, sending shivers of desire racing through her. The kiss ended. What was she doing? It was her own driving need that shocked her. But when he dipped his head and his lips touched her nipple with tantalizing possessiveness, she ignored the mocking voice, surrendering completely to his masterful seductions.

"M'sieur," a small voice called from the other side of the door.

Evon raised his head. Beau. "Christ!" He'd forgotten about Beau. He rose swiftly. He turned to Dominique offering her his hand, but when she didn't move he reached for her hand pulling her to her feet just as Beau opened the door and entered the cabin.

"M'sieur, I know I was supposed to wait for you

in the pilot's house, but I thought you'd forgotten so I came looking for you."

Dominique stepped from behind Evon. "Beau—" she began.

"Nicki!" he exclaimed. His eyes lit up when he saw his sister. "I didn't know you were here."

"I—I didn't want Hetty to worry. I wrote her a note—" she began in a choked whisper as she fumbled to redo the buttons on her bodice. Unable to remember whether they'd become unfastened during their feverish tussle, or whether Evon had unbuttoned them. She burned in remembrance.

Noting her discomfort, Evon came to her rescue. "Come on big guy. Let's go up to the pilot's house." He took Beau's hand in his. Then he winked apologetically at Dominique before turning and leading Beau from the cabin.

Dominique stared after them. What had gotten into her? Her thoughts swirled and she wondered if Evon's impression of her had been accurate. Was she, at heart, a loose woman?

Dominique straightened the coverlet. She stood and looked around the room. Suddenly the spacious cabin seemed to close in on her. She had to get out of there. She hurried from the room, and made her way quickly to the galley.

Dominique sat on the long bench at the table. Her hands were folded tightly. Had she encouraged him? she wondered guiltily. The sound of footsteps interrupted her train of thought. Looking up she saw Beau. He stepped through the arched doorway, and Evon followed behind.

"Nicki, M'sieur taught me how to ring the bells.

The big bell is a stop-and-come-ahead bell. And if you want to back the riverboat up you ring the little bell one time, but if you want to back up slow, you have to ring the little bell twice. And flanking is when the boat is floating with the current. M'sieur said I should be a pilot, cause a pilot makes a hell of a lot more money than a banker, and—"

"Beau!" Dominique exclaimed.

Evon saw the look in Dominique's eyes, and knew he was in deep trouble. "Now hold on, big guy. You shouldn't repeat everything I said," he admonished Beau sheepishly.

"Beau. Take Napolean and go to your room. I'd like to talk with M'sieur Forest," Dominique said. She shot Evon a penetrating look as she rose.

"It just slipped out," Beau shrugged apologetically as he obeyed his sister reluctantly.

"That was my fault," Evon apologized. He moved to the sideboard, and riffled through the contents. "Do you have provisions on board?" he asked glancing over his shoulder at Dominique.

"*Oui.* Hetty picked up what we needed at the market," she answered irritably. She tried not to curse in front of Beau, and she was angry with Evon for doing so.

"Aah *oui,* Hetty. I've decided that Hetty's place is here, on the riverboat with you and Beau," he said matter of factly.

"Oh," Dominique said. She bit her lip to stifle the cry of delight. Her surprise was evident, then her eyes narrowed. "What are you saying?" she asked suspiciously.

"Without Hetty here—well—I don't like the idea of Beau being left unattended," Evon said.

"Why on earth would I leave my brother alone?" she asked, noting his discomfort, but not understanding what it was Evon had implied.

"I was thinking of the evenings—you, aah—entertained."

"Entertained! What are you talking about?" Dominique asked, confused. Then it dawned on her that Evon still believed that she was a prostitute. That she would risk leaving Beau alone while she plied her trade. "Of all the low-down, sneaking—" she began, then paused as she realized that if allowing Evon to think the worst of her would mean he would bring Hetty back to them then she would let him think whatever he wanted. Cautiously she asked, "You're serious? Hetty can come home?" she was hopeful, but not altogether sure he had meant what he had said.

"*Oui.* I'm serious. I'll be leaving right away. And, I'd like Beau to ride along," he said.

While Dominique knew Evon wasn't asking her for her permission to take her brother with him, but merely stating a fact, she didn't want to say anything that would anger him and cause him to change his mind. "I—" she began, but hesitated. She did not like the idea of Beau becoming too fond of this man, but the thought of Hetty's return quickly lifted her spirits. She pushed the unhappy thought aside, and quickly agreed. "You're sure, M'sieur? What I mean is—" she began to explain, but her words were cut off.

"Hell—*non*—I'm not sure," he growled. She'd

left the plantation twice without his permission and Evon refused to let her make a fool of him a third time.

"Thank you, M'sieur," Dominique said simply.

"*Oui,* well, we'd better get going. It shouldn't take more than an hour to ride to Belle Terre and back. Hetty can throw a few things together and I'll see that she gets the rest of her belongings in a day or two," Evon explained slowly, but his mind was on the beauty standing before him. Then before he could change his mind he quickly turned and exited the galley leaving Dominique to stare after him.

# Seven

After Evon and Beau departed, Dominique left the confinement of the galley. She made her way to the upper deck where she strolled aimlessly around the walk, stopping to lean against an intricately carved post. Her thoughts were in a turmoil. She stared unseeing as the riverboats moved lazily in and out of the wharf. Dominique was relieved that Hetty would be back with her and Beau. Evon would return to Belle Terre, and she could begin the renovation. She was excited at the thought, but she still faced the problem of appropriating funds. Evon had control of her inheritance, and she couldn't go to the bank. The banker would refuse to loan her the money using the excuse that she was a woman. Such rigid standards infuriated her. Jules Harcourt was her only alternative, and she prayed he would not refuse her.

Suddenly, a disturbance on the *River Queen*, a

luxurious sidewheeler docked in the next slip, brought her out of her reverie. A shrill voice rent the air. Her eyes darted to the commotion below where an elegantly dressed lady was shrieking at a young Negro rouster. And when the lady lifted her parasol high into the air and brought it back down with such force over the boy's head, her mouth dropped open.

"How dare you soil my new traveling suit with your filthy hands." the lady screamed hatefully at the youth.

Dominique continued to stare as the captain of the vessel hurried up to the pair. The irate woman appeared inconsolable. She pointed to an area on her full-pleated skirt insisting that the rouster had smudged her garment. Dominique stared at the spot as did the captain. Dominique shook her head. In her estimation the woman was being petty and unreasonable, for it would have been extremely difficult, if not impossible, to notice anything amiss on the woman's traveling suit, for the outfit was a dark indigo.

Then when the nasty lady, as Dominique mentally described her, demanded the youth's dismissal, the captain looked at the boy and motioned for him to leave the riverboat, and Dominique felt sorry for the young rouster.

She continued to watch while the captain made a pretense of consoling the overwrought woman until she heard the familiar shout of a cab driver halting his team on the street below. She glanced at the hack and recognized the conveyance as the one Evon had rented earlier. She quickly realized that Evon and Beau had returned with Hetty, and her face lit up when she saw Hetty step from the cab.

"Nicki. We're back. And M'sieur Evon brought Hetty just like he said he would," Beau called excitedly.

Dominique nodded and smiled at Beau. Involuntarily, her eyes moved to where Evon was standing on the luggage rack as he swung Hetty's satchel down to the ground. He stepped down and as he did, his eyes met and held hers. The beginning of a smile tipped the corners of his mouth, and she noticed how his well-muscled body moved. His movements were swift and full of grace and virility. His stance as he paid the driver emphasized the force of his thighs and the slimness of his hips. He was devilishly handsome and she mentally caressed his qualities.

"Evon! Evon darling!" Yvette Renault called from the deck of the *River Queen*. Yvette waved and blew a kiss to Evon. Dominique looked from the lady back to Evon. Her eyes narrowed. She recognized the woman as the same woman who had, only minutes earlier, insisted that the young rouster be dismissed. Evon returned the lady's smile. Dominique watched in agitation as Evon set Hetty's valise down and walked toward the *River Queen* and the beautiful lady. But the lady didn't wait for Evon. She hurried toward Evon meeting him on the walkway where she threw her arms possessively around his neck. Dominique seethed inwardly as the lady kissed Evon, and she wondered if the lady was in fact kissing him or trying to devour him. Dominique was appalled at the woman's bold actions. She quickly glanced around at the people on the crowded wharf. The entwined couple had drawn a captive audience. When at last the woman lifted her head, she ran her tongue seductively over her lips, and proceeded to kiss Evon's eyes, cheeks, nose, and chin. When once more the woman's scarlet lips covered Evon's mouth, a swift shadow of anger swept across Dominique's face. Whatever did Evon see in that woman? Dominique ran her eyes down the length of the woman and admitted, although reluctantly, that the lady was not only fashionable, but beautiful. Dominique also saw that the woman was an aristocrat by the design of her trim traveling suit which Dominique noticed was cut from the finest European fabric. Unconsciously she ran her hands down her own plain, worn, and outdated gown feeling dull in comparison. She unconsciously lifted her chin. Dominique did not recognize the woman and wondered who she was. Was she Evon's fianceé? But, wouldn't he have said something to that effect? Suddenly she stiffened. The lady was Evon's mistress!

Hetty, too, had watched the passionate exchange between Evon and the beautiful lady. She studied the play of emotions as they danced across Dominique's lovely features. The first emotion registered Dominique's surprise which quickly changed to anger, and knowing the young missy as she did, Hetty smiled, for she knew the master was in for a real tongue lashing. "Missy, I'm going below to unpack. Beau," she called, "come along. I'll need you to help me with setting the table for supper." But, instead of moving toward her destination, Hetty continued to watch Dominique whose eyes were glued to the scene below.

"I'm coming, Hetty," Beau called from the other side of the riverboat where he'd been leaning over the railing watching a flatboat skillfully maneuver its way into the empty slip next to theirs.

Beau ran up beside Hetty and she called to Dominique, "Beau and I are going below. M'sieur will be here soon. I thought perhaps you would like a few words with him without the benefit of an audience." Hetty spoke with a significant lifting of her brows.

"I don't care if the whole damn city hears what I have to say to M'sieur," Dominique hissed under her breath.

Hetty didn't hear what Dominique said, but she knew what her charge was thinking. Dominique was unable to take her eyes off of Evon and the woman entwined in his arms. Evon slowly unwound the woman's arms from around his neck. Then he whispered something in the woman's ear and brushed his lips lightly across her cheek. He turned to leave and as though he remembered Dominique's presence, he glanced up at her. His smile made her angrier still. Why, she thought, the rogue acted as though this sort of thing happened to him every day! He acted as though having a woman throw herself in his arms was nothing out of the ordinary! And Dominique's expression was thunderous as she followed his descent. Her rage increased and she felt numb. She watched Evon nonchalantly pick up Hetty's valise and board the riverboat. On the upper deck he walked casually toward her. Their eyes met and locked. She heard Evon's quick intake of breath. A shudder ran through her, and she felt her anger dissipate. Then suddenly she wanted to run, to escape Evon's disturbing presence. Her eyes darted around the deck. She saw Hetty's retreating back and called out unsteadily to her, "Hetty, wait—I—" She took a step toward the tall mulatto, but the slight pressure of Evon's hand on her arm stayed her. When she didn't resist she felt herself being drawn back against his hard, warm chest.

Earlier, after Evon had left with Beau for Belle Terre, Beau was preoccupied with pointing out the various sights to Napolean, and Evon was left to his own ruminations about Dominique. Her stubbornness irritated him. She had been determined to stay on that damn riverboat, and Evon had known it would have been a waste of time to force her into going back to Belle Terre. With her willful nature she would have found another way to escape. But, hell, he thought, he couldn't just walk away leaving her alone and unprotected on the wharf. Evon would be needed at Belle Terre in the very near future. And it was imperative that D'Arcy remain at Forest Manor due to Evon's father's declining heath. He had no choice. Evon decided to send for Wyatt. In this, he trusted his brother's ability to watch over and protect Dominique's brother, her mammy, as well as the obstinate Dominique, herself. But it would take two, maybe three days before Wyatt could arrange to be in New Orleans, and Evon refused to leave his wards and their mammy alone until then. There was only one solution and that was that he would stay with them until Wyatt arrived. Evon knew Dominique would balk at his brother's coming. He also knew that Dominique would not welcome his presence no matter that he was thinking of their welfare. Now, staring into Dominique's green eyes he knew it was time to tell her his decision. It was not wise to put off the inevitable. And as he held her softness against him he thought of how she *should* react to his well-laid plan, thinking she should be beholden to him. Hadn't he, after all, just returned with her beloved mammy? And, he thought, having Hetty back should have lightened Dominique's feelings toward him. Smiling, he turned Dominique around to face him and prodded gently, "I have something to say to you. Let Hetty go below. She'll understand." He thought Dominique's expression had become wary, but she nodded and he relaxed.

"It's all right, Hetty. You and Beau go ahead," she called unsteadily. And when her mammy took Beau and disappeared down the steps, she heaved an affronted sigh and waited.

His grip tightened on her arms. His voice was

louder than he intended. "Hear me out before you say anything," Evon began, then he lowered his voice as he explained, "I've agreed to this preposterous notion of yours to live on this damn riverboat. I've even brought Hetty back, but I do not intend to leave the three of you alone and unprotected. So, my lovely *chérie,* I've come up with the perfect solution. One that will allow you to have your way. One, I might add, that will also allow me to sleep nights. Tomorrow, I'm sending for my brother. He'll be staying on the riverboat with the three of you. And—" his words halted when she opened her mouth in protest, but he pressed his finger lightly against her lips, and continued, "and, since it'll take a few days to make the arrangements, I've decided to stay here until Wyatt arrives. Then I'll return to Belle Terre." Evon smiled and removed his finger, and casually he draped his arms around her shoulders.

She licked her lower lip. Her rebellious nature got out of hand. "First it's you. Now it's your brother. I don't want your protection, and I certainly don't need your brother's," she spat at him while at the same time she jerked free of his embrace.

"Aah, but that is where you're wrong," he said as he raised one thick brow. "During the daylight hours, the wharf is bustling with activity and is quite safe, but when the sun drops behind the horizon the wharf is an unsafe den frequented by rapists, thieves, and murderers. You were safe, *chérie,* at Annie's, but Annie employs an army of big, burly men to guard the girls who work for her. Down here at the wharf you are no longer protected by Annie's henchmen. And I don't believe you realize the dangers of a woman living here with no one to watch after her but a defenseless mammy and a boy," he explained patiently. And, he thought, she hadn't realized when she'd made her decision to make her home on the riverboat that her brother and mammy would also become vulnerable to the riffraff who frequented the wharf.

*"Non!* You're wrong," she hissed venomously. Dominique felt trapped. Would she never be free of him?

"It is your decision. But if you refuse my condition, you will leave me no choice but to insist that you return to Belle Terre," he stated emphatically. Evon felt a twinge of remorse at the underhanded threat he'd made. But he quickly pushed his remorse aside. Dominique needed his protection whether she realized it or not. He would not relent.

"You have made your point, M'sieur," she concluded. He had won. She had no choice but to agree to his terms. She sighed. Then suddenly her spirits lifted. She could tolerate him for a few days. Then he would be out of her life. And she would decide what to do about his brother after his arrival. She smiled remembering Evon's description of Wyatt Forest. Wyatt was the direct opposite of Evon. And she decided, if need be, she could handle the lesser of the two evils. Having Wyatt

Forest invading her privacy was far more appealing than having Evon there to dictate her every move. "Who was that woman on the *River Queen*?" she asked, quickly changing the subject. "Was she your mistress?"

Her directness took Evon by surprise. "That woman? My mistress? If you're referring to the lady on board the *River Queen*, her name is Yvette," he answered noncommittally. His eyes narrowed, wondering what she was up to now. Dominique had surprised him when she had so easily accepted his terms to have first him and then his brother stay on the riverboat. He had foolishly relaxed his guard. And now, for reasons he didn't understand, he didn't like discussing Yvette with Dominique. But Evon recovered quickly, and he teased, "I hadn't realized that you were interested in my personal life."

Her mouth dropped open, but she quickly snapped her mouth shut, stunned by his bluntness. Then when she realized Evon had accused her of being jealous, she became angry, and she snapped, "I'm not interested in your personal life. A simple attack of woman's curiosity is all. I really could care less about you or that tart who threw herself at you. But, I must admit it was a shock to watch my guardian being mauled in broad daylight and being made a spectacle of before hundreds of people. But then true to character, you seemed to take such abuse in stride," she hissed at him. Her voice was heavy with sarcasm.

"Why, *chérie*. I believe you're jealous!" Evon

mused, as he raised one thick brow quizzically.

"Jealous? That's absurd, M'sieur," she sputtered. She was stunned by his cool appraisal. She trembled, but she told herself it was anger, and nothing more. His ridiculous accusation had raised her ire. How dare he accuse her of such a thing? He was the most exasperating man she'd ever known. When his eyes softened and he drew her back into his embrace, she struggled, not wanting him to think he was right, but when he tightened his hold she didn't resist.

"Forget Yvette. I want to talk about you," he coaxed.

He put his finger beneath her chin tilting her face back so that she had no choice but to return his gaze. *"Non,"* she choked. Her whole being stiffened as she became more uncomfortable by the minute.

"Why *chérie?* Are you afraid of me?" he asked, but the look in her eyes said something quite different, and Evon asked quietly, "Or, perhaps it isn't me, but yourself that you are afraid of."

His words were disquieting. "That's absurd!" Dominique gasped. She wasn't afraid of him. He was confusing her, and the knowing look he gave her made her cringe. Suddenly he loosened his hold on her. She quickly moved out of his embrace. She turned to leave, but she hadn't taken two steps when she felt his hands close around her midriff. He turned her around slowly, drawing her seductively against the length of him, and she gasped as she felt his hardness through the thin material of her old, worn dress. His head moved toward her. He was going to kiss her. Involuntarily her eyes closed as his mouth took possession of her lips. And when his tongue pressed against her teeth seeking entry, her lips, seemingly of their own accord parted. When his tongue delved into the dark, warm recesses of her mouth, she moaned and she purposely pressed her trembling body against his swollen shaft. His arm tightened around her midriff and his hand covered her breast. Evon raised his head and she opened her eyes. Her lips felt scorched. She wanted him to kiss her again. She wanted him to—*mon Dieu!* she thought, what did she want him to do? Dominique flushed at such thoughts, and she inhaled deeply as a shudder passed through her. As her misgivings increased, an oddly primitive warning sounded in her brain, and suddenly she pushed against him.

"Aah, *chérie.* We were just getting warmed up."

"Perhaps you were, but I—" she began shakily.

"You can lie to yourself. But you cannot lie to me, *chérie,*" Evon interrupted gently, but his words were firm.

Her composure was a fragile shell around her. She became increasingly uneasy under his scrutiny. She drew a deep breath and forbade herself to tremble as she asked hesitantly, "What are you saying, M'sieur?"

"I am saying, *chérie,* that you want me as much as I want you," Evon said truthfully. He watched the play of emotions on her lovely features and smiled. But when the color drained from her face, he flinched guiltily, and when she turned and ran from him he did not try and stop her. Instead he reached into his shirt pocket for a cheroot. He then struck the lucifer and lit the Havana cigar. After one long drag he flung the cigar over the railing where it sizzled and went out in the swirling muddy waters below.

# Eight

Later, the four ate supper in silence. Even Beau was unusually quiet tonight. And when the boy showed signs of falling asleep, Evon rose to lift Beau's light frame up in his arms as he turned to ask Dominique where to put the sleeping boy. Dominique looked to Hetty in alarm, but Hetty merely smiled refusing to come to Dominique's aid, and instead the older woman prodded Dominique to go with Evon to show him where Beau's cabin was. When Dominique quickly instructed Evon on the whereabouts of Beau's sleeping quarters on the pretext that she had to stay and help Hetty clean the galley Hetty, broke in and insisted it wasn't necessary that Dominique stay and help her.

It was late, and Dominique wanted nothing more than to escape the uncomfortable atmosphere. At last she agreed to go with Evon, thinking that after Beau was tucked in bed she would be free to seek out the safety of her own cabin. Dominique rose and led the way out of the galley.

In Beau's room, Evon gently laid the boy down on his bunk. Evon stood silently beside the bed while Dominique tucked the covers around her brother. Neither Dominique nor Evon had said a word after they left the galley, and when she had finished they tiptoed from the cabin.

Dominique hurried to her own cabin while Evon paused at his door, but he did not open it until Dominique had entered her cabin and closed the door behind her.

After a few seconds, Evon did the same, but once inside his cabin he did not go directly to bed, but paced slowly back and forth. When, later, he heard Hetty's door open and close he stepped out into the hall. In two strides he was at Dominique's door where he paused to listen and then knocked softly.

The door opened and Dominique stood just behind the enclosure. "I'd like to talk to you," Evon said briskly. He did not wait to be invited in, but barged into the room closing the door behind him.

He turned and their eyes met.

"M'sieur, I am not dressed," Dominique gasped indignantly.

"With a neckline like that you don't have to worry madam," he quipped irritably.

Dominique flushed, automatically covering her bosom with both arms as she explained heatedly, "I'm not dressed properly."

Evon angrily raked her with his eyes, then

suddenly he paused and his expression changed as his eyes boldly and seductively moved once more, but ever so slowly, over her body.

Dominique was not cold, but she shivered. "What is it you wished to speak with me about, M'sieur?" she asked. His bold scrutiny of her made her nervous.

"I think the time has come to talk about our feelings. To talk about you and me," he said as he reached for her hand. But Dominique quickly tucked her hand behind her.

"If your brother is anything like you I'm sure I should feel safer alone," she said taking a step backward.

"My brother is nothing like me. Don't run away, *chérie,*" he coaxed gently.

Evon took another step toward her. "Don't you dare take another step," she warned. He was too near. Her defenses were weakening. He seemed to enjoy her discomfiture. Her teeth were clamped together, but she forced her lips to part. "You, M'sieur, are a rogue," she said. Suddenly her eyes felt hot as tears welled up behind her eyelids. She did not want to cry in front of Evon. She sidestepped around him and through a blur of tears hurried to the other side of the cabin while she gained control of her emotions.

Evon watched as she retreated to the far side of the room. Had she bewitched him? he wondered as he stared mesmerized at the gentle sway of her hips. He knew he should leave, but he wanted to— hell—what did he want? "We are not strangers, *chérie.* We have shared more than a bedroom. And, I have seen you clothed with far less than that granny thing you have on."

She heard the soft click of the latch as Evon locked the door, and she spun around wide-eyed as he walked purposefully toward her. Suddenly she found her voice, "There is no need to lock the door. In fact," she paused raising her arm toward him as if she could hold him in place before she continued, "whatever it is you wish to discuss with me can be said with the door open." She knew she was babbling. Feeling trapped, she unconsciously bolted toward the door, but when she tried to go around Evon's tall frame, his arms snaked out, and he easily caught her around her waist.

He brought her up against him slowly as his eyes moved possessively over her delicately carved facial bones. Her breathing had become labored, and her long silky lashes swept downward. Her nose was exquisitely dainty, but when he saw her chin tremble he loosened his hold on her as he inhaled deeply, and stepped back.

His embrace had felt warm. When his arms suddenly fell away Dominique experienced a gamut of perplexing emotions which she could neither explain nor understand. Had she felt relief or had she been disappointed? She, too, stepped back and shrugged to hide her confusion. She lifted her chin a notch before asking hesitantly, "What was it you wanted to talk to me about?"

Evon shook his head slowly from side to side. "You must be a witch, *chérie,* for I can think of no other reason to behave as I do when I am near you. Or," he whispered, "perhaps you're a voodoo princess."

"A witch? A voodoo princess? Oh come, M'sieur, surely you're not going to start that again," she asked nervously. She waited, and when he didn't answer but continued to stare at her, she said, "I—I am very tired."

"I came here to give you assurance. To tell you that you will like my brother. He is not a man who would take advantage of a beautiful lady such as you. You will be safe with him. And, I think you and Wye will be well suited. But, be forewarned, neither is he easily misled. But nor was he born with my stubborn streak. And, I think you will be happy to hear that my brother's opinion of me will not rival yours," Evon stated flatly, then quickly smiled when Dominique's eyes widened slightly at his offhanded interpretation of his brother. He continued, "You will also discover that Wyatt and I are direct opposites. And, we look nothing alike. My hair is dark, his is blond. I'm sorry to say also that our personalities clash dreadfully. In fact I guess the only thing my brother and I have in common is our father's height." Evon winced. He knew he had not been completely truthful in his description of his brother, but Evon thought his family skeletons were better left where they were, buried deep in his subconscious. Besides, he didn't want to convey his feelings for his brother to Dominique. Once she met him she couldn't help but like him; everyone else did. *"Oui,"* he said thoughtfully, "I have no doubt you will find my brother more congenial than I. He is far more sympathetic to a woman's tearful plea. The ladies adore him. I don't understand why some lovely mademoiselle hasn't snared him before now. And, *chérie,* you will also find him sympathetic toward your cause after you tell him of my brutish behavior toward you. Wye is loyal, but he looks down his aristocratic nose at the rakehell reputation I've acquired," Evon informed her with a devilish glint in his eye. Then suddenly his expression changed, his eyes grew narrow, and his lips thinned as he said unconsciously, "But I give you fair warning that Wyatt takes his ancestry far more personally than I. Bastard is not a word anyone says lightly in his presence and gets by with it."

Dominique watched Evon turn and exit her cabin. Whatever was the man talking about? Once he had implied that he thought her a whore, then he had referred to her as a beautiful lady. And what had he meant when he said she and his brother would be well suited? Had he been entertaining thoughts of marrying her off to his brother? Well, she fumed inwardly, he'd best think again. He couldn't force her into marrying someone she didn't even know. Or could he? He was, after all, her legal guardian and the man had the same rights as a father—*mon Dieu!* He could force her to marry his grandfather if he'd a mind to. What would she do? Was she such a bad person that she deserved to be treated so? Even if she was, she thought, she was not going to marry Wyatt Forest. When and if she ever decided to marry, it would be to a man she loved, a man who returned that love. Suddenly Dominique shivered. The night sounds grew loud and she slid under the warmth of her coverlet.

Later, as she lay in the dark, she shivered as thoughts of Evon ran rampant in her mind. He was across the hall. So close—had he undressed? she wondered. Had he gone to bed? Did he sleep naked? She quickly chastised herself for such thoughts. Suddenly she threw the coverlet back. She decided it would be smart to wake Beau and have him spend the night in her room. She stepped out into the hall and made her way down the dimly lit area. She stopped at Beau's cabin, but when her hand closed over the brass handle, she froze.

"I just checked on him. Or are you afraid to sleep alone?" Evon whispered in her ear.

Dominique jumped at his words, but she quickly regained her composure as she answered, "*Non,* but I couldn't sleep, and strange thoughts were keeping me awake. I decided it would be wise to have Beau in my cabin tonight." She hadn't wanted to admit her fears to Evon. But the perplexed look on his face made her glad she had.

"I see," he said as he smiled at her quizzically.

"Do you, M'sieur?" she asked slyly.

Evon moved toward Dominique, but the look in her eyes brought him to an abrupt halt. Had he seen a flicker of fear in her eyes? He raised his hand in a silent sign of truce as he said softly, "There is no need to wake the boy. I promise to go to my cabin and stay there."

The following morning, Evon went to the livery in search of a boy to deliver the message to Wyatt at Forest Manor. He didn't like asking anything of his brother, but since D'Arcy was unavailable, he had no choice. At twenty-five Wye was a handsome man. There was a wall between the two brothers due to the circumstances surrounding Wye's birth that Evon refused to scale. And although Evon had never said the words, he loved his brother. Evon and Wyatt were sired by two separate men. Immediately after Evon's birth his mother had moved her belongings into one of the spare bedrooms. Shortly thereafter she and her husband's brother, Henri had had an affair. The affair continued for several years, and Wyatt was the result. A few years later, his mother died, but Evon never forgave his mother or his uncle for their deception. Evon knew that Wyatt was not at fault, but when he looked at his brother he saw the blond beauty of his mother intermingled with the handsome genes of his uncle.

Evon knew he could count on Wyatt. He handed the young Negro the envelope, and flipped him a coin. Then Evon hailed a cab. Evon's banker was supposed to take care of paying off the mortgage on Belle Terre, but had been unable to reach Jules Harcourt. Evon had also on two separate occasions tried to contact Harcourt, but to no avail.

The driver drew the carriage up to the curb, and Evon stepped down just as Jules was unlocking his door.

"Harcourt," Evon called as he paid the driver and hurried over to Jules.

"How dare you accost me in public!" Jules flared, giving Evon his back as he threw open his door, but when he would have closed the door in Evon's face, Evon shoved his foot in between the door and the doorjamb, halting his action. Jules's eyes blazed with hatred toward the younger man.

"Look, Harcourt, I wouldn't be here if it weren't a matter of utmost importance."

"State your business, Forest, and be gone."

"I've purchased Belle Terre from Emmett Chandler. I have with me a draft for the money Chandler owed you."

"That's impossible!" Jules exclaimed and then hissed, "Belle Terre is mine!"

"It's all right here," Evon said reaching into his pocket and withdrawing a manila envelope along with a cashier's check in the amount of the note Harcourt held.

"You can do what you want with the draft," Evon said as he tossed the envelope at Jules and turned toward the street where he raised his arm to hail a passing cab.

"Cheat! Murderer!" Harcourt hurled at Evon's back. Evon had heard those words before. He ignored the accusations Jules hurled at him. The hack pulled up beside him and he gave the driver directions to Forest Shipping Lines.

An hour later, after completing his business at FSL, Evon left the office where several weeks earlier FSL had purchased a large shipment of iron from a firm in St. Louis. The shipment was to be picked up and transported to the Cayman Islands. Evon had sent a draft for half the amount to St. Louis, but when his flatboats arrived to pick up the iron there was no cargo and no firm. FSL had been swindled out of a great deal of money and the plantation owners waiting for their material were, to put it mildly, irritated. Evon had sent his manager, John Dupree, to St. Louis to investigate the situation, but Dupree had returned to New Orleans empty-handed. At FSL, Evon had made arrangements with Dupree to purchase the promised iron from another firm, and personally they would escort the cargo to the Cayman Islands. Their clients had also paid half their bill for the cargo, and FSL couldn't afford to have three of the island's most influential plantation owners displeased.

When Evon's father's health declined, Evon had had to step in as FSL's president. It was now his responsibility to maintain the good name his father had created for FSL.

At the wharf, Evon paid the driver and turned to board the riverboat. He saw Dominique standing at the railing looking down at him. He smiled and raised his hand in a salute as he started up the walkway. He heard someone call his name, and paused and turned back to the street, but he groaned inwardly when he saw Yvette leaning out the window of her carriage. She called his name again and waved a pink, silk handkerchief in his direction. Evon stepped back to the street where her conveyance came to a halt before him. He reached toward the carriage door, but before his hand touched the handle the door burst open, and Yvette was out of the carriage and into his arms.

"Evon, darling," Yvette exclaimed breathlessly.

"Yvette! I thought you had left for St. Louis," he said. Evon frowned pointedly at Yvette.

Yvette ignored the look of irritation on Evon's face. "Oh pooh. After seeing you, I couldn't go to St. Louis," she whispered sensuously. Then she lowered her voice seductively, and added, "I missed you terribly. And we have a lot of catching up to do, *chérie.*"

Yesterday had been the first time that Evon had seen Yvette in weeks. "It has been awhile, Yvette," he agreed absentmindedly while his eyes unconsciously moved to the upper deck of the old riverboat. Suddenly Yvette grabbed Evon around the neck catching him off guard as she pulled him forward and kissed him hungrily. Although Evon knew that Yvette had intended the kiss to be sensuous, his eyes remained opened. Dominique continued to stare at him and Evon felt something akin to guilt. The feeling was one similar to how he'd felt when as a small boy he'd been caught stealing one of his mammy's hot pecan pies. But why should he feel guilty? And guilty of what? Hell, he thought, Dominique was the last person to condemn his or Yvette's actions. Having a madam as a personal friend left her little room to pass judgment on someone else's behavior. His arms tightened around Yvette and he took charge of the situation as he kissed Yvette passionately. Evon made the kiss appear a long and sensuous exchange.

Yvette was the first to break away. She stared dreamily up at Evon with the expression of a satisfied feline. Her breath came in short gasps, and she said huskily, "Oh *oui*, Evon, I have missed you, too. Your hardness speaks for you. Come, darling. Let's hurry. We can go to my townhouse. My bed is ready. And we're ready. Give the driver a fat juicy tip before we leave. That way he'll get us there in half the time or we'll have to make do with the backseat of my carriage," she urged as she tugged possessively on his arm.

Evon stiffened. He had meant to hurt Dominique, but he hadn't intended to encourage Yvette. "I'm sorry Yvette, but I have another commitment, and—"

"And—?" Yvette interrupted. She was visibly puzzled. She knew Evon wanted her as much as she needed him and she couldn't understand his sudden denial. He had not said what she had wanted to hear, and her mind swirled as she fought to find the words that would make Evon forget whatever it was he thought was more important than her. Suddenly her peripheral vision caught a movement on the upper deck of a dilapidated old riverboat, and when Yvette focused on the subject that had caught her eye, she felt herself staring at the loveliest creature she had ever seen. Yvette realized the young woman was glaring at her and involuntarily she drew her breath in. Yvette had always bragged that her woman's intuition had never failed her, and at the moment her intuition was telling her that the woman's sparkling sea-green eyes were alight with jealousy. Yvette's brown eyes narrowed. The beauty was acting as though Evon belonged to her. How absurd! Yvette thought as she blurted, "Evon. Who is that ragged young woman on that horrid boat?"

Evon had not taken his eyes off of Dominique. His lips tilted upward as he mused, "Aah. That is one of the commitments I mentioned earlier. Actually, there are two. Dominique and Beauregard Chandler. Emmett Chandler's children," Evon explained. He felt mesmerized by Dominique's silver-maned beauty. And as a slow knowing smile spread across his face, he winked up at Dominique.

Yvette did not notice Evon's gesture. *"Mon Dieu!"* Yvette gasped. "Emmett Chandler shot himself. Evon," she said turning to face him, "darling, how could his scandalous death possibly involve you? Or—his dirty urchins?" Yvette asked contemptuously. Then she turned once more to stare up at Dominique while she huffed to herself, that wretched urchin is certainly not a child, but a woman with all the right dimensions.

"Emmett Chandler appointed me their legal guardian," he replied as Dominique turned and left the deck. Evon turned reluctantly to Yvette. His lips brushed her cheek. "I'm sorry, Yvette, but I must go," he began, but his mind was filled with Dominique. Her fiery eyes, her slim hips. Suddenly he remembered Yvette, and he realized she did deserve an explanation. "I also purchased the Chandler Plantation and there are several legal matters requiring my immediate attention."

"Then you will be staying in the city tonight. Good. You can come by my townhouse. There is a matter of importance I must discuss with you," Yvette whispered mysteriously. She wanted to have Evon to herself. She wanted more than to talk with him. She wanted him. He was, by her own admission, the best lover she had ever had. Evon had upset her with his recent neglect of her. But she would forgive him. For one day, Evon Forest would be her husband. After seeing his newly acquired ward, she was determined not to let the twit interfere with her carefully laid plans. At least not without a fight!

"I'm afraid I can't make it this evening. I promised Beau to take him fishing in St. John's bayou tonight," he apologized. But secretly he was relieved to have had a plausible excuse. Yvette was a very persistent woman.

Yvette was not happy with his excuse, but she did not want to act selfish. Instead, she coaxed in a sultry voice, "Tomorrow night. Eight-ish." When she noticed the crease between his brows, she added quickly, "I need your opinion on an important business matter. I trust your judgment completely,

Evon." Yvette knew Evon well enough to know when he didn't want to do something, but she also knew her ploy would work—Evon could not refuse a damsel in distress. And when he nodded and reached for her arm, she accepted his proffered hand. Smiling, she stepped back up inside the coach.

Dominique had watched the tête-à-tête between Evon and his mistress. She had seethed inwardly when their kiss had lengthened and radiated a steamy aura around the couple. But as it became apparent that Evon was more than a disinterested participant, Dominique's green eyes had clawed him like talons. And when the kiss ended Evon had looked up at her. She saw amusement in his eyes, mockery. Then after the lady had turned to follow his direction, Dominique had felt her cheeks grow warm as she realized she had been eavesdropping. She had made a fool of herself. Scalding tears had welled up behind her eyelids and she had turned and stumbled blindly toward the safety of her cabin.

Inside the cabin, Dominique had thrown herself down on the bed, pounding her pillow with her fists. She was confused. Why had seeing Evon with his mistress upset her so? Hadn't she seen them in a similar situation the day before? A small voice said she had been upset then also, but she ignored it as she reasoned that Evon Forest was a womanizer. And not only was he handsome, but he was quite wealthy and a man like that probably entertained several mistresses who not only were willing to share his bed, but had hopes of one day sharing his name.

Dominique's chaotic feelings distressed her for she knew she was not a woman who could abide a man like Evon Forest. A man who was not only arrogant and domineering, but a man who had swindled her father out of her beloved home. Well, she thought angrily, Evon Forest could bed every last mother's daughter in the state of Louisiana, but M'sieur, you shall never bed me. And aloud she vowed, "and, M'sieur Forest, one day Belle Terre will again belong to me!"

Dominique rose and walked to the dry sink where she splashed cool water on her flushed face. She reached for the towel and patted her cheeks dry. Sighing, she walked back to her bed and lay down where she stared unseeing up at the ceiling.

Her thoughts whirled around in her mind and she wondered why Evon had done a sudden about-face and agreed to let her stay on the riverboat? Had he sounded anxious to be rid of her? Perhaps he realized the imposition of having them live with him at Belle Terre. Yes, perhaps it was the thought of a young boy and his grown-up sister and the lack of privacy that would create unforeseen problems with his mistresses. Then when a tiny voice whispered that it had been she and not Evon who had insisted they remain on the riverboat, and that again it was she and not Evon who had not wanted her to live at Belle Terre, she ignored it. This is what she wanted, her mind screamed, and she squeezed her eyes shut. She had more important things to think about other than Evon Forest. Tomorrow she would visit Jules Harcourt. She would ask, *non*, she thought, she would beg if necessary, her father's friend to loan her the money to refurbish the riverboat into a gambling casino.

# Nine

"Come in, *chérie,* come in," Jules Harcourt greeted Dominique. His dark eyes shone with delight at seeing the lovely girl.

Jules's enthusiasm eased Dominique's tension somewhat as her green eyes scanned the shabby interior of the small cubicle that was Jules's office. She had been shocked to discover that Jules, the owner of the grand mansion next to Belle Terre had his place of business in such a seedy section of the city. "M'sieur Harcourt," she greeted the handsome older man as he took her hand and brushed her dampened flesh with his thin lips.

"What a pleasant surprise. But my lovely *petite,* what brings you here?" he asked.

Hot tears rushed to her eyes at Jules's concern for her well-being and Dominique inhaled deeply before she explained, "I am no longer living at Belle Terre. I—I have moved permanently to Papa's riverboat. And—and—" she could not go on. Jules reached out and grasped her soft shoulders in his long tapered fingers, and drew her gently into his arms. Dominique felt warmed by his fatherly embrace, and she quickly brought her tumultuous emotions under control. Her own father had never showed her such compassion. Dominique swallowed and said softly. "I have come to ask a favor."

"You have only to ask, *chérie,*" Jules whispered as she stepped out of his arms. His tone was gentle, and his sad smile was filled with concern as he gazed at her.

Dominique felt encouraged by his kindness, and she inhaled deeply. "I would like to renovate the riverboat into a gambling casino, and I believe it will be a profitable business; but I am presently unable to withdraw my own funds, and—"

"You're living all alone on that horrid old riverboat?" he asked surprised as one dark brow rose.

*"Non, oui,* well there is Hetty and my younger brother, and—"

Jules quickly raised his hand to lightly brush a stray curly strand of her silver-blond lock from her forehead. "But you are still without protection. The dock is not a safe place for a lady such as yourself," he argued gently.

"We are presently under the protection of M'sieur Evon Forest, but he has sent for his brother who will remain with us until the riverboat is renovated at which time I plan to hire a gentleman to manage the casino," she explained. Her words were clipped and her silken brows narrowed visibly as she remembered how Evon had insisted upon staying on board without asking her permission. Evon, too, had been concerned for her safety. Now, with Jules repeating that same concern, she realized that perhaps Evon had been right. But it did upset her to admit it.

"Did you say Evon Forest? What does Forest have to do with you or any of this?" he asked angrily.

"He is the gentleman who purchased Belle Terre from my father before—before his death, and unfortunately for Beau and I, Papa also left M'sieur in control of our small inheritance, and that is why I am here," she explained.

"But how is this possible?" he asked indignantly.

"Papa appointed M'sieur Forest our legal guardian, and I cannot withdraw funds from our account without his signature.

"You mean the man will not allow you access to your own money?" he asked.

Dominique noticed the look of contempt on Jules's handsome features, and felt somewhat encouraged by it. "I did not ask him. We have had a difference of opinion. He does not like the idea of my living on the wharf. And I'm quite sure if I were to ask his signature to withdraw a portion of my inheritance he would refuse," she explained bitterly.

"Umm, I see. This is why you came to me. How much will you need, *chérie?*" he asked gently.

Dominique realized Jules was offering to help her, and she said breathlessly, "Only what it will cost to renovate the casino, and enough to hire at least twelve ladies to serve the gentlemen gamblers." Dominique held her breath. What would Jules think of her and her scandalous idea?

"But *chérie,* this is not permitted. A genteel lady such as yourself would do great harm to her reputation if she were to operate a gambling establishment," he reasoned, but open admiration at the courage Dominique displayed was apparent in his dark gaze.

"I realize that M'sieur, but I do not plan to operate the casino myself. As I said earlier, I will hire a capable manager," she explained with determination. Then as Jules nodded his head in agreement, she quickly launched ahead. "I would pay you the highest rate of interest." Dominique held her breath while she waited for his approval.

"Please, *chérie,* sit down," Jules insisted as he took her hand and led her to the only chair in the room. After Dominique was seated he turned, but did not take his eyes from the lovely girl before him. He began to pace slowly back and forth as he put one long tapered finger to his lips which he tapped lightly against his bottom lip. Then he cleared his throat and said matter of factly, "I see no reason to deny you the funds. But—our agreement will be between you and I. No one, not even your new guardian need know where the money came from. If that is agreeable with you then I shall contact my banker, and I'll have a draft for you tomorrow afternoon. I will meet you at my townhouse; here is the address. Say around three o'clock?" Jules asked as he quickly jotted down his

Bourbon Street address and handed it to her.

Dominique took the paper and tucked it into her pocket. She was relieved at Jules's kind offer. She rose from her seat, and smiled warmly at him as she thanked him with admiration shining from her misty-green eyes, "Thank you, M'sieur Harcourt. You shall not be disappointed. And I shall not tell anyone where the money came from."

"I'm sure our new venture will be most profitable in more ways than you realize, *chérie,*" he said as he once more took her hand in his.

Jules lingered over her hand, and Dominique felt uneasy when he didn't let her hand go after the customary kiss. But when she tugged gently he quickly released her hand. And she admonished herself silently, thinking she had read something evil into Jules's kindness making her feel guilty, and she smiled warmly at Jules as she said, "Thank you again, M'sieur." Dominique waited for Jules to open the door. But when he put his arms around her and drew her against him to touch her temple with his warm lips an uncomfortable feeling engulfed her. Then when Jules suddenly released her with a fatherly kiss to her forehead she once more chided herself for her foolish reaction.

Jules opened the door, and his thin lips broke into a warm smile and he said, "Until tomorrow, *chérie.*"

*"Oui,* I'll be there at three sharp, M'sieur," she said and walked away. Jules's warm smile had made her feel better, and she again chastised

herself for her earlier feelings of mistrust. But Dominique did not see the lustful gleam in Jules's dark eyes as she gave him her back.

The following day, Wyatt arrived and after making the introductions Evon left for Belle Terre.

Dominique's frosty greeting brought a crooked smile and a raised eyebrow from Wyatt, but he said nothing. Then after showing Wyatt to his cabin Dominique ignored Evon's brother, acting as though he were not there.

Hetty had shown her surprise when Dominique had explained that Evon had opened an account in her name at the bank and deposited a large portion of her inheritance. She hated lying to Hetty, but she didn't want to cause her mammy any unnecessary concern, telling Hetty she had to be at the bank at 3:00 to pick up the draft. She left, but instead of the bank she went directly to Jules's townhouse. After exchanging a few pleasantries with Jules and securing the draft, she hurried to Annie's where she repeated the same story to Annie that she'd told to Hetty: that Evon had agreed to put the funds in an account in her name. She knew how Annie felt about Evon and she didn't want to get into a long discussion over her guardian. She then explained to Annie that even though she wouldn't need any monetary help from her she would still need Annie and Lonzo to help her with the hiring of the workmen and the ladies to work in the casino and also the hiring of a capable casino manager. After which she and Annie with Lonzo's help made all the necessary arrangements to begin the renovation.

To Dominique's delight, two days after Wyatt's arrival, Lonzo brought several men in a flatbed wagon. The men began tearing out rotten boards and replacing the old boards with new lumber. The riverboat was humming with men singing and hammering as they worked. After instructing his men to do what was expected of them, Lonzo left to pick up the remaining supplies he had been unable to load in the crowded wagon.

Dominique was giddy with excitement. Then when Wyatt, caught up in the excitement, asked, "Is there anything I can do?" she smiled and quickly put him to work tearing out the rotted wooden railing.

The following morning, Dominique sat with Wyatt and Beau at the galley table while Hetty served them a delicious breakfast of ham and bacon with hot biscuits and steaming hot coffee.

"Hetty, this is the best breakfast I've had in a long time," Wyatt said as he speared another thick slice of ham.

"Why thank you, M'sieur," Hetty said as she smiled at the handsome blond-haired man. She liked Wyatt Forest and Hetty wasn't surprised when Dominique was not immune to his boyish charm. Hetty had loved Wyatt's father, Henri, for twenty years, but over the years she had caught only a glimpse now and then of his son. She sighed as she thought how proud Henri must be of his son.

* * *

Wyatt had been on board two weeks when he glanced over at Dominique and asked, "What do you think of my big ugly brother?" His eyes twinkled with mischief.

"Whatever made you ask that?" she asked. Her brow wrinkled. Evon had left for Belle Terre over two weeks ago, and during that time Wyatt hadn't so much as mentioned his brother's name.

"Oh, no reason in particular. But I somehow get the feeling the old man hasn't made a favorable impression on you. Unusual to say the least. I am curious though as to how my brother handled being rejected by such a beautiful woman."

"I'd rather not discuss your brother," she countered icily. Dominique had not seen Evon since his departure, but since their last encounter she'd had trouble falling asleep nights. After tossing and turning for hours she would drift into a restless sleep only to dream of dark turbulent eyes, a full, sensuous mouth, wide shoulders tapering to narrow hips and she would awake bathed in perspiration. Her dreams were becoming so real that one night she could have sworn that Evon had actually been with her physically, for she awoke with a burning fire between her thighs and her lips had felt scorched.

"Nicki, M'sieur Wye, and Hetty! M'sieur Evon is here!" Beau called from above.

Hetty smiled and grabbed for a towel and wiped her hands as she hurried out of the galley. Wyatt scooted his chair back and followed behind Hetty. But Dominique stayed in her chair. She couldn't move. She felt as though she was frozen. Panic consumed her whole being. Why had he come? Shakily, she rubbed her hands together. Her palms were damp and her breathing was irregular. What was the matter with her? She felt his presence before she looked up and saw Evon standing in the doorway. She stared into those ebony orbs. Her mouth felt like she'd swallowed a cotton ball and she couldn't speak. She stared mesmerized at him. *Mon Dieu,* she thought, but he was a handsome devil. He took a step toward her and suddenly her senses returned. She rose quickly, knocking her chair backward. "Please—don't come any closer!"

Evon reached down and righted her chair. "There's a problem out at Belle Terre and I need you to help me solve it. My first night at Belle Terre someone put a gris-gris under my pillow, and then last night I discovered Florrie in my room with a voodoo doll in her hand and," he paused, "there was a black hairpin on the floor beside my bed." He couldn't take his eyes off Dominique. He felt hypnotized.

*Non!* How could this be? A black hairpin! Florrie had put a curse of death on Evon? Dominique couldn't believe what Evon had said. But for all his faults she had never known Evon to lie to her. She had to talk to Florrie. Find out what was going on at Belle Terre. Then seeing the strange expression on Evon's face, she asked shakily, "Why are you looking at me like that?" A chill ran along her spine. Did he think she had something to do with the curse placed on him?

Several weeks had passed since Dominique had seen Evon. He wanted her to come to Belle Terre. She wanted to refuse him, but she feared for Florrie's safety knowing that many masters punished their slaves severely for death curses.

"I's don' care, Missy. Dat man done take dis hom' fom yous," Florrie cried, and tears splashed down her cheeks. When upset, Florrie reverted to the slave dialect.

"*Non! Non,* Florrie. What has happened between the master and me is not your concern. The master ignored the anger gris-gris you put under his pillow when he'd first arrived at Belle Terre, but he cannot overlook a death curse. He will punish you. He may even beat you!" Dominique said in a hushed tone. She loved Florrie.

Last year Florrie's mother, Blossom, had overheard her daughter singing *Li minuit tous moune a' l'eau—it is twelve o'clock all hands in the water,* Mamselle Marie Chauffez-Marie Lavernau. Blossom had realized the girl had been a participant in the festival on St. John's Eve, the yearly voodoo celebration out near Bayou Tchoupitoulas, and she had tried to dissuade the girl from attending another voodoo ceremony. But Florrie had refused to listen, and Blossom had then begged Dominique to speak to Florrie, but neither had Florrie listened to Dominique. And now the inevitable had happened, the new master was aware of Florrie's involvement in voodooism.

"Missy no wuhy. Fluries not mek death gris-gris, Fluries mek anguh gris-gris."

"But Florrie, M'sieur found a black hairpin beside his bed, and he thinks you put it there, that you put a death curse on him," Dominique explained fretfully. She knew plantation masters were familiar with anger gris-gris, and for the most part they ignored these harmless charms, but death curses were taken seriously.

"Ah dint. Fluries onlies mek anguh gris-gris, not wan' mastah dead," she said in a hushed voice. Suddenly her eyes widened as she realized the enormity of the accusation.

"Oh Florrie, they will punish you—he may even beat you!" Dominique whispered. She stared at the black hairpin Evon had given her, and she wondered if Evon was a kind master or a cruel master. Was he a compassionate master or was he a master capable of violence? Would he beat Florrie? Or would he . . . it was too monstrous, and Dominique was relieved when Florrie interrupted her train of thought.

"But ahs doan eban hab no haypens," Florrie said softly, as she envisioned the new master, with whip in hand, his eyes, red with fury, grabbing her gown and ripping it to the waist. Icy fingers seeped into every pore in her body and she trembled uncontrollably. The vision seemed a reality. The master raised the whip and brought it down to slash and tear into her soft flesh and she flinched as her teeth began to chatter. She whimpered aloud as she flung herself into Dominique's arms.

There was a deep, unaccustomed pain in

Dominique's breast as she hugged Florrie to her. She closed her eyes. She knew Florrie had told her the truth. Grief and despair tore at her heart. She had to convince Evon that Florrie had not put the hairpin in his room. Her only guilt was making a harmless anger gris-gris. Would he listen to her? She had to make him see the situation for what it was, that someone other than Florrie had put the death curse on him. Sighing, Dominique let the hairpin fall from her fingers as she gently pushed Florrie back. Dominique straightened her shoulders and lifted her chin a notch. She said with determination, "Don't worry, Florrie. No harm will come to you." She smiled, but a pain squeezed her heart.

"But what you gwine do, missy? What if the new mastah don't listen to you?" Florrie asked, drying her eyes on her skirt. Dominique's confidence in herself had lifted Florrie's spirits and her speech became more articulate.

"He'll listen, Florrie," Dominique said with conviction. Or, she vowed silently, I'll stand in Florrie's place. He'll have to punish me.

Evon had, at first, been slightly agitated at Florrie. He'd ignored the girl's first feeble attempt to put a voodoo curse on him. But when he'd caught her in his room with a gris-gris in her hand and a black hairpin on the floor beside his bed, he knew he'd have to reprimand the girl. He hadn't known what it was he'd done to make the girl despise him so. He couldn't recall saying more than hello and goodbye to the girl since taking up residence at Belle Terre. He'd discovered the girl in his quarters and had bridled his irritation while questioning her. But he'd become agitated when she'd shrugged and refused to say anything. The girl had intended to put a death curse on him, and he sadly realized that unless he found a solution to the problem, as master he would have to punish Florrie, but how? He'd never had a voodoo death curse to deal with before.

These last weeks Evon had worked from sunup until sunset. He was satisfied with the improvements already completed at Belle Terre. The exterior was near completion and so was the interior, with the exception of the water closet which Evon had put the finishing touches on the night before. The gas plant was also finished. The restored mansion was magnificent and he was proud of his accomplishments. But something was missing. He'd taxed himself to the limit, falling into bed, muscles aching only to lay staring wide-eyed into the darkness. Several such nights, he'd risen, thinking his restlessness lay with some detail he'd missed in the reconstruction of one of the outbuildings or in the plantation itself. He would return to his study where he carefully scanned each diagrammed sketch on the plan-table, tracing with his finger, the intricacies of each outbuilding, slave cabin, sugarhouse, stable, and even the silos to be repaired or added new, but he found nothing excluded. Then last night, he'd sat once more in his study staring unseeing at the wall above the plan-table and a vision of a lovely silver-haired creature standing on the upper deck of a brokendown riverboat appeared before him.

The scene had seemed so real that he swore he had felt her soft tender skin against his flesh, the aroma of her lilac scent stung his nostrils, arousing him, and jolting him back to reality. No woman had ever affected him so. He wanted Dominique and he swore he would have her if he had to kidnap her. He rose from his chair to pace back and forth while he envisioned himself abducting Dominique in one dashing scene after another. When his sanity returned, he'd rationalized that kidnapping Dominique would never do. No, he'd thought, he would have to think of a more civil way to coax her into making the trip willingly to Belle Terre, and into his bed. And it came to him. Florrie! He would ask Dominique to speak to the girl. Voodoo was a common practice among the slaves, but the girl had put a curse of death on him, and even though he did not believe such nonsense, he wanted it stopped. And when he went to bed he slept soundly for the first time in weeks.

The following morning, Evon had ridden in to the city on the pretext that he would not tolerate such extreme forms of voodooism from Florrie on his plantation, and an hour later Evon, with a smile on his face drove up the drive of Belle Terre with Dominique beside him.

Dominique walked slowly around to the back of the mansion. Her mind was in a turmoil as she searched for Evon. She would tell him the truth, that Florrie was innocent. And if he did not believe her she would convince him that beating Florrie would cause more harm than good. She would explain to him that Florrie was not a bad girl, that she was a hard worker, and besides, she reasoned she would show him that to beat the girl would most likely cause her terrible pain and she would have to be put to bed which would mean that Florrie's mother would have to carry the work load. Blossom would not only have the meals to prepare, but without Florrie to help, Blossom would have the burden of the whole house on her shoulders. And, she reasoned, what with the additional cleanup due to the renovation it would be unthinkable for Evon to expect Blossom to do more than she was doing. She sighed, wondering what would happen if Evon refused to be dissuaded. . . .

Evon stuck his head out the window and when he saw Dominique, he called, "*Chérie.* Up here."

Evon's voice interrupted Dominique's train of thought as she tipped her head to the sun, shielding her eyes as she called, "*Oui,* M'sieur?"

"Come upstairs, *chérie.* I have something to show you," he called pleasantly. The sunlight glistened on her hair making it the color of fresh cut wheat, and he smiled warmly.

His smile appeared genuine, and Dominique didn't want to do anything to darken his disposition. She returned his smile with a forced smile of her own and a nod of her head.

The time had come to confront Evon, and she hurried into the house and up the winding staircase.

Since leaving Florrie, Dominique had mentally

put together what it was she wanted to say to Evon. She reached the top of the stairs and he stood before her. Before she lost her nerve she blurted out her thoughts, questions, and solutions neither waiting for nor giving Evon time to answer or comment. As her hysteria rose she felt Evon's hands on her shoulders and her words died away.

# Ten

"I can what?" he exploded as he stared at her in disbelief. Then suddenly his features relaxed, and he asked gently, "You can't be serious, *chérie?*" He cupped her chin searching her face for an understanding of such a preposterous statement.

Dominique heard a trace of mockery in his tone and she stiffened, "You heard me, M'sieur," she stated belligerently, but her voice was shakier than she would have liked.

"You want me to beat you?" he asked bewildered. "Whatever gave—" he began, but she tossed her head and gave an irritable tug at her skirt, and he realized she had believed he was capable of such cruelty. Suddenly he threw back his head and let out a great peal of laughter, but at the look of surprise on her visage his mood became serious. He reached for her hand and coaxed gently, "Come, *chérie,* I want to show you something. We can discuss your punishment later."

Evon guided her down the long hallway and at

the end he let go of her hand and held his hand up, motioning for her to remain where she was as he reached for the brass handles of a newly installed set of double doors. He opened the doors in one sweep, and turning he smiled broadly at her.

After leaving Florrie, Dominique had felt alone and vulnerable. And now Evon's reaction to her words had left Dominique slightly confused. His anger had intimidated her, his laughter had surprised her, but when he took her hand in his, his gentle touch had helped to sooth her frayed nerves. It had given her a sense of strength and her despair lessened.

When Dominique had stopped at the end of the hall she had not known what to expect. And when Evon had thrown wide the French doors she had peered cautiously inside. Her eyes widened at what she saw. There was a huge porcelain tub against one wall and a washstand stood to one side of the tub. Her eyes swept the newly installed water closet and returned to stare at the unfamiliar-looking commode situated on the other side of the tub. Her cheeks colored profusely, but she ignored her discomfort as she looked up at Evon and whispered breathlessly, "It's beautiful!"

She was unaware of the captivating picture she made. Evon inhaled sharply. She was lovely with thick velvety lashes sweeping down over slightly tanned cheeks caused by being out on the decks more than she should. And he was glad he'd installed a window in the water closet above the tub, for in the sunlight her hair was the pale yellow of a field of grain. His eyes moved down to her firm high-perched breasts, and he felt a throbbing in his groin. He quickly averted his eyes, and stepped around Dominique to stand before the washstand where he reached for one of two brass spigots. He turned the spigot and a small trickle of water dripped from the spout. Turning it back he looked sheepishly at Dominique as he remarked casually, "A minor adjustment will correct the pressure problem."

His words helped to ease the tension that his earlier, silent appraisal had created between them, and Dominique sighed. His nearness unnerved her more than she cared to admit, and she looked up at him. Their eyes met and held. A silence filled the air and as it dragged out, Dominique struggled to think of something light to say to erase the newly mounting tension. Then shakily she said, "The house, I had no idea. You've accomplished a great deal in such a short period of time. I have seen improvement everywhere, but this . . ." her words trailed away as she swept her arm around the lovely blue and gold decorated water closet.

"You're beautiful, *chérie,*" he whispered.

His eyes were compelling, magnetic, and she said breathlessly, "Please, M'sieur." Her own eyes grew large and liquid. She took a step backward.

"Please?" he asked. And he reached for her.

*"Non,* M'sieur—" she protested, but he pulled her roughly, almost violently, to him as his mouth covered hers. His kiss was like a bolt of lightning sizzling its way to her very core. Then suddenly and without warning he released her and she stumbled back against the washstand.

"Do you still deny that your body comes alive when I touch you? Or has your profession conditioned you to respond to anyone? Please tell me I am wrong, *chérie*. Aah, say that you want me as much as I want you," he whispered hoarsely as once more he reached for her and enfolded her in a warm, protective embrace.

His words had been like a slap in the face and she stared at him with burning reproachful eyes. "*Non,* I do not deny that I want you and I despise you for it," she spat, and pushed hard against his chest.

"We would be good together, *chérie,*" he whispered as his hands moved in a circular motion on her back.

His words infuriated her. Dominique slapped him across the face. His expression grew thunderous and she wondered if he might not slap her back, but instead, she felt herself being picked up in strong arms as Evon carried her from the room.

"Put me down!" she hissed. But he remained silent while making his way purposefully back down the hall, pausing outside the master suite where he threw open the door. Inside the bedroom he kicked the door closed and walked to the side of the large four-poster bed where he dumped her without ceremony.

"Undress, madam, or I shall do it for you," he threatened ominously.

She stared disbelieving at his dark, angry expression. A suffocating sensation tightened her throat, and she began to fumble with the buttons on her bodice. Her eyes never left his. Then slowly his gaze dropped from her eyes to her shoulders to her breasts. Her fingers froze on the buttons, but she was strangely flattered by his interest. She unconsciously ran her tongue over her dry lips.

He inhaled sharply. Suddenly his eyes softened and he placed his finger beneath her chin and whispered simply, *"Chérie,* I want you." He dipped his head to taste her sweet lips, and when he felt her arms around his neck, he quickly and expertly maneuvered them onto the bed in such a way that Dominique was beneath him. Her breasts were flattened against his chest. He raised slightly and finished undoing the remaining buttons on her bodice.

In a passionate haze, Dominique realized that Evon had said that he wanted her and his words had sounded sincere, as though he cared . . . she panicked, as suddenly she wondered, had she mistaken lust for passion? But when Evon's mouth came down hard and demanding on her lips, she moaned, and when his tongue pushed against her tightly clenched teeth, she voluntarily parted her lips. His tongue probed the dark recesses of her mouth and her senses reeled uncontrollably. She ran her hands through his thick hair and down his back only to return to bury her fingers once more in his wavy locks, arching her body toward him as her breath came in short gasps. He had ignited something deep within her and she felt as though her whole body was on fire. "Oh M'sieur, please—"

"Slow down, *chérie,"* Evon whispered against her mouth. He raised his head to stare into her passion-glazed eyes as one hand outlined the circle of her breast. Then slowly he lowered his head and his lips touched her nipple with tantalizing possessiveness. He reached between them, taking her hand and guiding it to himself. "There is no turning back, *chérie*. We have gone too far to stop now."

She felt his flesh throb beneath her fingers, and suddenly she found his pants material too restricting and her fingers, with a will of their own, unbuttoned the fly of his trousers. She grasped his bulging rod. Evon's sharp intake of air made her release her hold on his swollen staff, thinking that she'd somehow caused him great pain. "I—I am sorry," she whispered uncertainly.

"Aah sweet angel," he said as raw and confusing emotions clutched at his insides. He wanted to bury himself deep within her warmth and he fought the urge to ravish her. He rolled to her side holding himself at bay and kicked off his pants. Then slowly he undressed Dominique and when he'd removed the last article of her clothing he quickly shed his remaining garments flinging them beside hers on the floor.

"We don't want things to end too quickly," he whispered, and he took one taut nipple between his teeth while his hand moved to the flat plane of her belly, easing downward into the furred Venus between her thighs. Rhythmically, he began to stroke the nubbin there. Her hand covered his in an attempt to stay his movements, but Evon covered her mouth with his and her body suddenly stiffened and convulsed repeatedly as beads of perspiration broke out to stand on her silken skin. "*Oui,* my lovely," he breathed into her ear, "you are everything I thought you would be and more, oh so much more." He raised his head to gaze into her passion-glazed eyes. "We are not finished. But then I do not have to coach you in the ways of love. Come my *petite.* As you know, that was only the beginning."

Dominique gasped in sheer delight. She tried to understand what Evon was saying, but his hands were once again upon her body. His lips trailed down the valley between her breasts pausing to tease one taut, dusky-pink nipple, and her mind simply wouldn't work. His tongue licked at her tender skin, and her body vibrated with liquid fire. His expert touch sent her to higher levels of ecstasy and she breathed in soul-drenching drafts as her impatience grew to explosive proportions and she cried out for release.

Dominique's hands were in his thick hair. She clutched his shoulders, she felt half fire, half flame and her nails raked his back. His breath was hot against her temple.

They had taken the time to explore, to arouse, to give each other pleasure, and Evon quickly covered her body with his. Dominique opened her eyes as Evon slid his hand between their damp bodies. He slipped his finger inside her warmth, and her eyes widened. Evon probed the walls of her Venus, feeling the dampness he sought. His entry was swift. But suddenly he stiffened and went dead still. "What the hell!" he exploded. His eyes flew open, but when Dominique's lips parted he quickly covered her mouth with his, silencing her cry of pain.

She felt a burning sensation deep inside her. Her eyes smarted, but when she would have cried out Evon's mouth covered hers in a gentle kiss that deepened, sending spirals of ecstasy through her. Dominique returned his kiss hungrily. He began to move slowly at first, then as he detected that the pain had subsided, his movements quickened. Evon picked up the tempo and Dominique matched him thrust for thrust until their bodies were in exquisite harmony with one another, soaring higher and higher until at last the peak of delight was reached.

They lay entwined for several seconds. Then Evon rolled to his side taking Dominique with him. Contentment and peace flowed between them. Evon had never felt so complete, so masculine, so male!

Dominique sighed contentedly. A few minutes later she heard Evon's even breathing and realized that he'd fallen asleep. She smiled and she, too, closed her eyes and within seconds succumbed to the numbed sleep of a satisfied lover.

Hours later, Dominique awoke. Where was she? She glanced around feeling somewhat disoriented. She tried to get up but a weight held her in place. *Mon Dieu!* she thought as what had happened earlier between her and Evon suddenly came crashing down around her. Dominique flushed profusely as she lifted Evon's arm which was draped possessively around her waist. She laid it back down gently upon his side. But when she tried once more to get up, his leg thrown over hers was another matter. She didn't want to wake him. Later, after what seemed like hours, she stepped to the floor, gasping as the cool night air touched her bare skin. She moved to cover herself with her hands and her foot touched something soft at her feet. She bent and searching like a blind person and at last she retrieved her wrinkled dress. She slipped it on and her shaking fingers fumbled at the tiny buttons. When she'd fastened all but one button, her fingers stilled as a large hand covered hers.

Evon turned her around slowly to face him and in the bright glow of the moon she saw the familiar passion blazing in his dark eyes and quickly stepped back. "*Non,* M'sieur," she said firmly. "*Non.* I cannot undo what has happened, but I guarantee there will not be a repeat performance."

"You can't mean that," he teased, but the determination he saw in Dominique's emerald eyes told him she had meant every word she'd said.

His expression was almost comical. Evon was looking at her as though he believed she'd taken leave of her senses. Well, she thought, she didn't care what he thought, and perhaps he was right. Earlier, he had filled a moment of physical desire, while she had allowed him to tear apart her soul.

Evon reached for her, drawing her into his arms, and before she could protest his mouth descended on hers. And when she felt her defenses weaken, she pushed with all her might against his chest. His arms dropped to his sides, and she ran from the room and out of the house.

She hurried to Florrie's cabin where she woke the girl insisting that Florrie return with her to New Orleans. After Florrie had dressed, the two made their way to the stables. Dominique quickly threw a bridle on Saladin, and together they rode out of the stable.

Dominique's anger mounted and she hissed scathingly beneath her breath, "He lied to me! Nothing happened that night in that damn cabin." And tonight? can you deny what happened tonight? a tiny voice asked, and she squeezed her eyes shut. "Tonight," she whispered aloud, "was a mistake."

# Eleven

"Maurice! Stop the carriage!" Yvette ordered in a shrill voice. The Negro coachman pulled back on the reins bringing the team to a halt as Yvette peered out the window of the phaeton.

She caught a glimpse of Jules Harcourt as he whisked a young woman inside the side entrance of his townhouse. "What's that little tart up to?" she mused, then called out, "Maurice, turn the carriage around. Drive out to Belle Terre." Yvette settled back against the plush velvet cushion. "I knew she was a deceitful little bitch," she hissed as she straightened her white silk bonnet and ran her hands anxiously over the skirt of her deep violet printed silk gown. "I can't wait to see his face when he hears this," she said arching one thin brow.

"Are you sure, Yvette?" Evon asked. There was concern bridled with anger in his tone.

"But of course I'm sure, *chéri,*" Yvette quipped sarcastically. "I saw her enter Jules's Bienville townhouse, and the familiarity with which they greeted each other said that she and M'sieur Harcourt are more than casual acquaintances."

Her words brought a frown to Evon's handsome features.

"Dominique and Harcourt? It doesn't make sense," he shook his head. Yvette had her faults, but he had never known her to lie. And she had seen Dominique and Harcourt together.

He had held Dominique in his arms, he had made love to her, and there had been no other man before him. Yet . . .

Yvette knew that Evon was questioning his ward's actions, but tiring of all the attention Dominique was receiving, she draped her arms around Evon's neck and moved seductively against him, determined to erase Dominique Chandler from his mind. When he continued to stare past her she became furious, but knew her anger would get her nowhere with Evon. She taunted coyly, "Why don't you ask her, yourself, *chéri?* Ask the little tart what she thought to accomplish visiting a man, alone at his private residence. One can only surmise what a man with M'sieur Harcourt's reputation wanted with—"

"Enough, Yvette!" he snapped angrily. He removed her arms from around his neck, but the pained expression in her dark eyes made him cringe inwardly. He knew he had no right to vent his anger on Yvette. She had driven all the way out here to Belle Terre to warn him of his ward's unseemly behavior, but then Dominique's behavior had always been questionable. Yvette, however, didn't know about Annie and the brothel. But, damn, he thought, why Harcourt?

Evon had a faraway expression on his face that Yvette considered unflattering to her feminine ego. Her arms snaked up around his neck and she leaned back to stare up at him. Sudden anger overcame her and unable to conceal the bitterness in her voice, she hissed, "Perhaps, *chéri* you should ask your ward why she would risk her reputation, not to mention the embarrassment she had brought to you, her guardian, with her whorish actions."

Yvette's words brought Evon out of his reverie, and she watched intently as her accusation penetrated his thoughts and his mood darkened at her words. She lowered her eyes not wanting him to see the gleam of satisfaction mirrored there. She had cleverly and quickly accomplished what she had set out to do . . . tear Dominique Chandler's reputation to shreds in Evon's eyes. And tomorrow, she thought, she would visit Jules at his townhouse and learn exactly what Evon's ward was doing there.

"That is exactly what I plan to do." Evon's anger did not go unnoticed by Yvette, and she was pleased with herself and her performance. But again she found herself anxious to rid them of their present topic, and leaning into Evon she moved her body seductively against his as she tightened her grip around his neck. But while her eager lips sought his mouth, Evon drew back and again removed her arms from around his neck. He set her aside and without a word turned and strode from the room calling to the butler to see her out. Yvette stared openmouthed after him and when she heard the door slam shut, her eyes narrowed and she whispered vehemently, "No one, not even Evon Forest ignores Yvette Renault for a slut like Dominique Chandler!"

*"Chérie,* I feel I have waited a lifetime for this moment," Jules whispered as he rained light kisses along the column of Yvette's slender neck.

"Don't waste time talking, M'sieur," Yvette gasped breathlessly.

Jules raised his head and gazed down at her swollen breasts. "They are lovely, *chérie,"* he whispered raggedly. "I had no idea—aah, *ma cousine,* why did we not think of this—"

Yvette felt impatient and insisted. "Now, Jules!"

Jules quickly inserted his swollen staff into her warmth. And then lay perfectly still as Yvette's eyes flew open. Jules chuckled and gazed into her startled expression before he smiled and began the age-old rhythm. Yvette, too, smiled, but his strokes were slow and deliberate, and she gasped. He watched her frustration and smiled in satisfaction, whispering, "Beg, *chérie.* Beg for the pleasure you know I can give you." His breathing was ragged, yet he waited.

Yvette's eyes flew open. Beg him! "Non, Jules. Yvette Renault does not beg any man. Men beg for Yvette's favors," she whispered fiercely against his mouth. His words had angered her, but the determination on his face made her squirm uncomfortably. "A cousin should not have to beg."

Jules's lips curved upward. Her anger excited him and her increased breathing told him what he had known all along—there was little doubt she would do his bidding. "Come my pet. Say the words and we will both be rewarded. I can satisfy this craving inside you . . . trust me," he whispered, but he was unable to conceal the glint of hatred that her words had inflicted on his very soul. He wanted to lash out at her, punish her for all the years she and her parents had looked down their noses at him and Reynard, treating them like trash, yet he waited patiently for Yvette to say the words he must hear. "Trust me, *chérie,* we are family."

Family? Jules and his dead brother had always been a thorn in her father's side and he had denounced them both years ago. Jules had won Harcourt Grove in a poker game or he wouldn't have that, or this—this townhouse as he called it was no more than a few sticks nailed together . . .

Damn him! she thought, her body was engulfed in flames. Her prime interest had been to use her wiles on Jules and therefore gain whatever useful tidbits of gossip that would help her destroy Dominique Chandler's reputation. And she had succeeded, but by doing so she had enhanced her own fiery nature. Jules, she discovered was a man capable of extinguishing the inferno Evon had ignited earlier. Besides, she reasoned, what were a few whispered lies between lovers? Jules had confided that Dominique was an excellent bed partner, but he'd refused to say more until after he'd been given the chance to compare her to Dominique. Yvette sighed. If giving in to Jules's request would keep her on Jules's good side and gain her condemning information against Evon's ward, then so be it. She would do anything to rid herself of that Chandler girl. "Please Jules, I need you," Yvette said huskily as she pulled his head down for a kiss. His lips parted and her tongue darted inside. Jules gasped his delight at her words and her sensuous action. He began to move and as his pace quickened, she smiled triumphantly and whispered words of love into his ear until she could hold back no longer. She met him stroke for stroke until she cried out. Jules, too, felt his release coming and moaned aloud as he lost all control of his senses and spilled his seed deep within her warmth.

Later, they lay entwined in each other's arms and Jules whispered against her ear, "You are to keep what I have told you in the strictest confidence, *chérie.*"

"But of course, darling. I will not breath a word to a single soul," Yvette promised faithfully. Her tone sounded sincere, but she was unable to hide the gleam in her eyes.

Jules did not notice the enmity shining from Yvette's dark eyes but he, too, smiled cynically. "We must do this again, *ma chérie.* I can expect to see you when?" he asked softly. He nuzzled her neck and added seductively, "I'd like to see you on a regular basis."

"Umm, I'd like that, too, but my stallion, we must wait," Yvette whispered huskily, trailing her fingers across Jules's chest and down the length of his firm-muscled stomach to his already hardened staff.

# Twelve

Dominique and Florrie had arrived back at the wharf a little after midnight and Dominique had made a pallet on the floor in Beau's room for Florrie until Hetty could ready one of the remaining fifty-three staterooms.

Dominique had changed into her nightdress and turned to walk to her bed when she noticed an envelope lying on the makeshift dressing table.

She picked up the letter and smiled when she saw it was from her cousin, Claire Chandler, who lived in North Carolina. Claire had written that her mother had died and that she would be moving into a tiny room over the millinery shop where she was employed. Dominique was saddened for her cousin. She put the letter on the tabletop and thought of Claire living in one room and stitching seams for hours at a time. Then she smiled. She would write a note to her cousin first thing in the morning and ask Claire to come and live with her. After all, she and Beau and Claire were the only three left of their family. She got into bed. Dominique soon closed her eyes, but suddenly Evon's face came into focus. Her eyes flew open. She tried to concentrate on Claire's letter, but the memory of Evon's arms around her, his mouth covering hers and . . . *non!* her mind screamed. She would not think of what had happened. With difficulty she drew her thoughts back to Claire's letter. She remembered her own father saying with disgust that his brother, Claire's father, had drunk away his half of the family fortune. And then after his death, Claire and her mother had been forced to live in near poverty.

Dominique's father had sent them a substantial allowance, but Claire's mother had used the bulk of the money to pay the debts her husband had accumulated over the years. *Oui,* she thought, she would write to Claire tomorrow and insist that she come and live with them on the riverboat. Surely Claire would find the roomy old vessel more to her liking than one tiny room. Dominique smiled sadly, and closing her eyes, she turned over on her side as darkness claimed her.

Who was talking to her? Was she dreaming? She was so tired. She tried, but she couldn't open her eyes.

"I said look at me!" Evon commanded harshly.

"What? Who?" Dominique asked hoarsely. She forced her eyes open and blinked and as the meaning of his words penetrated her groggy mind, Dominique suddenly sprang into a sitting position. The covers fell away, but she quickly drew them up beneath her chin. "What is the meaning of this, M'sieur? What are you doing in my room at this hour? If you think that what happened between us gives you the right to come into my bedroom uninvited, well you have another thought coming," she berated him indignantly. "How dare you . . ." but her words trailed away at the black expression on Evon's face.

"How dare you, *chérie?*" he said menacingly.

"How dare I?" she stammered. Her confusion was evident as she stared wide-eyed at him. His dark eyes held her mesmerized. Suddenly, his arms were around her and she was lifted from her bed as his lips covered her mouth.

Suddenly Evon remembered why he was here and he put her back down on the bed. He released his breath in an audible sigh as he stepped away. He needed some space between them. "What were you doing at Jules Harcourt's townhouse?" His words were loaded with ridicule.

"Jules? *Non,* M'sieur. That is none of your business," she said in a choked voice.

"None of my business? Aah, *chérie,* must I remind you that everything you do is my business?" There was a bitter edge of cynicism in his voice.

How had he found out? She had thought her visit had gone unnoticed. The shock of discovery hit her full force. Someone had seen her enter Jules's town house and had told Evon, but who? His mistress? "If you must know, I went to see Jules to get the money he offered me to refurbish my riverboat into a gambling casino," she admitted haughtily.

"You did what?!" he fairly exploded. He stood

there tall and angry and his eyes were black and dazzling with fury.

Startled, Dominique leaned backward in her bed, but in two strides Evon was beside her, gripping her arms. "Please, M'sieur, you are hurting me!" she cried. His reaction to her words terrified her and she feared what he might do if angered further. Her heart thundered in her chest. Was this the same man who had held her tenderly and whispered words of love in her ear?

Evon gazed down at Dominique. The fear he saw in her eyes made him cringe. His intent had not been to make her afraid of him; far from it. He had wanted her to tell him that Yvette's words were a lie. Jules Harcourt was his hated enemy. But she hadn't denied it, no. Instead she had readily admitted to being there. Suddenly he realized what she'd said, that Harcourt had given her money! Why would she go to Harcourt? Why hadn't she come to him? There was more than enough money to have the damn riverboat repaired, remodeled, or whatever she wanted to do. Hell, he thought, she had enough money to buy five riverboats if that was what she really wanted. This was ridiculous. "I don't believe you. What you are saying doesn't make any sense," he said gruffly.

"I don't care what you believe, M'sieur. And guardian or not you have no right to question my motives or—"

"As your guardian, I have every right. I am responsible for your behavior, your—"

His domineering manner made her furious. "And who, M'sieur, is responsible for your behavior? Is it your duty to teach your ward the art of lovemaking?" she snapped, but was immediately sorry she had spoken such mean and spiteful words. As quickly as she'd said them she wished she could take them back.

"You were not an unwilling participant, *chérie,*" he retaliated. But at the hurt expression on her beautiful features Evon sighed. Her taunt had triggered his anger and he had spoken before he'd realized the effect his words would have. "I am sorry, *chérie,* but what happened between us has nothing to do with this recent mishap. And—" He gazed at her lovely features: her eyes were as green as emeralds and her pert little nose was tilted slightly upward. His eyes dropped to her slender neck and lower still to the full firmness of her breasts. "Why did you go there without a proper chaperone?" he asked perplexed. He wanted to believe her, that she had gone to borrow money from Harcourt, but why would she ignore the dictates of society? If it had been as she had said, that she merely went to secure a loan, why hadn't she taken Hetty with her? But he already knew the answer to that—Hetty would have refused to accompany her. Hetty hated the riverboat and Dominique would never have made Hetty do anything against her will. And had she asked the banker, he too would have ignored her request. Suddenly he realized her appointment with Harcourt had been legitimate and he knew he had had no right to badger her.

"If you don't mind, I'd like to get dressed," she said and hastily looked away.

"Of course," he said as his hands dropped to his side. Evon didn't move and Dominique quickly looked at him. He seemed to be peering at her intently and then his gaze dropped from her eyes to her shoulders and to her breasts.

There was a tingling in the pit of her stomach and a blush like a shadow ran over her cheeks. "M'sieur . . ." she could say no more.

"I'll be in the galley," he said in a deep-timbered voice as he turned and left the cabin.

Dominique stared after him. What had she done? She had allowed Evon to take her very heart and soul, a man who disapproved of her, a man who didn't love her.

She brought her emotions under control and dressed quickly and made her way to the galley where Evon waited with two cups of café au lait on the table. Also there were two *beignets,* left over from the morning before, that Hetty had brought back from the Café Du Monde.

Dominique kept her eyes averted as she sat down across from him. She bent over her cup.

"Dominique," he began, but paused as he stared at the crown of her silver-blond head. "Christ! Why Harcourt?" he asked, but subconsciously he already knew the answer; had she come to him he would have refused. But he couldn't admit that to her. "You could have asked Annie, or—"

"Or what, M'sieur?" she asked bitterly.

Evon didn't answer right away. He was still having trouble with the thought of Dominique alone with Harcourt. But he couldn't deny the fact that he had made his position clear to Dominique.

He did not approve of her living on the riverboat, and had she come to him with this new notion of a gambling casino, he would have exploded. "Why Harcourt? Why not Annie?"

She did not miss the criticism in his voice. "Annie? Annie does not have that kind of money. And had I gone to the bank, the banker would have snubbed his nose at a woman asking for a loan. The why, M'sieur is that M'sieur Harcourt was the only person who stood beside my father and offered to help him when everyone else turned their backs on Papa," Dominique said bitterly.

Friend! Harcourt? Were they talking about the same man? Evon's dark eyes narrowed and his back became ramrod straight. Harcourt was a cheat and a thief. How could she defend a man like that? The man had destroyed her father, yet she sat across from him telling him what a kind and generous man Harcourt was. Why, the man was the devil's own advocate. Or perhaps Yvette had been right, perhaps there was something between Dominique and Harcourt.

"What you have done is inexcusable, *chérie.* If word were to circulate that you and—"

"If? Oh come now, M'sieur. I am not stupid. Your mistress may have insisted that you are the only one she had told of my indiscretion, but surely even you know better," she spat at him.

"Yvette will tell no one. But enough. I fear I, too, have compromised your reputation and I'm willing to marry you, but there are complications."

"Marry me! How dare you patronize me. I wouldn't in a million years marry a conceited, arrogant rogue like you," she hissed venomously. Who did he think he was? Willing indeed. If she never saw him again it would be too soon, and to think she had lain in his arms, and been haunted by dreams of this man. Suddenly she rose and marched from the room. As she entered the gangway a firm hand clamped around her upper arm, she was spun around, and warm lips covered her mouth hungrily. The blood pounded in her brain, leapt from her heart, and made her knees tremble. She was shocked at her own eager response. A warning alarm sounded, but his hand unbuttoned her blouse, his fingers icy, but the palm fiery hot making her senses reel. Her emotions whirled and somersaulted and she pushed the warning to the back of her mind. Gently his hand circled the outline of her breast and the gentle message sent currents of desire through her. He reclaimed her mouth and she drank in the sweetness of his kiss.

"Aah, *chérie*. Marry me and I'll give you whatever you wish. You can forget this damn riverboat, and—"

Forget this damn riverboat! She snapped her eyes open as she fought to bring her tumultuous emotions under control. She took a deep breath and kicked Evon in the shin as she pushed with all her might against his rock-hard chest. Her sudden and unexpected actions surprised Evon and his hands fell away. He reached down to rub his aching shin.

His quick release threw Dominique off balance, but her flailing hands found the narrow walls of the gangway and she steadied herself.

Dominique paled. She was appalled at Evon's words, he had proposed to her while in the same instance he had insulted her. "I do not want to marry you, M'sieur."

"Aah *chérie,* what can I say? I am in need of a wife and although I am not proud of my part in this, you are in need of a husband," Evon explained softly realizing his part in jeopardizing Dominique's reputation. Evon ignored the foreign feeling in his chest as his thoughts raced ahead. If Dominique were dressed in the proper attire *and* they were physically attracted to one another and if Dominique would agree to his terms, he knew that together they could pull off the charade necessary to fool his father and gain his inheritance. "Dominique. Our marriage would be in name only. If you will come back to the galley I will try and explain," he coaxed gently.

"There is nothing you have to say that I want to hear, M'sieur," she spat angrily.

"Aah, *chérie.* Please reconsider?"

Evon Forest was an exasperating man. First he demanded, then he pleaded. She wished he would do one or the other. His actions confused her. "In name only?" she asked puzzled. Now what did he mean by that?

"If that is what you want," he answered.

"*Non,* M'sieur. We have said all there is to say. If you'll excuse me." Her inquisitive nature wanted to hear more, but she turned and fled before she did something dumb like reconsider his offer.

Once inside her stateroom, she quickly slid the

bolt in place.

He did not go after her, but walked back inside the galley and sat down. He took a sip of the tepid liquid and bit into a *beignet*. Aimlessly he went through the motions of chewing and swallowing the tasty pastry while contemplating ways to persuade Dominique to accept his marriage proposal. Time was running out. And he would lose his inheritance if he didn't marry before his thirtieth birthday. Suddenly his mind's eye created a silhouette of Dominique in his arms in his bed and an idea struck him. Then he frowned, realizing it would take some ingenuity on his part to talk her into going along with his scheme.

# Thirteen

"Claire!" Dominique shouted, and threw her arms around her cousin.

"Oh Nicki, it's heavenly seeing you again. I know you weren't expecting me until next week, but after I'd written that I was coming, there really was no reason to prolong my stay in North Carolina."

Dominique held Claire at arm's length and exclaimed, "Let me look at you." Her eyes swept over her cousin, and Dominique felt shoddy by comparison. Her own brown silk day dress was limp and faded while Claire's soft white muslin made her cousin the more stylish of the two. Claire was the shy one even though she was a few years older. Dominique was the bold one, and, when necessary, took the initiative.

Suddenly they were talking and laughing at once, and unconsciously brushing at the dampness on their cheeks until Dominique called out, "Hetty! Beau! Florrie! Claire is here." She smiled tearfully at her cousin and said, "I'm so glad you are here. We're going to have a wonderful time together."

Hetty and Beau called to Claire as they hurried over to where she stood beside Dominique.

Florrie remained at a distance.

After the greetings, everyone began talking at once, and at last Dominique held up her hand and motioned for quiet. "Enough," she laughed. "I'm sure Claire would like to freshen up and she's probably starved. Come, let's go below and Hetty will make Claire something to eat, and Beau, you can carry her satchel down to the cabin Hetty and I prepared for her."

Later, in the galley, and after both Hetty and Beau had retired for the evening, Dominique and Claire sat catching up on each other's lives during the two years since Claire had last visited Dominique at Belle Terre.

"So much has happened since we last saw each other. Your father and my mother—" she began.

"Yes," Dominique broke in, "they're both gone, but we have each other, and Beau and Hetty." Her eyes misted and she sighed and said, "You must be exhausted, Claire, I think it's time we went to bed and tomorrow we'll talk more. She smiled warmly at the cousin she'd always felt was more her friend than her cousin.

"Thank you, Nicki. I am a little tired," Claire agreed. They walked out of the galley arm in arm and made their way down the narrow hall to their cabins and said goodnight.

The following day, Dominique gave Clair a

tour of the riverboat, smiling at Claire's enthusiasm.

In a few days, the two along with Hetty and Florrie combined their efforts and cleaned several staterooms while Beau with Napolean occupied himself on the main deck watching the painters as they put the finishing touch on the outer walls of the Texas deck. "Claire, are you sure you worked in the millinery back in North Carolina?" Dominique straightened and arched her aching back while rubbing gently at the sore spots. She glanced over at her cousin and laughed. Claire stared up at her from the floor she was scrubbing, but before she could answer, Dominique continued, "Seamstresses stitch all those dainty little rows and the modistes I've seen dress and walk so prim and proper and are all so damn stuffy. And you, you fit right into the prim and proper scenario, but stuffy, never! Just look at you, you're as mussed and dirty as the three of us. And we should be ashamed of ourselves! We've made you labor like a Missouri mule since you've been on the riverboat. Claire," she groaned, "you must slow down! It isn't necessary that you work at such a pace; I'm having trouble keeping up with you, and Hetty and Florrie seem to be lagging behind, too. Besides we have the majority of the cabins finished. The remaining staterooms we'll ready as we need them or can squeeze the time in to do them. And there's no rush, I might add," she smiled.

"I haven't done any more than either of you and you're embarrassing me," Claire said, but grinning good-naturedly she added, "besides, this is my home now and I want to do my share. It's the least I can do to show my appreciation for all you've done for me."

"You don't need to thank me, Claire. Your coming here means everything to me. And Hetty and Beau and Florrie love having you with us," she assured her cousin.

"It's late. Let's stop for now. The workers assured me their work would be finished in a few more weeks, so tomorrow we'll tackle the grand saloon. They say save the best for last, and in this case it'll be the hardest, but I think we'll all find it the most rewarding," she smiled.

Five weeks later, the riverboat sported a new coat of paint and was outfitted with new curtains, hand-sewn by Claire and Hetty. The faded velvet draperies had been cleaned and pressed and the casino opened for business.

Earlier that same day, Annie brought twelve girls to act as hostesses for the casino's opening, and Lonzo had brought Lance Martin, the casino's new manager. Lance was a quiet, handsome gentleman in his early thirties who could be trusted—according to Annie and Lonzo.

They stood outside the swinging doors—Dominique, Claire, Beau, and Hetty—watching excitedly while the saloon filled to bursting with rich planters, merchants, and bankers. They were anxious to try their luck at the new casino's faro, poker, and blackjack tables. Men stood five deep around the roulette wheel calling out their numbers, and as the big wooden wheel slowed and finally came to a halt, muttered curses and groans were heard as the men placed another wager hoping that the next turn of the wheel would make them a winner.

The crowded bar boasted five bartenders. Men sat four to a table playing monte while they eyed the daringly dressed waitresses bringing glasses of whiskey, brandy, and bourbon.

"Oh Nicki! I hope the boat doesn't sink," Claire remarked. Although she smiled, there was a seriousness to her tone.

"It wouldn't dare, Claire. Look at that crowd! We'll make a fortune if this keeps up." Dominique felt a light tap on her shoulder. Startled, she turned and was caught unaware as she stared up into a set of dark eyes. Her blood soared with unbidden memories and she sucked in her breath.

"I'd like to talk to you, alone," Evon said, and his tone brooked no objections. He'd reluctantly put in an appearance tonight and one look at his ward made his blood boil. "Where the hell did you get that dress?" His eyes raked her down and back up to stare disapprovingly at her breasts straining against the too small bodice. "From Annie?"

"*Oui*—but I had nothing el—"

"You borrowed a bundle from Harcourt. Don't tell me there wasn't something left over to outfit yourself decently," he snarled at her. "Well . . . ?"

Her thoughts raced, why was he always finding something wrong with everything she did, or didn't do? He was acting like a jealous husband . . . jealous? She stared at him—*non*—impossible! She turned, but then looked back at him—damn! she thought, even when he was angry and berating her every movement she was reminded of his sexual attractiveness. She nodded her head slowly as she turned and allowed him to tuck her arm through his as he led her out on the promenade deck. They walked in silence all around the deck and when Evon hadn't said a word, she paused and turned to face him. "You said you wanted to talk to me?" she asked.

"I would rather take you in my arms and kiss your lovely mouth, I'd rather—" his husky words trailed away as he took her in his arms and his mouth claimed her slightly parted lips. He raised his head and gazed into her lovely features. "I'd rather make love to you in the soft glow of moonlight while—"

Dominique had gone with Evon thinking to prevent a scene. Or so she had told herself, yet walking beside him she fought to control her swirling emotions. A barrage of confused thoughts and feelings had assailed her. He had boldly spoken his thoughts aloud and reality set in as she fumed heatedly, "You are a rogue, M'sieur, and you have insulted me for the last time!" Lusty bastard! she fumed silently. Jealous, indeed! she mocked her previous thought.

"Oh, but *chérie,* that was no insult. My intentions are honorable," Evon said firmly.

"M'sieur, really!" she blustered, and pushed away from him. She turned and walked quickly away.

Evon watched her go and reached inside his vest

pocket for a cheroot. He struck the lucifer and dragged deeply on the imported Havana. He leaned his hip against the banister and blew the smoke out into the mist that hung low over the dark flowing Mississippi. His thoughts were in a turmoil. That damn dress! If she bent over, those luscious orbs would spill in plain view of everyone in the casino. Is that her intent, to attract every man in New Orleans?

Dominique hadn't believed him. He hadn't lied, he wanted Dominique. She affected him in a way no other woman ever had. He wanted her lying beneath him with her hair spread out over a satin pillow and her arms around his neck. He could almost feel her slender fingers winding their way through his hair as she brought his head down to meet her parted lips. He inhaled sharply. "You're in trouble, Evon," he said aloud. *"Oui,* M'sieur, you're in a whole hell lot of trouble." He threw his cigar over the side railing and turned and strode in the same direction as Dominique.

"Nicki, are you all right?" Claire asked as Dominique joined them outside the saloon.

Dominique was furious. "That man is despicable. He is a rakehell and a rogue and a—"

"Who is he, Nicki?" Claire asked curiously.

"The devil, himself!" she said, her eyes wide and her breath coming in short gasps. She turned away and after inhaling deeply she turned back to her cousin and apologized, "I'm sorry, Claire, but he makes me so mad." Dominique took another deep breath. "His name is Evon Forest and Papa appointed him guardian over Beau and me. He also owns Belle Terre."

"However did all this come about?" Claire asked.

"I'll tell you later," she said, and turned to Hetty. "Will you take Beau below? It's past his bedtime, Hetty. Where is Florrie?"

"Of course, *chérie,*" Hetty said, but her lips quirked slightly and the lifting of one thin brow went unnoticed by Dominique. Then realizing Dominique had asked her about Florrie, Hetty answered disgustedly, "That lazy girl's already asleep."

Dominique walked through the double doors preceded by Claire. Lance Martin walked up to the ladies and, bending his elbow, offered an arm to each. Dominique smiled and slid her arm through his, but Claire hesitated until Dominique nodded for her to follow suit. He escorted them to a table and pulled out a chair for Claire. He turned back to Dominique and in an undertone he asked, "What do you think?" He swept the crowded room with his arm.

Dominique couldn't hear him what with all the merriment in the smoke-filled room, and she leaned forward, her ear near his chin as she said in a raised voice, "I'm sorry, Lance, but I can't hear a word you're saying."

His lips to her ear, he rephrased his question, "I would say that the casino is a success, don't you agree?"

"I hope you're right, and that these gentlemen aren't just being inquisitive," she said, as she glanced around the crowded saloon. Suddenly she felt a large hand grip her soft wrist in an iron-clad vise.

"Come with me, Dominique," Evon demanded.

She looked up and her eyes took in Evon's powerful presence, but he didn't give her a chance to answer as he turned and pulled her in the direction of the exit. Suddenly Dominique dug her heels and skidded to a stop. "Release me, immediately, M'sieur," she insisted indignantly.

"Dominique. There is something you and I have to settle before this gets out of hand," he inclined his head toward Lance Martin who stood staring after them.

"Lance?" she sputtered. "What *are* you talking about?"

"If you don't mind airing dirty laundry in front of half the population of New Orleans—" he began, but at Dominique's startled expression he paused and waited for her to make the next move.

"Don't be ridiculous, M'sieur."

"I am not a man who allows his future wife, no matter the arrangement agreed upon, to trifle with another man whether it be in a public place or a private residence," he said, knowing the insinuation would infuriate Dominique to the point of retaliation. Even Dominique would not want to chance the gentlemen sitting within hearing distance to be apprised of the expletives he was sure she would hurl at him.

"Of all the—come on." Fury almost choked her as she spun around and led the way to the small alcove she and Lance used as their private office. Dominique entered the office and whirled back to face Evon. "What exactly were you implying, M'sieur? I have never met a more wretched or annoying man than you. What right do you have to come here and accuse me, belittle me—how dare you!" she spat at him. Was this the same gentle man she'd shared her most intimate moment with? How could he be so, so . . . her thoughts were jumbled and as she glared at him, she saw a hint of mockery in his dark eyes. "Future wife indeed! One mistake, and I repeat, *one,* for it will never happen again, and you presume to dictate my very life. M'sieur, you are despicable, you are the most irri—"

"Aah, *chérie,*" he crooned as he reached out and drew her against him, his mouth devouring her and cutting off her words.

She was caught off guard at the sudden vibrancy of his kiss as wave after wave of shock slapped at her. His hand moved to the swell of her breast and she inhaled sharply as her blood soared with unbidden memories.

Evon sensed the awakening flames within her and his own ardor was mounting at a very rapid pace. He lifted his dark head. "Come with me, *chérie.*"

Her heart was hammering, her breathing ragged. She paused to catch her breath. Suddenly warning spasms of alarm erupted within her and she felt ill-equipped to handle the situation she found herself in, knowing that if she went with him she would be lost. "I—non, I can't," she choked and pushing with all her might against his chest, she insisted, "Let go of me."

His hands fell away and Dominique escaped into the crowd of gentlemen placing bets and milling around the crap tables. Evon sighed. He'd taunted and bullied her and forced her to come with him, but in the end she had refused to be intimidated. He wanted her more than he'd ever wanted a woman in his life. Evon walked out of the office and seeing a vacant chair at one of the poker tables, he sat down and threw in his ante as the dealer began dealing the cards. Several hours later, after Evon had won several thousand dollars, he stood and raked his winnings into his hat. He took a step away from the table, but paused as Lance Martin suddenly blocked his way. Martin was an attractive man, he had to admit, and although Martin was not a tall man, his broad shoulders and narrow hips made Evon realize why he was so popular with the ladies. And Dominique? he frowned as he brooded silently, had he truly shocked her with his earlier implication that there was something between Martin and her, he wondered, or did she really feel something for him? Was she, like so many others he'd seen, fooled by his sophisticated good looks, his charm?

"Looks like you had a good night, Forest," Lance commented congenially nodding toward the bills in Evon's hat.

"Not bad, Martin. I've had better nights, but then again I've had worse," Evon said matter-of-factly as he eyed Lance speculatively.

"Have a good evening, and come back. Your money as well as your markers are always welcome on the *City of New Orleans,*" Lance remarked casually and stepped over to the next table where he made idle talk with a gentleman planter from Slidell.

Evon knew that Martin's reputation afforded him his choice of the top managerial positions on any one of the hundreds of riverboat casinos up and down the Mississippi River. Yet he chose Dominique's casino to work in, why? His eyes narrowed. If Martin thought Dominique was one of the fringe benefits included in his new position, the bastard had another thought coming. Evon spun about and strode from the casino.

# Fourteen

"Wyatt!" Dominique called as she ran down the gangplank and threw her arms around the man's neck. "It's so good to see you. We missed you opening night!"

"It's good to see you, too, Nicki," Wyatt said as his hands rested uncomfortably on Dominique's waist. "One of our ships was damaged in a storm. I was at the shipyard all night," he explained, and smiled apologetically.

"I had no idea you two had become such good friends, or do you welcome all visitors with such enthusiasm?" Evon asked sarcastically. Damn! he thought, for someone who refused to acknowledge his presence when Dominique had first met Wyatt, she was acting as though he was suddenly her best friend. Hell, he realized, she was pleasant with everyone, except—he growled, and unconsciously he'd interrupted his own train of thought.

Dominique hadn't seen Evon standing behind Wyatt. She frowned and ignored his remark. Her arms slid awkwardly down Wyatt's chest and she drew them away, threading her fingers together behind her back. "What brings you—both of you—here?" she asked slowly. Evon's presence was disturbing as usual. Why did he always appear out of nowhere and make her feel guilty as though her behavior was being questioned?

Wyatt cleared his throat. "I don't know about Evon, but I was over at Forest Shipping checking on a shipment due in earlier today, and thought I'd drop by to say hello," Wyatt explained, and tugged uncomfortably at his collar.

"Lunch should be about ready. Would you like to stay and join us?" she asked. Then she remembered Claire, and added excitedly, "Besides there is someone I'd like you to meet, Wyatt." At last, she thought excitedly.

Evon cleared his throat. "I, too, had business here in the city." At Evon's words, she glanced up at him and nodded and as an afterthought, reluctantly extended her invitation, "You're welcome to come along, too, that is, if you're hungry—" She purposely left her invitation unfinished hoping he would take the hint that she was merely being polite.

"Thank you. I'd like that very much. Of late, when in your company, I'm always famished, *chérie,*" he said softly as his eyes raked the length of her. He looked at his brother with a dark scowl.

Wyatt, however, refused to acknowledge Evon's none too subtle hint by offering Dominique his elbow, and when she slipped her arm through his the smile he bestowed upon her was dazzling.

In the galley, Dominique introduced Wyatt to Claire and smiled when he pulled out a chair next to his and her shy cousin had no choice, but sit beside him.

Dominique turned to Hetty and asked, "Where is Florrie?"

"She said she wasn't hungry and asked if she could take a walk. I didn't think you'd mind," Hetty answered. Hetty did not practice voodoo and disapproved that the girl did.

"Of course," she agreed, and aware of Hetty's dislike of the girl she added, "Florrie misses Belle Terre."

The mulatto clucked her tongue and Dominique looked up, but Hetty had her back to her and Dominique sat down.

Dominique smiled all through the meal and Evon couldn't help but wonder what was on her mind. Knowing Dominique as he did made him suspicious. "You are in an unusually pleasant frame of mind today, *chérie*. Has something happened that you would like to share with the rest of us?" he asked leisurely.

His words shattered her happy mood. Why did he come? she fumed. She had been anxious for Claire to meet Wyatt, thinking each day that Wyatt would stop by the riverboat, but she hadn't contemplated Evon's being there when she introduced two of her favorite people. She put her fork down and glared up at Evon who sat across the table from her. She said nothing as tension built to a crescendo between them with an intensity that everyone in the room could feel, even seven-year-old Beau glanced nervously first at his sister and then at Evon, but Hetty tapped him on his shoulder with her wooden spoon and he quickly lifted his fork to his mouth.

Wyatt stared at Evon while Claire looked pensively at Dominique, but neither spoke and finally Hetty turned from the sideboard where she was adding more gumbo to the empty bowl. "Eat up, there is more."

The tense lines on Dominique's face relaxed and she silently thanked Hetty for the interruption and she spooned more gumbo onto her plate relieved to have something to do and an excuse to take her eyes from Evon's. Her relief was short-lived as Evon interrupted her concentration.

"So, *chérie. The City of New Orleans* is a success—" he said unable to quell the sarcasm in his voice.

Dominique looked up at Evon. Sparks flew from her eyes. She inhaled deeply bringing her anger under control. "I believe the take was favorable, to say the least."

"The take?" he exploded. "Where the hell did you pick up an expression like that? Never mind. I can guess." His own expression grew thunderous, and he silently cursed Lance Martin.

"Your home is where, Claire?" Wyatt quickly broke in attempting to change the subject.

"North Carolina," Claire answered quickly. She felt her flesh color, but her eyes never strayed from Dominique's strained features or Evon's mouth which dipped into an even deeper frown as he glared at Dominique over his plate.

Suddenly Dominique rose. "M'sieur, you have overstepped your authority, and—"

Evon's brow rose. He admired her spunk. He'd been rude. And he was somewhat ashamed of his behavior. After all, he was a guest at her table. He quickly apologized, "I am sorry. Please sit down and finish your lunch."

Dominique flushed angrily, but she did sit down. Would she never learn, she asked herself angrily? And as usual he'd had the last word.

"And what do you do for a living, M'sieur Forest?" Claire asked Wyatt hesitantly as she tried to ease the tension at the table.

"Please. Call me Wyatt. I, *chérie,* am Vice President of Forest Shipping," Wyatt returned proudly, looking over at his brother, but when Claire did not respond and instead spooned a mouthful of gumbo, he, too, returned to the thick, tantalizing concoction Hetty had made.

They finished lunch in silence and afterward Hetty shooed everyone out of the galley.

As they were leaving, Hetty told Beau that it was his turn to help and as everyone walked up on deck they could still hear Beau's protests.

Wyatt took Claire's arm and drew her hand into his and invited her to stroll around the deck. When she nodded, Dominique sighed and stared after them. Evon's snicker made her turn, and seeing his mocking expression, she glared at him and spat, "You're impossible, M'sieur." She chastised herself for her behavior, but despite her fears, she felt a hot and awful joy standing so near Evon.

"Aah, *chérie,* why do you insist on doing this?"

"Doing what! M'sieur," she started as his words broke into her thoughts.

"This!" he fairly exploded with a sweep of his arm. "This riverboat, the casino!" he emphasized pointedly.

"Why, M'sieur, it is a way of making a living for the three, now four of us. We have been over this before—"

"And, I repeat—there is no need for you—to make a living—as you call whatever you're doing—I can support all of you, and besides, at Belle Terre you would—"

"I will not take your money, nor will I stay under the same roof with you!" she hissed at him.

"Why, *chérie?* Are you afraid you may like living with me?" he whispered as he slowly lifted a finger and gently touched her breast, sending sparks through her.

She inhaled sharply and stepped back as a shudder passed through her. What was wrong with her, she asked silently. It was broad daylight. Surely . . . she turned away, but firm fingers clamped around her wrist and she was spun back around bringing her up against a hard, well-muscled chest. "M'sieur, please, everyone will th . . ." She let her words trail off. What could she say to this giant of a man holding her so near to his thudding heart while her own heart hammered erratically inside her own chest. "Please . . ."

Evon jerked his hand back. Abruptly, he turned, his one thought to put distance between him and Dominique, and jamming his hands in his pockets he strode to the other side of the deck. He stood staring out over the populated harbor as he brought his rioting emotions under control.

Christ! he thought, every time he was near Dominique he acted like a schoolboy. If he hadn't walked away . . .

Dominique didn't move. She couldn't. Her back was to Evon and she closed her eyes denying that what she felt for Evon was passion, refusing to admit that the very thought of him sent her emotions into orbit, rejecting the fact that the very sight of him made her heart take a perilous leap. But she couldn't—not any longer. She bit her lip, and without turning around she knew he was there.

"Come with me, *chérie?*" he asked softly as he stepped around to face her. Dominique started to refuse, but he raised his hand in a truce sign. "I will not force you to do anything you do not wish to do. But if you will come with me I promise you only have to ask and I will return you to the riverboat."

Suddenly Dominique felt very tired. She felt drained. "Alright, M'sieur," she sighed.

Dominique sat with her back rigid. She had not known she would have to sit in front of Evon on Marengo's back or she might have refused his invitation. And although his arm lay casually around her waist she held herself erect and strained slightly away from him. Then suddenly Marengo leaped over a small log in their path and his arm tightened. He pulled her snugly against his chest and memories of their night together flooded her thoughts. Then another thought intruded on her confused musings, what would she do if . . . if at this very moment his seed grew within her? What will you do? She shook her head slightly to clear her tumultuous thoughts as the gelding slowed to a walk and Evon guided him down the path to the river's edge. He dismounted and clasping her waist, he lifted her from the saddle and slowly he let her softness slide sensuously down the plane of his body. His hooded black eyes were filled with passion. "M'sieur!" she gasped.

"I haven't broken my promise, *chérie*. You are fragile and I wouldn't want you to slip and fall," he explained roguishly.

His look was one of pure innocence, so ridiculous that she was sure she had been mistaken and Dominique could not prevent the corner of her mouth from curving upward. She had never seen this side of Evon. His lips inched toward her mouth, but she turned her face away. Evon released her slowly, taking her hand and entwining his fingers through hers, silently urging her forward. He walked beside her toward the coffee-colored water of the Mississippi River lapping at the sandy-loamed shore. "Marry me, *chérie.*"

Dominique was lost in thought and his words brought her to a sharp halt. "What did you say?" she asked, and when he paused beside her, she looked up at him.

Evon urged, "Say *oui.*"

"I can't," she insisted as she withdrew her hand and turning she hurried back in the direction they had come. Evon sighed and followed after her. She stopped beside Marengo. She waited. She felt his hands on her shoulders and his warm breath near her ear. She shivered.

"Don't run away, *chérie,*" he said as he dipped his head and kissed her slender neck. His hands lingered on her soft flesh. Then slowly he turned her to face him. His eyes took in her disheveled appearance. During their ride her pins had come loose, freeing her thick wavy locks. Wispy curls surrounded her flushed cheeks while one loose tendril lay against the swell of her breast. He reached up and stroked the silky texture. "We are good together, *chérie.* As I have said, I would make no demands on you. Marry me, and you shall have everything. Belle Terre will again be yours. If you will let me explain—I must marry before my thirtieth birthday." He paused at the frown on her lovely features. She would expect an explanation, and rightfully so, but he was reluctant to tell her the truth. He said instead, "My father is very ill and that is his final wish—that I marry, and—" he was reluctant to add that his father also wanted an heir in the making.

"And?" she ask simply.

"And, he insists an heir will prove the union is—" he began, but he saw no need to finish. Dominique's surprise equaled his own. He had not meant to tell her.

She couldn't believe her ears. An heir? "That is preposterous, M'sieur. We would have to—that is—"

*"Oui,* we would. Wouldn't we?" he agreed and found the idea to his liking. "Indeed we would," he whispered.

*"Non!"* she insisted. There is already a strong possibility that you are already carrying his heir, a voice whispered back at her, and she choked, *"non . . ."*

His hand found her breast, and he heard her sharp intake of air. She was not immune to his touch. He smiled.

She felt blood coursing through her veins like an awakened river. She couldn't think as an undeniable magnetism was building between them. Her mind told her to resist, but her body refused to listen. Suddenly she was crushed against his chest, and she wondered how she had gotten there. Had she gone into his arms willingly? And she realized it didn't matter how she had gotten there, only that she was in Evon's arms and for now that was where she wanted to be. She felt safe and protected. His mouth sought her lips and her thoughts were of Evon and the delicious stirrings he evoked in her. His teeth pulled gently on her lower lip and she parted her lips and ran her tongue over his mouth.

He eased her to the ground, "Aah *chérie."* Lifting his head, he stared into her glazed eyes, "You make me feel things I've never before felt with another woman. And you make loving you so much easier, what am I to do with you?" His words trailed away and he recaptured her lips while his hand continued to probe until Dominique wrenched her mouth free and gasped. She dug her nails into his back as she moaned and squirmed beneath him. His other hand unbuttoned the bodice of her gown and slipped the fabric aside, and as he dipped his head his tongue caressed one swollen globe. His hands explored and she was engulfed in flame. When she could stand it no more she pleaded, "Please . . . oh please . . ." He shed his trousers and covered her and as he entered her hot, wet velvet he lay perfectly still savoring the warmth of her, but her impatience grew to explosive proportions. "Please . . . Evon!" And Evon began to move. His strokes were steady and then he stepped up the tempo. Dominique moved with him until their bodies were in exquisite harmony and as Evon's movements quickened so did Dominique's. Skin to skin, they were one as they soared higher and higher until the peak of delight was reached by both and their pleasure was pure.

As their breathing returned to normal, Evon moved to lean on an elbow taking some of the weight from her slender form. He brushed her lips with his mouth and trailed a path down her neck, but Dominique stopped him as she held each side of his face in her hands and whispered, "I would like to go back now, M'sieur."

Evon sighed, but he nodded his head in agreement. He rose. They dressed and walked in silence to where Marengo stood cropping at the tender grass.

She felt his hands on her waist and he lifted her up into the saddle and stepped up behind her. In silence he reined the horse's head around and nudged him forward. On the ride back to the city she tried without success to ignore the strange aching in her limbs. Evon nudged the horse into a gallop and she was jolted backward. His arm tightened possessively around her. Her feelings for him were intensifying. He had struck a vibrant chord and she could fight her emotions no longer. She relaxed as she drank in the comfort of his nearness. Her acceptance of her feelings for Evon quickly melted her resolve and suddenly she *wanted* the protectiveness of his arms. His appeal was devastating and her body felt heavy and warm, and she sighed as she closed her eyes.

"Think about what I said, *chérie,* and we'll talk about it again after you've thought it over. After my father's—after my father is—gone—you will be free to leave."

His words had been sad, and she wanted to say something to ease his pain at the inevitable, but before she could assemble the right words her eyes snapped open. She felt as though she were suspended in air and then she hit the hard-packed path. Her body rolled over and over until she came to a halt against a fallen tree trunk. She realized the high-pitched screams were not hers, but Marengo's, and she knew she had been thrown from the horse's back. She moved and a pain shot up her leg. Her thoughts raced, what had happened? Where was Evon? With great effort she lifted her aching head and looked around. Marengo stood several yards away. His head was down and he was nuzzling a dark figure lying on the ground. Evon! her mind screamed and she tried to get up, but her leg wouldn't hold her. A sudden fear struck her that Evon was badly injured or worse. Using her hands and elbows she crawled to where he lay.

She managed, with difficulty, to drag herself to a sitting position.

She swiped at the wetness on her cheeks and lifted his head onto her lap. There was blood oozing from a deep gash on his forehead. She tore a strip from her petticoat and dabbed gently at the gaping wound. When the dark liquid continued to drain his life's blood from him she applied pressure as she'd seen Hetty do once. "Evon, please . . . open your eyes. Look at me, Evon. Please, please say you are all right," she sobbed close to his cheek. Evon groaned and Dominique whispered his name over and over until at last he opened one eye. The other was swollen shut and when she lifted the torn piece of cloth she saw that the bleeding had slowed to a trickle. She replaced the material as Evon stared up at her. His eye was glazed, but he lifted his arm and his fingers encircled her waist. His grip felt firm as he eased her hand with the stained cloth away from his injury. With his other hand he touched the cut gingerly and tried to sit up. *"Non!* Don't move. You've been hurt . . . it could be bad," she insisted, but her relief shone brightly as she stared down at Evon.

"What the hell happened?" he asked hoarsely.

"I don't know. I think something spooked Marengo and we were thrown from his back. I—I thought you . . ."

"I heard a shot, and that's the last thing I remember," he explained as he raised his hand and touched his forehead gingerly, and then added, "My head hurts like hell."

Unconsciously, Dominique rubbed her aching thigh. "I know what you mean, M'sieur. When I tried to sit up I had no feeling in my leg. Evidently I landed on my leg and it was numb until now."

"Here let me take a look at that leg," his own injury forgotten in his concern that Dominique's leg had been broken. His thoughts had been on the man who had tried to kill him and he hadn't noticed the strained expression on her lovely face as she tried to hide her pain.

*"Non!* M'sieur, you must lie still, you have started the blood flowing again, and you have already lost a great deal of blood."

"Ssh, *chérie,* when you raise your voice you make my head throb like the devil," he groaned aloud, and he struggled to a sitting position with a little help from Dominique. He reached for her leg and flipped her gown up to her waist. She gasped and he smiled crookedly as he said, "This is no time for modesty, *chérie."* He glanced around. He had no idea how long he'd been unconscious, but he knew their attacker had fled the scene evidently thinking he had done what he had set out to do, and he had a good idea who was responsible for this deed. His hands moved over her soft flesh while his fingers probed gently, yet carefully. "I think you'll be all right, cherie," he said after he finished her perusal and was satisfied that there was no serious injury or broken bones, but his hands lingered on her soft flesh, and he eased her to the ground.

*"Non,* M'sieur. The bleeding has started again and the time has come for us to leave this place and

seek medical attention for you." She smiled up at him, but her tone said she would brook no argument from him.

"You're right, *chérie,*" he said softly, but made no attempt to move.

"Evon I can't get up with you on top of me," she coaxed.

"Umm, how true," he teased and with some effort and an occasional groan he stood. Finding his feet firm on the ground, he felt stable enough to reach down and help Dominique to her feet.

Evon called to Marengo and within minutes they were on their way back to the city.

# Fifteen

A short while later, Dominique pulled back awkwardly on Marengo's reins. "Wyatt!" she called. Then she half turned in the saddle as Evon nearly slid from the horse's back. "Evon!" she cried, grasping him around his shoulders and holding onto him for dear life.

"Evon? Nicki? What the hell happened?" Wyatt yelled, grabbing Evon around the waist and letting him slide slowly down Marengo's side. He laid him on his back next to the gangplank. "He's been shot! Who did this to him?" he insisted as he examined his brother's wound. The gash was to the bone, the flesh jagged, but upon closer examination, he could see the bullet had grazed Evon's forehead and had not lodged in his flesh. "He's lost a lot of blood, and his breathing is irregular. We'd better get him inside," Wyatt commanded, but he needed no help as he lifted his brother and carried him up the gangplank and followed Dominique below.

"Did I hear—oh dear me, whatever has happened to M'sieur Forest?" Hetty asked wiping her wet hands on her apron.

"Wyatt?" Claire called softly as she, too, followed Hetty out of the kitchen galley. "Oh!" she gasped as she saw Wyatt carrying Evon's limp body along the narrow hallway.

Inside the vacant stateroom, Wyatt put Evon on the bed. He leaned over his brother, checking his pulse and shaking his head at Evon's pallor. "Hetty, would you fetch me a pan of water and needle and thread. A few stitches and he'll be as good as new. What is one more scar, eh Evon?" he muttered.

"You'll do no such thing. I'll have Beau run over to Toulouse Street and summon old Doc La Rue," Dominique decided as she turned to Hetty and instructed, "And Hetty you get our herbs and supplies from the galley."

"No doctor," Wyatt said with determination.

"What do you mean, no doctor?" Dominique asked.

"Evon will want me to sew him up. He doesn't trust doctors. Besides, I'm getting pretty good at this sort of thing," he muttered, and winked at Claire.

"I'll just bet you are," Dominique said stiffly, but as she stared down at Evon's pale features, her brow knitted together in a worried frown. She asked haltingly, "Who could have done such a terrible thing? And why Evon? He is going to be all right, isn't he Wyatt?"

"I'm afraid this isn't the first time an attempt

has been made on Evon's life, but Ev is the one to ask—and—*oui,* he's going to be just fine," Wyatt said and turned to Claire, "Why don't you take Nicki to the galley and make her something to drink. I'll be a while here and I'm sure Hetty won't mind staying and helping me, will you Hetty?" he asked gently.

"Of course not, M'sieur. I'll be happy to stay," Hetty said.

"But—" Dominique began not wanting to leave Evon.

"Come, Nicki, Beau, you too. We'll let these two do what must be done. M'sieur Evon needs attention and we're taking up time that should be spent on M'sieur," Claire said, taking charge. She had seen the worried expression on Wyatt's handsome face and knew he wanted to concentrate on his brother and his condition. With Dominique standing so near and asking so many questions she knew it would be better for all if they were out of the way.

Dominique paced back and forth. "What is taking so long?" she asked.

"Nicki, you have asked that same question at least ten times and my answer is the same, stitching flesh is not different from stitching garments and the task is a time-consuming one if the result is to be a pleasing one," Claire smiled wanly. She did not take another person's pain lightly, nor had she meant her words to sound trivial, but she was worried about both Evon and Nicki.

Dominique paused. She stared at Claire as if she had never seen her before. "What did you say, cousin?"

Claire's cheeks flushed. "I'm sorry, Nicki. I know this isn't a time to jest, but I thought to lighten your mood, and—" She paused and then whispered, "Perhaps lessen your pain."

Dominique covered the short distance between them and put her arms around Claire and hugged her fiercely. "You are a prize, Claire. I love you, cousin."

"A prize?" Claire asked, puzzled at Dominique's choice of words. Her cousin's vocabulary sometimes confused Claire, yet she envied Dominique's straightforward way of saying what she thought when she thought it. How she wished she had even a smidgen of Dominique's self-confidence.

"A gem, a treasure," Dominique said gently. "And one day, cousin, a gentleman is going to come along and snatch you away." Dominique smiled as she saw tears shimmering in Claire's lovely amber-colored eyes, and she added softly, "I am so happy you accepted my offer to come and live with us. I don't know what I would have done without you these last weeks."

A tear slid down her own cheek and Claire choked, "No, I am the fortunate one, Nicki. You and Hetty and Beau, and—" She smiled and continued, "Well, the activity has helped me through a trying time in my life. The work *has* helped keep both our minds from our sorrow."

"*Oui*, you're right, Claire. The added work load of this old tub has made us both too weary to dwell on our sorrow." Dominique said thoughtfully. Then her brow rose as her thoughts returned to Evon.

The sudden tensing of Dominique's jaw betrayed her deep emotions, and Claire immediately knew that her cousin's thoughts had returned to Evon Forest. "He's going to be as good as new, Nicki."

Claire's words broke into Dominique's thoughts and, startled, she asked, "What did you say?"

"M'sieur Evon," Claire said softly.

"You're probably right, Claire. Evon is thick-headed, and he's—"

The door opened and Dominique's eyes darted to Wyatt.

"He's been asking about you, Nicki. Go on in. But heed my warning—he's in a terrible temper," Wyatt said with an exaggerated frown. Then his face split into a wide grin, and he stepped aside and Dominique brushed past him.

Inside the cabin, she hurried to the bed where Evon lay. Her eyes anxiously moved to the bandage on Evon's forehead.

*"Chérie?"* Evon whispered.

"Are you in a great deal of pain?" she choked. His eyes were closed and he was so pale.

"Aah *chérie*. I feel as though I have a hangover that exceeds all hangovers. My head throbs—but enough about me. I'll feel fine by tomorrow. How is your leg?" he asked. His eyes remained closed.

"Oh. My leg is just bruised, I'm sure. In fact, I had forgotten all about it," she said and realized it was true. Her concern for Evon had made her forget her own pain.

"Good. I am glad," he whispered.

"You know who shot you, don't you?"

"Oui, *chérie.* I know," he sighed softly.

"Who did this terrible thing?" she choked.

"You wouldn't believe me if I told you—please—*chérie,* can we talk about this later?"

Dominique nodded and his hand moved to cover hers. Just as she started to ask if she could get him anything she realized he'd drifted off to sleep. Dominique knew that sleep would aid his recovery and she tiptoed from the room.

The following day, against the advice of Dominique, Wyatt and even Claire, Hetty, and Beau, Evon left for Belle Terre. He had to leave. Dominique was so near, so unattainable, that when the desire to hold her and an aching in his loins far exceeded the throbbing pain in his head he sought the solace of the plantation.

At Belle Terre, he dismounted slowly and smiled as he remembered the bewildered expression on Dominique's lovely face when she had insisted he was too ill to travel or to take care of himself after his arrival. Then he had asked her to make the trip with him. To continue her nursing skills, of course. Her face had turned a deep crimson as she sputtered her refusal.

"Aah, but soon, *chérie.* Soon you and I will share the master suite of your birthplace," he said aloud as he threaded the reins through the hook of the iron post, and with effort made his way up the stairs of the old mansion.

* * *

A commotion in the hallway brought Evon to his feet and he made his way to the closed double doors. When he reached for the brass handle the door burst open banging back against the wall. "Evon?" Henri questioned as he gazed at Evon.

His worried expression was not lost on Evon. "Word gets around," Evon said disgustedly as he turned and made his way back into his study.

"Wyatt knew I would want to know—who did this? Harcourt? We're all aware of the man's vendetta against you. He is a vengeful man," he growled and began pacing back and forth in front of Evon. Linking his hands behind his back he said, "You are no longer in this alone. Wyatt and I—"

"Will do nothing! It is over and no harm was done."

"No harm! The bastard could have killed you," Henri exclaimed as he spun around to face Evon. He frowned. "Look Evon, I know you are not concerned with my opinion in this, but hell this is what, the second or third attempt that devil's made on your life? The first time you were almost paralyzed for life. The next time you may not be so lucky," he stated emphatically.

"This is none of your business. And you keep a tight rein on Wyatt or—" He didn't finish. A man like Harcourt didn't play by the rules and he knew without a doubt that neither Wyatt nor Henri were a match for Harcourt and his underhanded tactics. "My majordomo will see you out," he said and gave Henri his back.

"Of course. I'm relieved it wasn't more serious

than it is—" he paused. "I'm sorry for the intrusion—I—I had to see for myself." Henri turned and hurried from the room.

Evon exhaled. Why the hell had Wye told Henri? Wye was a product of Henri and their mother. He had their mother's blond hair and sky-blue eyes, but otherwise he was a carbon copy of Henri. And he frowned, it was impossible to distinguish Wyatt's rich baritone from Henri's voice.

Why then, at his uncle's departure, did he experience this heaviness within his chest, almost like a pain? Was it guilt? Ridiculous, he scoffed. Henri was the guilty one. Henri was the one who had heaped an injustice on his own brother, Jacques, Evon's father. Henri had betrayed him, and Evon. And his mother? He refused to think of her—not after that day so long ago when she'd been laid to rest in the family tomb—he had vowed he would not mourn her death. And Wyatt? What were his feelings toward their mother and Henri? Did Wyatt feel the pain, the unfairness of it all, the hate? Was his brother bitter? Jacques had been fair where Wyatt was concerned. He'd made Wyatt second in command at FSL and Wyatt would inherit half of everything except Forest Manor. Jacques had put aside cash in Wyatt's name to make up the difference, but—if Evon didn't marry . . .

The following day, Evon stood outside of Saladin's stall stroking the nervous stallion's neck. "You need exercise, big boy. My head's killing me or I'd oblige you. You miss her, and so do I, but I don't know of anything short of kidnapping your mistress—" He paused and his brow lifted. His soft words and gentle touch calmed the horse, but his words had an unsettling effect on Evon. "Umm. Why not?" he mused and there appeared a mental picture of himself tossing Dominique over his shoulder and whisking her away to some secluded rendezvous and he smiled as he shook his head. Then he sobered. Why not? he thought, he would be leaving soon and—sequestered together on the island—a more romantic setting couldn't be found if he searched the world over . . . "Jorgee! Saddle Marengo—no wait—saddle Saladin!" Evon called, and a dark-skinned man of medium height with a slight crook in his back hurried out of a stall. He carried a shovel and bobbed his head and smiled as he agreed, "Yas suh. Dat blek debbal shor' cud youse som' ex'ciz'." He leaned the shovel against the stall, and picked up a bridle from a peg with the horse's name above and walked the few steps to Saladin's stall.

# Sixteen

"You're leaving tonight? But—I thought you were waiting until Friday. John can't leave until after the *Wyndward* is unloaded," Wyatt remarked. His surprise was evident. He wanted to make this trip with Evon. He had even rehearsed what he would say to his brother.

"I've changed my mind—is something troubling you?" Evon inquired. He still had to pick up a few things at his townhouse and he was in a hurry to be on his way.

Wyatt wasn't one to make idle chitchat, and therefore Evon knew he had something he wanted to discuss with him.

"I'd like to make this trip with you," he said.

"You'd like to *what?*" Evon fairly exploded. His brother's rejoinder took his by surprise. "That's out of the question," he said brusquely.

Evon cared a great deal for his brother, but his idea of brotherly love was not being sequestered for several weeks—and especially not this trip—with Wyatt.

The brothers held equal shares in FSL and each had his own duties; their paths rarely crossed within the operation of the company. Wyatt was brilliant with figures while Evon was a skilled engineer and he doubled as the company's major troubleshooter. "Wye—I don't think—"

"I never interfere. Whatever decision you've made—" Wyatt interrupted. "And I've stood behind you during those rare occasions when your father—well—let's just say I've always been on your side—and—you owe me, Ev," Wyatt said quietly as he straightened his shoulders. He wasn't being fair and he knew it, but he didn't care. He wanted to go. This trip was important to him. He was going—with or without Evon's approval. All the years he was growing up Evon had been his idol. It had hurt him that Evon had ignored him. Later, after he'd learned that his parentage was the fault, he'd understood. But now they were adults and he wanted Evon's respect, and he wanted his brother's love. This trip, he felt, was his chance to right their relationship. To make Evon see that he had no part in what had happened all those years ago. He wanted to be Evon's brother in the true sense of the word. "I'm going."

"Fine," Evon agreed, and he chuckled as he thought of his brother's reaction when he discovered the reason for his hasty departure. *Non,* he thought, he saw no problem in Wyatt's tagging along. No problem whatsoever.

"You agree?" Wyatt asked, but frowned as he continued, "I'm not sure I like the tone of your voice, but I'll not argue the why. Thanks, Ev. You won't be sorry," he concluded.

"I never thought I would be," Evon said.

Evon was serious, Wyatt thought, but he said, "Good. I'll pack and be on board within the hour . . ." He waited for Evon to clarify their departure time.

"That's plenty of time. We'll sail in two hours."

"See you then," Wyatt said as he turned and exited Evon's office. He hadn't a minute to spare. He had to stop by his townhouse and pack his clothes. He also wanted to stop by the riverboat. He and Evon would be gone for weeks, and he wanted to say goodbye to Claire. After he'd met Claire, she had been in his thoughts on more than one occasion. This journey was important to him, but he knew he would miss Claire. Claire, he thought, wasn't beautiful in one sense of the word, but she had an inner beauty that to Wyatt rivaled the ladies he had known. Her eyes—her eyes were an unusual shade of amber—fool's gold. He smiled at his own interpretation. And her lashes. Her lashes reminded him of the finest velvet, long and thick. When Claire looked at him, she made him feel as though he were ten feet tall. In the past, the women he'd known lacked strength and character, but not Claire, he thought. Oui, he thought, he would miss her.

"I wouldn't do that again, little brother," Evon growled as he raked his fist across his bruised cheek.

Wyatt stood over his brother, both surprised and amazed that he had reacted so rashly to Evon's deplorable behavior. "Kidnapping is against the law, brother, in case you weren't aware of the fact. But then laws were made to be broken, isn't that the code you live by, Evon?" Wyatt panted. Unconsciously he rubbed his skinned knuckle as he glared down at Evon.

"Now just a damn minute," Evon snarled, rising to his feet in one fluid movement.

*"Non!* You wait a damn minute. You've gone too far this time, Evon. I won't stand for this," he insisted heatedly.

"Now that you are aware of the situation, what do you propose we do? We're miles from shore and I'm not turning the ship around, so—"

"She is not a prisoner, and you will not treat her so. Nor will I stand by while you use her for your pleasure, Evon. I swear by all that's right and holy that I'll—"

"Of all the fool . . . do what you will," Evon spat and turned and stalked away.

"I wouldn't have believed it if I hadn't seen it with me own eyes," the first mate, Stumpy, guffawed.

Wyatt inhaled deeply, but he smiled at the first mate. "Nor would I." Wyatt turned and hurried below and quickly made his way down the hall to Evon's cabin. At the cabin he paused. Then he reached for the handle and once more he inhaled deeply and quickly turned the knob.

"Wyatt! What are you doing here? Whose ship is this?" she asked puzzled.

"How did you get here?" he asked gently.

"I was on a side street. Someone grabbed me from behind. I didn't see who the heathen was," she explained and flushed angrily. Earlier, she had dressed in her disguise, and had been on her way to Annie's when she had been kidnapped. She had been gagged and thrown over a well-muscled shoulder and brought to the wharf where she was taken on board a ship and deposited in this spacious cabin. She had not been tied up and after the man had left she had removed the gag and yelled and pounded on the door until she was hoarse and her fists were bruised. She was confused as she stared back at Wyatt Foster. The ship swayed gently. "Wyatt what is going on? Did they kidnap you, too?" she asked and tears glistened in her eyes.

"Dominique—I—" he began, but he couldn't go on. How did you tell someone—Nicki—that the cause for her being swept from her home, the cause of her being on a ship bound for the Cayman Islands, for kidnapping her and for the horrible fear—that his own brother who had always been an honorable man had committed this heinous crime? "Nicki . . ." he began again, "Evon—"

"Evon? What has Ev—he did this? Where is that bastard?" she hissed and stormed past Wyatt and out of the cabin determined to find and confront him. How could he do such a thing? It was deplorable even for Evon, but when she reached the stairway and saw Evon's expression as he came toward her, she knew and she stopped abruptly and waited. She glared at him, and at that moment she wanted more than anything to slap his face, to hurl expletives at him, to beat her fists against his chest. Then suddenly his large frame blurred and her legs felt rubbery, and as they folded beneath her, her eyes closed and she slumped to the floor.

Dominique's eyes rolled back in her head as Evon reached her and folded in a heap at his feet. He gasped and knelt, then lifted Dominique in his arms and retraced her steps and carried her through the doorway where Wyatt still stood in the center of the room. "She fainted," he explained as Wyatt glared at him. "I was coming down to apologize, but—"

"What did you expect, after what you have put her through?" Wyatt asked disgustedly.

"Whatever I expected wasn't that she'd faint dead-away at my feet," Evon shot back. He moved around his brother and laid her on the bunk where he clumsily began to remove her clothing.

"Now look Ev—"

"You are supposed to do this when someone faints."

"I'll get Cook. He'll know what to do for her."

"Fine! Fetch him and be quick," Evon demanded. "She's so damn pale."

Wyatt watched the gentle way with which Evon's hand brushed back a loose tendril. He'd never seen his brother look so worried. It was as though he . . . Wyatt shook his head. This was not the time to stand and analyze his brother's actions. He turned and hurried from the room.

Evon stared down at Dominique. She was so lovely. He had expected her fury when she saw him, but not that she would faint. He gazed at the fullness of her breasts. Haltingly, he reached out and ran a finger over one flushed cheek. Perhaps, he thought, she was sick? Yet her skin felt cool. He exhaled. Dominique was not a woman to faint at the slightest provocation—but, he reminded himself, you *did* kidnap her. "So?" he said aloud. She was made of stronger stuff than that. Besides he had witnessed her many moods, happy, sad, and he had been the brunt of her anger on more than one occasion. He'd seen her tirades—and—she had never fainted. His eyes moved to her midsection and he lay his hand on her slightly swollen abdomen. He inhaled sharply. His eyes darted to her lovely face and her eyes fluttered open.

# Seventeen

"What happened?" Dominique asked weakly. She made an effort to sit up, but the pressure of Evon's hand on her shoulder was enough to restrain her.

"You fainted," Evon explained worriedly.

"Fainted? But that's impossible. I've never fainted in my life!" she exclaimed huskily.

"I didn't think you had," he said, and his dark eyes studied her intently.

"Then why—?" she sputtered searching her mind for an answer.

"I thought perhaps you could tell me, *chérie,*" he interrupted, then let out a long, audible sigh.

Her eyes moved reluctantly to where his hand lay on her abdomen. She drew in her breath sharply. When had she had her last monthly? Seven—eight weeks ago! *Mon Dieu,* she was what? Two months late! "I am pregnant! This is all your doing, you bastard," she hissed at him.

"All my doing, *chérie?* As I recall, you were a

willing partner," he said.

There was a lethal calmness in his eyes. "How dare you! You have stolen my home, compromised my reputation, a shot meant for you could very well have killed me, you bring me here against my will, and at this very moment your seed grows in my womb—and you have the nerve to hurl insults at me?" she flung back at him.

"Now just a damn minute. I did not steal Belle Terre. Your father approached me and I paid what he asked. And might I remind you, the bullet hit me, not you, and if you want to accuse anyone look to your friend Harcourt. As for the child—I am an honorable man. I will marry you," he said tersely. He knew he had said it all wrong. Instead he ached to hold her in his arms and he would rather drop on bended knee if she would have agreed—but—she had refused him before and he would not chance another rejection.

At his words, her anger soared. Fire smoldered in her emerald eyes. "Honorable? Honorable!" she sputtered.

*"Oui,"* he said.

His smugness infuriated her. "How gallant of you. You may have brought me here against my will, but you cannot force me to marry you, M'sieur," she said haughtily.

"Not only can I, *chérie,* but I will," he paused, and then added, "You forget, this is my ship, and—if necessary—"

"What do you propose? Am I to be bound and gagged?" She hissed, unable to hide the disbelief in her voice.

"That won't be necessary, *chérie,*" he said. His voice though quiet, had an ominous quality. "If you refuse to participate—it isn't necessary that you participate," he hedged and he felt a pang of guilt in the pit of his stomach.

She shivered. "Whatever are you saying? It takes two to make a wedding, and I will not go along with this—this farce," she spat.

"As I said before, it is your choice. The ceremony will take place—by proxy—if that is the only way." His tone was steely and he felt a slight twitch in his jaw.

"Even you wouldn't stoop so low," she said scathingly.

"I'm going up on deck to make the arrangements. I'll be back within the hour—how we do this is up to you, *chérie.*"

He rose and turned to leave and her feet touched the floor and her eyes swept the room until she glimpsed his hairbrush on the oaken desk. She hurled it at his back and it glanced off his shoulder, but he continued out the door.

Dominique heard a key turn. He locked her in her room! After several deep gulps of air she balled her hands into fists and seethed aloud, "Can he do this? I will not agree to—but unwed and pregnant—it was unthinkable. But hadn't she in the past done the unthinkable and lived through it? Hadn't she turned up her nose at propriety when she opened the casino? She frowned. Unwed and pregnant—she would be ostracized! She lifted her chin slightly—but what of the child? an inner voice whispered. Should he be made to suffer because of her actions? She clamped her hands over her ears. Then slowly she let her hands fall away as another thought interrupted her. Why? Why was he determined she marry him? He had mentioned honor—was it honor—or the inheritance—of course—that was it—his inheritance! It didn't have a damn thing to do with honor. She was furious. And then she sobered as she realized that she needed Evon Forest as much as he needed her.

The captain had gone below to get his Bible. Evon stood staring out over the deep blue water as wave after wave of churning sea rolled before him. He had held Dominique in his arms. He'd made love to her. She had made him feel as no other woman before her had made him feel. He didn't want another woman. He wanted Dominique. He had proposed to her twice, but she had refused to marry him. She would not refuse this time.

The captain stepped on deck with his Bible in hand. His eyes moved to Evon and Evon nodded as he turned and went below.

Evon opened the cabin door and Dominique rose and walked slowly toward him. She said nothing as he extended his arm, but stepped past him and walked stiffly up on deck where the captain waited.

Two weeks later, they arrived on Grand Cayman Island. During that time Dominique had only had an occasional glimpse of Evon. Wyatt had been considerate of her needs which had been few. She remained for most of the voyage in her cabin, going up on deck when Wyatt had insisted her health would suffer. Her cabin was spacious and elegant, but she barely noticed. She was married, yet she did not feel married. Evon was her husband, yet he did not speak to her, nor did he take his meals with her, and he slept in Wyatt's cabin. He acted as though she were a leper, and she felt that he abhorred her very presence. She was so alone.

Upon their arrival at Evon's two-story Georgian mansion they were greeted by servants and an Irish wolfhound, Wolf, who bounded up to Evon and Wyatt. Then the dog, apparently taking an immediate liking to Dominique, nuzzled her hand and after circling her several times sat at her side. She petted the large head and for the first time since leaving New Orleans, she laughed.

Later, in the upstairs suite of rooms Wyatt had said would be hers during their two-week stay on the island, Dominique stood in the center of the room and looked around admiring the soft pastel colors and the elegant furnishings. Suddenly she sighed and walked to the opened French doors. She stepped out onto the veranda. Her eyes scanned the beautifully manicured lawns and the view above the treetops was magnificent. The setting sun shimmered across the aquamarine Caribbean. She frowned. She wondered what she would do during these next two weeks?

"Nicki?" Wyatt called softly.

She turned and smiled as Wyatt stepped through

the doorway. *"Oui?"* she asked, trying to hide her despair.

"I want to introduce you to someone. You'll find her a wonderful companion while you're here on the island. Her name is Sophie and she's Evon's housekeeper. I know you'll like her and she'll love you."

"I really have to unpack—" she began hesitantly.

"Sophie will help you unpack and get settled. And she'll be a good friend to you—Sophie loves Grand Cayman and she's fascinated by the pirate history of the island—so be warned: And if there's anything you want while you're here, just ask and Sophie will see that you get it. Come with me," Wyatt pleaded eagerly. He bent at the waist, extending his arm in a wide sweep, courtly fashion, making an exaggerated show of gallantry.

Dominique laughed and then quickly sobered as she dipped into a deep curtsy and then straightened. She tossed her head back and haughtily thrust her nose toward the ceiling while at the same time she scooped up her skirts to glide past Wyatt as she swept out into the hall. "Oh!" she squealed as she collided with Evon. Caught off balance she clutched at his sleeves. She felt his arms encircle her waist and she inhaled as he drew her up against his chest. She looked up and he smiled as he quirked one brow.

She opened her mouth to apologize, but no words were forthcoming. Then his smile was replaced with a frown and he quickly released her. She fell back a step. Suddenly she realized he could not bear to touch her and she cringed beneath his stare. She felt icy fingers seep into every pore and she stiffened. Without a word Evon turned and strode to his own apartment, closing the door behind him. She stared at the closed portal.

"Evon!" Wyatt admonished his brother for his inexcusable behavior. Then he turned to Dominique. "Nicki?" he said softly, and gently touched her elbow.

*"Oui,* I'm coming, Wyatt," she said haltingly. She felt the sudden hammering inside her chest and a weakness in her legs as she turned to take Wyatt's proffered arm. How long since Evon had held her, or since—*non!* she gave herself a mental shake, she would not allow herself to dredge up painful memories. She smiled brightly at Wyatt. Memories, that until now she had locked away in a dark corner of her heart. Evon had married her and he was now her husband—but theirs, she knew, was a marriage in name only.

"You've changed, Ev," Wyatt said breaking the silence of the last half hour.

Due to the missing shipment and lost shipping orders, the brothers had ridden out early that morning to meet with the plantation owners to go over sketches of the still unfinished manor houses and outbuildings. Evon was determined to fulfill the order and assure the plantation owners that his company was aware of and would fulfill its obligation and ship the necessary material as quickly as possible. FSL had already received a draft for half the purchase price. Evon had realized that the only way these men would continue to do business with Forest Shipping Line was to travel to the island and personally talk to them. If given the go-ahead, he would make copies of the original blueprints and draw up new contracts, guaranteeing them a definite delivery date.

"Oh! In what way are you referring to, Wye?"

"You know damn well what I'm referring to," he began irritably. Then he added, "In the way you treat Nicki."

"My relationship with my wife is none of your concern, little brother," Evon shot back and drew back sharply on the reins bringing his horse to a halt.

"Of course it isn't. But hell, Ev, you haven't seen the look in her eyes, the hurt—the pain when you—"

"Let it go, Wye, you don't understand," Evon said tersely, but his own thoughts had been running in the same direction and he felt a pang of guilt and frowned. Aah *chérie,* he thought, if only you would let me love you, if only there wasn't this between us, this marriage of convenience. He sighed.

Wyatt watched his brother and saw Evon, too, suffered. Suddenly he realized what it was he had seen in Evon's features on the ship—it had been concern—and *oui*—pain. His brother loved his wife! "You're right, Ev. It's none of my business." Wyatt's voice faded, losing its steely edge.

Evon mumbled an agreement, unaware of his brother's raised brow as Dominique invaded his thoughts. She intrigued him with her fiery temper, bull-headedness and determination, and although she would deny it, her tender side. When he held her in his arms and kissed her he unleashed a passion so great it not only astonished him, but—*oui*—overwhelmed him. He burned with remembrance and he ached to hold her, to kiss her . . .

# Eighteen

The days passed quickly and Dominique realized she was in love with Evon. Her stay on Grand Cayman was pleasant, and Wyatt had been right in his interpretation of Sophie. Dominique did not know what she would have done without her.

Sophie had given her a grand tour of the island, taking her to the little hamlet of George Town and then to Pirate's Cove. They stopped the carriage in Bodden Town and Sophie pointed out the island's first public building, a courthouse with jail. "Look Dominique!" she exclaimed, "that is where the famous pirate, Neal Walker—we call him Neddie—made Bodden Town his headquarters. He was a very close friend of old Governor Wood. And because of Bodden Town's close association with pirates, it is firmly believed that there is much treasure hidden along the coast and in the nearby caves. But legend has it"—Sophie leaned toward Dominique and whispered—"that sites of many treasure troves were known to the early inhabitants, but they were afraid to interfere with these, because of the belief that they were haunted by dead pirates who had "volunteered" to remain behind to guard them. It was feared that violent death would be the fate of anyone who dared to molest a treasure and that near relatives would suffer untold miseries as well."

Later, that same day the two women sat relaxing in the two wicker chairs on the veranda. They talked and sipped tea while Dominique munched on mangos, plantains, and Sophie's delicious Pavlova cake. Dominique grew drowsy and closed her eyes and Sophie rose to instruct Cook on the dinner menu.

Dominique awoke when Sophie returned to her chair. Then, Dominique, her curiosity getting the better of her, could not help but ask Sophie, "How is it that you came to live on the island—to work for M'sieur Evon?"

Sophie smiled. "I lived in New Orleans where I worked in an apothecary shop. The owner was an elderly gentleman and one day he decided he'd worked long enough and simply closed the shop. M'sieur Forest and I had a mutual friend who told him of my predicament. He explained he was desperate for a housekeeper, but he told me there was a catch—he put it most delicately—explaining that I would have to move to the island—permanently. He wanted to give me several days to think about this, but I had no job, and no family—so—I gave him my answer then and there—I've lived here five years, and—" She shrugged. "I am thankful every night for M'sieur Evon's generosity. I am comfortable in my work, and I love the island." Sophie smiled brightly.

A week after their arrival on the island, Dominique and Sophie again sat side by side in their wicker rockers. Sophie had pricked her curiosity and she turned to the plump woman. "You are happy working for M'sieur Evon?" Dominique asked nonchalantly.

"Oh *oui.* He is an easy man to work for. And M'sieur has a pleasant disposition. He is a kind man, Dominique," Sophie insisted and smiled sadly at Dominique. "He really is a fine man," she added, not unkindly.

Dominique stared at the housekeeper. She really was fond of Sophie, but her description of Evon—well—the words irritated her. Evon had certainly fooled Sophie or perhaps he hid his deceiving nature when he was around the softhearted woman, she thought, *and* he was definitely a man of many faces. He had duped as well as deceived her—hadn't he? Suddenly Dominique felt a violent need to be alone. She quickly rose and, mumbling, she excused herself and hurried down the steps and along the now familiar path leading to the ocean. Wolf rose and stretched and followed along after her. When Dominique neared the beach she was aware she was out of sight of the mansion house and she slowed her steps.

She knew she had been rude to leave Sophie like she had, but she had had an overwhelming urge to be alone with her thoughts. Her eyes misted. She missed Hetty and Claire, and she missed Beau. She knew her disappearance had most likely devastated all three. And Evon—what had happened to make him change toward her? He had wanted her before their marriage—but now—well, she would make him want her again!

Dominique had been on the island a week and a half, during which time she and Wolf explored the beaches. They swam in the shallow water and romped on the warm white sand.

Dominique had hurled pieces of gnarled driftwood high into the air, laughing as the big dog fetched the wood and brought it back to her, and when she tired she napped in the shade while Wolf lay beside her. Today was no different. The two went through their usual routine, and when she awoke she walked along the beath where she discovered a path leading into the woods.

She and Wolf had gone on about half an hour when she sighted an old, dilapidated hut. She squealed in delight. Crimson and lavender Bougainvillea covered the side of the thatched structure and a narrow stream ran along the back of the building. Dominique stepped inside the hut and gazed around the tiny room. A dusty pallet lay in one corner and in the center of the room she saw an overturned table and two chairs. She righted the table and set the chairs upright, testing their sturdiness. Debris was scattered across the hard dirt-packed floor. She scanned the room and spied a crude makeshift broom standing in one corner.

She picked up the broom and began sweeping the rubble into a pile in the middle of the floor. Dust particles filled the room making her eyes water. She sneezed. Then with Wolf's help, they dragged the bedding outside where she beat it with the broom. Leaving the pallet to air Dominique went back inside to finish.

Later, she stood the broom in the corner and stood back to admire her effort. She stepped back outside and called to Wolf to join her. "Come on, boy. Let's wade in the stream while the dust settles." Dominique was hot and tired, but she smiled as she and the shaggy dog quickly made their way to the edge of the water. Dominique grasped her skirts in her fingers and tucking the material into her waistband tested the stream's temperature with her toes. She laughed and stepped into the cool water calling to the dog to join her. She splashed water on Wolf and the giant dog dashed in and out of the stream all the while barking and lapping up water. "Shaggy beast!" Dominique laughed at the great dog's antics while brushing droplets from her face.

Dominique returned to the cabin. She yawned and looked longingly at the pallet. She lay down to rest a few minutes before starting back. She closed her eyes.

Several hours later, she awoke with a start. Wolf growled deep in his throat and suddenly she was wide awake.

"What is it, Wolf?" she whispered tremulously. Her eyes darted around the room and she realized the sun had gone down. She rose quickly and rushed from the hut where she collided with what felt like a brick wall. She was still queasy at being abruptly awakened and on impact she screamed.

"Everyone has been searching the island for hours fearful that something happened to you. You have upset the entire household with your thoughtlessness!" Evon barked at her. Yet he clutched her to him in a tight embrace.

Dominique heard the sharpness of his voice, but her face was buried against his shirt and she did not see the anxious expression on his face. His harsh tone made her angry and she pushed against his chest.

Evon sighed, and reluctantly released her. "I did not realize I was a prisoner. If I had I would have reported my whereabouts before leaving the compound," she returned heatedly, her fear forgotten.

"You did not return for the supper hour and Sophie became worried that something had happened to you. She sent two house servants to search for you. When they returned without you her concern grew and when Wyatt and I entered the house the woman was almost hysterical," he ground out between clenched teeth. He did not add that his own concern was far greater and at finding her safe and unharmed his relief had been so great as to weaken his limbs.

"And how is it that *you* had no trouble finding me?"

Her scathing words angered him. "I know every inch of this island," he said harshly. He did not tell her that on more than one occasion he had followed her and watched, at a distance, as she swam and frolicked with the shaggy dog on the beach. Or how he had envied the dog swimming beside her in the cool, blue-green ocean or how he had longed, each time, to go to her, to hold her, to kiss her, yet knew he had forced her to marry him and she would not welcome his company.

Almost savagely Evon had retraced her steps that afternoon, finding footprints along the outer edge of the beach. After careful examination he found the path where she and the dog had entered the woods. Fearfully he had followed their trail to the deserted cottage. When she had burst through the doorway and into his arms, his relief had been short-lived. He had bristled at the emotions her warm body evoked in him. And now he gazed at her and his dark-brooding eyes raked over her body.

Her hand suddenly went to cover her mouth.

He could not help but notice a trace of fear mingling with the red-hot anger as she glared at him. His expression softened. Obedience was not in his wife's dictionary—*non,* he mused, theirs would not be the usual type of marriage—she would ever be a mystery to him. But he kept his tone harsh as he demanded, "Come. The night air grows cool."

Who did he think he was that he could order her around? She ignored him and stomped back inside the hut.

"Dominique!" he roared. She stepped through the entrance and Evon was right behind her. He reached out and jerked her around to face him.

"What do you think you're doing?" he asked angrily.

"You are no longer my guardian. I do not have to do as you say," she hissed, her breath ragged in impotent anger. He was too near. She could smell his male scent.

His eyes were black and dazzling with fury. He stood there, tall and angry. Her breath burned in her throat.

Wolf whined and tried to step between them, but there was no room and he backed up and circled around them.

The silence became unbearable. Evon had a fiery, angry look that was unfamiliar to Dominique. She inhaled and tossed her head. "I will leave when I'm good and ready and not before," she said insolently.

Evon remained silent. He reached out and lifted her in his arms. She gasped and glared at him. "You are right *chérie*. I am no longer your guardian. I am your husband," he whispered and instead of leaving the hut he carried her toward the pallet, his eyes never leaving hers.

His touch upset her balance. "*Non*. Put me down," she insisted warily. His look was so galvanizing it sent a tremor through her and her cheeks colored under the heat of his gaze. When he dropped to his knees with her in his arms her heart thumped uncomfortably. "You mustn't," she squeaked.

"Ssh," he whispered against her mouth.

She opened her lips, but his mouth smothered her feeble protest. He maneuvered her to her back as his tongue slipped inside to explore the recesses of her mouth and she ran her fingers through his thick hair.

He lifted his head. "Should I stop, *chérie?*"

Their eyes locked as their breathing came in unison. "I—I—" she paused. She felt drugged by his clean and manly scent. Her mind told her to resist, but her body refused, and pulling his head down, she kissed him with a hunger that belied her outward calm.

His mouth left her and caressed her neck. Moving down he nudged the bodice of her dress aside and his lips touched one small globe, its pink nipple marble-hard. His tongue caressed the sensitive swollen peak. Her senses reeled as if short-circuited. Blood pounded in her brain, leapt from her heart, and made her knees tremble.

His hands searched for pleasure points. Her dress crept up onto her thighs as she moved closer to him. His hand moved under her dress to skim her hips, his touch light and painfully teasing. His hand moved to her raised mound to caress the nubbin between the springy curls. The gentle massage sent currents of desire through her, and she caressed the length of his back. He paused to kiss her, whispering his love for each part of her body.

Evon unbuttoned her blouse with trembling fingers and pushed the material aside. His hands lightly traced a burning path over her breasts. He undressed her slowly, worshipfully. When he'd finished he quickly shed his own garments and she watched his urgency meet her own lusty, unsatiated needs. His hands began a lust-arousing exploration of her soft flesh. She writhed beneath his touch and he took her hands, encouraging them to explore. She haltingly ran her fingertips over his flat nipples and when she heard his sharp intake of air she moved her hand down the hard plane of his abdomen and paused at his navel. He covered her hand with his and urged her to continue. She inched her way down until her fingers brushed against his hardness. He groaned and quickly covered her body. Her breasts tingled against his hair-roughened chest and she writhed beneath him. Skin to skin, they were as one. He quickly inserted his throbbing staff and as he began to move she felt passion rising in her like fire. He increased the pace and her body began to vibrate with liquid sensations. She moved in unison with him until together they soared to an awesome, shuddering ecstasy.

She lay in his arms and savored the feeling of satisfaction. His had been a raw act of possession and she sighed in pleasant exhaustion.

Evon rested his chin against Dominique's temple. A smile ruffled his mouth. "We are good together," he whispered tenderly. He held her in his arms. One hand covered her breast while the other hand caressed her bare thigh.

She was surprised to hear his words echo her own thoughts. She could no longer deny herself his touch and she found the thought very satisfying. She didn't care why, only that he had married her. Contented, she succumbed to the numbed sleep of the satisfied lover.

Evon rose on one elbow and rested his head in the palm of his hand. His eyes moved over her lovely face. She looked more delicate and ethereal than ever. Her beauty was exquisite, fragile. He lowered his head and brushed her lips. Her eyes fluttered open and she smiled and turned in his arms and looked at him. "We have to get back. They'll be worried," he said and kissed the tip of her nose.

Evon got to his feet bringing Dominique with him. He kissed her gently.

Evon lifted his head. He sighed and reluctantly released her. They dressed quickly and walked outside into the cool night air where Wolf lay with his paws tucked beneath him. Evon whistled and the big dog got to his feet stretching languidly and then trotted after them.

Dominique yawned and Evon swept her weightless into his arms. She laid her head on his shoulder and wrapped her arms around his neck. Her lavender scent wafted into his nostrils. She shifted in his arms and her breast pressed lightly against his chest. If he didn't get back to the mansion and soon . . . he smiled and quickened his pace.

# Nineteen

A glimmer of light from the house came into view signaling less than a hundred yards to go. Evon sighed his relief. He had had to call upon all his restraint while fighting to gain control of the riotous emotions her nearness had caused to erupt and he was fast losing the battle. He couldn't seem to get enough of her. His breeches were stretched to their limit and with each step his passion grew to explosive proportions until both he and the seams of his trousers had reached the end of their endurance.

They reached the mansion and Sophie and Wyatt ran down the steps to meet them. They fussed over Dominique and she assured them she was all right. She explained she had fallen asleep and lost all track of time. Evon continued past them and on into the house. He carried her up the stairs and into the master suite where he laid her gently on the bed. His gaze met her wide-eyed stare. He winked and his smile was roguish as he turned and instructed Sophie to prepare a warm bath—for both of them. Sophie blinked and Wyatt lifted one brow and the two stared first at Dominique and then at Evon. Wyatt cleared his throat and excused himself and Sophie nodded and quickly left the room.

"Am I to understand we are to share this room, and—" Dominique began.

"This bed," Evon finished and removed his shirt and draped it over the back of a chair. He paused while his eyes caught and held hers. "That is agreeable, is it not?" he whispered and began a slow walk toward the bed. The door burst open and Sophie hurried inside with an armful of linen. Her intrusion brought him to a halt. "What the—"

I brought the bath cloths and your bathwater will be ready in a few minutes," she said breathlessly and set the linen down on a stool next to the large copper tub. She reached for the folding screen standing in one corner.

"Leave it, Sophie," Evon said. His words were clipped but his tone was not unkind.

Sophie looked up and her hands paused in midair. "Of course. I'll be back later with your water." Her cheeks colored and she quickly exited the room.

Evon smiled and quickly stepped to the side of the large four-poster. He bent one knee and rested it on the edge of the bed and positioned his hands on either side of her as he leaned over her and ran his tongue over her dry lips. Her eyes widened. He recaptured her lips and lifted his hand to cup the back of her head. Suddenly the door opened and in marched a parade of servants each carrying a bucket of steaming water. Bringing up the rear was Sophie. She clapped her hands, and instructed, "Over here, hurry." Sophie glanced at the couple, and then she quickly averted her eyes. The servants emptied their buckets and Sophie herded them from the room. She closed the door behind her.

*"Mon Dieu!"* Dominique breathed. "What must they think seeing us like this?"

Evon chuckled and lifted her in his arms and carried her to the tub. He released her legs and she slid sensuously down the length of him. She felt him against her and she gasped. "You are my wife, *chérie*. Have you forgotten so quickly?" he asked and touched her lips with the tip of his finger. She ran her tongue along her bottom lip.

Suddenly she felt shy. She stared at his bare chest and swallowed. "Evon—I'm not sure this is a good idea," she choked. "Perhaps you'd like to bathe first and I'll—"

"First?" he said and lifted one brow.

At his inquiry she looked up and when he smiled her eyes widened. *"Non."* She began to back away.

Evon drew her back against him. *"Oui,"* he whispered and began slowly to remove her clothes. When he'd finished he quickly stripped out of his trousers and lifted her into his arms.

*"Non!* There is not room for the two of us. We can't—"

Evon ignored her and when he stepped into the warm water she grasped his neck tightly. "Relax *chérie*. There is plenty of room. You will see." He sat down and positioned her with her legs around his waist and brought his knees up behind her. "A perfect fit."

His swollen member rested against her abdomen sending shivers of delight through her. *"Oui,"* she whispered against his mouth, breathing in his male scent. His hand explored the small of her back and suddenly the touch of his hand was more than she could bear. She put her arms around his neck and buried her face against his neck. His hand slid between them and he cupped her breast and she had no desire to back out of his embrace as she wound her fingers in his hair and lifted her head seeking his mouth. She touched his lips gently and his arms came around her as he opened his mouth and slipped his tongue between her parted even teeth. She moved her tongue in unison with his and suddenly he grasped her hips and lifted her and positioned her above him. She felt him, hot and stiff, as he inserted his swollen staff into her warmth. She gasped and clasped his shoulders in her hands. He moved her slowly up and down the length of him, instinctively, her body arched toward him. His tormented groan was a heady invitation and she began to move in unison with him, meeting him stroke for stroke until waves of ecstasy flowed through her and together they shattered into a million glowing stars.

"Aah *chérie,"* he breathed and let his head fall back to rest on the copper tub while she rested her head against his chest.

After a few minutes Evon raised his head and

picked up the scented soap and a cloth on the stool and began to wash first one breast and then the other. "This is foolish," he said and moved Dominique back and rose in one fluid motion. He lifted her in his arms and stepped from the tub. "We can bathe later." He smiled and carried her to the bed.

A few days later, with the signed document and an extension from the plantation owners and a date of three weeks from FSL to deliver the necessary material to the plantation owners, both Evon and Wyatt with Dominique between them boarded the ship for the return trip to New Orleans.

Evon and Wyatt carried their luggage below while Dominique stood at the railing and waved a tearful farewell to Sophie. The ship moved out to sea and when she could no longer see Sophie's silhouette she turned and went below. She would miss both Sophie and the beautiful island.

"What's this?" Evon asked as he stared at the folded paper Wyatt had handed him.

"Read it, big brother. I had it drawn up several months ago. I—let's just say I wanted you to have it before you returned to Forest Manor," Wyatt explained, and shrugged.

Evon quickly read the letter. "This says you relinquish all rights to Forest Manor," Evon said and stared at his brother.

"Forest Manor is yours, Ev. I never wanted it," Wyatt said.

"I don't know what to say," Evon said slowly.

"Yeah, well—" Wyatt shrugged again and began to unpack his things. Then he straightened, but he didn't turn around as he said, "How is Jacques doing, Ev?"

"He's under the weather more than not these days. I'd like to ride out and well—to be honest Wye, I'd like to take Dominique out to meet him and stay for a few months, but—"

"But you're not sure Nicki will go. Ask her. She might like the idea," he offered and turning his head toward Evon he smiled and asked, "You love her, don't you Ev?"

Evon stared at Wyatt. "You say the damnedest things at the damnedest time." He walked slowly out of his brother's cabin shaking his head as he went, but his thoughts were in a turmoil as he admitted Dominique certainly made him feel as he'd never felt with another woman—and there had been many—causing him to say and do things that he didn't ordinarily say and do, like sounding angry when in fact he was anything but. She made him feel ten feet tall—he wanted to make her smile—to protect her—and he'd felt something akin to jealousy when he'd seen her with Lance Martin. In fact, he admitted, he couldn't bear the thought of her in the arms of another man.

Dominique stood in the middle of the cabin she had used during the trip to the island, but she and Evon would share the cabin on their return voyage. She looked up and Evon stood in the doorway. She smiled. He continued to stare at her. Puzzled, she frowned and quipped, "Would you rather I move my things to another cabin, or—"

Evon did not let her finish. He took two steps and she was in his arms and the kiss he bestowed on her took her breath away. He lifted his head.

"Does this mean—" she began.

He quickly recaptured her swollen lips.

Later, Wyatt was on deck and Evon had taken his maps and joined him. Dominique hummed a tune and had finished unpacking Evon's clothes. She closed the drawer of his chest and she noticed an envelope on the shelf and the seal was broken. Curious she reached for the document, but she quickly drew her hand back. Then haltingly she picked up the single sheet and began to read. Her eyes widened and she nibbled at her bottom lip. "Wyatt has relinquished all rights to Forest Manor?" she said aloud. It was dated several months earlier. "He didn't have to marry me!" she breathed aloud.

The return voyage was everything Dominique could ever have dreamed a honeymoon could be.

They had encountered no storms and mild winds saw them docked in New Orleans on schedule two weeks later.

Wyatt left to attend to business at the FSL office, and Evon hailed a cab directing the driver to take him and Dominique directly to the riverboat.

Inside the coach, she looked out the window. "You married me—why?" she asked. She'd wanted to ask Evon that question since she'd first read the document in the cabin on the ship, but each time she'd tried Evon had taken her in his arms and she'd lost her train of thought. The ride to the riverboat seemed an ideal time. Would he declare an undying love—

"What?" he asked. His thoughts had been on his father. He'd known for years his father had wanted him to marry and produce an heir, and when his health had failed his father had added the codicil in an attempt to rush things along.

"I said—" she began.

"I heard what you said, *chérie*. I was lost in thought, and—aah *chérie*—we are married—it is more than I dared hope would happen," he said realizing the truth in his statement.

"I read the document Wyatt gave you," she said.

"Aah. So that is what this is about," he sighed.

"And—" she prompted. This was not what she had wanted to hear.

"And—Wyatt handed me the document the day we left the island, and—"

"The day we left?" she gasped unable to hide her disappointment.

*"Chérie—"*

*"Non*. Don't say another word." He reached for her, but she pulled away. "Don't touch me," she hissed. He hadn't known! Her mind screamed the words. She had thought he had married her because—because he had wanted to—because he cared for her . . .

Why had he left that paper lying around? Damn! Evon swore silently. They had had two glorious weeks. The return trip had been everything a man could ever dream. He and Dominique had had it all. And now—where the hell did they go from here? Would she go to Forest Manor with him? Or would she insist on staying on that damn riverboat? "Dominique. I have a proposition I would like you to consider before refusing—" Dominique started at his words and he paused. Then he continued. "I'd like you to come to Forest Manor. I would like to see my father and—and announce our marriage." He hated it that he had not chosen his words more carefully. He knew his words sounded cold and unfeeling. She would most likely refuse to accompany him, and he couldn't blame her if she did. He had told her earlier of the stipulation his father had added to his will. That he marry before his thirtieth birthday or forfeit his inheritance. He wished he hadn't told her, but he had. He sighed. "I would like you to meet my father."

She was furious with him, but then his words penetrated her fury and she realized he had told her the truth. Had she wanted him to lie? She had known from the beginning that his inheritance depended on being wed before he turned thirty. Oh but, her mind cried, I wanted more—so much more . . . "I would like to meet your father," she said stiffly. She did not look at him, she couldn't. She was going to have his baby and he had wed her saving her from public ridicule and she in turn had given him back his inheritance. They had married for all the wrong reasons, but perhaps with time . . .

"You will come with me?" he asked, and he was unable to hide the awe in his voice.

*"Oui,* I will. And—" she paused and wondered,

do either of us have a choice? "I'm sure your father will be pleased when we tell him his grandson will arrive in the spring." Her lip quivered. She was glad he couldn't see her face.

"My father will be most pleased when we tell him," Evon said and he realized he would be proud to tell his father of his marriage to Dominique and of their child.

"I hope he will not suspect we were not married when—I mean I don't want him to think ill of me or think me a loose woman—or that—"

"I know what you mean, *chérie,* but be assured that my father will not count the months—my father will love you on sight. How could he not?" Evon asked gently. He realized that what he said was true. His father, like him would be captivated by her beauty and charm. He would love her immediately. His father would be proud that she was his son's choice, his father would also be proud that it was Dominique who carried his grandchild. *Oui,* he knew his father would be proud to call her his daughter. Evon cleared his throat. "We'll go by and pick up your things and we'll have to pack a few things for Beau to take with him."

"What will I say to them?" she wondered aloud.

"Who?" he asked.

"My family. Hetty, Claire, and Beau," she said sadly.

"There is nothing to explain. I talked with them before we left. They knew you were going with me," he remarked casually, ignoring a spasm of guilt in the back of his mind.

"They knew?" she gasped and spun around to face him.

"Why are you angry?" he questioned her.

His words held a no-nonsense tone and she glared at him, but when she saw the slight lifting at the corner of his mouth, she bit back the retort that had been on the tip of her tongue. Suddenly she burst out laughing.

It was Evon's turn to stare at her. He had expected her anger, her wrath, but he hadn't expected her to think his actions comical. He reached for her. "So, you think me a clown, do you? I'll teach you to laugh at your husband, you little minx." He, too, laughed as he drew her up against him. She gasped, and Evon became serious as the laughter died in his throat. He dipped his head and captured her mouth savoring the taste of her. His hand covered her breast. Suddenly his need was so great he felt as though his loins had burst into flame. He had not known such passion existed in this man's world.

Dominique sensed that Evon was going to kiss her and the laughter died in her throat. When his hand found her breast she was shocked by the impact of his gentle grip. Her nipples hardened and a delicious shudder heated her body. His tongue urged her lips apart and slid into the warmth inside. Her pulse quickened at this speculation. Then when the driver called out their arrival, she tensed.

Evon lifted his head and smiled warmly at her.

"We are at the wharf, M'sieur," she said anxiously.

"It would seem so, *chérie,*" he whispered, but he did not release her. He turned his head to nuzzle her ear and to nip gently on the tiny lobe.

"Evon! *Non!* The driver, the people—someone will see," she whispered hoarsely. But his hand once more was upon her swollen breast. She felt his chin push away the material that shielded her soft skin and his scalding mouth quickly covered her exposed breast sending flames of desire soaring through her veins. She was lost to the passion his actions instilled in her, the driver, the crowded wharf . . . she wanted more—she wanted so very much more . . . then Evon raised his head and he released her. Startled, she watched as he fell back against the leather seat. His eyes were closed and he inhaled great gulps of air, and she realized that she, too, was having trouble catching her own breath. Unconsciously, she lifted her hands to her bosom and with trembling fingers she fumbled with the bodice of her gown. "M'sieur?"

"Shh, *chérie*—give me a minute," he said between breaths. He opened his eyes. Suddenly he realized where they were—and in a damned rented carriage. He sat up. Then he slammed his fist forcefully against his palm. His mood grew dark. Christ! He had almost lost control. He'd come close to ravishing Dominique—and in a god-damned hack! *"Chérie.* This has got to stop. It is time we had a serious talk," he grated between clenched teeth.

Evon's sudden movement startled Dominique and she jumped. What was he talking about? What had she done? "What are you saying, M—

M'sieur?" she asked him haltingly.

"This!" he hissed angrily and flung his arms out wide.

She ducked fearing he would strike her. "This?" she asked puzzled. Then suddenly her anxiety turned to anger as she snapped, "And exactly what do you mean by 'this'?" His words had both confused and embarrassed her. Who did he think he was that he could speak to her in such a manner?

"This! This backseat romance of ours. I will not go back to stolen kisses, baring your breasts—this—"

She gasped. "M'sieur! How dare you speak so crudely, so, so—"

"Truthfully?" he asked softly.

"You are an inconsiderate man," she said. He had insulted her and she felt the heat on her cheeks and looked away.

He reached for her and pulled her back against him. "You're my wife. I want it all. Everything that goes with the title. *Chérie,* I want to share all I have with you, my home, my table, my bed." He wanted what they'd shared on the ship. Evon rested his chin against her forehead.

But not his heart, Dominique thought disparagingly. And, for how long? she wondered sadly. Could she do as he asked? Could she share all of those things and—after his father's death—what then? Would he ask her to take their child and leave? Would he say that he no longer needed her or that he no longer wanted her? Could she just walk away . . . a sob tore at her throat and unconsciously she clutched at his lapels. She inhaled several deep breaths while at the same time she blinked rapidly, and then she choked, "You are right, M'sieur. I'll stay until your father's—" She knew she was being heartless, but she quickly lifted her head and as she stared into his eyes she continued. "Then the arrangement will end." Her words sounded hollow, hard, as she realized that these last weeks had meant nothing to Evon. Unconsciously she released his lapels and when her fingers brushed against the bulge of his trousers, she stiffened. Her cheeks flamed and she inhaled sharply as her thoughts raced, the lusty bastard. His loins had prompted him to take her in his arms—the soft-spoken plea that she accompany him to Forest Manor.

Evon heard the flatness in her acceptance. He realized her condition and not a great love for him had influenced her decision—what had he expected? Hell, he thought, he'd asked her to marry him—she'd had no other alternative and now . . .

# Twenty

"But sir, you must. What will the doctor say if you refuse?" Dominique insisted nervously.

"I don't care what the old coot says. I hate that nasty stuff, but if you leave the bottle I'll take it later," Jacques Forest said gruffly. One bushy, black brow rose expectantly.

"*Non* M'sieur. Yesterday you poured the dosage out and this medicine is very expensive. It is sinful to waste it," she insisted. Her expression along with her stance was as determined that Jacques would take his medicine as his scowl was that he would not. Then she smiled slyly and added, "Of course if you refuse—you did want me to push you out onto the balcony—I was going to read a few verses—but then I could always finish the sweater I was knitting and—"

"Harumph. Give me that damn bottle—and the spoon if you expect me to take that unsavory stuff," he growled.

Jacques's gruff exterior didn't fool Dominique

for one minute. It was a facade. He was really an old softie. And she had seen right through him the first day she had arrived with Evon at Forest Manor. It was a trick he used to get his way, whether with the servants or his valet and yes—even with Evon. And if Jacques was dying, then, she thought, she was not into her sixth month of her confinement. She looked down at her protruding abdomen and chuckled. *Non,* Jacques Forest would most likely outlive them all. She certainly hoped so. She loved the older gentleman. And that was what had prompted her to take over administering his medicine after discovering his little secret. Besides, she smiled, he couldn't fool her. She wouldn't allow it. "All right. I'll leave it, but none of your tomfoolery. I'll be back in a little while," she agreed. She spoke in a no-nonsense tone and left the room confident he would take his medicine.

"Bossy little wench," he grumbled after her. And when she continued on out the door, he smiled and rolled his eyes upward as he reached for the uncapped bottle his new daughter had left on the bedside table. He picked up the bottle but stilled his movement as he pictured how Evon had stood at the foot of his bed and introduced his new wife who was, Evon had informed him, already carrying his child. Jacques had known Evon had said this for his benefit—and Evon's—it was after all Evon whose inheritance depended on the authenticity of the two of them being able to pull this off. Evon needed to convince him their marriage was legal and not a hoax. But Jacques knew better. He chuckled. You did it this time, boy—bringing the wench here and having her pose as your wife—but you forgot it was all pretend—sampled the goods did you? Got caught! *Non,* Evon hadn't fooled him. Jacques had seen Evon's intent right from the start. Evon had falsified their marriage document. But, Jacques had to admit, Dominique's swollen abdomen was evidence that the two had been intimate. Foolish boy, caught in your own trap—but Jacques had become fond of the girl—perhaps, he mused, since they obviously had *something* in common unless—had Evon been duped by the wench—was the girl perhaps already with child when Evon arranged this little farce? The old man threw his head back and roared. "If that's true—it would serve you right, boy," he mused aloud. He sobered and his eyes darted to the door, but seeing the closed portal he sighed and his still-handsome face relaxed. He had added the codicil to his will because he was concerned by Evon's single status—but if the girl was carrying another man's child . . . but if it were Evon's child she carried—suddenly he sat bolt upright in bed. His spirits lifted and he whispered aloud, "A person should make the best of a situation." He lifted the bottle to his lips and, grimacing, he gulped the bitter liquid while in the same instance the door opened and Evon walked in. Jacques sat the bottle down. "Come in. Come in, boy," he said and looked anxiously at Evon.

"Father," Evon said softly. He couldn't deny that his father never looked better and he knew

Dominique was the reason for his father's improved health. Suddenly he noticed the odd expression on Jacques's lined face. "Have I suddenly grown horns or is there something on your mind?" he asked.

"It isn't going to work, you know," he said sarcastically, annoyed that Evon would think he could be duped so easily.

"What isn't going to work? Did I miss something or—"

"I'll admit she's a beauty and likeable to boot, but you haven't fooled me for a minute. She isn't your wife and if by some underhanded chance you really did marry the woman, the child she carries is most likely some sailor's by-blow."

"What the hell are you talking about? I married Dominique aboard ship while we were enroute to Grand Cayman. And I can assure you that the child is most definitely mine."

"Documents can be falsified and the woman is the only one who knows positively who the sire is," he bellowed, and then added, "I want more proof that you've complied with my wishes, or, by God you'll forfeit your inheritance."

"To tell you the truth, Father, in the beginning my mind did run along that very same course, but somewhere along the way, the estate, Forest Manor, all of it suddenly became less important and Dominique and our child is what is important. If that's the way you want it then there's no hard feelings, but if you want to hear it from someone who was there and witnessed the ceremony, ask Wye. He's never lied to you," he said and turned and walked out of the room closing the door behind him.

"Damned if it isn't true!" Jacques boomed aloud.

Later that same day, Dominique stood in the kitchen sipping the refreshing iced tea the housekeeper, Harriet, had given her. "Are you sure M'sieur Jacques needs that horrible tasting draft the doctor insists he take?"

*"Oui,"* Harriet Sinclair said. She smiled sadly.

"But he seems so—"

"Healthy?"

"He is pale and somewhat weak," she admitted, "But it is most likely attributed to his being confined indoors, and to taking orders rather than giving them," Dominique reasoned heatedly. "I can't see that his pain is related to his heart or any other serious condition other than possibly irritation. A man like Jacques is a man who has spent a lifetime in the saddle and in his fields laboring beside his slaves and working his land. I realize Jacques is short-tempered but understandably so. He should be made to feel like a man, not an invalid. He is reduced to thinking his last days are numbered. The only thing wrong with Jacques is that he has given up," she finished softly and her eyes burned with unshed tears.

Harriet had not been happy when Evon had brought the young miss to Forest Manor, but these last months she had warmed to Dominique. Harriet's feelings had deepened until she loved the woman standing before her trying to reason away Jacques's debilitating illness with her youthful logic. And Evon, she wondered, what were his feelings for the wife he'd brought home to his doubting father? Evon cared for Dominique. Of that Harriet was certain, but she'd seen the mockery in the old man's dark eyes and, she realized now, she too had felt uneasy when Evon had introduced Dominique as his bride. But her doubts were immaterial. It was Jacques Evon had to convince. And—if Jacques did not believe Evon—would Jacques carry out his threat? Would he turn the estate over to Wyatt? She shuddered to think of what *that* would do to the brothers' already shaky relationship.

"You bitch! You're lying!" Jules roared. He raised his hand and slapped Yvette with all the anger and frustration her words had instilled in him.

*"Non!"* she screamed, and fearing his wrath she jerked her head back, but she wasn't fast enough and she felt a stinging sensation on her cheek. He had dared to strike her. Suddenly she flew at him with her balled hands. She struck his chest with her fists, shrieking obscenities. He caught her wrists in an iron grip and pulled her hard up against his length. She stilled, gazing into his eyes. His lips claimed her mouth in a bruising, yet tantalizing kiss, and all the fight went out of her. Her arms encircled his neck and her hands were in his hair. She moaned, as she slid a shaky hand down his chest stopping at his waist where her fingers groped eagerly the buttons of his trousers.

Jules lifted his head. He allowed her to free his swollen member, but when she began to fondle him he reached down and stilled her hand.

"Jules!" she sputtered.

Her frustration excited him, but he had more important matters to see to. Yvette would keep. He smiled bereftly at her. "You bring me gossip that my beloved Dominique has been betrothed to that bastard Forest and without thought of how your tale has affected me—expect me to put my feelings aside merely to satisfy your lusty appetite." He snarled at her and shoved her away from him.

"But—but Jules! What of my feelings?" she cried as she slumped to the floor. "That little slut of yours stole Evon from me. I swear to make her pay for her wickedness!" Yvette hissed up at Jules. She rose and brushed the dust from her red velvet gown. She smiled maliciously and she looked at Jules with such hatred the man cringed and she grated, "You profess to love the whore, Jules, but I am the one who makes you hard and I am the one who brings out the stallion in you. You will not find such pleasure with one so meek as the ice angel." Yvette stomped from the room. She slammed the door with such force that the windows rattled.

I shall no longer need you, my spiteful little Yvette. After we have disposed of Forest, I won't need you. I'll have Dominique, and your body will no longer tempt me. Then the stallion will rear and mount my Dominique who will pleasure me far beyond feisty Yvette and . . . visions of Dominique invaded his thoughts . . . she was naked beneath him. Jules's hand moved to the fullness between his legs. He rubbed his aching staff. "Soon, *chérie*. Soon you will be mine," he said gutturally and turning he gazed at his reflection in the hall mirror. He lifted one brow. He smiled an evil smile. His eyes gleamed. He was proud of the satanic expression staring back at him. Jules turned and hurried into his study. He was anxious to put his plan into motion and there was much yet to do before he plunged his brother's sword into the heart of Evon Forest.

Dominique walked along the hallway humming softly. She opened the door to the suite of rooms she shared with Evon. She and Evon were married, and he had introduced her as his wife to his father. She was the mother of his unborn child, and she wanted what they'd shared on the island; but since their arrival at Forest Manor over three months ago, Evon had worked long hours in the fields and when he returned and on those rare occasions when he made love to her, it was as though demons drove him. His actions were feverish, almost reckless, and afterward he would fall immediately to sleep.

"We'll be leaving in the morning. That is if it's all right with Dominique, but I'm sure when I ask her she'll be relieved to return to New Orleans and Claire and Hetty. How about you?" Evon asked Beau as he put his hand on the boy's shoulder. They had ridden out to check the fields and he'd wanted to let D'Arcy know of his plans, but he also wanted to include Beau in their conversation.

"I guess so. I do miss Hetty and Claire, but I'll miss my new friends and I'll miss Jacques, too," Beau said. He suddenly realized he might never see Jacques again and a tear slipped unnoticed down his tanned and freckled cheek.

"I'm going to miss you, too," D'Arcy said to Beau, and he turned to Evon, and added, "I hate to see the three of you leave. You've all been good for the morale around here."

"Thanks my friend, but I have to be in New Orleans by Monday because we've a big shipment going out and Dupree will need my help with the paperwork," Evon explained, but his mind was not on his friend or the paperwork. His mind was on Dominique, and his heart sang at the thought of having her all to himself and the tranquility of the townhouse.

After his father had become ill the work load had fallen on him and when he'd become involved with Belle Terre and his guardianship he'd turned everything over to D'Arcy. But D'Arcy was one man whereas before it had taken all three of them to see to the running of the plantation.

D'Arcy had for too long attempted to do the work of three men and things had gotten behind. Now things were once more running smoothly and knowing D'Arcy could handle things for a while Evon couldn't wait to get to New Orleans and his townhouse where he could catch up on his rest and be a husband in the true sense. He'd neglected Dominique, but things would be better once they returned to New Orleans.

Evon had asked Dominique the night before, at the dinner table, if she would mind traveling to New Orleans and staying at the townhouse while he conducted his business. She had had mixed feelings similar to Beau's, but she had readily agreed knowing that family businesses were run by family members and Evon was the president of the company. They would be leaving in a few days and she still had several preparations to attend to before their departure.

The doors of her armoire stood open and she walked over and stooped to reach for the new riding boots Evon had had made for her after their arrival. Suddenly she saw the boots she had left behind that day at the cabin. She rose as tears glistened behind her eyelids. She still found it hard to believe that all the dresses in the armoire were hers. Evon had seen to it that she had a new wardrobe and he had even anticipated the thickening of her waistline. He had instructed the seamstress to stitch the gowns in such a way that they could—how had he put it?—grow with her. She frowned. He was thoughtful and kind and polite—to the point of making her want to scream. She wanted to throw herself in his arms, to creep into his room, to sit in the middle of his bed—and demand he love her. *"Non, chérie,* he would say, this will never do," she said aloud and swiped at her cheeks and smiled at a mental picture of Evon's shocked expression.

"You find your new gowns humorous? And who is *he?"*

"What? Evon! *Non—non,* M'sieur," she denied.

She had not noticed Evon sprawled leisurely on her lounge chair. And caught unaware she colored fiercely and stepped quickly to her dressing table and picked up her brush and vigorously ran the stiff bristles through her already immaculately coiffured hair. He could have knocked, she thought angrily. "I thought you were in the fields."

Evon had known he had done Dominique a great injustice. After their arrival his decision to allow her time to get used to not only being married, but to get used to him, had seemed reasonable. He had had good intentions and had worked himself from dawn until dusk in an attempt to keep his resolution, and until today he had kept his word. But today he had been unable to think of anything or anyone but Dominique—suddenly he had to see her—to hear her voice—to hold her in his arms—"What mischief are you up to?" he asked, his voice fading, losing its steely edge while his eyes boldly ran down the length of her and then back up to rest broodingly on her lovely face.

*"Non!* I do not think you would find my thoughts at all amusing, M'sieur," she insisted nervously. Suddenly she thought of his reaction to such a statement and bit her lip to keep from dissolving into a fit of laughter. She inhaled sharply. What was wrong with her? She'd been upset when he'd attributed their inconsistent lovemaking on her delicate condition. Delicate indeed! How could he say such a thing after all she'd gone through? Why—she'd looked forward—suddenly her cheeks grew hot and then she tilted

her head back and admitted silently, *oui*—she'd looked forward to lying with Evon, and she was proud to be his wife, but she wanted more—she wanted him as he had been that night on the island—on their return voyage. He was her husband—but she also wanted him as her lover.

Evon stared at Dominique. She had changed. She had changed, and not just her physical appearance—she'd put on weight—but even on those rare occasions when lying beside her when he had been unable to control the emotions she'd evoked in him, and he'd turned to her—she'd never—not once, had she refused him. She was no longer critical of his every word, she was more tolerant—more loving? Dominique?

What was he thinking? she wondered. He did not have to be so obvious. He thought her fat, ugly—humph, she thought. Is it no wonder then that he worked long hours—he evaded her, he could not abide the sight of her! Suddenly a sob tore at her throat and she quickly dipped her head and set the brush down. She did not want him to see the tears that threatened to spill forth. *Non! Mon Dieu!* she prayed silently. I will not make a fool of myself. She had to get a grip on her emotions. She took several deep breaths and blinked rapidly, determined to act as nonchalant as Evon.

Dominique was fighting for control. Why? Evon wondered silently. He watched her fight for control and mused, aah, this is more like the Dominique I know. Then he sobered. "Is something wrong, *chérie?*" he asked softly. He rose and walked to her side.

Had she heard concern in his voice? She quickly swiped at her flushed cheek. *"Non,"* she denied. He was most likely laughing at her. Then she sighed. Evon may find her form unsightly, but she knew he would never laugh at her.

Evon reached out and took her chin between his fingers and gently turned her to face him. She kept her eyes down, refusing to look at him. Then she realized she was staring at the button on his trousers and her eyes darted to his.

He held her with his dark stare. He seemed to be peering at her intently. She opened her mouth to speak, but no words came out. Slowly she lifted her hand and placed it on the sleeve of his white lawn shirt. He released her chin and as his fingers curled around the soft flesh of her upper arms in an iron-clad grip she felt herself being lifted before him. He remained silent. Something intense flared through her entrancement. Her heart jolted and her pulse pounded. He was so disturbing to her in every way . . . "Evon?" she choked.

"Evon. I like to hear you say my name. The formality of M'sieur mocks a relationship such as ours, don't you agree, *chérie?"* he asked and his hand moved up to cover her breast. His fingers massaged the hardened nub.

Dominique gasped. She tried to step away but he held her firmly. "And how would you describe our—relationship, Evon—"

He began a slow perusal of her facial features and when she could stand it no longer, she asked, "Evon?" There was a tinge of bitterness in her voice. She waited.

He ignored her question. Instead he leaned down and nudged her gown aside and took one firm globe in his mouth. Dominique gasped. Yet it was her own driving need that shocked her. He lifted his head and she could not deny the passion she saw in his eyes. She pushed all doubt from her mind. There was only the here and now—and Evon was here. She exalted in his male strength, his cleanliness, and his masculinity. Suddenly liquid fire flowed through her veins and her body vibrated. When his mouth once more claimed hers her lips quivered in unspoken passion. She shook with desire. Evon lifted her in his arms to lay her gently on the bed. He lay beside her leaning his head in his hand while his arm rested on his elbow. He gazed at her thoughtfully. Dominique raised herself up on her elbows, her lips were within a hair's breath of his mouth. "I want, I need—that is unless . . ."

"Unless?" he asked hoarsely.

"Unless you find—"

*"Oui, chérie?"* he whispered. His eyes moved over her lovely visage. She was beautiful. Her cheeks glowed and her smile melted his very heart.

She had never smiled so often nor had her eyes glowed as they did now. "Unless?" Evon asked again.

"You find me fat, ugly, and repulsive—"

"What? *Non chérie,* you have always been perfection and now you are more lovely than ever—to me you are the most beautiful woman in all the world and, madam, if it weren't for your advanced condition I would make mad, passionate love to you this very minute and—"

"You would?" she whispered and pulled him back down beside her.

"Dominique—" he croaked. "You tempt me sorely—if you need help with the packing just ask Harriet to get help," he offered in a hoarse whisper as he gazed into her soft eyes. He found it impossible to hide the light of desire illuminating from his own dark eyes.

"I tempt you, do I? What packing?" she asked seductively.

"The hell with the packing."

# Twenty-One

"Oh Jules, you're wonderful!" Yvette exclaimed delightedly. "When? Soon, I hope." She pulled the sheet up over her ample bosom and clasping her upper arms with her hands she hugged herself.

"Tomorrow night. And that is where you will be most helpful," Jules said slyly. His eyes narrowed into tiny slits, and he added, "After their arrival Evon is scheduled to meet Wyatt at their shipping office and that's when you're to call upon the lovely Dominique. I'll be waiting in the shadows when you and Dominique leave Forest's townhouse. Then after I have Dominique in the coach I want you to leave immediately and go to Wyatt's townhouse. Make yourself look as though you have been roughed up a bit. Then bring him back here. I'll do the rest." Jules unconsciously ran his hand down his stomach to his manhood. Lost in thought, he caressed his swelling member.

Yvette watched and bewildered she said, "But darling, Wyatt is not stupid! He will become suspicious if I bring him here." She worried that his obsession with the slut, Dominique Chandler, was making him careless.

Jules raised his hand and stroked her breast through the sheet. "If you'll hear me out I'll explain what I have planned for Evon's bastard brother," he grated. The vision of Evon Forest filled his thoughts. He cursed violently beneath his breath. Spittle rolled down his chin, and when Yvette laughed he jerked the sheet from her naked body and rose menacingly above her. "Enough!" he roared and took one nipple between his fingers and twisted cruelly.

She flinched. "Jules! That hurts." She rubbed her hand over the top of his and smiled tremulously and with her other hand she brought his head down to her and she kissed him, sliding her tongue inside his opened mouth where she moved it in and out in the age-old rhythm of generations past. Jules pulled back and she frowned.

"It was meant to hurt, you little fool. Cease this foolishness. I want your full attention," he spat. She attempted to wipe the spittle from his chin, and he jerked his head to one side. "Leave it!" he sneered. "Listen!" He rose from the bed pacing back and forth. "When the younger Forest arrives I will instruct him to bring Evon—"

Yvette hated Jules, yet watching him pacing naked before her caused heat to course through her, igniting a flame between her thighs and she listened to his instructions halfheartedly. When, at last, his words died away, she rose and stepped in front of him. She did not want to raise his ire but she had been inattentive and had only heard what he had said about Wyatt. She blurted, "Whatever good can Wyatt Forest be to us?" Her eyes were glued to his swollen staff erect and seemingly beckoning to her, and as though it had a will of its own her hand reached out and stroked him. Unaffected, he stayed her hand. She moaned, but Jules continued with his monologue as though nothing out of the ordinary had taken place. Suddenly she realized he acted as though she weren't there.

"You are to appear slightly hysterical when you inform Wyatt that Dominique has been kidnapped. I will then instruct the younger Forest he is to bring his brother to the wharf where I will be holding Evon's wife. If you do not follow my instructions to the letter, I will be forced to . . . you *will* do exactly as I say, or . . ." he explained, emphasizing the fact that he would brook no mistakes on her part. He allowed his thoughts to drift to Dominique—ah *chèrie,* after he is dead. Yvette moved beside him. She stroked his bare chest and when her hand moved downward she abruptly interrupted his train of thought. Jules gritted his teeth. Yvette was becoming boresome. Yet, he needed her to carry out his deadly plot—For the time being he must be tolerant of her. Let her think once he had his beloved Dominique that devil's spawn, Evon Forest would be hers. Jules relaxed and smiled at Yvette. Realizing his mood had mellowed, Yvette once more plied Jules with her magical talent, but it was not Yvette he saw before him, but his beloved Dominique and he groaned aloud as his passion soared.

Later, Jules lay beside the sleeping Yvette and his thoughts returned to that misty morning when Evon Forest had run his sword through his brother, Reynard. Jules had vowed to avenge Reynard's death. He had tried on several occasions to kill the bastard, but each attempt had ended in failure. This time he would not fail. His revenge would be complete. He would kill Evon Forest!

Yvette stretched and yawned. "Wyatt is to be a pawn to lure Evon to the warehouse, but I still don't see how—"

Her husky voice cut into Jules's deliberation and when he glanced over at her puzzled expression, he grinned lewdly. "You will, *chèrie*. You will. If you do exactly as I have instructed—soon, *chèrie*—once again your stallion"—he paused, as he thought, I am the stallion, but he realized if his plan was to work he must act out the scene—"will again ride above you," he finished. "Now the time has come for you to concentrate on pleasuring me, or—" he grated venomously.

Yvette quickly rose and positioned herself above Jules. She skillfully ran her hands down his length while at the same time with her lips she trailed soft kisses on his pale abdomen. Her mind filled with thoughts of Evon. Jules's plan would insure her a future with Evon. His tone brooked no argument and Jules's implications left no doubt in her mind that if she wanted Evon she must keep Jules happy, obey his every command. But soon she would be free. He would replace her with his slut . . . her lips caressed his swollen staff. Then she paused as she realized she, too, must have a plan—what was to guarantee her that Evon would come back to her? If Jules carried out his plot to kidnap the Chandler woman and take her away with him—Evon was loyal. He would search to the end of the earth and—*non,* she thought, I have waited too long already. I will not wait forever for the man I love. But if the Chandler woman was dead . . . and Jules . . . Suddenly she felt Jules's fingers bite cruelly into her breast and she returned to the present. She raised her head and whispered, "Oh *oui, chèrie.* I will perform as never before." Yvette's lips covered his throbbing staff and within seconds her ministrations erased all else from his mind and his climax was such that his cry carried out the window of his townhouse to the street below where two prostitutes paused, glanced up, and gave each other a knowing smile. One mused gruffly, "Ah 'lieves we done losed dat one." The other arched one penciled brow, sniffed indignantly, and said bawdily, "Wonna effen Miss hyah an' mitey gibs lessens?" They laughed raucously and walked on, their minds returning to their previous task. Then a carriage stopped, and a large, heavyset man opened the carriage door while he impatiently motioned to one of them. She smiled a toothless grin and hurried over to the open door. He motioned her to get inside the darkened interior and, nodding, she stepped up and into the carriage. He slammed the door shut.

Dominique paced back and forth. She was

packed and her trunks sat near the bedroom door. She had helped Beau pack his small trunk earlier that morning and she was anxious to get under way. She had missed Claire and Hetty, and of course Annie and Lonzo, but she felt a tinge of regret at leaving Forest Manor. She would miss Jacques and Harriet.

She smiled as she remembered the expression on Claire's face when she had put her in charge of the casino. Claire had sputtered and refused, telling Dominique she was not capable of such an elaborate business. Dominique had assured her cousin she would stand in her place and that it was Lance who would actually be in charge, and Claire had given in.

And Hetty, bless her heart, hadn't fooled Dominique for a moment. She had tried her best to look appalled after Evon had announced their marriage and had added that they would be leaving for his father's plantation, and Beau was to go with them. Hetty had put on a pretense of objecting—using the excuse that she and Claire could not possibly handle a casino without Dominique's help. She had waved her arms and insisted she and Claire were incapable of such a task. But Dominique had seen the look of satisfaction gleaming in Hetty's almond-shaped eyes. Dominique knew from the beginning her mammy had hoped for a match with Evon, and Dominique was aware that Hetty was secretly pleased with the way things had turned out. At first Beau was apprehensive about leaving Hetty. But shortly after their arrival at the plantation

Beau had quickly made friends among the slave children and his pain lessened. When he wasn't fishing or swimming with the children he was riding his new pony along between Evon and D'Arcy as they rode about the plantation. Beau had loved every minute of their stay at Forest Manor. Dominique paused in her thoughts. She realized sadly that her young brother had also seemed somewhat reluctant to return to New Orleans and the adult world that had surrounded him there. But she reasoned that they would only stay at the townhouse a short while, and Evon had almost six hundred slaves at Belle Terre, and her young brother would soon make new friends.

Later that same evening, the trio and several servants arrived at Evon's townhouse where they would stop over for a few days after which they would continue on to Belle Terre.

Evon carried Beau upstairs. He deposited the sleeping boy, fully clothed, on the bed. Beau's room was at the end of the hall. He left the room to return downstairs where Dominique waited.

Dominique fidgeted while she waited for the two Negro houseboys to bring in her luggage. She felt cold and although the foyer was warm a dampness hung in the air.

Shortly after leaving Forest Manor it had begun to rain. And an hour later they had had to detour around a large section of the road that had been washed away by the driving rain. Then when lightning struck a tree nearby and fell against one of the carriage wheels it broke out several spokes and had to be replaced. After they were once more on their way the coachman reined in the horses and peering out the carriage window she saw a tree lying across the road. It took over an hour to unhitch the four horses and rig up a makeshift harness around the tree and drag it to the side of the road.

Where was he? she wondered as she glanced nervously up the stairs. What was taking him so long? Perhaps he wasn't coming back downstairs. Perhaps he didn't want to share his suite with her. Perhaps—as he had on the island—he thought to evade her and have one of his servants escort her to an apartment where she could "have her rest." Well she didn't need—nor did she want to rest! *Non!* She needed her husband! And *mon Dieu,* she would have him . . . She looked up and Evon was coming down the stairs. "I am well rested, M'sieur," she said haughtily.

Evon made his way down the long winding staircase. Unconsciously he rubbed his hand over his face. Suddenly at her words his hand fell away. "What—"

"You heard me. I said I do not need to rest." She took her bottom lip between her teeth. She tapped her foot as she waited as Evon paused and then continued toward her.

One brow rose as Evon came at a snail's pace down the stairs. From the look on Dominique's face he knew she was irritated and he also knew he had unknowingly caused that irritation. She looked ready to pounce on him and he took his time reaching the bottom of the staircase. Her ever changing moods puzzled him. He blamed it on her pregnancy. He was aware of the unpredictability of women during their confinement. But something had riled her and he picked up the pace and quickly stepped onto the cool marble floor.

In one step she stood before him. He looked past her. Did he think if he did not look at her she would go away? she wondered and fumed at her own question. "Where am I to sleep?" she asked tersely.

"I will have Samson show—"

"I think not!" she spat at him.

"Oh—and why not, madam?" he asked politely, raising one brow. His surprise was obvious.

"I prefer that you show me to our suite," she parried.

"Our? As you wish—" Evon said indulgently, while at the same time he clicked his heels together, military style, and crooked his elbow offering her his arm. His eyes bore into her. She pursed her lips, slipping her hand through his bent elbow, and silently he escorted her up the long, curving staircase. Evon paused outside a set of double doors. He removed her arm and opened the portal. He stood back waiting for her to precede him into the room. Dominique took a hesitant step as her eyes darted around the dimly lit interior.

"If you are not comfortable here other arrangements can be made," he explained patiently. He wondered if he had been too quick in his decision. Suddenly, he felt an overwhelming desire to take her in his arms. To cover her mouth with his. To silence the protest he feared was forthcoming. He knew she had not been comfortable sharing his bedroom in the past—yet here at his townhouse where he stood and waited for her to refuse, possibly even demand separate sleeping quarters. when she said nothing, he added, "I believe it is customary for married couples to share—"

"I find this most suitable, M'sieur," she interrupted brightly. She turned and walked to the bedside where she turned up the lamp. Her eyes marveled at the masculine furnishings. She smiled her approval. Her eyes moved to the large four-poster. Unconsciously she visualized herself lying in Evon's arms and she smiled warmly. Momentarily lost as she was in her secret ruminations, Dominique did not notice Evon's frown which was quickly replaced with a smile. Suddenly it had struck him that she was not displeased with the arrangement. He was puzzled at her attitude and wondered was he wrong or was she happy with the arrangement? Did she understand his intention? He had given her more than enough time to adjust and the time had come— Suddenly his thoughts were invaded with a mental picture of Dominique lying beneath him. His loins ached. "I have to see to our luggage." He knew if he stayed their trunks would remain in the foyer. If he hurried he could be back in a matter of a half an hour. "Don't move. I'll be right back," he said and hurried from the room whistling a love song he'd overheard Dominique humming on the ship.

Evon reached the bottom step just as Wyatt burst through the door. His hair was mussed and his shoulder pad was torn and hanging loose. He weaved slightly and Evon reached him as Wyatt collapsed in his arms. "What the hell happened to you?" he demanded, thinking his brother had had too much to drink and had most likely gotten into a brawl. He was both aggravated and concerned at his brother's untimely appearance.

"I returned home this evening and found a note saying it was of the utmost importance that I meet you at your office, and—" he rasped weakly.

"Note? What note? I didn't send any note!" Evon exploded furiously. He had a vague understanding of where this was leading.

"I realized that, brother, *after* I awoke and found myself lying on the floor of your office." He rubbed the back of his head and winced. "Someone hit me from behind when I walked through the door. From the mess your office is in I must have walked in while it was being ransacked," he explained. He ran a hand over his face. "Damn, my head hurts like hell."

Evon examined the lump on Wyatt's head. "From the size of that knot I'd say you're lucky whoever did this didn't split your skull open." Evon helped Wyatt to his feet and put his arm around his neck and led his brother to the stairs. "Let's get you upstairs. I'll send one of the servants to get something cold to put on that lump. We can talk about this in the morning."

"Wyatt!" Dominique exclaimed. She hurried out into the hall where Evon and Wyatt were making their way slowly past her open door.

"If you'll turn down the covers in that end room, and fetch a servant, I'll get him in bed," Evon instructed.

"What happened?" Her eyes followed Evon's and she hurried to the closed door and opened it. She rushed inside. The room was dark, but she followed the stream of light filtering into the room from the hall. She quickly turned down the covers as Evon and Wyatt reached the side of the bed.

Evon steadied Wyatt and lifted him onto the bed. "I'll get him undressed while you go—"

His prompting reminded her of his earlier request to fetch one of the servants and she hurried to do as Evon asked assuring him, "I didn't forget. I'll be right back."

Later, after they'd taken care of Wyatt's needs and he had drifted off to sleep. Evon and Dominique returned to their suite. "Who could have done this awful thing to Wyatt?" Dominique asked, rubbing her temple.

"I don't know for sure, but I can make an educated guess," Evon growled and ran a hand through his hair. "If the bastard wants me I'll gladly oblige him, and he sure as hell better leave my family alone. So help me—"

"Evon! Who? You suspect someone—who?"

He ran his hand over his face. "I don't want to fight with you tonight, *chèrie . . ."* He sighed as he unbuttoned his shirt.

Dominique walked to where Evon stood in the center of their bedroom and placed her hand on his bare chest. "Evon. Please tell me." Her eyes moved over his face as she waited.

He sighed. "Jules Harcourt." Her lips parted and she frowned. When he put his finger over her mouth she snapped her mouth closed. She didn't believe him. "I'll see what I can find out first thing in the morning—if Jules is innocent he has nothing to fear from me." His lips brushed her forehead. She shivered, and he said softly, "Wyatt is going to be fine. When he was ten he fell from the roof of the stable and broke his arm. It was far worse, believe me, and then a week later he was caught climbing back up on that same roof."

*"Mon Dieu.* Was he injured again?"

Evon chuckled. "He didn't fall again, if that's what you're thinking, but after Mammy got through with him he couldn't sit down the rest of the day."

*"Oui.* And he could have been killed tonight," she said and was relieved that he wasn't.

*"Oui.* I will find who did this to Wyatt."

She nodded and sighed. Then her thoughts returned to their earlier conversation. Evon believed Jules had hit Wyatt over the head, but why would he do such a thing? Evon had to be wrong. She knew Jules and Jules was not a violent person. Then she remembered Evon's promise to investigate the matter and she relaxed. He would find the real culprit and realize that Jules was innocent. She made her way slowly over to her dressing table where she sat down and began to remove the pins from her hair. She brushed her wavy locks until they gleamed. When she had finished, she turned to stare shyly up at Evon.

Evon watched as she brushed her hair and when she'd laid the brush down he moved to stand near her. He had shed his jacket. His shirt was unbuttoned and hanging loosely from his trousers. His chest was a swirling mass of dark hair. His bronzed skin glowed in the dimly lit room. Her breath caught and when Evon closed the distance between them he lifted her to stand before him. His touch burned her skin. He enfolded her in his arms. A delicious shudder heated her body.

His hands moved over her back massaging the tense muscles. "Cold?" he whispered against her temple. His breath was harsh and his loins ached with longing. He had to go slow, her delicate condition required he be gentle. "We can—I will not hurt you or the child?" he asked hesitantly.

"*Non*. The doctor says there is no need for concern. But he would like us to abstain during the last four weeks—and at least the same length of time after the birthing," she said breathlessly. His hands had become urgent and he gripped her buttocks drawing her against his throbbing member. She smiled tremulously as she realized the bulge she felt wedged between her thighs was proof that he did not find her shapeless form repulsive.

He lifted her with ease and lay her gently on the bed. He made no move to lay beside her. He stood allowing his eyes to glide the length of her loveliness. The addition of their child growing within her womb made her more lovely than he had thought possible. "You are beautiful, *chèrie*," he breathed, his sultry eyes never leaving her. He slipped the top button of his trousers through the buttonhole.

Relief flooded through her and any doubt she may have had concerning her condition dissolved with Evon's words, his eyes, his . . . Sitting up, she covered his hands with her hands. "Allow me," she said. He remained silent. He nodded, and she began with slow deliberation to complete the task he had begun. She undid the last button and curled her fingers around his swollen member while with her other hand she slid the trousers down. She inhaled sharply. Were all men this large? She had lain beneath Evon, yet she had not seen his manhood. The hard, erect rod stood proud and she marveled at the masculine beauty of her husband.

Evon watched Dominique. He had never been ashamed of his body, and had been silently proud he was so endowed. And now, seeing the expression as she released his manhood made his chest swell with pride. At times he'd known he'd made her unhappy, but in this he knew she did not find him lacking. He bent his knee and leaned on the edge of the bed. He drew Dominique in his arms and maneuvered them so that he was beneath her and positioned her knees on either side of him. With one hand he cupped her buttock and drew her down to nuzzle the valley between her swollen breasts. Then he rolled to his side taking her with him. He sat up and with slow deliberation he removed each article of her clothing. He gazed upon her nakedness. "Aah, *chèrie,*" he breathed, "I have dreamed of this moment and I shall savor each and every second until—" He took a pebble-hard globe between his teeth and rolled it around, slavering it with the tip of his tongue. Dominique moaned and he covered her body with his. He put his knee between her thighs and gently nudged her legs apart. She spread her legs and his hand caressed her. His fingers parted the tight curls and when he stroked the tiny nubbin within she moaned and he slipped a finger inside. "Umm you are ready, *chèrie*. You are wet and oh so ready. He slid a second finger inside her warmth, to explore, to probe until she lay panting, her body squirming beneath his. She moaned, "Evon—please—" He withdrew his fingers and stroked the swollen bud and when she gasped and cried out—never taking his eyes from hers—he expertly inserted his erect staff. He did not move but savored her warmth. Then he began to move, slowly until he heard her breath, quick and whispery against his ear and he lengthened his strokes and picking up the pace he wrapped her legs around his waist. She matched him stroke for stroke. Their movements were harmonious and together they soared through the universe. Suddenly, Dominique arched and her nails raked his back. She breathed in deep soul-drenching drafts and she felt as though she were shattering into a million glowing stars. Evon groaned. His pleasure was pure and explosive as he released his pent-up passion into the mysterious cavern she had encouraged him to explore. Their breathing slowed and returned to normal. Evon propped himself on his elbows and kissed her reverently. He moved to lie beside her and taking her in his arms he drew her against him. He said nothing and soon he heard her even breathing and knew that she slept. He wanted to remain where he was, but the sky was streaked with predawn light, and his concern for his brother and what had happened earlier made him realize he had to find out who had accosted Wyatt—and why?

Reluctantly he eased his arm from beneath her head and rose and quickly dressed. He looked down at her and with a sigh he turned and slipped silently from the room.

# Twenty-Two

Later, that morning, Dominique awoke and stretched languorously. She ran her hand over Evon's pillow, but she felt only the satin covering. She sat up and stared at the emptiness beside her. There was a dent where Evon's head had been, but that was all the proof that he had been there earlier. Then she arose and quickly washed and dressed. She smiled as she stepped out into the hall and closed the door behind her. He was probably sitting at the table sipping café au lait and waiting for her to come down and join him. But when she reached the dining room she stopped and stared disappointedly at the empty table. The servant had set two places and Evon's had not been touched. He had left and she worried that if Evon discovered who had caused his brother's injury, he would not think twice about going after whoever had hurt Wyatt. She nibbled on her bottom lip. She had to find him—stop him. She would plead with him to go to the authorities. A servant came in with her breakfast, but she took one look at the steaming poached eggs and thick slices of ham and her stomach rebelled. "Did M'sieur Evon say where he was going?" she asked, praying he knew *and* would tell her. "Massa say he gwine to FSL. Then he gwine nose 'round ribbafunt," the dark-skinned man proudly disclosed with a broad grin. "I'm going out," Dominique announced. "When M'sieur Wyatt wakes up tell him I'll be back this afternoon." She ignored the servant's obvious concern and rushed out into the hall where she snatched her bonnet from the hall tree and hurried out the door.

"I can't believe the little bitch played right into our hands. I still can't understand what she was doing in that section of town."

"Umm. She has saved us precious time. She made the abduction a simple task," Jules remarked calmly. Jules didn't want Yvette to see how upset Dominique's condition had made him. Silently he mused how he would punish Dominique for her deplorable behavior, but it was Evon Forest who would die a slow and unpleasant death for stripping her of her innocence and, he sneered inwardly, impregnating his beloved.

Suddenly Jules spun around and placed his shaking hands behind his back. "Come, Yvette, there is a sudden and unbearable ache in my groin. Your expertise is needed to erase the pain. Come," he coaxed. He wanted Dominique, but he needed time to come to terms with her loss of innocence.

She belonged to him—as did her virginity. His need was almost unbearable, but he feared he would lose control and harm or perhaps kill his beloved Dominique. *Oui,* time was what he needed and then when he had done away with her bastard husband, then he could forget, forgive . . . Yvette! She must not suspect, not yet. But soon it would not matter. Soon . . .

"Oh *chérie,* must I? I'm really not in the mood. Besides, the slut is in the next room. These walls are thin. She will hear—" she pouted. She watched Jules thoughtfully. He frowned and she cringed fearing his ire. He was a cruel man when angered. But, she thought, he had promised when he had the slut they would quickly execute the remainder of the plot. She saw no reason for delay. And pleasing Jules was time-consuming. He was a poor excuse for Evon, but he had served her purpose. He had the Chandler woman—she wanted Evon. She wanted to be with Evon when he discovered the note saying that Dominique had run away with Jules. "Let me write the note and—" she began.

*"Non!* There is still much to do and haste causes mistakes. Nothing must spoil the ending. You must be patient, *chérie.* If you do not do as you are told—perhaps a change in the final act—your obedience depends on it. I wrote the script or had you forgotten?" he threatened bitterly. Spittle dripped from his chin. He rubbed his crotch suggestively.

"But, Jules! You promised! You have the girl. I want Evon Forest," she pouted. Her thoughts were filled with Evon. She pictured him naked and beckoning her to him. Then suddenly and without further prompting from Jules, Yvette began to sway her hips and slowly and seductively she shed her garments, smiling as she sauntered over to where Jules stood. Without hesitation she reached out and fondled his limpness through his trousers. Jules gasped bringing Yvette back to the present. She remembered Dominique in the next room bringing a feral smile to her opened lips. Suddenly she *wanted* the bitch to hear their mating sounds. Her eyes hazed over and she threw her head back and laughed. She heard Jules's chuckle and she tore the buttons from his pants as her passion blossomed and soared to explosive proportions.

"I think before I turn you over to Forest it would be wise of me to beg you to teach my innocent *chérie* the arts of your craft. You, Yvette, are a woman with talent—" Under her expertise Jules hardened and she smiled seeing him drool uncontrollably. She dropped to her knees and closed her eyes. Jules cupped the top of her head with his palm. He squeezed cruelly. His overlong nails dug into her scalp. She gasped in pain and released him. Jules grabbed her cheeks in a painful grip and she opened her mouth and Jules quickly inserted his throbbing rod. He smiled down at her. She hated him. And suddenly she wondered if Evon was worth her suffering Jules's sadistic overtures? She realized her own sexual desires far exceeded the normal, but Jules was insane. He was a vile man who found release through the pain and torture of others. A feral smile slithered across her face and she vowed this would be the last time she would play the part of Jules's whore. The thought relaxed her, and she rationalized; because of Jules, she would soon have Evon all to herself. Perhaps she did owe Jules, and when several minutes later she heard his familiar gasps and felt his body convulse . . . she smiled. Half her debt was paid. She smiled and released him. His eyes were glazed and he trembled violently. She reached out and stroked his limp staff. Her fingers closed around him, and she whispered against his wet lips, "And now, *chérie* for the second half—"

"Hell no, I'm not being rational! Dominique has been missing for two weeks. We've torn this city apart looking for her and we still haven't a clue as to where she is or what happened to her. I can't find one goddamn thing to be rational about—can either of you?" Evon seethed. Anger he could handle, but this deep-seated feeling of helplessness frustrated and angered him until it became a scalding fury. "Someone kidnapped my wife and when I get my hands on the bastard, so help me—" he said and gritted his teeth and began to pace back and forth. "So help me I'll kill him with my bare hands!" He raised his hands and squeezed his fingers together in such a way that both Wyatt and Henri cringed at the implication. They knew without a doubt that Evon would make good on his threat.

Henri studied Evon's face. He watched it take on a satanic look and he felt Evon's pain.

"Evon, what about the crib whores? Have you and Wyatt talked to them? Have you asked if they've heard or seen anything out of the ordinary?" Henri asked intently.

"Hell, Henri," Wyatt began, "we've asked everyone in the whole damn city if they've seen Nicki. The answer was always the same—*non,*" he finished. Sighing he walked to the liquor cart and poured himself an ounce of bourbon. He looked down into the amber-colored liquid, swirled the contents, and remarked casually, "If I rode out to Forest Manor, D'Arcy could be here by tomorrow afternoon—"

Evon's head snapped up and he halted his pacing. His first thought when he'd discovered Dominique missing had been to send for D'Arcy, but he knew D'Arcy was needed at the plantation and—his father needed D'Arcy. His thoughts raced, he couldn't sit by while—God only knew what Dominique was being subjected to . . . He refused to think further. "I thought for sure there would be a ransom note," he choked bitterly. This not knowing—he had to do something!

Had he seen tears in Evon's eyes? Henri gasped and he and Wyatt exchanged a worried look. "Evon. Let me do it. I could stay with Jacques—"

*"Non!"* Evon thundered. He ran a shaky hand over his face and held out his hand to stay both Henri and Wyatt's words. He didn't want that—Henri at Forest Manor. His father— "Give me a few minutes alone. We will talk again," he said in a hushed whisper and both men nodded and left the study. He had to come to terms with more than

Dominique's disappearance. Evon crossed the room and sat heavily on the leather couch. He dropped his head in his hands. Dominique! Their unborn child! He knew he was being irrational, but Dominique's disappearance—not a clue—the frustration—he was acting like a half-crazed idiot. He had to get a grip on himself. If Dominique were still alive . . . the time had come to set aside this feud. The time had come to bury his pain, his hate. He had to concentrate on his wife and their unborn child. Wyatt had come, *Henri* had come . . .

The following evening, Evon held the door open while Wyatt with D'Arcy right behind him came through the door. Once inside Evon clasped his friend to him and then ushered both men into his study where he offered them a seat.

"Thirsty?" he asked stepping next to the liquor cart. He didn't want a drink himself, but he realized the long ride had been a dusty one. He picked up the bottle of bourbon, but both men declined. Evon put the bottle down and moved to sit behind his desk.

"Wyatt filled me in on all the details. He's explained the situation and I'd like to do all I can to help find the little missy," D'Arcy offered gruffly. He'd met Dominique when Evon had brought her to Forest Manor. He'd liked her from the beginning and although his duties kept him busy and away from the house, he'd discovered riding beside Evon that his first impression had been accurate—Evon was in love with Dominique. Oh, he hadn't said the words aloud, but

D'Arcy saw it in Evon's eyes, in his voice, like a caress, when he spoke her name. D'Arcy smiled. *Oui,* he thought, he was glad she was Evon's wife. D'Arcy watched while she took over the care of Jacques. That took courage. He saw her weave her way into the old master's heart—that was a feat in itself. The young missy had brought life and meaning back to Forest Manor. The fact that Henri had come to Forest Manor—the little missy had definitely changed Evon's thinking. She was everything Evon needed and more—much more. She was responsible for bringing the Forest household together. They were a family again. And, he vowed, he would do everything within his power to bring Evon's wife safely back where she belonged.

"You know what you have to do?" Evon instructed the large mahogany man sitting before him. "We've hit a snag with the crib whores and you're our only hope," he sighed raggedly.

D'Arcy detected the desperation in his friend's voice and nodded. "They're scared," he said, but he knew fear wasn't the real reason the prostitutes wouldn't talk to Evon. *Non,* the real reason lay in Evon's being white and the woman he'd questioned were black.

"It's more than that. But we both know that. And the sooner we get started . . ." Evon stood.

Wyatt and D'Arcy followed suit and the three men left the study in silence.

# Twenty-Three

"It's almost over, *chérie*."

Dominique stared at the half-crazed man before her. She fought against her restraints and bit furiously into the knotted rag Jules had stuffed into her mouth. Her mind raced nonstop, one minute screaming obscenities at Jules, then praying that Evon would come for her, release her from this madman! If only she could loosen the bonds, she would scratch the monster's eyes from their sockets—and the woman, his partner, who was she? Dominique had heard their vile passion through the thin wall. Each time it had been the same. He had told the woman of his needs and the woman had administered, never seeming to satisfy the man's perverted appetite. And the guttural sounds they made each time they coupled brought bile to her lips to choke her. She had tried to block the sounds out of her mind. She had tried to think of Evon, and more pleasant times. But her hands were tied behind her and she could not cover her ears, she could not block out their rutting noises. Each time she had bit her tongue until she gagged on her own blood. Her face was swollen and eyes bruised. The woman had come into the room and slapped her repeatedly. The room was kept dark and Dominique could not see the woman's features, nor did she recognize her voice. The woman waited until Jules left and then she would enter the room to hurl obscenities and heap abuse on Dominique. Dominique felt sure the woman thought she could identify her for the woman went to a great deal of trouble to disguise her voice. But she couldn't imagine who would stoop so low as to team up with a scoundrel like Jules Harcourt. Jules—whom she had believed was a true and loyal friend of her father's—

Jules turned the wick up and returned her thoughts to the present. The dim light from the lantern cast an eerie glow on his face, and she looked at him with hatred in her swollen eyes.

Jules saw the hostility she fixed him with. He sighed. "As I was saying, my *chérie,* soon it will all be over. Evon Forest will be dead and you, my darling, will be mine—all mine. I'm going to remove the gag and you will not scream or—you do understand, *chérie?*" he asked softly. She nodded and he pulled the rag down below her chin. "Try and see things from my point of view, *ma petite.* I had worked very hard and you would have been mine had your father not played such a vicious trick on me. Belle Terre was mine until he signed it over to Forest—and when he made that devil's spawn your guardian, that was too much.

Things had gone along as scheduled until that time. You do see that I did everything for us, *chérie,* and then when your father took his life, I was elated. So convenient. But then he ruined everything by involving Forest and that's when I had to devise a new scheme to have you." His eyes moved to her midsection. "I wish there was a way to rid you of this burden, but after the birthing—well *chérie,* I can't allow you to keep the child of the bastard who not only killed my brother, the man who I have vowed would die by my own hand. He is also the man who took Belle Terre from me. But most of all, he took you, *ma petite.* And when Yv—when I discovered he had whisked you away to that damn island of his, and"—he was losing control and became excited—"and I will save the how for tonight, *chérie,*" he breathed and fought to regain his control. He stood above her. His eyes moved over her and froze seeing her extended abdomen. Jules's eyes narrowed to slits and one hand shot out and grasped her breast. He squeezed her cruelly and when she whimpered he smiled and quickly released her. He stepped back. "You must be punished, *chérie.* I am your master now. I must punish you. It is not really your fault, but it is your belly his seed grows in, and—"

Dominique blinked back hot-molten tears as she stared at him. "You're mad!" she whispered. "Evon was right, you are the one who hit Wyatt over the head. You're the one who shot Evon and—"

Jules saw the hostility she fixed him with. "Oh

*oui,* I shot him. It's a pity my aim was not as accurate as his was when he killed my brother, but his time has run out. Wyatt? What are you saying?" he asked suddenly realizing she was accusing him of something he knew nothing about.

"At FSL, you bastard, you hit Wyatt over the head," she spat and when Jules stared at her, she continued, "You could have killed him, but then what's one more dead man—"

Dominique lost control and when her voice rose hysterically Jules jerked the rag back in place.

Tears welled up in her eyes. How could she have been so blind? Jules spun around and left the room. She stared incredulously after him. Then her eyes moved to the window and when she could not see the tiny pinhole near the top of the drapery she knew the sun had set and soon it would be dark and the woman would return. But first, the woman and Jules would have their time together. She squeezed her eyes shut. How much longer? And what had Jules said? That he would kill Evon? *Non!* She had to do something! She twisted her wrists, already bruised from similar attempts, but she could not free herself. She had to get away, warn Evon—Jules and the woman had already set their vicious plot into motion, and she realized they would lure Evon here—using her as the bait. She sent up a silent prayer: please—*mon Dieu*—keep Evon safe. Don't let these monsters hurt him . . . she was so hungry, she was so tired—her head lolled on the dank floor and merciful darkness claimed her.

Dominique awoke with a start. She felt a burning sensation on her cheek. Her eyes flew open.

"Enough!" Jules commanded hoarsely.

Dominique saw two shadows as they scuffled in the darkened room. The woman was panting loudly and Jules flung a string of obscenities at the furious woman. It was then, in a daze, that she realized the woman had slapped her across her cheek. She struggled to stay conscious, to erase the cobwebs, to return to the present, the living hell she had endured these last few weeks. Unsure of the time or even the day. "She made a fool of you!" The woman shrieked hoarsely at Jules. "She went willingly with Evon—she married him *and* she slept in his bed—her swollen stomach is proof that his seed is planted deep in her womb . . ." she hissed at him.

"Quiet! I will listen to no more of your crude lies. She was forced. He made her do his bidding and *ma chérie* had no choice but to obey that bastard!" Jules yelled at the woman.

"Surely you don't believe that?" the woman taunted.

"She would not—" Once more Dominique lost consciousness.

Yvette was tired of Jules's ranting and raving. She was tired of obeying him, of groveling at his feet. This madness must end. She wanted Evon, but this was absurd. "Your little whore jumped into his bed. She opened her legs and begged him to pleasure her—as hundreds of woman have begged Evon before her—as I have begged Evon," she said smugly, and gave him a wicked smile.

Jules could not see her face, but he heard her every word. He refused to listen to her lies. He turned and stalked from the room. "Cease your prattle. There is much to do. You must find the younger Forest. You will tell him she is here. That he is to bring his brother before the midnight hour or she will die," he instructed her over his shoulder. Tonight would see an end to it all. Jules smiled. An end to Yvette's depraved ranting. He heard her steps behind him. He inhaled. The time had come to avenge his brother's death. This night Evon Forest would die—and Yvette—perhaps he would take Dominique away from all this. They would live at Belle Terre until after the birth. Evon Forest had filled her head with lies, lies about him. Forest had taken her by force. He had gotten her with child. But now, Jules thought, she was his. He would take her away—he would make her forget what that bastard had done to her.

"Hetty, Claire," Evon greeted as they walked into the galley. "You both know Wyatt, but you haven't met D'Arcy here." He pointed to D'Arcy who stood between him and Wyatt. "D'Arcy, I'd like you to meet Dominique's mammy, Hetty, and her cousin, Claire." After the salutations, Evon asked, "Could we have a cup of that hot coffee?"

"Of course, M'sieur," Hetty said and hurried to the counter where she poured three cups and set them on the table.

Wyatt walked over and put his arm around

Claire's shoulders. "We'll find her, don't worry, *chérie.*"

D'Arcy continued to stand. But when Hetty motioned impatiently for him to sit across from Evon, he smiled and pulled out a chair and sat down.

The three men quickly drank their coffee and rose to leave. "We knew you two would be worried, so—" Evon began, but words evaded him and he let his words trail away.

Hetty understood and quickly stepped forward and covered his hands with hers as she said, "Thank you, M'sieur. We—We'll pray and—" she began, but tears filled her almond-shaped eyes and Hetty bowed her head unable to go on.

"Where have you been?" Jules asked irritably as Yvette came through the door and discarded her cape on the back of a worn chair. "Come here, *chérie.* I need you—I need you now!" he croaked and when she smiled and stepped into his arms he feverishly undid the frogs of her emerald green velvet gown and slipped his hand inside her bodice and squeezed one firm, ripe breast. Her hands moved over him and her lips parted and she slipped her tongue inside his mouth. Jules sucked gently and then lifted his head. "You are good, *chérie.* The best. Whoever instructed you knew perfection," he said and when she reached down and fondled him he gasped and together they made their way to the rumpled bed where they quickly divested each other of their clothes.

"You're not bad yourself," Yvette purred, returning the compliment as she moved seductively against his naked thigh.

"Who was he, *chérie?*"

"Really Jules, this is not the time—" she began, but when he put his arms behind his head, she snapped, "Oh all right. Maurice was my instructor. Are you satisfied?"

"Not quite. There must be more, tell me, *chérie.*"

Her eyes narrowed, but she knew when Jules wanted something it was useless to try and deter him. "Oh all right. When I was twelve I accidentally stumbled upon Maurice in the attic with one of our young maids—and being the inquisitive brat that I was I threatened to tell my father what I had seen if Maurice didn't let me watch. Afterward I insisted he do to me what he had done to the maid. Poor Maurice was not only shocked, but my threat had scared him out of his wits, and then when I began to remove my clothes he quickly shooed the maid out the door. The things he did to me—and let me do to him—aah, but too quickly it ended, and four short years later Maurice was too old, his tool limp and useless. Then when he caught one of the servant's sons in my room he brought Jouet to my room and with great care and patience he taught him well—" She paused.

"Jouet! You must be joking. Your toy? Your plaything?" he roared with laughter.

*"Oui.* And I was very pleased with him, but—"

"But?" he prompted.

"But Jouet grew lazy and when I became pregnant Maurice was furious and he quickly replaced Jouet with a new young groom father had hired," she finished. She sighed and shook her head regretfully.

"The child?" he asked curiously as he smiled and took one pink globe and rolled it between his fingers.

"Maurice took me to the widow Paris. And afterward Maurice insisted the widow see to it that I was not inconvenienced again."

"And after the groom?" he asked excitedly.

"I liked variety and Maurice saw that I was kept busy, but now—"

Suddenly Jules turned her over on her stomach. She looked back as his fingers curled around the base of an empty wine bottle on the bedside table. Her eyes widened.

Later, Jules sat on the edge of the bed. "Would Maurice approve, *chérie?*" he asked and stared into space.

"Aah *chéri,* Maurice would have been proud of you," Yvette purred.

Jules was not listening. He was thinking of Dominique lying on the cold, damp floor and suddenly he realized he had prolonged the end of this scenario as part of Dominique's punishment. But, he realized, it was he who was the one being punished. How he ached to hold Dominique, he wanted to make her his, he wanted to rid himself of the vendetta against Evon Forest. He wanted Forest dead! It was he who was hurting, it was he who suffered Yvette's constant whining and all the while Evon Forest was free— "Free!" he roared aloud and fell back on the bed.

"What?" Yvette screeched fearfully. She stared at Jules. His features were distorted and he began to rock back and forth as though he suffered some severe pain. Yvette inched to the side of the bed.

Jules felt the bed give and as Yvette stepped to the floor he rolled and bellowed as his fingers circled her wrist and he jerked her back onto the bed. "Non, *chérie.* There is no need to fear the stallion, not when the mare is so willing to please," he growled. Then as every fiber in his body screamed at the unfairness he endured, and as his mind filled with scenes of his brother lying on the ground, his white shirt turning red as his life's blood flowed from his veins, the loss of Belle Terre, and—after all he'd done—the bad investments, the burned barns, the loan he gave Chandler and then called back . . . He couldn't take direct credit for Chandler's suicide, but he knew he was indirectly responsible. And who had ruined everything? Evon Forest! It was Forest who had killed his brother on the dueling field, shooting him in the heart, and it was Forest who now owned Belle Terre and had married his beloved Dominique. But, he smiled lewdly, it was he who would have it all—it was he who would avenge his brother's death, and after he'd killed Evon Forest he would not only have Belle Terre as his own but he would have Dominique. But first he must kill Evon Forest! Why not end things quickly? He had Dominique. There was no need to prolong—the child! He had to wait until after the child was born before he could—wait—the widow Paris! Of course and it was Yvette who had supplied him with a solution. He would wait no longer. There was but one person standing in his way . . . he had to slow down, he was too close to accomplishing all he'd set out to do, and there was still Yvette. She must not suspect . . . "Pleasure me, *chérie—*" He felt as though he would burst with excitement, but when he looked at Yvette he saw the confusion, the fear in her eyes, and he said softly, "I need you, *chérie.* Do this for me."

Yvette haltingly reached out and began to stroke him. He smiled and she relaxed and within minutes her expertise had him teetering on the brink of climax. He stilled her hands and croaked, "Slow down, *chérie,* we have the rest of the night." She kissed him and when she resumed her ministrations his passion escalated and he quickly rose and straddled her thighs. Sliding his hands beneath her silken smooth buttocks he lifted her and bent and laved her with his tongue. She moaned and arched against him. He lifted his head and commanded hoarsely, *"Non chérie.* Not yet." Then abruptly he released her and rolled onto his back.

"Jules?"

His breathing slowed and he barked, "You are the best, *chérie,* but Dominique will be better."

"Wha—why you bastard! Insult me all you want, Jules, but she is no better than me. She is no longer the virgin you dreamed her to be. Evon has been there before you."

"I want you to bring the widow Paris here."

"You're crazy! Marie Lavernau does not make house calls."

"She must!" he roared angrily. He sat up and grabbed a handful of Yvette's dark locks in his fist.

Yvette could stand no more of his cruelty and although he held her in a painful grip she raked his face with her nails. He yelled in pain and released her. Then he covered his face with his hands and rocked back and forth.

Yvette's hands flew to her face, but when nothing happened she removed her hands slowly and stared at Jules. She watched and as his shoulders shook she suddenly realized that, madman though he was, Jules loved Dominique Chandler. Evon had married the bitch and Jules was in love with her, and when she felt hysteria bubbling up within her, she fought for control. After a few seconds, she smiled and could not resist heaping additional pain upon her lover, and she taunted softly, "You still cannot accept the fact that Evon had that little slut before you, that's what hurts isn't it, Jules?" She sighed as she realized that, at last, their relationship was nearing an end. The thought elated her, and suddenly she felt Evon's presence. And it was Evon, not Jules, beside her, splendid in his nakedness. Unconsciously she reached out and ran her hand down Jules's chest to the coarse curls between his thighs.

At her touch Jules's hands fell away. "She belonged to me! No one, and especially not that devil's spawn, had a right to take—to violate what is mine," he snarled. In a flash his hands reached out and before Yvette realized his intent his fingers closed painfully around the soft flesh of her neck. He began to squeeze and as she opened and closed her mouth and there was no sound, he was fascinated and quickly applied more pressure and he laughed eerily as her eyes grew wide and seemingly bulged from their sockets. "You thought me a fool. Did you think I would not know when your thoughts turned to *him*? You were the fool to think you could use me as a ready substitute for your horny stallion." Her terror excited him and when her hands flew to his he felt her strength dwindling and he threw back his head and roared at her feeble attempt. "You are no longer useful to me, and it would be foolish on my part to allow you to live. I have all I'll ever want and need in the next room, but—"

Suddenly he loosened his hold and she gulped great gulps of air back into her lungs and as her strength returned she clawed his hands until her nails broke and there were deep grooves and trails of blood on the backs of his hands. Then she brought her knee up and he easily leaned forward escaping the blow, and when her nostrils flared, his breathing increased and he urged, "That's it, fight, *chérie*." Then her hand snaked out and she slapped him hard across the face. He smiled and said, "Your theatrics no longer amuse me." His fingers tightened and as he watched her face turn from a deep pink to crimson and then take on a purplish hue, his excitement soared and spittle filled his mouth and spilled out to run down his chin where it dripped onto the valley between her breasts. His passion escalated, and when he felt her go limp he stared down at her. He shook her and when she did not respond he lifted her and hurled expletives at her puffy features. He released her and when she fell back on the mattress he let out a strangled cry and in a frenzy he plunged his throbbing staff into her. When he at last felt himself begin to climax he feverishly pumped until he expelled his seed into her still form. Spent, he slumped over her. When his breathing at last slowed and returned to normal he rose and stepped to the cold floor and without a backward glance he pulled on his trousers and reached for his shirt.

"What the hell is going on here, Jules?"

Jules looked up. "Need I explain?" He shrugged, and pointedly ignored the heavyset man.

"Christ! She looks dead—Jules, answer me. Yvette was my cousin. *Mon Dieu,* she looks dead—" John Dupree gasped.

"And what of me? Am I not also your cousin?" Jules spat, finished dressing, and nonchalantly walked to the bedside table and opened the drawer. He stood with his back to his cousin and slowly withdrew the dagger. Clutching it he eased his hand behind him and turned back and smiled. "Forget Yvette. There are more important things at stake. It will be over after tonight. And—within the month you and I, cousin, will have it all. Everything we've ever wanted, and more. I have decided to kill both Evon and Wyatt Forest and with their father on his deathbed—you are next in line to take over the business," he commented as he moved slowly toward the heaveyset man. The man frowned and when John Dupree would have spoken, Jules put his hand up to stay his words as he continued, "If you're worried about Henri don't—it has been many years since his name was on the Forest properties, and since there is no heir—nor will there be—and with the brothers dead and old Jacques gone, you—will inherit it all. The company will be yours."

Sweat ran down Dupree's fat jowls. He shook his head. "I don't know, Jules. Three deaths—" he said shakily as he reached into his breast pocket and retrieved a handkerchief.

Jules watched him intently.

The man ran the cloth over his face. Suddenly Jules brought the dagger from behind his back and raised it high above his head and plunged it into Dupree's thick chest.

# Twenty-Four

*"Mon Dieu!"* Dominique screamed silently. The woman is Yvette and Jules has killed her and in a fit of madness he has ravished her dead body and now he has killed another! She held her breath and listened. Silence. What now? Would she be next? Would he rape and kill her also, she wondered in terror. Suddenly the door was flung open and crashed against the wall startling her out of her reverie. She looked up and in the dim light she saw Jules's silhouette as he paused in the doorway. She strained to free herself. Then Jules moved to stand beside her and when he knelt down she froze. With lightning speed he reached out and cupped one swollen breast while at the same time he slid his other hand under her tangled skirts. Suddenly he pinched her tender flesh cruelly. She flinched and he smiled.

"You are shaking, *chérie.* You heard," he whispered, and moved his hand to the small rise above her womanhood. Then when he suddenly dipped one finger inside she gasped and clamped her knees together.

*"Non, chérie,"* he crooned softly. "There is no need. I am not ready for you—it is too soon after Yvette or I would show you just how feeble your effort is—" He paused watching her intently and when her eyes widened fearfully he smiled, satisfied that she understood his implication. He sighed before continuing, "There is still your husband to dispose of and afterward you and I will visit the widow Paris who will—" He paused once more, released her breast, and ran his hand over her swollen abdomen to emphasize his intent. When her eyes widened and quickly filled with tears, he soothed gently, "There, *chérie,* do not cry. You will find that after we leave the widow Paris, your punishment will end and you shall find me a forgiving master. Your sin will be forgiven . . ." he croaked, rose, and spun around and hurried to the open doorway. Suddenly he paused and returned to slip the gag back in place. Then he was gone.

Dominique sobbed against the rag and then she felt her body go limp. He was going to kill Evon, and bound and gagged as she was there was nothing she could do to stop him.

Suddenly she heard a muffled sound. She tensed. Had Jules returned? She heard a moan. Yvette! There was a soft scraping sound and suddenly she saw Yvette on all fours crawling through the doorway. Then Yvette suddenly slumped to the floor. Yvette stirred and with great effort she rose once more and as she inched toward Dominique, Dominique noticed a blankness in her eyes. What was she doing? Would Yvette blame her for what Jules had tried to do to her? Was Yvette going to kill her? Then she was beside Dominique and as she struggled to a sitting position she whispered hoarsely, "He thinks I am dead and you are his, but he is wrong—sooo very wrong." Yvette reached across her and Dominique cringed, but as she felt Yvette's fumbling fingers on her wrists she realized her intent and she eased forward. Suddenly she felt the rope fall away. She was free! Then when Yvette fell forward across her Dominique shuddered. She quickly removed the rag from her mouth and eased Yvette off of her. Yvette's eyes now stared, unseeing, up at the ceiling, and Dominique rose quickly. The weeks of inactivity and inadequate nourishment had left her weak and she stumbled and fell against the wall. She paused for several seconds and then quickly crossed herself as she said a brief prayer for Yvette's soul. She knew Evon's life depended on her warning, and she called upon all her willpower while she also prayed she was not too late. She slowly and purposefully inched her way out of the room and out of the house into the cold night air.

At eleven o'clock that same night, D'Arcy walked back to the carriage where Evon and Wyatt waited. He opened the door and stepped inside. He sat down and stared at his hands. "I thought you said Harcourt was in St. Louis," he asked, and exhaled.

Evon and Wyatt exchanged glances and swung their eyes across to stare at D'Arcy. Evon said, "Yvette said Jules left for St. Louis a few days before Dominique was abducted. He was my first suspect. Yvette had been at my townhouse when I returned from FSL. That's when I discovered Dominique was missing, and that is when Yvette had told me Harcourt was in St. Louis. Then where has he been these last weeks?" Suddenly he felt a tightening deep within his gut and he knew he would not like the answer.

"I've questioned three women so far. Two of them admitted to hearing uh—sexual sounds coming from an open window at Harcourt's townhouse. From all they've said it was the same night the missy was kidnapped. The third prostitute insisted she'd seen a woman dressed in a dark cape with a hood draped over her head go into Harcourt's residence earlier this evening—"

"The lying bitch!" Wyatt exclaimed. He rose swiftly and grabbed the leather strap. Evon's hand stilled Wyatt's actions and halted his exit from the carriage. Wyatt turned and stared questionably at his brother.

"Wait!" Evon barked. "Let's think this through. There can be no mistakes. Dominique's life may depend on our keeping our heads," he said in a steady voice, but his mind raced ahead. They had to take action, but their plan had to be foolproof. Yvette! When he found that deceiving bitch he would—his concern at the moment was not Yvette. He had to concentrate on getting Dominique out of the clutches of that madman, Jules Harcourt.

Several seconds went by and Evon said finally, "We'll talk with the Renaults— *non,* on second thought, Wyatt, you go to Yvette's house—see what you can find out from her parents. And D'Arcy you come with me. We'll wait for you outside Harcourt's townhouse, Wyatt," Evon instructed, and both men nodded and Evon opened the carriage door.

Dominique crept around the side of Jules's townhouse. She was almost to the front when she felt a hand slapped over her mouth and she was dragged back inside. "Where did you think you were going? You cannot run away from me, not now, not when everything is falling into place and the end is at last in sight. *Non chérie,* you are mine now and always," he whispered against her ear as he dragged her back through the door and into the room she had only recently escaped.

*"Non,"* she screamed. Her sudden outburst surprised Jules and when she felt his grip on her relax she seized the opportunity and broke free and stumbled out the door. She heard his steps behind her and she slipped into an open archway. It was dark inside. She felt her way along the wall and moved until she could go no farther. She stood with her back to the wall and held her breath. Then she heard footsteps and she froze. The footsteps grew louder and when Jules entered the archway she moved around reaching out with her hands while at the same time she scraped her bare

feet on the floor searching for something—anything—she might use as a weapon. Her leg brushed up against wood and she reached out and ran her hands over the rough surface. Her fingers touched something cold and hard and she realized it was a metal object, about the size of a small branch. She gripped the rod tightly and raised it high above her head and advanced toward the archway. She heard Jules breathing within inches of her and she took a step forward and brought the rod down with all her might. There was a loud thud and a strangled moan. The rod fell from her hands and she heard Jules fall forward and felt his hand swipe her ankle as he fell at her feet. She screamed and stepped around the still form and stumbled out of the building. Her unsteady legs felt as though they would not hold her, but she continued to run along the side of the house. She collided into something. She was brought to an immediate halt. She felt arms go around her waist and she screamed and collapsed in a dead faint.

"D'Arcy. Over here," Evon called.

D'Arcy hurried to where Evon stood.

"It's Dominique," Evon choked. His heart sang joyfully as he eased her to the ground.

"Is she—?" D'Arcy couldn't finish. She was so—limp.

Evon lifted her gently and lay her on the grass as fear gripped his insides. He leaned over her and put his ear close to her mouth while at the same time he lay his palm over her breast. Then he looked up. He exhaled, not realizing until that moment he'd been holding his breath. He looked up at his friend and said, "She's alive. She fainted."

D'Arcy also released his breath. He threw his head back and mouthed a silent prayer of thanks. Suddenly his head shot back to Evon. "Harcourt!" he yelled.

Evon's head shot up. Before he had time to comment, D'Arcy had moved off in the shadows. He retraced Dominique's steps.

D'Arcy eased inside the house moving quietly. He was looking for the man who was responsible for Dominique's disappearance. He found the opened portal and slipped inside, but in the dimness he saw only an outline of bare furnishings in the room. He moved to the window where he threw back the drapery and light from the half moon filtered through the dirty window. He saw Yvette's still form and kneeled down and put two fingers on her bruised neck. She was dead. He stood and looked around the room glimpsing a crumpled blanket on the floor and a piece of knotted rope. He bent to pick up the rope and felt the dampness there. He dropped the hemp and made his way back to the doorway, but he stepped on something and bent to pick it up. A poker. He shook his head and quickly moved out of the room soundlessly. As he stepped into the room across the hall he discovered Dupree's body. He left the room to search the remainder of the house before returning to Evon and Dominique.

Her eyes opened and she sucked in her breath. "You're safe, *chérie.*"

"Evon!" she choked and flung her arms around

his neck. A carriage drew up to the curb, but she didn't hear it as she sobbed against Evon's shoulder.

"Is she all right?" Wyatt asked as he knelt beside Evon.

"I think so," Evon said as he lifted Dominique up and carried her the short distance to their carriage.

"What did you find out, Wye?" he called over his shoulder, but his thoughts were on Dominique. Her arms were around his neck, and tiny hiccuping sounds came from her bruised and swollen lips. He would kill Harcourt! He would strangle him with his bare hands. If he had to search the world over he would find him! He stepped up into the carriage. "Maurice gave me a note from Yvette. It said you were to come to Harcourt's townhouse at the midnight hour. Not a minute before. Not a minute after or Harcourt would kill Dominique," Wyatt said between clenched teeth. "The man's an animal. And Yvette"—he paused wishing Yvette had been there—"Yvette had gone out earlier and I didn't take the time to find out where. I came as fast as I could." He stepped up behind Evon and D'Arcy followed and closed the carriage door.

Evon sat down with Dominique on his lap. "Any trace of him?" he asked his friend.

*"Non,* but I found two dead bodies. One was Yvette and the other—"

"The other?" Evon asked puzzled.

Wyatt blurted. "There were two?"

*"Oui,"* he said answering Wyatt first. "It was

your manager from FSL, Dupree."

Suddenly things began to fall into place. "It had to be Dupree who hit you from behind, Wye. He was involved from the beginning—it all falls into place, the lost shipment—" Suddenly he didn't care that Harcourt had escaped—he had Dominique beside him—she was safe. Right now Dominique needed him.

"We'll find him. He can't get too far," Wyatt said and leaned back against the hard leather seat and closed his eyes.

D'Arcy was silent for a moment, then he said, "I want to be there when you catch that bastard, Ev."

"We'll all three be there," Wyatt said and sighed.

Evon nodded and rested his chin against the top of Dominique's head and his arms tightened around her.

The weeks sped by and Dominique's bruises healed. And the cruelty she'd suffered at the hands of both Jules and Yvette began to fade. She gained weight. The infant grew rapidly in her womb. The months sped by. She counted the weeks, and then the days until her child was born. And then at last she was in her final week of confinement.

Dominique stood in the nursery staring down at the tiny apparel she'd knitted for the baby. She closed the drawer of the chest and walked over to the cradle D'Arcy had made and ran her hand over the smooth railing. Suddenly and without warning a pain stabbed her. She grimaced and her hand went to her side. She looked up and Evon stood with his hands braced on either side of the door. Their eyes locked and she smiled. He was so handsome. "Spying on me?" she asked impishly. Her pain was forgotten as her thoughts slipped back to the last months and she realized that it had been one long and continuous honeymoon—well very nearly, she thought. The doctor had insisted upon separate sleeping quarters after the ordeal she had suffered. For the sake of their child they had moved her things out of the master suite and into another apartment. She wondered if Evon felt like she felt, if his pain was anywhere as great as hers? Did he toss and turn losing hours of sleep thinking of her as she thought of him? Or, when at last he did close his eyes, was it to dream of her as she dreamt of him? Did he ache to hold her, to kiss her—unlikely, a small voice intruded into her thoughts, and she sighed as she realized how foolish she was being. Not only did she fall asleep to dream of Evon, he filled her thoughts during the daylight hours. Her thoughts drifted back to the day after the doctor had left, and she realized she had been sparring with Evon every day about one thing or another. Nothing serious, but when Evon had suggested they move her things to the adjoining room she had declined, fearing not Evon's, but her own traitorous emotions. And it continued, bickering back and forth over non-consequential matters until even the servants cringed when they had to be in the same room with them. Why, she remembered, they had even argued over the sex of their child. Evon had been adamant that their child would be a girl, with her mother's beauty and hair and eye color, and she had rebuked his words insisting the baby was a boy and would definitely be a replica of his father. Their sparring continued, until even the servants avoided them.

Annie and Lonzo had made weekly visits as did Claire and Hetty, and all had been subjected to their squabbling. Even Wyatt had thrown up his hands and left seeking the tranquility of New Orleans. But, all in all, at least she and Evon resided under the same roof and not miles apart.

But then Jacques had suffered a serious setback and she knew things would change. Soon, she realized, their arrangement would have to end and she and the child would be asked to leave to return to the riverboat. If only the doctor hadn't insisted on separate sleeping quarters. She sighed and walked to where Evon stood in the doorway.

It was remarkable, Evon thought, she had been so frail, so battered and abused. Yet, she had bounced back those first weeks at Forest Manor. He marveled and was thankful that no harm had come to their unborn child. Dominique's due date was only a few days away and soon, he smiled, he would have Dominique back. She had become the center of his universe, and he wanted his wife back.

He caught her around the waist as she attempted to duck past him. "Where do you think you're going, *chérie?*" he asked. He pulled her against him. He inhaled her scent. She smelled of honeysuckle. "Have you been in the garden again?" he whispered against her ear.

*"Oui."* Her simple answer sounded flat even to

her. Then suddenly she didn't care. She was tired of pretending to be unaffected by their strange arrangement. She was tired of pasting a smile on her face each time she left the privacy of her apartment. She was tired of always feeling tired. Tired and fat and ugly. A lone tear escaped and slid down her flushed cheek. "Oh!" she exclaimed. And then again. "Oooh! Please put me down. I must use the water closet. I—I—" she insisted, and then realized she was too late as she felt a warm trickle run down her legs. Her eyes widened and her already flushed cheeks colored a deep, dark crimson.

Evon looked down and stared at the puddle surrounding their feet. Realization struck him and he lifted her and turned to leave. He ignored her protests and carried her into the master suite where he lay her gently on the bed. "I'll be right back."

"*Non*. I can't stay here. I'll ruin the coverlet. I must use the water closet," she cried, and struggled to sit up, but as an onslaught of nausea washed over her, she lay back down and covered her face with her hands. She had wet all over herself, and in front of Evon.

Evon paused. "You are where you belong. And you shall stay there until after the birthing. You will have our child in our bed, *chérie,*" he said, and his tone brooked no argument.

The child! What was he saying? Did he think her time had come? This was ridiculous. She had to go to the water closet. Besides, she would know of such things, and she felt no pain, only that twinge. Suddenly a sharp knifelike pain tore through her and she squeezed her eyes shut and gasped aloud. *"Mon Dieu!"* she whispered.

Nineteen hours later, Evon placed their sleeping son in her arms. He had refused to leave her side and when she had become drenched in perspiration and was too weak to open her eyes, Evon had bathed her face with a cool cloth. After the birth, Evon had kissed her forehead and taken their son and she fell into an exhausted sleep.

# Twenty-Five

Dominique sat in the cool shade. Six-week-old Jacques lay on the quilt, asleep beside her. She reached down and smoothed his dark unruly locks from his forehead. He was a beautiful child and he'd gained two pounds since birth. She looked up and Evon stood a few feet away. She gasped and her eyes widened. Then Evon dropped his gaze to the child and she chastised herself for her foolishness. Yet, she reasoned, she could have sworn she had seen something unusual in the way he stared at her. Need, passion? *Non,* she silently rejected her ruminations. She realized that the hour had grown late and she rose and reached out to the sleeping infant. Strong fingers circled her wrist and she froze. Why was he here? His touch was more than she could bear. "I have to take him in. It is late and I'd like to feed him before the supper hour."

"Wait. Only a moment. I have to tell you—I've just come from Father's room, and—"

*"Non!"* she breathed and jerked her arm free and began to run toward the house. *Non!* she screamed silently, *non* . . .

She stood outside Jacque's closed door. Jacques—she had known him only a short while, but during that time she had enjoyed sparring with him. She'd grown fond of him—she'd come to love the older gentleman. She opened the door and slipped inside.

The room was so quiet. Jacques lay so still . . . Her hand went to her mouth and she sobbed aloud as she ran to his bed and threw herself across his lifeless form. She cried until there were no more tears and at last she rose and kissed his cheek. Then quietly she left the room closing the door softly behind her.

Dominique came down the stairs slowly. She did not notice Evon waiting at the foot of the staircase. He held their child in his arms. She reached the bottom step and then she looked up. Seeing the pain in his eyes, her eyes filled and tears flowed down her cheeks. As Evon reached out to her she stepped into his arms and sobbed until there was only an occasional hiccup.

Jacques squirmed between them and Evon whispered, "It is over, *chérie.*"

She lifted her head and nodded and she took the baby from him and without a word retraced her steps back upstairs.

The funeral was two days later and more than two hundred people attended. Dominique had, against the protests of both Evon and Wyatt, insisted on helping to prepare the body for viewing.

Dominique lay in her bed already missing Jacques terribly. The funeral was over and the friends and neighbors had left and everyone had retired hours ago. Her mind returned to the hours she'd sat reading to Jacques, and how proud he'd been when she and Evon had told him they'd named the baby after him and how he loved it when she brought the infant with her to his room. She wanted so desperately to comfort Evon at this time and she needed to be comforted.

The doctor had cautioned her against having marital relations the month before the birth of the baby. After she'd given birth, he had once more repeated this same warning. Now, she thought, it had been a little over six weeks and Evon had not indicated in any way that he was dissatisfied with their continued abstinence.

Unable to sleep she rose and padded barefoot across the room. She made her way down the stairs. The kitchen was lit up. As she stepped through the portal, she paused. Evon sat with his arms braced on the counter with a cup of café au lait in his hands.

He looked up and smiled sadly. "Come in, *chérie.*"

She felt herself stiffen. He was so handsome. His presence was electrifying. She shook her head slightly. She had to get a grip on her emotions. It was over. Jacques was dead.

# Twenty-Six

"I'll be leaving before the end of the week," she said and unconsciously lifted her chin. She had known from the beginning that Evon's inheritance had been the reason he had married her. Now that Evon's father was dead there was no need to keep up the pretense. He had used her. But a small voice whispered, are you without guilt? He, at least, had been honest while you—*non!* She fumed silently. Why should I wait and give him the satisfaction of treating me like excess baggage. He is a scoundrel, a rogue, a womanizer of the lowest rank. Her eyelids grew hot and refusing to allow him to see how hurt she was, she spun around.

He did not want her to go. She was his wife. He knew they had married for all the wrong reasons—she to save her reputation and give their son a name and in the beginning to assure him his inheritance.

"It is your decision," he sighed and jammed his

hands in his pockets. Suddenly he felt an overwhelming desire to take her in his arms, to kiss her—but he knew he couldn't force her to stay.

"My decision! That's a laugh. This is all your doing! I have had little choice, but to go along with the ridiculous charade." She glared at him. She couldn't believe she'd said the words aloud. As the tension stretched ever tighter between them, he shook his head, and then when he opened his mouth to speak she quickly snapped, "I have to see to the packing." Yet she didn't move as he continued to hold her with his bold gaze. What was he thinking? she wondered angrily. Was he relieved? Perhaps even overjoyed to at last be rid of her? Evon was probably thinking that with her out of his life he could resume his—his rakehell activities: gambling, carousing, womanizing. Suddenly she stiffened. So, she realized, that is how it is, is it! Her anger escalated. If he thought to rid himself of her so quickly he had another thought coming! She would take her own sweet time and leave at her convenience, and she blurted, "I have changed my mind. There is much to do and I can't possibly leave so soon. I'll be staying until the end of the week." Her tone was heavy with sarcasm and she thought that should set him back on his heels. But when he remained silent and merely quirked one brow at her, she wanted to slap his arrogant face; instead she marched past him with her nose in the air.

"What the hell was that all about!" he shouted. He wanted to go after her, to tell her how much he wanted her to stay, to tell her he was nothing without her, to tell her that she and their son were all that mattered to him. He wanted to tell her that he loved her—he paused and whispered aloud, *"Oui."* Suddenly he knew it was all true, he realized he had loved Dominique from the very beginning when he'd first laid eyes on her lying unconscious on the cold, damp ground. Suddenly he wanted to tell her all those things to make her see just how much she meant to him—would she laugh at him? He knew she didn't share his feelings and he had been inconsiderate of hers. Dominique's father entrusted his daughter to his care and he had not lived up to Emmett's expectations, having proved a poor excuse for a guardian. Perhaps he had done all right by Beau, but not Dominique, having forced her to marry him. He flinched as he realized he'd been a terrible husband. If only she would give him the chance he would make it up to her. He would—suddenly her words penetrated his thoughts—she'd changed her mind. She'd said she wasn't leaving until the end of the week! This was the chance he'd been hoping for. He would get her to reconsider—perhaps she would agree. Yet she'd made it clear that she wanted to leave, in fact, was anxious to go! He had been the one who insisted on this devil's bargain and although at first she had been reluctant, he readily admitted she had held up her end of their bizarre arrangement. If he asked her to stay would she think him ridiculous? Could he blame her if she *did* laugh in his face?

Evon moved slowly into the hall and when Dominique opened the door of the nursery, he called out to her, "Dominique, wait." Suddenly he didn't care what her reaction was. He had to let her know what was in his heart. He hurried after her.

Dominique heard Evon call but she ignored him and went into the nursery.

Evon strode down the hall stopping outside the nursery where he paused and leaned with both hands on the doorjamb. His eyes moved around the room settling on her where she stood removing their son's tiny garments from the top drawer of the intricately carved chest of drawers. "Dominique," he whispered and moved into the room.

Dominique heard Evon enter the room and she quickly swiped at her damp cheeks. She didn't give a damn what he wanted or didn't want. She had done all she could do. What did he want from her? He had his damn inheritance. She had given him a son. She had loved him. She had nothing else to give him. She would not prolong—

*"Chérie?"* Evon called softly, but his mellow baritone was edged with control. When she continued with removing the infant's things he took a step toward her. Then he said, "Why are you deliberately ignoring me?"

Dominique heard his footsteps as he made his way slowly toward her. His actions reminded her of a lion stalking his prey, and she straightened and turned around. At the expression on his face she realized that was exactly his intent. To scare her into submission. Suddenly she felt like a cornered animal about to be snared for a feast. She stiffened. Her thoughts raced. Then suddenly her fear turned to anger. She would not be intimidated by him, and pulling herself up to her full height she noticed a familiar gleam in his eyes and she fought to keep her heart cold and still as she evaded his question, saying, "I don't know what you mean, M'sieur." Her tone was matter-of-fact, while she held back tears of disappointment, of what might have been. Her mouth felt like old paper, dry and dusty, and her throat seemed to close up.

"The hell you don't! And why are you addressing me as M'sieur? Have I been demoted? We're hardly strangers. I don't like it. In fact, I don't like it one damn bit. How many times are you going to change your mind? Are you or are you not leaving at the end of the week? What I want to know is why are you leav—"

"How dare you?" she interrupted him. Her eyes blazed with mounting rage.

"How dare I what? If you'd let me finish just one sentence. I was trying to ask you why the hell—" he began.

"You know perfectly well what!" she seethed. She knew what he'd been about to say. Why the hell don't you leave right now! Well if he wanted her out of his house, then so be it! Of a sudden she realized the end of the week was an eternity away. She nearly choked on her fury and her green eyes blazed at him. "I have changed my mind. I will be gone within the hour," she threw the words at him like stones.

"Domi—" he began as he took a step toward her, but her burning, reproachful eyes halted his action. Swallowing his apology, he said instead, "If your mind is made up, far be it for me to try and change it." He stared at her only a second before he turned and strode from the room, berating himself for his foolish actions. "You were a fool to think she would stay," he thought heatedly. "Christ! you damn near made a complete ass of yourself in the bargain," he hissed aloud as he entered the hallway.

Dominique stared after him. She couldn't make out his words, but she guessed that he was saying good riddance to a bad bargain. As she felt hot moisture gathering behind her eyelids she slammed the top drawer of the tiny chest closed and one lone tear escaped unnoticed down her cheek. She quickly reached into the armoire and pulled out a satchel and began stuffing things into the bag.

"Are you sure you're all right, Nicki?" Beau asked sadly.

"I'm fine, and you will be, too. Just wait. You'll see. Now that you've passed your eighth birthday you get to stay up an hour later, and now that we're back on the riverboat, we have the cleaning, the cooking, the casino—well, I'll need you to help me with Jacques and—"

"You mean I'll be watching him all by myself?" he asked.

"I know you can handle him, but if you think he'll be too much trouble," she stated and paused.

*"Non,* Nicki. Jacques won't be any trouble at all," he insisted, his face glowing with pride. "I'll take real good care of him," he promised.

"I know you will, *chérie.* And now I have to see if Lance needs me to help him with any last minute preparations in the casino. We're opening in an hour," she smiled, and tussled his bright red curls.

A few minutes later, Dominique walked into the little alcove. Lance was sitting at the desk. "Can I do anything?" she asked.

Lance looked up and smiled. "Not offhand," he answered, but suddenly his mind was no longer on the inner workings of the casino. "You look lovely this evening, Nicki," he complimented. In the beginning he had sworn that the boss lady was off-limits, but now—his eyes moved appreciatively over her trim figure. He sighed, and forced his eyes back up to her lovely green eyes. "You're beautiful. Nicki, I—"

Dominique had always felt comfortable around Lance. She knew his reputation as a ladies' man, but theirs had always been a strictly professional relationship. However, his unexpected appraisal had been less than professional and it made her very uncomfortable. "Thank you. But since I'm not needed here, I'll see if Claire or Hetty need my help in the galley." She quickly left before she said something that would make them both uncomfortable.

When Dominique walked into the galley, Claire was humming to herself as she arranged jumbo shrimp on a large platter. Dominique walked up just as Claire began to sing the words from a popular ballad. "Claire, you have a lovely voice. I had no idea. I just thought of something, Claire. Oui, you'd be perfect, and you're exactly what this place needs!" She smiled at her cousin. "Absolutely perfect!"

"Perfect?" Claire asked and laughed. "Nicki, whatever are you talking about?"

"To sing on the casino stage," Dominique exclaimed excitedly.

"To sing—" Claire shook her head back and forth. "Nicki, you must be joking. I'm a seamstress, not a singer," she insisted. Then her voice rose an octave, and she asked, "Whatever will you think of next, cousin?" A glint of humor returned and she stared at Dominique, musing silently, how one person could concoct, and on the spur of the moment, such outlandish schemes. Imagine Nicki thinking she could sing on the stage in front of all those men! Why the idea was not only preposterous, but scandalous! She smiled and on impulse gave Dominique a quick hug before saying, "Hetty is almost finished with the last platter and that should do it." She picked up one of the trays and, confident that the subject was closed, walked out of the galley.

"Ummm," Dominique pondered thoughtfully.

"It isn't as ridiculous as you seem to think, sweet, innocent Claire." She visualized her cousin standing on the stage of the casino. Claire had a lovely voice and if she could convince her cousin to sing, the added attraction would definitely be a plus for business.

Dominique left the galley and hurried to the casino where she jotted down a message and handed it to a porter to give to Claire. Then she made her way to her cabin.

Later, Claire read the note the porter had handed her. *Please, cousin, do this for me. Love Nicki.*

"Sit still Claire. I have one unruly curl to pin in place and then I'll be finished." Dominique held several hairpins between her lips and her speech was garbled.

Claire strained to understand her gibberish. She was unable to make out what Dominique had said. "I can't believe I let you talk me into this! I'm still not sure I can do it," Claire insisted, but Dominique ignored her.

"Ouch!" Claire complained after Dominique pinched her cheeks. Claire looked in the mirror and admitted the pain she'd suffered had added color to her pale cheeks. Suddenly her stomach felt queasy. "This is not going to work. I simply can't go through with this. I can't stand up there and sing before all those gentlemen—"

"Of course you can. And you will. Now. Let me

see you," Dominique said and stood back to inspect her handiwork. "You look beautiful—almost serene," she breathed and she meant every word. Claire was lovely and with the added lip rouge—*oui,* she determined, her cousin looked somewhat—provocative. "What do you think M'sieur Wyatt will think when he sees you? I'll bet he'll whisk you right off that stage and carry you off to some dark romantic setting where he'll—" Dominique gave her cousin a wicked and exaggerated wink.

"Nicki! What a sinful thing to imply. And you a wife and mother—" The sudden flash of pain in Dominique's eyes halted her words. She had not meant to hurt Dominique. "I'm sorry, Nicki," she apologized quickly. Her thoughts went back to the day Dominique had returned to the riverboat. She had carried Jacques in her arms while Beau had walked along beside her. Dominique had held her head high. And, as though nothing had transpired in the months she'd been away, she seemingly eased back into her previous role, but Claire knew it had taken a great deal of courage to make the transformation. They had never discussed why Dominique had left Evon. But Claire knew Dominique loved Evon Forest and although she put up a good front, she knew Dominique was not happy and never would be without Evon. Then suddenly she blurted, "Nicki, what happened between you and Evon?" She quickly realized she'd overstepped her boundary and her hand flew to cover her mouth. When she saw the stunned expression on Dominique's face, Claire found herself asking softly, "I mean what went wrong?" Her tone was gentle as she added, "I know Evon loves you and I believe you love him—"

"You're wrong, Claire," Dominique corrected her cousin. Her memories of him were pure and clear and his name lingered around the edges of her mind as she unconsciously rearranged one tenacious curl on the top of Claire's head. Her thoughts filtered back to the day she met him. "Did I tell you the first time I met Evon I awoke naked in a strange bed and—" Dominique looked in the mirror at the startled expression on her cousin's face. She smiled and quickly changed the subject as she whispered eagerly, "Come. You're scheduled to begin shortly. We'll have to hurry or you'll be late for your debut."

Claire rose and slowly followed Dominique out of the cabin. She was no longer upset that she'd allowed her cousin to talk her into this. No, she thought, Nicki's pride kept her from talking about her misery, and although Dominique's words had shocked her, Claire knew Nicki needed her. If only Nicki would— "Pride can be as dangerous as jealousy. It can eat away at your insides until there's nothing left but a shell," she muttered.

Dominique paused and turned to stare at Claire. "Pride? Whose pride?" she asked.

"Yours!" Claire said angrily.

"Mine? Whatever are you talking about, Claire?" And when Claire didn't answer, Dominique continued toward the casino.

The customers were overjoyed with Claire. Dominique had divided her attention between Claire and Wyatt. While Claire sang her eyes continually strayed to Wyatt sitting in a front row table. Wyatt's first reaction after Claire had walked out on stage had been one of shock, but he soon relaxed and his eyes never left Claire. Dominique looked up and watched as Claire's nimble fingers danced across the keyboard of the piano. Dominique smiled as she realized that each song Claire sang she sang as though it had been written especially for Wyatt. Claire finished her last song, and Wyatt stepped forward to escort her from the stage.

Dominique watched as Claire and Wyatt exchanged glances, and she wondered if they shared a special message—a message two people share who are in love. She had to stop thinking like this. She sighed and turned away and hurried through the crowded casino to the tiny office. She felt drained, hollow, lifeless, but she had a mountain of book work to do before she could retire for the night.

An hour later, Dominique closed the ledger and leaned back in the straight-backed chair. She stretched and rolled her head back on her shoulders. She should get up and go to bed, but she continued to sit behind the desk as she nibbled on the end of her pen. "Pride?" she whispered aloud and shook her head. Impossible! Claire was mistaken. Claire wasn't aware of the unusual condition upon which their marriage had been based. She didn't know how wrong she was or how far from the truth she'd been when she had said Evon loved her. Claire had made it sound as though all she had to do was go to him and Evon would welcome her with open arms. Claire made it sound so simple and easy, but that wasn't the way of it, *non,* if it were she would run all the way back to Belle Terre and Evon's arms. She sighed and lay her head down on the desk. *Mon Dieu,* she thought, why had she complicated her life by falling in love with Evon?

Dominique raised her head and rubbed her eyes. She thought of Evon and what might have been. A sob tore at her heart and she covered her face with her hands. As far as Evon was concerned she was no longer necessary, no longer a part of his life. Why can't I forget? Put him out of my mind as he has me? she wondered painfully. "Because I love him," she whispered aloud.

The following day, Claire went in search of Dominique, and when she stepped onto the promenade deck she saw Dominique staring out at the cool, muddy water and she felt a heart-wrenching pain and realized the time had come to try and reason with her cousin. She walked over to Dominique. "Nicki, please—talk to me," she pleaded softly.

Dominique gripped the railing until her knuckles turned white. "What should I say, Claire? That ours was not a real marriage—a mockery—an arrangement—and both Evon and I were caught up in circumstances that made it necessary to marry? Then after Jacques's death there was no reason to continue with the role we'd been playing, not even the birth of our son. I didn't want to go along with Evon's offer, but I was already carrying his child and I had no choice. I had no idea what it would cost me—the humiliation, the embarrassment, the pain . . ." Her voice caught on a sob and she couldn't go on. She had not known she would fall in love, nor that he would take her heart, her very soul, and toss it away. She could not look at Claire as she asked, "Is that what I should say? Make a complete fool of myself—"

"Nicki—" Claire sobbed. She had never seen Dominique this way—shattered. She took her into her arms. Her cousin's sorrow was her sorrow and hot tears welled up and spilled onto her cheeks. "I am so sorry. I have intruded where I had no right," she apologized sincerely.

Dominique felt hot moisture gather behind her lids. She blinked rapidly. She would not cry. She would not shed another tear over the likes of a man who had practically pushed her out of his house. Evon wanted his freedom, well, she thought angrily, he could have it! She didn't care—not anymore. "It's over, Claire," she said flatly. Then she inhaled deeply, and added shakily, "Besides, whatever would I do on a plantation where servants do all the chores? Why," she said brightly, "I didn't even have to do my own hair, and I had a personal maid who even washed my back for me." Silently she had to admit that she had enjoyed being pampered, she had even become adept at planning meals and supervising the household servants. And, she thought sadly, after seeing the way Jacques had outwitted the servants, she had taken over his care—loving a challenge. She had coddled and taunted and, *oui*, she had even tricked Jacques into taking the awful tasting medicinal draft he hated. Under her close scrutiny he had eaten his meals and she had rewarded him by reading his favorite verses, and she had insisted on naming their son after his grandfather. After his birth she'd seen to it that her son became as familiar with the exterior of the plantation as she had become, and when she took the infant in to see Jacques he would smile and play with the baby for hours. She would miss Jacques. And Beau had loved being at Forest Manor. He loved Evon and D'Arcy. He'd beamed at being allowed to accompany the two men on their daily field inspection. And—she remembered—he had gained weight. Beau had been happy at Forest Manor and he had acquired an appetite to match D'Arcy's—well, not quite, she admitted, perhaps she was exaggerating a bit. No one could eat as much as D'Arcy, not even Evon who was definitely not a slouch when it came to food. She smiled and a tear slipped unheeded down her cheek. And then there was the pony Beau had had to leave behind. Evon had given Blackie to Beau his first morning at Forest Manor. She knew Beau missed Blackie—and D'Arcy—but most of all she knew her young brother missed Evon. She missed Evon and above all else she had enjoyed being near Evon. Dominique sighed. This was something she had fought against, this reminiscing. She stepped back and smiled at Claire. "I think I'll check on Jacques. I put him down for a nap and Beau is watching him. It's been over an hour and I'm sure Beau would rather be here on deck, putting Napolean through the paces or commandeering an imaginary ship, than sitting in the cabin watching his nephew."

"If you should need to talk again—I'm a good listener," Claire offered.

Dominique nodded. Suddenly she felt her spirits lift and she hugged Claire fiercely.

# Twenty-Seven

"Forest Manor?" Henri exclaimed puzzled. "But, but—" he sputtered. Henri stared incredulously at Evon. Had the boy lost his mind?

"Forest Manor is yours, Henri," Evon repeated patiently. "I want you to have it. You can move your things in immediately. I'll be leaving tomorrow. If—if you should need anything I'll be at Belle Terre."

"I don't know what to say. Does this mean you—"

"Does it really matter?" he interrupted. "What happened was a long time ago. I've recently discovered how futile it is to dwell in the past." Evon sighed.

"I loved your mother with all my heart, Evon. No wait!" he insisted and held up his hand. "I want you to listen. To hear—all of it. Please," he asked and when Evon remained silent he continued, "It started a long time before you or Wyatt were born. I—I fell in love with your mother when

Celeste was still a young girl—it seems I loved her all her life. And that love blossomed and grew until I thought I would die with wanting her. And—however hard this is for you to accept—your mother returned that love . . ." Henri paused as a wealth of memories flooded his thoughts.

"Really Henri—I don't see how this is going to do either of us a damn bit of good," Evon said tersely. He glared at Henri.

Evon's interruption intruded on Henri's reverie. Henri cleared his throat and quickly insisted, "Hear me out. I wanted to marry your mother—but marriage was out of the question—at least in Louisiana. So I tried talking her into going away with me, up North—where no one gave a damn. I—I begged her. We could have married and our children—" He stopped abruptly glancing up at Evon. Evon was gazing at him intently, but he said nothing and Henri sighed and continued. "We could have had so much more than—"

"What the hell are you saying, Henri?"

"My father and your maternal grandfather had betrothed Jacques and your mother the day Celeste was born," he explained. And he thought, even now, all these years later, he still felt the pain, raw and piercing . . . He sighed once more. "And when, two days before the scheduled wedding, my father discovered me and your mother together, he forbade me to see Celeste again—ever. I had no choice but to obey him. He was my father. And then nine months after their wedding—you were born. We knew—Celeste and I—"

"You lie!" Evon glowered. His face darkened

and he balled his hands into fists. "You stand here and think I would believe such a blatant lie?" he seethed, and he trembled in anger. He would listen to no more and he gave Henri his back and strode from the room, slamming the door with such force the walls vibrated. In the hall, Evon paused momentarily, then he took the stairs two at a time and walked briskly down the hall to his apartment. Inside his bedroom he stuffed several items of clothing into a satchel. His thoughts raced. He had to get out of there. Snapping the valise shut he left the room and retraced his steps back downstairs. As he passed the study Henri stepped out in front of him. He did not break his stride, but sidestepped Henri. When Henri called out his name Evon walked out the front door and didn't look back. Distance, he thought, distance . . .

Evon stepped down from the horse's back. He let the reins trail behind him. He made his way to a small rise and stood and gazed out at the even and gently flowing rows of sugarcane standing in the field. He sat down and drew his legs up draping his arms over his bent knees. He'd lost his father, and his wife had left him and taken their son.

Henri's words came back to haunt him. Henri and his mother—Jacques wasn't his father. It wasn't true—it couldn't be true. And Dominique—how he missed her and their son and Beau . . .

During the weeks after Dominique had left, he'd been unable to sleep, unable to eat. He'd been back at Belle Terre a week. His nights had been filled with memories of Dominique—her softness, her passion—and during the day he saw her in every room. And then there had been Henri's words. Doubt plagued him—his father—his mother—his brother—Henri—and his son. And always Dominique . . .

He reached down and picked up a handful of soil. He sifted the rich soil through his fingers. "Dominique," he whispered aloud. And suddenly he wondered if perhaps his mother and Henri had felt as he felt? Had they loved as he loved? Was their pain unbearable as his was . . . ?

He rose and brushed the dirt from his trousers. He straightened and pausing he envisioned Jacques as a young man standing in the shadows of his marriage while his wife and brother betrayed him. Evon shook his head, but he was unable to free himself as memories of his youth flashed precariously in and out of his mind's eye—carefree, happy—and then his discovery—the crushing blow he'd suffered when he'd found his mother in the arms of his uncle. And later, Henri arriving at Forest Manor and Jacque's arm around Henri, unsuspecting. Dominique suddenly interrupted his thoughts—she was in his arms, his mouth covered hers, and then . . . suddenly he was no longer himself, but Henri, and Dominique transformed into a vision of his mother. Had Henri been truthful? And his father—business trips when he had been away for weeks, months at a time—and when he returned, there had been gifts for everyone. And then he realized he'd never seen his father take his mother in his arms. He'd never seen his father kiss his mother . . . Had his father known? His head throbbed. He raised his head, pursed his lips, and gave a shrill whistle. Saladin trotted up to him. Evon inserted his foot in the stirrup and stepped up and swung his leg across the stallion's back. He clamped his knees into the horse's sides and Saladin dug his hooves into the soft sandy loam.

Back at the stable of Belle Terre, Evon rubbed the blanket vigorously over Saladin's damp hide.

On the ride back, Evon had given the stallion his head, and the wind in his face had helped relieve his aching temples and helped somewhat to vent the tension of these last few months. Evon ran the coarse material down the stallion's leg. When he'd finished he stood and tossed the blanket over the top rail of the saddle rack. Then he led Saladin into his stall. He called to the groom and asked him to brush the horse, and when the groom appeared Evon handed him the lead rope and left the stable.

Later, in his study, Evon studied the glass he held thoughtfully. His vision blurred. He smiled. It had been a long time since he'd overindulged. He leaned back in the plush leather chair. Unconsciously he swayed the chair back and forth. The rhythm soothed his frayed nerves. He yawned and relaxed, closed his eyes and fell into a deep and, for the first time in months, dreamless sleep.

"Evon!"

Evon awoke with a start.

"Here you are." Wyatt laughed as he walked through the door and flopped onto the sofa across from where Evon sat at his desk. Wyatt loosened the top button of his shirt. He reached for the half empty bottle on the desktop. He picked up a glass and for the first time he looked at his brother. Wyatt let out a long, low whistle. "You look bad, real bad, big brother. Tied on a good one, huh," he said good-naturedly and chuckled as he splashed an ounce of bourbon into his own glass. Wyatt leaned back and sipped the amber-colored liquid all the while gazing over the rim of his glass at Evon. Wyatt swirled the fiery liquor around the inside of his mouth and swallowed. Unconsciously he took another sip and then rested the empty glass on his knee. "Want to bend my ear?" Wyatt asked and gave Evon a lopsided grin.

"I hear you're not the only bastard in the Forest family," Evon snarled, and reached for the bottle.

"Ev—" Wyatt began and his expression sobered.

"Tell me—am I the last to hear? Imagine all these years, everyone laughing their asses off behind my back."

"I'm sorry, Evon, but you refused to listen. You didn't want to believe—and, *oui,* I suppose there are those who have guessed at the truth."

"I don't give a damn who—Wye—I—"

"Don't Ev. Hell, does it really matter whose seed was planted and who—"

"You're damn right it matters! It matters that Henri waited all these years to bare his guilt," Evon growled.

"Would you have listened? Henri loved our mother—" Wyatt poured himself another drink and then he glanced up at Evon and flinched at the naked pain he saw in his brother's eyes. Evon sat staring into his own half empty glass, and Wyatt cleared his throat. "You can't change what happened, Ev. Henri and Mother found themselves in an impossible situation. Besides, it didn't seem to affect Jacques or his life," he paused. "Hell, Ev, Jacques never complained. He had everything he wanted and needed a few hundred miles up the river. His mistress has been dead about ten years now, but his son and daughter still live in St. Louis—let it go, Ev."

"Mistress? Son and daughter?" Evon asked incredulously of Wyatt. Then he choked, "Is there anything you'd like to add? Another tidbit you'd like to toss my way?" Had he been blind? All those years! He slammed his fist down on the desktop. "How the hell—"

"You looked the other way. Ev. Henri tried on several occasions to tell you, but you never gave him the chance to set the record straight, to clear the air. You hated Henri, and you hated our mother. You shut them out—and you shut me out," Wyatt accused softly.

Unable to hide the bitterness in his voice, Evon insisted, "I'd like to be alone." He refused to look at Wyatt and he didn't see the pain on his brother's face.

Wyatt stood. He stared at his brother's haggard visage and shrugged. "You know where to find me . . ."

* * *

"Walk on deck with me, Claire," Wyatt said and offered Claire his arm.

Claire had sung her last song and when she stepped down from the stage Wyatt had been there to escort her through the crowded casino. He steered her through the crowd in the direction of the swinging doors. Her heart was thumping inside her chest and her fingers ached to reach out and draw his head down to hers. When he asked her to walk on deck with him she didn't answer but slipped her arm anxiously through his. His gaze held hers as he pushed open the door and together they strolled along the promenade deck.

Later, Wyatt paused in the dim light and gazed into her amber-colored eyes. "Fool's gold," he murmured and he took her in his arms and, groaning, he covered her mouth. He raised his head and pulled her gently against him and whispered against her temple, "I think I'm falling in love with you, Claire."

Claire inhaled sharply. "Oh Wyatt!" She breathed aloud. She'd wanted so much to hear him say those words. "I love you so—" she began. She couldn't believe that Wyatt, so handsome, so suave, so— "But that's not possible, I mean you're so—and I'm not pretty and I'm much too tall and—"

"You're beautiful, *chérie,*" he said and quickly added, "and if we stay here much longer I'm afraid I'll do something we might both regret later. I seem to be having trouble keeping my hands to myself." Wyatt exhaled audibly.

Claire could not believe his words. Her heart sang. When Wyatt again tucked her arm through his, she sighed and squeezed his arm and they moved out of the shadows and strolled once more among the gamblers and hostesses.

Evon waited until the last passenger had left the riverboat. Lance Martin stepped on deck and as he held the door for Dominique, Evon lifted a brow. When Lance took her arm and tucked it through his and moved with her toward the gangplank, Evon's eyes turned dark and threatening. Then when Lance paused and turned to Dominique and took her hand from the crook of his arm and bent and kissed it, Evon's mood turned thunderous. It wasn't the customary kiss that bothered Evon. It was the way Lance lingered over her hand that was making him see red! His patience had worn thin and he stepped from the shadows. "Good evening." His voice, though quiet, held an ominous tone.

"What?" Lance blurted. Startled he jerked his head around to where Evon stood behind him.

"You were leaving?" Evon insinuated.

"Umm," Lance mused, staring at the fire flashing from Evon's eyes. When he looked back at Dominique and noticed the brightness that hadn't been there a moment before, he frowned. "So it seems." Lance exhaled and stepped onto the boarded walkway, and in doing so he gave a wide berth to Evon who quickly stepped past him.

*"Oui."* Lance smiled. "So it seems." Somewhat reluctantly, Lance took another step and lit a cheroot. Then tossing the lucifer away he walked down the gangplank and stepped onto the street where he hailed a passing cab. He didn't look back.

"How dare you be so—so insulting, so demanding?" Dominique hissed and spun around, but his fingers on her wrist brought her back and up against him.

"I dare, *chérie,* because you happen to be my wife," he said huskily.

Fire flew from her eyes and when she would have protested he quickly dipped his head and captured her parted lips in a bruising kiss. Dominique made fists and beat on his arms. And then suddenly his lips gentled. When he slipped his tongue between her teeth she felt her heart leap precariously and vibrate against her breast and her pulse skittered alarmingly. Slowly he lifted his head and looked into her eyes. His gaze was so compelling she felt riveted to the spot. Her breath was coming in short spurts and she felt her control slipping. She probed into his glazed stare. Her heart did a flip-flop. Mirrored in his dark eyes—was it passion she saw? Lust? And—there was something else. *Non!* she admonished herself mentally. Foolish woman, she chastised herself silently. You are imagining things. He does not love you. But somehow she wasn't convinced—she had seen something—something tangible. Perhaps, she reasoned silently, lust and love were so closely related that she could not tell the difference. And suddenly she did not care what she had or had not seen in their depth—Evon wanted her. She could feel it, and accompanying it was an overwhelming sense of well-being, a closeness with this man who held her in his arms. And she wanted to remain in his arms forever, to— Was she being foolish? Ask him, an inner voice cried. Ask him? *Non.* Then before she lost her nerve, she blurted, "You don't want me, but you don't want anyone else to have me. Is that it, Evon? Is that how you feel? Well, let me tell you I won't stand for you stepping in and out of my life when the mood suits you," she choked as she twisted out of his grasp to stand haughtily before him. Who was he to think he could toss her out of his life like so much excess baggage only to walk back into her life, to dictate her comings and goings when the notion struck him. Well, he had another thought coming! "And furthermore, M'sieur—"

"You talk too much, *chérie,*" he whispered and before she realized what was happening he drew her back into his embrace. "Umm, you smell good. You feel so soft and warm and—I want you so badly I can't sleep, I can't eat—I need you. Come with me, *chérie.* Come back with me to Belle Terre."

She drew her breath in sharply. "You want me! And what am I to be? Your whore? You have gone too far this time. What you ask is too much, M'sieur! Release me—release me now or I shall scream," she demanded. Her body was stiff and her voice shook.

"My whore? *Non, chérie,* I am not asking that

you be my whore. I want you. I want you and our son. I want you for all the reasons a man wants his wife at his side. I want you with me always. I want your body beneath me—" he moaned and recaptured her swollen lips.

Her eyes stood open and her body trembled at his words. How was it she had thought she loved this man?, she asked herself silently. She felt his fingers hot and scorching on her bare skin as he undid several of the tiny pearl buttons. The audacity! She gasped and brought her hand up in protest, but when his tongue entered her mouth and he covered her breast with his palm, her hand paused in midair and all her anger dissolved. Suddenly it didn't matter. *Non,* nothing mattered except that he was here, and she was in his arms. She closed her eyes and pressed her length against him. When he held her he made her feel warm and protected. And if he didn't love her, she knew he was attracted to her—and knowing that he wanted her, for now was enough . . .

He lifted his head. "I want you and Beau and Jacques to leave with me, now, and return to Belle Terre," he whispered. There was a gruffness and a husky undertone in his voice.

"I can't just leave—Claire and Hetty need me . . ." Dominique whispered. Her thoughts raced. If she went with him would he tire of her, and then what? He walked in and out of her life wrecking her stability and ripping her very soul apart to suit his fancy. And when he had once more had his fill of her—what then? Return to the riverboat once more? While the days had been filled with the activities of the boat, the nights had been torturous. Each night she'd dreamed of Evon and had awoken, her body drenched in perspiration. Those dreams had left her trembling. *Non!* she screamed silently. She would not go through that again. Yet she heard herself saying, "I'll need help with the packing and—both boys are asleep and—" Had she really said those things? *Non,* she protested inwardly, I can't subject myself to that again . . . She squeezed her eyes shut praying silently for strength to overcome whatever it was that drew her, like a magnet, to Evon. Yet she found herself wishing with all her heart that he loved her, that he take her in his arms, that he make love to her. Suddenly she knew she would not let him use her—and then—

"I want you, *chérie,* and you want me. There is our son to think of—and Beau," he reasoned quietly. He ached inside. His loins burned and he moved suggestively against her. What did he have to do to make her understand how much he loved her? "This is no place to raise Beau or our son," he growled. Somehow he had to make her realize how much she meant to him. Then he stiffened. She would come with him. She was his wife, he determined silently.

So that was it. His concern lay with the unsavory atmosphere of the wharf. He had not thought twice when he had sent her back to the wharf, but now it wasn't respectable enough to raise their son!

*"Chérie?"* he prodded her gently.

He was looking at her so—and his voice was

almost a caress as though he really felt—her skin tingled at the possibility. Stop it! a small voice admonished her silently and she scoffed at her own wishful thinking. She had been quick to condemn Evon after he'd admitted his need of her. Yet, what of her own riotous emotions? He stood so close she felt heat radiating from his body, and a delightful shiver ran through her. Suddenly she was glad he had come. She would go with him and when he tired of her—*Non!* He would not tire of her, she would see that he didn't. Evon was here and she must concentrate on now—later would take care of itself . . . And if things didn't work out she would worry about that when the time came—perhaps, just perhaps she could make him fall in love with her again. She could play the coquette . . . "You'll have to help me with Jacques," she said, and quickly swallowed past the lump in her throat and prayed with all her heart that she'd made the right decision.

# Twenty-Eight

"That's wonderful, Nicki, but I shall miss you terribly," Claire said tearfully. Wyatt had walked Claire to her cabin, and his lips had brushed hers. Afterward she had fairly floated into her room where she had changed into her nightgown. Unable to sleep she heard Jacques wail and had opened her cabin door. Evon had blocked the way. He held a whimpering Jacques. He smiled and had motioned her into Beau's room where she watched while Hetty and Dominique quickly stuffed articles of the boy's clothing into a bag. As her eyes moved to where Beau sat half asleep and half dressed on his bunk, she quickly realized that Dominique and the boys were leaving with Evon. She smiled.

"Belle Terre is less than an hour's drive. You and Hetty are welcome to visit whenever you want," Evon said in a low voice so as not to wake his now sleeping infant son.

*"Oui!* And I shall find a million excuses to

return to the city and we can shop and have lunch and—" Dominique said in a rush until her voice broke. Claire knew her cousin would miss her and Hetty, and she also knew she would again be in charge of the riverboat. The added responsibility would be worth it if it meant Dominique would be happy. Smiling tearfully, Dominique hugged Claire and then turned and took Jacques from Evon.

Their ride to Belle Terre had been a silent one. Jacques had remained asleep, and Beau had fallen asleep as soon as the carriage moved away from the wharf. Dominique had held Jacques on her lap while Evon had sat on the seat across from her with Beau's head resting in his lap. After making sure that Jacques was comfortable she'd leaned her head back against the plush upholstery and closed her eyes.

Less than an hour later, the carriage pulled up in front of Belle Terre and stopped. "Can you manage our son? The servants have all retired, but if he's too heavy I can carry Beau up first and come back and relieve you of our little Hercules there," he mused softly.

It was the first time either had spoken since they'd left the city. Although she was exhausted, she smiled at his humorous remark.

"Non. He's asleep and I don't want to chance his waking up. He would not want to go back to sleep," Dominique said.

Evon stepped down and Dominique waited for the coachman to assist her from the carriage. Evon waited until she was beside him, he smiled, and together they carried the sleeping boys up the steps and into the house.

The following morning Evon was up and about before Dominique had awakened. After she had fed Jacques and had peeked in at the still sleeping Beau she had made her way downstairs and into the dining room.

"Missy!" Blossom cried when she saw Dominique coming through the doorway. She set the steaming platter of bacon down and hurried over to hug Dominique. "Ah's so glad yous hom'."

"Oh Blossom. I'm so glad to see you and it's good to be here," Dominique said softly.

"Heah. Set yousef down and et," the dark-skinned woman said, and bustled about the kitchen. After Dominique was seated, Blossom smiled brightly and hurried from the room to fetch her mistress's eggs and biscuits from the warming oven.

Dominique reached for the silver pitcher and poured herself a cup of café au lait. She sat and sipped the hot coffee. Then a few minutes later, Blossom hurried back into the room and set two platters on the table. "Ah's sho glad y'all hom', missy. Yas ah is. Dis ol' hous' wuzn't de sam' widout y'all."

"Thank you, Blossom. I was so exhausted last night that after I tucked the baby in his crib, I fell into bed with all my clothes on and I can't remember laying my head on the pillow," she laughed.

Evon had gone to bed shortly after Dominique. She was already asleep and he'd smiled and cradled her in his arms and held her there the remainder of the night.

Evon had drifted off to sleep a little before dawn, and when he'd awoken a few hours later, he'd remembered that D'Arcy would be arriving within the hour. He had not wanted to disturb Dominique, and he had eased his arm from beneath her shoulders and rose and quickly donned his clothes. He'd frowned as he realized sadly that he would not see her again until the supper hour and bent to brush his lips lightly over hers, lingering until he felt a familiar tightening in his loins. Before he changed his mind he straightened and quickly strode from the room.

Blossom left the dining room, and Dominique picked at her food as she wondered how she should go about attracting Evon, making him interested in more than just her body. She decided to ask Florrie to watch Jacques and keep an eye on Beau for a few hours—she would ride out, find Evon . . .

Blossom bustled into the dining room just as Dominique pushed back her plate. The large woman frowned but cleared the dishes from the table. "Yous dint et much, missy, but ah'll fix yous a big lunch. Ah's sho glad yous hom'—yas ah is."

"Me too, Blossom," Dominique said brightly. And then suddenly she sobered. She had made up her mind and she was anxious to put her thoughts into action. She would pursue Evon relentlessly, and if need be she would seduce him— Stop it! You're here, can't you be satisfied with that? a voice nagged. *Non!* she fumed silently. She would make him love her . . . "I wasn't very hungry," she mumbled, and then with renewed confidence she asked, "Is Florrie at the cabin?"

"Naw'm, dat chile don' run offen," Blossom said sadly.

*"Non!* Ran off? But where would she go?"

"Ah's don' rightly knows, missy. Mebbe she wid dat voodoo queen, Marie Lavernau," she said, and the huge woman lifted her apron and dabbed at her tear-filled eyes. "Massa gonna whoop dat chile good wen he finds 'er."

*"Non.* Blossom. No one is going to beat Florrie," Dominique said firmly. She turned to leave, but when she felt Blossom's hand on her shoulder, she paused and turned back to the dark woman.

Blossom reached into a fold in her skirt and pulled out a crumpled scrap of paper. "Ah's cain't red, but—"

Dominique took the piece of paper and stared down at the scribbled letters. She read it quickly and gasped, "I have to go out for a while." Dominique hurried out the door and in her haste the crinkled paper slipped from her fingers.

"So. You came. But then I knew you would." Jules said and jerked Dominique inside, sliding the door closed and sliding the bar back in place. He turned and grabbed her by the shoulders and brought her up against him and devoured her with his mouth. She gasped and he slid his tongue between her teeth, but when he felt her gag he flung her away from him. "You'll get used to a lot more than my tongue, *ma petite*. If you think to balk I'll be forced to punish you—umm," he mused as he walked around her and rested his chin in the palm of his hand. "Or better yet I'll punish, what's her name?" When Dominique remained silent, he said, "Florrie, isn't it?" He withdrew a long-bladed knife and Dominique's eyes widened fearfully. He smiled and grasped Dominique's wrist and dragged her through the foul-smelling warehouse. At the far end lay Florrie, tied and gagged. Jules released Dominique and when she attempted to go to Florrie, he restrained her. Jules then walked to where Florrie lay on her back and with the toe of his boot he rolled the frightened girl onto her side and bent down and sliced through the rope binding her hands behind her back. He jerked her to her feet, but he did not remove the gag. "You are to bring Evon Forest back here, to me. Do you understand?" he demanded as he glared at Florrie with burning, reproachful eyes.

Jules's temper when crossed became uncontrollable, and when the girl did not immediately answer him, but looked pleadingly at her mistress, he reached out and jerked Florrie to him and slapped her across one cheek. Dominique gasped, but Florrie didn't make a sound. Instead she moved her head up and down. "Go! And be quick. Your mistress's life depends on you doing and saying exactly as I've instructed," he taunted. He smiled ferally at the girl and gave her a violent shove. Florrie stumbled, but she managed to regain her balance and without a word ran from the building.

Jules turned back to Dominique and said, "You know what I must do, *chérie.* Turn around. I have to leave, but first I must tie your hands and make sure you can't scream and alert any of the rousters working nearby. I'll be back before the girl returns with your stallion and with luck your husband will bring his brother—" He paused and watched her puzzled expression. "That way the authorities will think the brothers fought over the girl and then they killed each other." Jules watched as tears gathered in her eyes and slid down her cheeks. Then he threw back his head and laughed raucously and turned and left Dominique to stare after him.

Dispose of Evon? *Non!* she screamed silently and twisted her wrists viciously. Jules was a madman! After he had kidnapped her that first time she had discovered that he was not the man she had thought him to be. She knew he was insane and as she thought of the trap Jules had set for Evon and Wyatt she increased her struggles to free herself. When her body became drenched in perspiration, to her relief she felt the rope loosen and she slipped her hand through the knot. She gasped. She was free!

Dominique scrambled to her feet and ran toward the other end of the warehouse. She was within a few yards of the entrance and freedom when she heard the scraping of the iron bar as someone slid it back. The door opened and Jules stood in the doorway. She froze. *"Non!"* she screamed. "I will not be your prisoner, nor will I suffer your vile ravings again."

She began to run toward Jules, unsure of what she would do when she reached him, but determined to escape—to claw him, to fight him with every ounce of strength within her. She determined that he would have to kill her to prevent her from leaving.

Jules paused and as he stared at her, she flew at him and attacked him with all the pent-up anger and frustration she had kept bottled inside her since Jules and Yvette had imprisoned her all those months ago. She clawed his face and kicked his shins. Her violence had momentarily stunned him, but he quickly recovered as her nails bit into his cheeks and he roared in pain as he grabbed her arms restraining her and slapped her hard across the face. She stumbled back and fell to the dirt floor. Before she could clear the cobwebs from her head he was upon her. His mouth came down hard on hers and his hand fumbled with her skirts. She could not move. She was pinned beneath him and sheer black fright swept through her until she thought she would faint. Icy fear twisted around her heart, but she refused to give in to this maniac. As she fought to remain conscious she was gripped with a sudden strength, and she began to struggle. She brought her knee up hard between his thighs and she felt a whoosh of air on her cheek as her knee connected with his genitals. Jules rolled from her and grabbed himself. She got to her hands and knees and as she gulped great deep breaths of air she quickly began to crawl on all fours away from him. She prayed silently, only a few feet and—but she felt him as he dove for her and grasped her around the waist. He held her in a death grip and rolled with her until she was on her back with him astraddle her. He slapped her several times. Bells sounded inside her head and her eyes glazed over and she felt herself losing consciousness as she weakened beneath him. Her head lolled from side to side and her vision blurred, but she remained conscious. In one sweep he tossed her skirts aside and he fumbled to undo his trouser buttons. Dominique blinked several times and as her senses returned she felt his throbbing member hot and hard against her naked flesh. Terror gripped her as he groped for her breast through her gown and squeezed painfully all the while probing. She screamed. He fell over her and devoured her with his mouth, plunging his foul-tasting tongue inside her mouth. Suddenly she clamped her teeth together and as her mouth filled with his blood, she gagged, but refused to let go.

He roared in pain and his hands came up and closed painfully around her neck. His fingers dug into her soft flesh cutting off her air and she knew she was going to die. Her thoughts turned to her infant son and to Evon.

Suddenly Jules was lifted from her and she rolled to her side. Inhaling deep gulps of air, oxygen flowed back into her lungs as she rolled away from the men.

"You lousy, rotten son of a bitch!" Evon spat out as his fist landed in Harcourt's face.

*Mon Dieu!* she thought as relief washed over her in waves. She struggled to her feet as Jules staggered backward. Before Jules regained his balance Evon was on him again, pummeling him with blows to the face and head. The sound of bone splintering sent a shiver along her spine. Evon came back with several blows to Jules's midsection and Jules doubled over. In the same instant, Evon brought his knee up and caught Jules square in the face. Jules crumpled to the dirt floor like a rag doll.

Dominique flew to Evon's side and he automatically curled an arm about her, his breath coming in short gasps.

"You are safe, *chérie*. That animal will never touch you again."

Her eyes wide, a residue of fright still mirrored there. "Is . . . he dead?" she whispered.

A twisted smile curved Evon's lips. "I don't think so, but I don't really care."

Dominique nodded, starting to shake with reaction. "*Mon Dieu!* I was so frightened. But you came . . . just when I needed you . . ."

He held her tightly for a moment. "I was almost too late," he whispered hoarsely.

A noise broke the tense moment and they looked up to see Wyatt, followed by D'Arcy and some uniformed policemen, bursting through the doorway.

Evon growled, "Lock the bastard up and throw the key in Lake Pontchartrain."

"I was afraid we were too late," Wyatt breathed. His face was pale as he slid his gun back into the leather casing beneath his jacket.

"What the hell's going on, Evon?" the lieutenant asked as he too holstered his weapon. He glanced back at Harcourt and sent one of his men to get a wagon.

Then Dominique heard someone sobbing softly somewhere behind the group of men. She stepped back and drew Evon's attention so he would release her.

Dominique hurried toward the heart-wrenching sound and discovered Florrie crouched down with her face buried in her hands. Her shoulders shook and Dominique bent and gently lifted the girl to stand before her. Florrie peeked between her fingers and seeing that her mistress was safe, she sobbed louder.

"Ssh, Florrie. It's all right," she soothed.

Hearing her mistress's kind words, Florrie put her arms around her and sobbed out all her guilt and sorrow.

Watching, Evon choked, "I returned to Belle Terre and Blossom handed me a note from Harcourt to come to a warehouse on the wharf, he didn't specify which warehouse—Christ! If Florrie hadn't found me when she did . . ." He let his words trail away, and ran his fingers through his hair.

Jules tried to open his eyes, but one was swollen shut. After a moment, his good eye focused on a gun belted on the hip of one of the officers. Evon's voice filled him with hatred. Evon and his brother stood before him—alive and well—while his own dear brother—his Reynard, the only person who ever cared what happened to him—lay dead in a damp, cold grave not eight blocks from this very spot. White-hot rage ran through his veins. Slowly he struggled to his hands and knees and then he was on his feet. He did not want to alert the men, and slowly he took a step forward and then another until he stood in back of the officer. An icy calm washed over him. He raised his hand and his fingers curled around the butt of the pistol. Without hesitation he slid the revolver from the policeman's worn holster.

At last he would avenge Reynard's death. First he would kill Wyatt Forest, determined that Evon watch as his brother died a slow and painful death. And it would be Jules who decided when to fire the fatal shot. Then he would kill Evon Forest. He would torture Evon in exactly the same manner as his brother. He would kill them both—suddenly the officer's hand flew to his empty holster. He spun around.

"What the hell do you think you're doing?" the policeman yelled.

Startled, Harcourt took several steps backward.

He ignored the man's question as the group turned, but his grip tightened on the gun. "Step out M'sieur Evon! Bring M'sieur Wyatt with you. Step out where I can see you," Harcourt demanded hoarsely.

Evon had been explaining the events that had taken place to Wyatt, D'Arcy, and the authorities. He had forgotten about Harcourt. He turned and cursed his carelessness. His eyes moved past the uniformed officers to where Harcourt stood.

Christ! Evon thought as he stared over the officer's shoulder at the half-crazed man. Harcourt's smile was grotesque in his swollen face. Evon inhaled and let it out. His mind raced. He had to get the gun away from Harcourt. Hell, he thought, he was the one Harcourt wanted. He took a step toward the gunman, but his way was blocked when the lieutenant stepped in front of him. He drew his brows together angrily and glared at the lieutenant. The lieutenant shook his head and turned toward Harcourt.

"Throw the gun down, Harcourt," the lieutenant called loudly.

Harcourt hissed, "Never!"

"You bastard!" Evon ground out between clenched teeth as his eyes moved back to glare at Harcourt. Evon stared at Harcourt. The man was unsteady as hell and at any minute his legs could buckle. If he collapsed the gun could discharge! A stray bullet—Dominique, Wyatt, or one of these men—any one of them could be shot, killed! He refused to stand by and do nothing. *Non,* he thought, he *would* not . . .

"Step aside gentlemen. The time has come to take *ma chérie* and leave," Jules said hoarsely as he waved the pistol back and forth at the men to emphasize his authority.

Evon stiffened at his words. He refused to think of what would happen if Dominique were to leave with him. He would not stand by and let that crazy lunatic take his wife—he had to do something! He had to get his hands on a weapon. His eyes darted around the circle of men. D'Arcy? *Non,* he knew D'Arcy had no weapon. He felt the hair rise on the back of his neck. And then he glanced at Wyatt! Wyatt was armed.

Evon moved forward a pace, putting Wyatt behind him.

Wyatt took this opportunity to slip his hand beneath his jacket until his hand touched the pearl-handled revolver. Slowly he lifted his gun from the waxed leather casing. Then he slid it downward until he felt Evon's hand cover his—expediently the brothers made the exchange.

Evon gripped the cold metal in his hand. His dark eyes sparked with white-hot rage as he glared past the officer's shoulders at Harcourt. He had to force himself to remain calm. Not to pull the trigger and shoot the crazed maniac before him, and his voice was cold and lashing as he commanded, "You're free to leave, Harcourt, but if you want to walk out of here alive, you'll leave alone." Evon's intent was to divert Harcourt's attention.

"How dare you threaten me! I am the one with the gun. You are a fool, M'sieur. I will leave with *ma chérie*, and no one will stop me," Jules roared.

Before anyone could stop him, Evon stepped away from his brother and the uniformed policemen. "Dominique is my wife. Mine, Harcourt!" he said coldly.

Harcourt raised the gun to take aim at the perfect target Evon presented, but his arm shook with pain.

Evon's arm snaked up and he squeezed the trigger, surprising the crazed man.

There was a flash and an explosion.

Harcourt blinked. He heard voices, but they were far away. He stared straight ahead—and then his knees buckled and he collapsed in a heap on the floor.

Dominique watched the hideous events take place as if in a dream. She gazed in horror at Jules, lying dead on the floor, and shuddered. It was finally over!

Suddenly, Evon was there, taking her in his arms, kissing her until her trembling stopped, until she grew warm beneath his touch.

He lifted his head and gazed into her eyes. She pulled his head back down and kissed him.

When the kiss ended, he cupped the back of her head and tilted her backward, and as his mouth grazed her earlobe, he whispered softly, "Not only has your affection aroused my passion, but I'm afraid it has stretched my trouser seams to near bursting. *Non!* do not step away . . . it could prove embarrassing . . ."

"What?" she asked. She knew she had been impulsive, and she was hurt by his reaction to their kiss. She thought Jules had severely injured—or perhaps even that he had killed Evon. She had been relieved beyond distraction and she'd had to touch him—to hold him, to kiss him, to—Suddenly the full meaning of his words penetrated her thoughts and her eyes widened and she felt her cheeks grow hot.

At her stunned expression, Evon threw back his head and roared with laughter. He felt a sharp twinge on his upper arm and when he realized she had pinched him, he quickly sobered and gazed into her brooding eyes. Softly he said, "I am sorry, *chérie.*"

# Twenty-Nine

After a warm bath Dominique had donned her nightdress and climbed into bed and was propped against the pillow.

She waited anxiously for Evon to come. She tingled at the thought of what this night would bring. He would be here soon, he'd said he would.

The police had taken Jules's body to the undertaker, and Evon, along with Wyatt and D'Arcy, had taken Dominique to the riverboat where Evon had instructed D'Arcy to take Beau and Jacques after he'd discovered Dominique's disappearance.

After a tearful reunion Evon had insisted that Beau and Jacques remain on the riverboat until the following morning. When Dominique had disagreed he'd hinted that he thought she needed to rest. When she'd shaken her head and indicated with her hands that she felt fine, he'd pulled her out into the gangway and whispered, "Please, *chérie,* give me this one night." She stared at him, and he'd taken her in his arms and pleaded, "That's all I ask, just one night." Unable to hide her smile she'd nodded her consent. Now the door opened and brought her out of her reverie as Evon appeared.

Their eyes met and locked.

Evon kicked the door closed with his heel and began to move slowly into the room, never taking his eyes from her. Evon's gaze swept over Dominique's body, taking in every exquisite curve. She had given him this night and he would use every minute to convince her that she was where she should be, where she wanted to be, and where she belonged—with him—forever.

No one could compare with Dominique. She was perfection in every way, and she was his. He would make her see that he loved her as no man ever loved a woman. She was his *chérie,* his Eve. He gazed at her lovely features and unbuttoned his shirt and flung it away. He quickly shed his remaining garments, and in two strides he was beside her.

"Aah, *chérie,* at last I have you all to myself," he whispered as he leaned over her and braced his hands on either side of her. He'd thought her lost to him, first when Harcourt had imprisoned her and then when she'd left him. And then when she'd been in the clutches of that madman a second time he'd nearly lost his mind. In a huskier voice, he added softly, "And, *ma chérie,* I mean this night to be one you'll remember and treasure always."

He held her mesmerized. A passionate fluttering arose at the back of her throat, she swallowed and took a deep breath and tried to relax. Her hands, hidden beneath the covers, twisted nervously. He kissed her gently on the mouth and her breath caught in her throat. Her heart thudded noisily within her. She loved him so. She sighed and prayed to be everything he expected—and more. She ran her eyes over his nakedness. His body, firm and hard with his staff swollen and standing erect, was proof that she affected his passionate side, and she knew he wanted her. And, she thought, she would make him continue to be attracted to her, every night for the rest of his life! Then she faltered, and before she could squelch it, doubt crept into her mind and unconsciously she frowned.

"What's this?" he asked. One brow rose slightly as he took her chin between his fingers. "Are you suddenly sad?" he asked softly. He knew that being unable to speak would frustrate a weaker person, but this was Dominique, and he felt certain mere frustration could not make her frown so. "Would you rather I didn't touch you? Perhaps after what you have been through you would prefer to be alone?" he questioned as he silently cursed his insensitivity, his selfishness. She had been pawed and nearly raped by that bastard and here he was wanting to prove how virile he was! "Damn!" he swore aloud, angry with himself. Then he stared down at her. "I am sorry, *chérie.*"

Leave her alone? *Non!* She shook her head back and forth. *Non,* she wailed silently. He frowned and she feared he would leave. Suddenly, she reached up and grasped his head between her hands and raised up and kissed him softly.

She released him and his insides flamed, but he called on all his restraint as he inhaled and said, "You have suffered greatly. I wasn't thinking. I realize that the touch of a man—any man—at this time would—hell, *chérie,* I can see how being in the clutches of that crazed pervert had to have been a nightmare, but with time you'll feel differently, and when that time comes you will honor me—"

She did not want his sympathy. She wanted him. When he reached up and she felt his fingers close on her wrists, she tightened her grip around his neck, refusing to turn loose until he understood what she had to explain to him.

Evon made a strangling noise and gently he tried to remove her arms. *"Chérie,* I think you misunderstood my mean—"

*Non!* If he left now all would be lost. She had to make him understand—that he wasn't Jules, that she wanted him to touch her, to make love to her, to— "Pl—please, don't leave me," she whispered in a garbled voice, and for a second she thought she'd wanted it so much that she'd merely said the words silently. But when he pulled back she saw the awesome expression on his handsome face and she knew she'd said the words aloud.

"Please . . . *ma cherie,"* he breathed, and crushed her to him, and when she would have pulled away he tightened his grip.

She had said the words aloud and she was glad she had. She felt her cheeks grow damp. She pulled her head back and smiled tremulously at Evon.

"Aah *chérie.* I want you. I need you. How I love

you," he whispered.

"What—What did you say?" she asked haltingly.

"I said I wa—"

*"Non!* You said—"

"I love you," he said simply. "I have loved you from the beginning."

Once more she was speechless, but it had nothing to do with fear. Her gaze was first one of surprise, then awe, and finally joy.

At her startled expression he smiled sadly and added, "I didn't realize—*non*—I wouldn't admit it, but—aah *chérie,* I know it now. I feel it every time I look at you, every time I hold you in my arms, every time I kiss your sweet lips, and *oui,* every time I make love to you. My heart sings when I am with you, and it hurts like hell when you're not with me," he said. Then he smiled and added, "And if ever you should even think of leaving—be warned *chérie*—by comparison, Jules Harcourt was a lamb."

"A lamb? Ummm, then you M'sieur—do you know what you are? You are a lion—my lion," she said sensuously.

"M'sieur? *Non*—lion? Ah *chérie,* I like that," he said softly as they lay back on the bed and he dipped his head and nuzzled the hollow of her neck. The caress was a command. She moaned and a shudder passed through her. Then he lifted his head and when his mouth swooped down to capture her lips, she felt buffeted by the winds of a savage harmony. He slid his tongue inside her mouth sending shivers of delight coursing through her and when his hand began to roam over her body, pausing to explore her sensuous parts, she began to move seductively beneath him. His hand closed over her breast and he sought and found the vee between her thighs with his other hand. She cried out and clutched his head in her hands. He gently massaged the tiny nubbin hidden within the soft curls, and when he slipped one finger inside she gasped. Her body trembled and she pleaded, "Evon, oh Evon." Her pleasure brought a groan to his lips and he took one rosy globe in his mouth and sucked gently. He released her breast as his tongue laved her hot, moist skin, trailing down her abdomen. He removed his finger and grasped her smooth silken buttocks and lifted her, her musk drawing him ever closer, and he kissed the inside of each thigh. Then his tongue flicked out, finding her secret place that she shared with him. She gave a little cry of pleasure and he sucked until he felt her body convulse again and again.

As the last wave of ecstasy washed over her and her breathing slowed he lifted his head and gazed longingly upon her lovely face, and whispered, "You are ready, *chérie.*" Moving over her he entered her swiftly. He paused, glorying in her hot, wet tightness. Then he began to move.

She felt his rod pulsing against her warmth and she emulated him as he picked up the pace and drove into her faster and faster. Love flowed in her like warm honey. She breathed in soul-drenching drafts as she felt herself being lifted and hurled out into space where her body melted against him and she fantasized an even greater ecstasy. She gasped in sweet agony as suddenly she shattered into a million glowing stars.

Evon heard her gasp and when he felt her release he, too, climaxed as his pleasure pure and explosive overwhelmed him and he felt himself throbbing inside her, over and over as he spilled his seed into her.

Later, with Evon's arms around her, Dominique lay drowned in a flood tide of the liberation of the mind and body. She sighed closing her eyes as contentment and peace flowed between them. She felt drowsy and she replayed Evon's words again in her mind. How I love you. She smiled.

Evon's eyes were closed. He held Dominique against him never wanting to let her go. He'd nearly lost her. He would not tempt fate again. He swore to watch over her and protect her with his life.

Unconsciously he rubbed his chin against her forehead and then he brushed his lips over her temple. He held one firm breast in the palm of his hand. He ran his thumb over her nipple and when it became taut he felt himself harden. He inhaled and tried to bring his fast growing desire under control, but when Dominique's eyelids fluttered open and she smiled lazily up at him, he brushed his mouth across her lips. When her lips parted and he felt her naked thigh on his leg he rolled to his back taking her with him. She lay on top of him.

Slowly and deliberately he pushed his tongue between her straight, white teeth and sensuously moved his tongue in and out. He released her mouth and gazed into her eyes. "You are the most beautiful woman in the world, *chérie.* You are my life, my soul, my very existence. Without you to share my life I would shrivel up and waste away. I shall love and cherish you always. I love you with all my heart."

"I will never again leave you. You are the man I love, my champion, my lion, and the father of my children," she said softly. Her love shone brightly in her eyes.

"Children? What are you saying, *chérie?*" he asked, puzzled. And when she smiled shyly, he took her face between his hands and gazed intently into her eyes. She nodded and blushed. "You are with child?" he whispered softly.

*"Oui."* She touched her fingertips to his lips.

"How far along are you?" he asked excitedly and took her hand in his.

"At least two months."

"You were pregnant when you left Forest Manor to return to the riverboat."

*"Oui,* but I did not realize it until a few weeks later and then I thought it was too late, and—"

"Aah *chérie.* I should have insisted you stay."

"Your father had died and I thought you had no further use of me—the bargain—"

"That damn bargain. Never, and I mean this literally, never should either of us ever mention that ridiculous agreement again. I never meant to hurt you."

"Nor I you, but if not for our arranged marriage we would not be here tonight."

"Umm," he agreed. "Perhaps it wasn't so ridiculous after all," he said. "And if my father—Jacques—hadn't added that damn codicil, and me trying to outwit him—*non*, you are right."

"Why did you say Jacques?" she asked puzzled. She had never heard Evon refer to his father as anything but Father.

"Aah *chérie*. It seems we have things to discuss. Jacques was not my father. Henri is my father," he sighed.

"What are you saying?"

"Henri and my mother were lovers."

She saw the pain on his handsome features and her heart ached. "Oh Evon! Does it really matter? You had the best of Jacques and if you'll let him—Henri is a good man. I don't know what happened, but I'm sure the years have been as hard, perhaps even worse, for Henri than for you and Wyatt."

"I realize that now more than ever. If I hadn't met and fallen in love with you, *chérie*, I would never have known the joy of loving and being loved. I could never have understood what Henri and my mother had gone through. My mother and Jacques were betrothed at birth—she was forced to marry, not the man she loved, but his brother. She carried Henri's seed on the night of her wedding and—and Wyatt isn't the only bastard to carry the Forest surname, and—"

"And it doesn't matter, Evon," she said softly.

Suddenly he recaptured her mouth. After several seconds he released her and whispered hoarsely, "*Mon Dieu*, I love you. I want you."

"Love me, Evon," she breathed against his mouth.

Evon slipped his hardness inside her. Their passion quickly soared and escalated until their bodies were in exquisite harmony. Together they reached the peak of delight and exploded in a downpour of fiery sensations.

Later, as they lay side by side, Dominique rested her head on Evon's chest. "Hetty is fond of D'Arcy. Did you know that?" she said, and stifled a yawn.

Her words broke the silence. Evon chuckled. "I think D'Arcy is smitten with your mammy. He asked my permission to call on her and soon."

"What did you tell him? Did you give your permission, or—" she began excitedly and sat up.

"Whoa!" he interrupted her and raised a hand in the air. "I told him it wasn't up to me, that that decision was not mine to make. *Chérie,* I want to give Hetty her freedom. I have signed her papers, and as anxious as D'Arcy appeared I knew D'Arcy would get them to her quicker than I could," he chuckled.

"You signed her papers? You gave her her freedom?" she interrupted him breathlessly.

*"Oui."*

She looked at him and her eyes filled and tears ran down her cheeks, "Thank you," she whispered.

He wiped her cheeks with his thumbs and then he kissed her gently. "There is something else you should know, if you don't already suspect—a wedding to celebrate—and soon," he said impishly.

Her eyes widened and she shook her head as she disagreed, *"Non,* they have only just met. They do not know each other well enough to get married."

*"Non, chérie.* I am not talking about D'Arcy and Hetty. I was referring to my brother and your cousin."

"Wyatt and Claire! Oh Evon, do you think so? How exciting. I had so hoped—*mon Dieu,* our family will grow—and oh Evon, I feel so—so—"

"I know *chérie,* I know." His eyes wrapped her in a cocoon of euphoria. He drew her into his arms.

She whispered, *"Oui,* my lion." He showered her with slow, drugging kisses and she knew that at last she was where she belonged. He rose above her and her body began to vibrate with liquid fire and the hot tide of passion once more raged through her veins.

Evon entered Dominique and hurtled them, once more, beyond the point of return.

The following day, Evon and Dominique returned to Belle Terre, bringing with them Beau and Jacques. Evon opened the carriage door and stepped down. Beau bounded to the ground right behind him and ran to reacquaint himself with his friends. Evon shook his head and laughed and turned back and held out his hand for Dominique. She tucked her hand in his and held the baby in her other arm while Evon assisted her from the coach.

When both her feet were on the rich, black earth, she paused to gaze up at the grand mansion. She smiled and took a step forward, but suddenly she felt herself being lifted and swung into the circle of his arms. His lips brushed hers ever so lightly and he kissed their sleeping son's forehead.

Evon inhaled and walked up the steps. "We are home, *chérie.*"

Jigger opened the door and when Evon carried her through the door, her heart filled to bursting as she realized this was where she belonged, with Evon, loving him and bearing his sons and daughters. She had come home.